WHERE IS

TONY BLUNT?

Book 2 in The Atrocities Series

by JOSEPH MITCHAM

ISBN: 9798697250624

Isaac,

Catch Cho

Nov '21

i

Acknowledgements

The text of this book has benefited from the knowledge, experience and attention to detail of Ollie, Adam, Ele, Ben, Kev, Phil, Derek and Col Matt. Support to the artistic elements of the project came from Jonathan and Stephen. Thank you all.

The views and opinions expressed are those of the author alone and should not be taken to represent those of Her Majesty's Government, MOD, HM Armed Forces, or any government agency.

This book is dedicated to the memory of John Jeffries 1922-2020 – veteran of Arnhem; he always had the brightest smile and was loved by all who met him. Rest in peace John.

Contents

1

Prologue

Sangin, Afghanistan 6 June 2008 – 2 Section of 4 Platoon, B Company, 2nd Battalion The Parachute Regiment is patrolling the area north-east of Forward Operating Base Robinson.

"BLUNT, GET UP HERE." the Section Commander bellows as he takes a knee in the fine, powdery sand at the edge of the roughly worn track. The other members of the ten-man team laugh as Tony runs past them from the back of the patrol snake as fast as he can under the weight of his body armour, webbing, daysack, rifle, and helmet. Even the attached medic and signaller shake their heads at him disparagingly as he doubles past them.

"GET FUCKING MOVING." Screams John, the section second in command, a full eleven years his junior and not an ounce of respect or empathy for him. Tony runs by without acknowledging him.

"Yes, Corporal." Tony blurts in exhaustion. He knocks into the patrol commander as he falls to his knees beside him.

"Get the fuck off me, Blunt." Corporal Gibbons says, shoving him on the shoulder. Tony is already off balance and falls sideways to the ground. "What the fuck are you doing Blunt, you fuck-wit, get up."

"Yes Corporal, sorry Corporal." Tony just wants to do well, that's all he's ever wanted to do from the day he joined up, but he puts himself under so much pressure - his limited intellect and ability to coordinate himself, mean that he's made one mistake after another until his colleagues have lost all confidence in him one by one.

"Get a fuckin' grip, Terry might be watching." Corporal Gibbons uses the ever-valid threat that 'Terry Taliban' could be about.

"Yes, Corporal."

"Right, sacrificial ginger time." Corporal Gibbons laughs as if it's a joke, but it's not a million miles from the truth. "Rick's spotted something up front; I want you to get forward on your belt buckle and confirm it, that's if there's anything there, okay?"

"Yes, Corporal." says Tony obediently, and he immediately throws himself flat on the floor and begins to leopard crawl forward towards the lead scout.

"Tony, you fucking twat, you don't need to crawl until you get past Rick – switch on."

"Yes, Corporal." Tony gets back to his feet.

"Ditch your daysack and webbing too, leave it with Rick."

"Yes, Corporal." Tony unclips the large plastic buckle of his belt kit and pulls his right arm out of the shoulder strap of his pack and the yoke of his webbing. The straps tangle with his rifle sling and he finds himself in knots.

"Seriously, Blunt? You're a fucking cluster. Why don't you just take yourself off with that rifle and fucking end it? It'd be safer for the rest of us."

"Sorry, Corporal." After a painfully long period of reorganisation, he has himself ready, rifle re-slung, daysack and webbing gripped in his left hand by the straps. He walks the proven route to Rick who is laid prone on the ground. The track extends before him with a thin, rough, prickly bush line to the left and an open and empty yard to the right.

*

As he approaches the lead scout, the peacefulness that Tony has enjoyed for the last ten seconds is broken. "THIRTY METRES, QUARTER RIGHT OF AXIS – BUILDING WITH RED DOOR, SAY SEEN IF SEEN." Rick shouts in a perfectly clear voice, without looking around.

"Seen." says Tony, following the target indication voice procedure as taught.

"Two fingers left of the base left-hand side of the building, see a linear disturbance in the ground, slightly darker than the rest of the track." Rick guides Tony onto what he has observed in the most efficient way possible. Tony raises his rifle into the aim to make use of the four-times magnification sights and walks forward a few steps.

"ARRRGH, FUCKING HELL TONY, you fucking useless cunt." Rick fumes as Tony quickly lifts his boot from the back of his right ankle.

"Sorry Rick, didn't see you there." Tony says, feeling a deep inner pain as he messes up again, impinging on the impeccable conduct and professionalism of Rick, who he holds in the highest regard.

Rick is on point for a reason; Cpl Gibbons has selected him for his innate level of awareness and soldiering skills. One to watch for the future; Rick is one of those soldiers who is made for Special Forces, and has the personal drive and desire to get there in an almost automated fashion, not at all uncommon in the Regiment.

"I've cleared up to here with the Vallon, you need to do the rest. Stop short five metres before the building, then get down and start prodding, got it?"

"Got it." Tony replies nervously, the seriousness of the task dawning on him as he places his kit down next to Rick and takes the detection device from him.

"Blunt, your rifle." Rick nods at Tony's weapon.

Tony lifts his rifle strap over his helmet and begins to put it down on top of his webbing.

"Tony, for fuck's sake. Sling it over your back."

"Oh yeah, sorry." Tony leans the Vallon against his leg and takes the shoulder strap of his rifle in his left hand and the other length of the sling that follows the body of the rifle, in the other. He pulls the strap in his right hand to bring them to equal lengths, then puts the rifle on like a rucksack.

"Tighten the sling so it doesn't slide off your back." Rick advises him. "Sorted. Now be careful you bell-end." he says with enough endearment to put the faintest of smiles on Tony's face for just a second.

"Thanks Rick." Tony steps forward waving the Vallon side to side over the ground in front of him.

"Slow down, nob 'ead, and move it in bigger arcs." Rick says with real concern for his incompetent colleague, who, whilst he does not like, or want to be friends with, is still an Airborne brother. "Take your time and don't give all your focus to the sweep. Think about what's going on around you and other possible threats." Rick has taken up a kneeling position looking forward down the track and covering to the left. A fellow Para moves up slowly behind him, keeping a couple metres between them and is scanning the right of arc. Tony knows that these guys are his eyes and ears whilst he concentrates on the Vallon and the possible IED.

*

The edge of the building gets ever closer and Tony thinks about changing to the prone position - if whatever awaits him should function; he'll be less likely to 'cop it' if he's out of the likely upward blast cone that it will send up. He takes a knee, places the Vallon on the ground beside him and takes his pocketknife from the left map pocket of his combat trousers. As he is about to get on his belt buckle he sees a twitch in the bush to his left.

"COMMAND WIRE, TAKE COVER." he shouts and launches himself into the cover offered by the corner of the building. He hunkers down in the fetal position and braces for the explosion, but it doesn't come.

"BLUNT YOU FUCKING MONG, WHAT THE FUCK ARE YOU PLAYING AT?" Corporal Gibbons is already up to Rick's position, moving forward to let his displeasure be fully known to his sacrificial ginger. Tony gets himself up to a solid kneeling position at the building's edge ready for what's coming. "Sorry Corporal," he says for the umpteenth time today, "I thought I saw a command wire." He points back to the spot - there is a wire, now clear of the dirt that had concealed it, and again it begins to show the unmistakeable signs of lateral movement. Tony doesn't know what to say, Corporal Gibbons is almost upon him and doesn't look pleased. "But Corporal…"

Scything clicks snap through the air, Tony recognises the sound instantly from previous enemy contacts. High velocity rounds pepper the air around him as the echoes of the AK47s' muzzle blasts clatter around the immediate area. "CONTACT LEFT." Rick shouts to the rest of the section.

Unsure of what to do, Tony looks to Corporal Gibbons - *he's already taken cover*. Tony drops to the ground, hoping that it will swallow him up. "What shall we do Corporal?" He edges a little closer to receive counsel from Corporal Gibbons, but Gibbons doesn't respond. "Corporal Gibbons." Tony knows in his heart that Corporal Gibbons is the last man in Battalion that would let this battle opportunity pass him by, the last man on earth who would freeze when faced with the enemy. Tony reaches out in anguish and grabs his shoulder, slowly pulling on the collar of his body armour to roll him over. The 7.62mm AK47 round has done what it was designed to do - entering the Junior Non-commissioned Officer's face, just on the left side of his nose, it had ripped the entire right side of his face off on its way into the cranial cavity and taken most of his brain with it as it tore out the back of his head, leaving the top of his skull, scalp and short brown hair hanging down into the gaping hole that is left.

"MAN DOWN, GIBBO'S DEAD, GIBBO'S DEAD." Tony shouts.

"MAN DOWN...MAN DOWN..." the message passes back down the section of fighting troops.

"ALRIGHT, ALRIGHT, TONY, GET INTO COVER." Rick shouts back to him.

Tony moves back and to the right, into the limited safety offered by the building, but rounds are still coming his way, exposed by the downward slope that presents him to the enemy. He can see shapes in the bushes moving to improve their arcs of view, putting him in further danger. There is a door into the building just behind him, he moves back towards it whilst wrestling to get his rifle off his back. He gets to his knees and leans against the door. It gives a little, but there is something behind it. He pushes harder and it opens enough for him to enter.

*

He holds his rifle in the aim as he finds himself in a sparsely furnished terracotta room. As dust clears and his eyes adjust to the low light, he sees people, a family, old and young. They are cowering in the corners and murmur in terror, terrified of what the westerner will do to them. He drops his rifle down to let it hang freely by the sling and raises his hands, showing them his gloved, but empty palms. "It's okay, I don't want to hurt you." he says softly.

The old man in the corner says a few words in Pashto that Tony does not understand. A young girl of about thirteen answers him, then says to Tony, "My grandfather says you cannot stay here, they will kill us all if they find you with us."

"I'm sorry, I don't want to get you in trouble. I'll protect you while I'm here, please let me stay, just a few minutes until it quietens down." He smiles at the girl; she smiles back at him.

"Shouldn't you be out there fighting with your friends?" she asks.

"They're not my friends."

The girl gives him a saddened look. "Let me speak to Grandpa."

The family discuss the situation at length, talking about Tony, pointing and gesticulating at him as though he is not there. His focus moves from their unintelligible chatter to the noise of the battle raging outside – he feels a sweat of guilt come over him for abandoning his comrades, but then the feeling of shame leaves him as he thinks about how they treat him; like shit, making him feel worthless to his core. Eventually the young girl turns to him and says, "If you're staying, we will need tea."

The family make themselves comfortable around Tony, the elderly ladies sit off to one corner and Tony sits close to the Grandfather in the middle of the room on the carpet. The young girl sits with them as the only bi-lingual member of the family. Grandfather seems nervous and not concerned about joining in conversation. "So where did you learn to speak English?" Tony asks the girl.

"My brother, Ismal, he learned so that he could work as an interpreter with the Americans, he taught me as he was learning.

"The Americans? Not with the British?" Tony enquires.

"No, the Americans were here first, first the soldiers, then the contractors. The British came two years ago, but you do not pay as well." She laughs lightly. "Ismal moved north to Kabul to follow the Americans' money. My name is Malala. What is your name?" she asks coyly.

He smiles at Malala. "My name's Tony, but I get called a lot worse. Malala - that's a beautiful name, maybe I'll call my baby Malala."

"It is a sad name really, it means 'grieving one'. My Mother gave me that name, as my father was killed just before I was born."

"I'm sorry, that's so sad. It wasn't us was it?" Tony says naively.

"No," Malala says with a laugh, "it was the Taliban. They were fighting for power and were killing anyone who resisted. My father was a local leader and would not give in to their ways or demands, so they killed him."

"That's terrible."

"Yes, there are lots of girls my age named Malala, it's becoming more common these days too."

"Is it usual to invite gunmen to join you for tea? I burst into your home with a rifle, and you welcome me for a brew." Tony says with a smile.

"Of course," says Malala, "wouldn't you welcome a stranger into your house back home? Especially one in danger, one who is fighting your enemy?" Before Tony can answer, Grandpa says something. Malala answers him with a shout.

"What did he say?" Tony asks. Malala is blushing.

"He is teasing me, he asked me if I want to marry you."

"And what did you say?"

"I told him you are married, expecting a baby."

"Well, you are a very beautiful young lady. If I wasn't already fixed up and you were ten years older; you can tell your grandpa that I would have snapped you up, but I must try and get back to my friends." Tony stands and turns towards the door. Grandpa starts to shout and wave him back away from the door.

"What's the matter?" Tony asks.

"He says that you cannot go out there, if they see you leave, they will kill us all."

"I have to go."

"Then let me check that no one is there before you show yourself."

"Okay." Tony accepts the compromise, despite the sound of the odd gunshot still audible from outside. Malala opens the door enough so that she can see what is going on, watches for a few seconds, and then reports back to Tony; "Your friends are in trouble, the fighters are shooting the ones who are left from the high ground through the bushes, we are behind them, they will not see you. Go if you must."

Tony looks at Malala as if expecting further orders, but she just gazes back at him. He takes her place at the doorway and has a look for himself. The steep hillock on the far side of the track, that had channelled his patrol towards the house, gives the fighters a commanding position over what is left of his team, though he can only make out two of them. He sees Rick's body lying still and prostrate a few yards back from where he had been when Tony had stood on his leg. "Stay here." he says to Malala.

*

Tony creeps from the doorway to the corner of the building. He turns and walks a little further down the track, forgetting about the failed improvised explosive device, remembering as he steps onto the darker dusty soil that Rick had pointed out. He is lucky; there is no secondary switch to detonate the charge – if there is, it has also failed to trigger. He walks on a few more yards until he finds an easy route into the dry, spiky bushes - he penetrates them, emerging at the foot of the enemy's bank. The fighters have consolidated in a short baseline at the top of the hillock, there are three dead slumped amongst them. The remaining fighters are raining down rounds onto the remnants of the section. Tony knows that his rifle is made ready, and that he has a full magazine of thirty rounds, he gives it a shove on the base to ensure that it is correctly fitted and will not drop out at the vital moment. He firmly presses the change lever down to automatic – at close quarters and with at least four enemy fighters on the brow of the hill, his trigger finger is not quick enough to double-tap all targets on the 'single shot' setting; one of the fighters would surely react in time – Tony dares to dream of this as his 'Budd VC' moment - could he become a legend, as Brian Budd of 3 Para had done four turns of the Afghan handle ago?

Tony feels his heart pounding in his chest beneath the weight of his heavy body armour but focuses his attention on his route to the enemy. The ground is rough, rocky, and dusty. He clearly remembers the technique he was taught in basic training; he plants each foot carefully before putting his full weight onto it, moving slowly and lightly. There are no twigs to snap here, like on the slopes of Brecon, but plenty of rocks that will make as much noise if dislodged. The gradient of the slope increases steeply, making a slip more likely, he navigates the worst of it and the ground begins to flatten. As the brow of the hillock plateaus, he finds himself no more than ten metres from the line of Taliban fighters, who are all one hundred percent focused on firing on the few remaining British soldiers. As Tony raises his weapon and makes the decision to open fire, the fighter in the middle of the group removes his magazine and looks behind him for a fresh one, he sees Tony and shouts to warn the other insurgents, but it is too loud and it is too late. Tony grasps his weapon tightly and pulls the trigger. He arcs his shoulders from left to right, cutting through what turns out to be five live targets, judging his steady movement to ensure that the barrel points at the last man, just before he is able to turn and return fire.

He stands frozen in position, shaking with bewilderment at what he has just done, amazed that he didn't fuck it up. A smile spreads across his face as he watches for movement from the enemy. "POSITION CLEAR." he screams.

2

Rejected, but accepted

"If you're so keen to go after terror suspects, then why were you seen in London talking to a group of them?" The big man asks. Then, slam – a huge over-hand right smashes Tony across the bridge of the nose. The blow delivered by the infamous man he knows from years ago. He falls backwards on the soft grass of the old church yard. The third man looks up and down the street outside of the brick wall perimeter to check for any approaching potential witnesses as Craig and John stand over Tony.

"What happened to you, Blunt? I thought you sorted yourself out?" the hawk-like thug asks. Tony doesn't reply, he just eyeballs John with contempt, recycling the hatred that had built up over years of being treated like a nobody by him, and people like him. Tony once more finds himself powerless - bullied, dominated, vulnerable. He hates this feeling of a complete lack of control, of being at the mercy of others. He imagines himself being on the winning team; he visualises John on the floor, surrounded by him and his new friends, but Tony knows that he is fighting a losing battle on this occasion – *where is my power? Why don't I get to have power?*

"Why are you here?" Craig asks, "Why are you interested in what we're up to? Who are you reporting to?" Again, Tony says nothing. He thinks through what he has heard about their mission to steal the UK Terror Watch List – *would I be on it? They know I met with my contacts in London, will they be targeting me? Are my new friends on their list?*

"He's just a fucking idiot, Craig. He doesn't know anything, let's just fuck him off." says John.

Craig takes his time, giving Tony a long hard stare. "Whatever you know, or don't know, you just forget it, okay?" Craig gives an uncharacteristic snarl as he goes on, "If we see or hear of you again, you're a dead man. Do you understand?" Again, Tony remains silent, a mixture of his hatred and feeling petrified.

John bends down to Tony, grabs him by the collar and hauls him to his feet. "WELL, FUCKING ANSWER. DO YOU FUCKING UNDERSTAND?" John pushes Tony back on his heels and then yanks him forward again, straight onto his forehead. Tony's nose explodes into a gushing mush of blood which oozes out over and into his long ginger beard. John follows in with crunching hooks to the ribs, finishing with a fully loaded uppercut to the jaw. Tony spins around with the force of the blow and slumps to the ground on all fours. "NOW DO AS THE MAN SAYS AND FUCK OFF."

*

Tony has managed to stop the blood flowing from his nose but cannot stop the tears flowing from his eyes, or the involuntary sobs. His physical pain pales into insignificance next to the mental pain of being battered and rejected by a supposed 'Airborne brother'. Regardless of their different aims and perspectives, despite John's expected hate and lack of respect for him, it hurts Tony to be pitted against someone that he respects - admires even. All Tony had ever wanted was to be accepted by the team that he chose to join, and he now finds himself on the opposing side from it. He switches his thoughts to the love and warmth that he has felt from his new friends and acquaintances; he begins to feel a whole lot better. He has been welcomed, revered, and been made to feel like he belongs.

Sitting under a tree at a quiet edge of the Parkway green, he thinks back to the ten minutes that he had spent with Malala and her family, how he had been the centre of attention, how they had treated him; their kindness. He feels the same love flow from his new friends, never once insulted or disrespected, certainly never shouted at or rebuked.

His mobile phone buzzes in his inside jacket pocket. The incoming call is from a stored number listed as 'K'. He answers without hesitation. "Salaam Murshid."

"Salaam, Brother, how are you, are you fine?"

"I'm okay Brother, a little bruised but okay." Tony considers how to break the news of his failure. "I am compromised, they knew of our meetings, Brother."

"I know, and you did well to hold your silence, you have done well, Brother, this was not your fault."

"You know, already?"

"Yes, Brother, I had eyes on you." Tony looks around him, wondering if he is being watched now. *"You must forget this episode; you are no further use to this mission. Go to London; we will provide you with a place and security. You are safe now, Brother."*

"Thank you." Tony says with a deep sincerity.

"Is there anything at your home that might provide any clues to your activities with us?"

"No, Brother."

"Then do not return there, if you are compromised, others may come for you. Throw your phone in the nearest bin, then go directly to the train station and take the next train to London, you will be met there, my Brother." The line goes dead. Tony feels buoyed and rejuvenated. He walks south towards Adderley Park, his tears replaced with a smile.

*

Boarding his connection to Euston, Tony is pushed aside by a group of young lads as they run to get the last empty table in the carriage. "Be careful, fellas." They stop and look back at him, faces full of menace.

"Or what, you beardy bell-end." the bravest one replies. Tony says nothing but continues to stare at the gobby teenager. "What are you looking at; fancy me do ya? PAEDO." The boys begin to chant, "PAEDO, PAEDO, PAEDO." Tony feels everyone on the train looking at him; he decides to remove himself from the situation. He turns away and heads for the next carriage. "Yeah, fuck off you dirty bearded paedo."

He takes a seat in the barely quarter full carriage, picks up a discarded newspaper, and begins to while away the seventy-four minutes of the journey. He quickly scans the main articles, finding nothing interesting. As he moves further through the paper, he sees more and more advertisements for attractions and events in London over the summer months; Hampton Court Garden Festival, BBC Proms, Wimbledon, London Pride, the list goes on. Tony thinks about the hundreds of thousands of awful people and their kids, like those in the next carriage, flocking into the capital, and how he'd like to wreak his vengeance against them. He flicks backwards and forwards between the advertisements, like a catalogue shopper, looking at the dates and considering the capacities of each of the events, until he has a half-formed plan in his mind for the perfect target.

knows that this conversation is important, he knows that he needs Alex on side.

"I've been talking more to some of the top boys, mostly the handlers that weren't in London." John says with enthusiasm, hoping to ignite Alex's interest.

"All chomping at the bit no doubt?" Alex says disparagingly.

"Actually no, not right away. They wanted to know if you were on board… said you brought a lot to the party; you gave us that edge of security."

"Really? Alex gets the feeling that his ego is being massaged, not something that he thought John could be capable of. This puts him further into two minds about giving John's offer any further consideration.

Alex checks over his shoulder again for any unnoticed newcomers to the café. "So, what would be your proposed scheme of manoeuvre?"

John hunkers down lower to the table and goes on; "I reckon we form a fresh committee, bring in Cliff, Spence, and maybe Blakey, then start tracking down this Interest Group."

"What? You four blokes are just going to bimble about looking for them with me providing comms?" Alex mocks John, goading him, knowing exactly what's coming next.

"No, don't be a twat; we'll need to get some decent intelligence." John says shyly.

"You mean you need me to get Lucy back on the team?"

Lucy is a sore topic for Alex; he considers her as perfect in every way, not just physically, but as an ambitious Intelligence Corps Corporal, big into adventurous sports and taking wild chances, she is a real handful. With her brash, uncompromising personality and no-nonsense attitude; she has it all. Unfortunately for Alex, she had ended things with him straight after the Millbank bombing. Being switched on to how the intelligence community works; she knew that continuing to keep company with Alex would significantly increase the chances of their team being tracked down, and there was no way that she was going to let that happen.

"I won't do you any good, John. I'm in the past tense as far as Lucy is concerned. She binned me off as soon as the mission was over. She's a cold fish; once she was bought into the mission, that was all she cared about. She only let me shag her to get me to go through with it."

"Really? You really believe that Alex?"

Alex doesn't answer, just searches his soul a little, though not as deeply as he has done over the past week.

"Well, you tell me that you're not looking for an excuse to get near her again, and I'll tell you that I don't want her for her intelligence." John's stern look turns to a smile, Alex's smile breaks in turn. He is impressed at how John seems to have developed and matured in the few days since Craig, their leader and friend, had met his demise in London. John now seems more considered - to have a deeper intellect to his conversation.

"I would like to see Lucy again, but we may have a better option." says Alex, causing John's right eyebrow to rise, and ears to twitch, a trait that Alex had not noticed before.

"What are you thinking?"

"Another source, a better connected one."

4

The plot thickens

The sweat rolls off his body; it runs from his scalp, down his forehead, dripping from his brow. It seeps through his long, course, red beard as he pushes out press-up after press-up in the thick, musty air of the darkened room. Conditioned by years of training in the Second Battalion, the gym had been one of his only friends.

As he comfortably completes the set of one hundred repetitions, he rests face down, breathing heavily on the dirty, dusty carpet of the anonymous and unremarkable flat. Tony feels comfort in being tucked away in the estates of North London, with no connection to the outside world, but for his new, clean, and fairly disposable mobile phone and an internet connection that also carries no link to his identity. The only other person on the planet that knows of his presence here is his mentor.

Tony manoeuvres himself onto his backside and pivots on the spot, swinging his legs around to hook his feet under the cross beam of the ancient-looking oak table; he begins a set of sit-ups. His brain goes into a semi-conscious state of meditation, in which he can think through his ideas and partially formed plan, whilst counting his sit-ups. His thoughts strengthen as he excites himself with new concepts, and he loses count, time and again, going back to the last number that he can recall, *a method of destruction that requires no explosives? Where was I? 220, 221, 222.* He continues to bob, down and up, in a perfect rhythm, like a metronome.

His phone rings from the sideboard, which is as old and battered as the table. "Shit." He says as he gets to his feet, unable to feel too annoyed, as he has been anticipating news; his soul purpose is to act on that news when it arrives – it has been for over a week, and he hopes that it is this call that will provide it. He picks up the new mobile handset and answers; "Salam." He awaits the reply with bated breath.

"*Salam, Brother.*" Tony is delighted to hear this voice, though it is not the voice that he is waiting for.

"How are you?"

"*I'm fine, but I only have limited time.*"

"How did you get my new number?"

"*Our friends got it to me through the network. Do you have any news for me?*" The voice on the other end of the line sounds calm but nervous.

"No news yet, but I have made a proposal to avenge your incarceration. This will make the Birmingham attack look like a walk in the park."

"*It was.*"

Tony laughs aloud at the quip, but quickly stymies it, as it is not reciprocated at the other end of the line by the caller.

"What I have proposed will dwarf Birmingham and rob everyone in this land of their sense of security. I hope that it will signify the beginning of our war."

"*Birmingham was the beginning, Brother Tony, do not rob me of that. The blast in London locked us in; my part in this must not be over-looked.*"

"You did well, my friend, you executed your part in the plan expertly. Do not be blinkered to your tactical role, my Brother, you are a vital part in this operation, as we are smaller parts within our broader strategy. Call me again in a few days; hopefully, I will have news for you by then." Tony ends the call and places the phone back on the table. He clears his mind as he settles back into the monotony of his endless sit-ups.

*

Beginning to fester in his own juices after completing his workout and cooling down, Tony pulls a chair up to the table and opens the lid of a nearly new laptop. The internet browser is open on the screen with multiple tabs to the websites of numerous tourist attractions; he clicks on a few of them, sneering at the images of crowds of people enjoying themselves. He clicks on the blue 'W' on the task bar, bringing a text document to the fore – his summary list of the high-profile events programmed to take place in London this summer. He looks over the dates of each of them, he mulls over the ripeness of opportunities, the multiple attractions that will draw ever larger crowds as dates overlap – *"It will be then."* He makes no further notes and deletes all the text in the document and then re-saves it as an empty page under its existing title 'TASK 3'.

Tony picks up the digital landline handset from its station and dials a number from the 'recent calls' list.

"Salam." comes the answer, barely audible from a whispered voice.

"Salam, Murshid. Are you well?"

"I am surviving, just about. Have you had word from our soldier?"

"Yes, a short while ago; he is strong. I will let him know that you asked after him. Do you have word from the council on my idea?"

"Yes, it is agreed that your plan will proceed. You have impressed everyone, young man. You have proven to be a most valuable servant to us. Do you have everything that you need for this task? Money? A workforce?"

"Thank you, Murshid. The beauty of my plan is that it is low cost and relatively low effort. The generous fund that was left for me here will be more than enough, and the more people that are involved; the greater the risk we have of being discovered. Though there is one special item that I would like, that purchasing myself might raise suspicions."

"Consider it done - I will make arrangements. Have you selected a date for your mission?"

"Yes Murshid, the third Saturday of next month."

"Very good, that is perfect timing. My team here should have the boy's copy of our list unlocked by then, and that shall be the day that we reach out to our new crop of soldiers."

5

New beginnings

Alex arrives outside the modern office building situated deep in the industrial parks of Solihull. He cannot help but be impressed by the professional look of the premises, towering above its surrounds, standing out from the older buildings with its gun-metal grey panelling. The shiny acrylic sign, posted in the lush green lawn, reading 'Contingency Group' - *contingency for what I wonder.*

He walks up the path to the door and gives it a push; it doesn't move. He pulls it, but still it remains firmly closed. *"Good morning, Sir. Do you have an appointment?"*

"Yes, Alex Gregory to see John Gallagher." Alex looks around the door frame and further up the face of the building trying to spot a camera as he waits for a response.

"Thank you, Mr Gregory, Mr Gallagher will be with you in a minute, please take a seat in the reception area." Alex hears a feint click from the electromagnetic mechanism at the top of the door and pushes it open.

The reception area meets expectations set by the building's exterior. The voice from the intercom had likely come from the smartly dressed lady standing behind the high desk to the left of the impressively large space, her uniform similar to that of an air hostess. The reception hall is dominated by a huge spiral staircase that rises from the centre of the room, the white enamel-painted steel structure curling through 360 degrees between each of the three floors above ground level, with a meticulously engineered, brushed aluminium banister and stanchions separated by perfectly arced panes of glass, or more likely Perspex. The room is brightly lit, and the white walls enhance the glow of the place. There are three enormous grey sofas, set up in an open square, facing the reception desk, placed around a beautifully crafted oak coffee table. As the only visitor, he selects the optimal position on the centre sofa affording him views of the exit, the staircase, the lift doors behind it, and the not unattractive receptionist who he now faces directly.

"Can I get you a drink, Mr Gregory?" The receptionist asks in the sweetest of voices. Alex isn't sure how long he will be waiting and doesn't fancy navigating more than one flight of those steps with a full cup of coffee.

"No, thank you." He waits patiently for five minutes, letting his phone keep him company to pass the time.

"Oye oye, nob 'ead!" The receptionist smirks, looking up at John who is leaning over the balcony of the third floor.

"Hi John." Alex replies, shaking his head and frowning at the receptionist, making out that John's laddish behaviour is beneath his standards. John runs down the stairs two at a time like an excited kid. Alex stands and walks around to his right to the open space between the back of the third sofa and the foot of the stairs as John bounds down the last few steps. Alex extends his hand, which John grasps as he lands on the immaculate slate floor tiles. His momentum is curbed just in time to stop him colliding with Alex but leads into a good strong man-hug.

"Welcome to our new headquarters." John says as he steps back away from Alex and releases his hand.

"What, all of this?" Alex asks.

"No, no, just the third floor; I'll give you the tour. You've already met the lovely Sandy." He gestures towards the receptionist.

She smiles back at him, "You owe me a fiver, Mr Gallagher."

John laughs quietly. "Stairs or lift?"

"Stairs." Alex says as though there were no other option. "What do you owe Sandy a fiver for?"

John leads Alex up the spiral carpet, talking as he goes. "I told her to expect a smooth little bastard this morning. I bet her that you'd be asking for her phone number within five minutes of walking through the door."

"I'd wondered why you'd kept me waiting."

John goes on to explain what he has set up so far as they pass the first-floor landing; "Contingency Group is a security company, providing specialist services to client organisations around the world. It's owned by an old mate of Craig's." Alex feels a pang of upset at the mention of the fallen boss man. "When he heard about what went on in London; he was one of many straight on the blower, wanting to know what he could do to help. I said we needed somewhere to run future operations from if we were going to find out who was behind the real Interest Group. He said we could have a chunk of this place."

"Wow, that's handy." Alex says, slightly out of puff at the unexpected shock to his lungs provided by the stairs.

"What's the matter with you? Not kept up with your training?" John says as they reach the third landing. The entrance to the office space is off to the right of the lift doors. John strides towards the single, solid looking, finely sanded oak door. He wrenches down on the handle and ushers Alex in.

*

"Gents, look who's joined us." John says loudly as they enter the large, open plan room. There is a huge table in the centre of the considerable space, which is being used as an operations 'bird table', there is an over-sized map of the United Kingdom spread across it, with a sheet of acetate pinned over it. Alongside, to the right of the table are four desks with PC monitors, keyboards and not much else on them. Three of the desks are occupied by Spence, Cliff, and Blakey; they all stand and move to greet Alex.

"Hello young man," Spence says in his rasping Northern Irish accent, despite his Scottish roots. He grab's Alex's hand and grips him just above the elbow with his slender left hand. "Good work with taking down that fecking piece of shite." He says, referring to Alex's part in apprehending the Millbank bomber. Alex smiles solemnly back at the almost gaunt looking man, who's jet black hair flops down over his forehead.

"Thanks Spence, but I can't really take the credit for that. It's good to see you." he says modestly.

Cliff, towering over him from the left, clutches Alex around the neck lovingly. "Yeah, good effort Alex, shame you never got the chance to finish him off though mate." Alex can feel the bulge of Cliff's bicep pressing into the back of his neck. He looks up at the hulking man standing over him, his stubble growing into tight black curls, many of them greying.

"Hi Cliff, are you shrinking?" Alex says with a fond laugh.

"Come here, lad." says Blakey, patiently standing, waiting his turn to say hello to Alex. He envelopes him with his enormous arms and hugs him tight. "You did a great job for us that night." Blakey says over Alex's shoulder, with deep emotion in his voice, clearly still raw after the shock of losing one of his team in Leeds. Alex had been a strong voice of support, even if only at the end of the phone line, and had helped Blakey to refocus on the task in hand.

"Mate, that must have been rough at your end." Alex says with sympathy.

"All right, Blakey fella, put him down." John says mockingly. Blakey eventually releases Alex and pats him on the shoulder.

"Right, let's take the rest of the tour." John says, walking around to the right of the bird table. "This is the main operations space, clearly." he says waving his arm over the desks and table. He approaches the first of two doors on the wall on the right side of the room. "Through here is the conference suite."

"Nice." says Alex, peering in, but not entering.

"And in here," John closes the conference suite door and moves along the wall to the next one, "there are toilets, a storeroom and a kitchenette – do you want a drink?"

"Always." Alex knows the importance of having a brew to chat over when he's with this gang.

"On the other side," John points to the opposite side of the room, the top half of the wall is windows across its full length. Alex can see more windows and passageways through them, "there's a variety of different sized offices, but I don't think that we'll be using those, unless you want a comms office? Or if you can get us an intelligence source; a G2 cell? John references the old Army 'G' categorisation of file headings, G2 being intelligence.

"Wouldn't have thought so." Alex takes brew orders from Blakey, Cliff, and Spence while John gets some mugs together.

*

The five sit around the bird table sipping their teas. There is an air of hesitation, no one quite knowing where the conversation might start or what the agenda might contain. Craig's direction is missed, and John's sense of leadership is yet to be fully realised in this context. Alex decides to get the ball rolling. "The real Interest Group, then - do they exist? If they do; where are they and how are we going to find them?" There is no reply from his Special Forces-trained group of friends. "If we find them; what are we going to do with them."

"Well that won't take a lot of imagination." Cliff offers, chuckling to himself. "Seriously though, some form of higher group must exist. What happened in London was well-planned, if not incompetently executed. Though they still did the job on us." Cliff grinds his fist into the palm of his hand, and snarls at the thought of his lost friends.

"The bunch in the conference centre were definitely the bait, not the real players. Zafir's the only survivor, and we'll not get near him to find out anymore." says Spence. There is a frustrated pause as the men consider what they know against what they need to know.

"The only other partial potential lead we have to them is Tony Blunt, if, indeed, he is connected to them." Alex says, conscious that this may be a touchy subject to bring up with John, who had mistakenly included his former 2 Para colleague in the trawl for operatives for the previous mission. Unbeknown to John, Blunt had been radicalised and looks to have been attempting to subvert their campaign against members of the UK Terror Watch List.

"We've looked for him - he's disappeared." John responds.

"How hard though, John?" Spence asks. "We were pretty busy juggling other business at the time. Is it worth re-visiting?"

"Yeah, you've got a point, Spence. I think the lads only did a bit of passive investigation – we might be able to dig him out with a bit more of a 'hands on' look." John concedes.

"Right, that's action point one. What are the work strands?" Blakey is keen for something tangible that he can get stuck into.

John pauses for thought. "From what my guys found; he had a place somewhere in Solihull, so we can check that out. His mum lived locally too, and he was always close to her from what I can remember - we could speak to her, and he had been working in a metal shop; they'll have some record of him there."

"Brilliant. What else?" Blakey asks.

"I have an intelligence connection that I might be able to reopen." says Alex.

"A pair of legs that you might be able to reopen more like." John laughs.

"Not that one." Alex says sharply.

"Ooh, touchy!" John laughs a little more. Everyone else joins in, even Alex.

"No, seriously, this is a different source; she did help out on the last mission but was only on the peripheries."

"'She'? See, I told you, he's at it again." John says, again raising a raucous laugh from the lads. Whilst mildly embarrassed, Alex revels at being included in the banter with these men. Craig had told him that he would not earn their respect lightly, and that it might take significant time for them to bond, if ever. Within barely two weeks of knowing them, after such shared experiences, and with Alex doing, and going through, so much; he had begun to feel like one of theirs. Alex thinks about what useful intelligence he might glean from Agent Thew of The Security Service.

"I can request access to Zafir's phone data, if they are connected; that might give us some clues. Blunt may not be on their radar, he appeared in the images from an Interest Group meeting in London, the ones that helped us to discover him, but we don't know if the security services ever followed up on him, or if they have; whether or not they have identified him." Alex is sure that more will come to light once he gets talking to Agent Thew, but first he must work out the best way to establish contact with her.

"That sounds good, Alex." John says, ending the pause and breaking Alex's concentration. "You have a sniff at that," again everyone laughs at Alex's expense, "and I'll speak to Blunt's mum. Spence, you locate his place and check it out, Blakey and Cliff, you look into his employment, the foundry and wherever else." Everyone nods, "Right, no time like the present. Do what research you can on the computers, and then hit the streets. We'll reconvene here Sunday, 1000hrs."

Not one for computers, Spence disappears straight out of the door. Blakey and Cliff take seats at the two middle desks and start tapping away... slowly. John perches on the edge of the bird table, takes out his phone and begins scouring social media for Blunt's mum.

*

Alex takes a moment to explore the spare offices on the left side of the ops room. He follows the corridor that circles the larger proportion of the floor. There are lots of small offices and several multi-occupancy rooms. As he heads back to where he entered the corridor, he selects and walks into the last single-desk office, takes a seat, and removes an immaculate, new, but cheap phone from his trouser pocket.

"Hello, Whitehall Operator, how may I direct your call?"

"Hi, could you put me through to Agent Charlie Thew at The Security Service Headquarters please."

"One moment, Sir... Please hold while I put you through." Alex thinks through his strategy as the poor-quality recording of Beethoven's Moonlight Sonata kicks in. He has never spoken to Charlie before, only knowing what he has picked up from over-hearing conversations between her and Lucy, and what he has learned from what Lucy has said about her. In his mind, she is as head-strong and pragmatic as Lucy, and possibly a little more mature - she would seem to have an equally single-minded attitude towards taking down those that need taking down.

"Who's this?" the curt, sharp voice is a jolt in Alex's ear from the light music that he was beginning to enjoy.

"Hello, Agent Thew?"

"*Yes, I know who I am, who are you, y' fool?*" She sound's irritated and fiery.

"My name's Gregg, I worked with Lucy, you were chatting with her a week or so ago." Alex is careful to give her enough information to let her know his potential significance, but not enough to implicate himself in anything that happened.

"*So not Alex then? Alex Gregory?*" Agent Thew says angrily. Alex panics and gasps for air as he desperately tries to come up with a response. "*Don't try and fuck around with me sunshine, I'm no one's mug.*"

"No, no, Charlie, I'm not fucking with you, I'm just trying to protect myself while I'm working towards the same thing as you."

"*Well remember who you're talking to.*" This woman exudes confidence, with a carefree air to her casual north-eastern voice. "*Why am I talking to you and not Lucy?*"

This stings Alex, he wishes that Lucy were here with him building the intelligence connections. "Lucy and I are no longer working together, she had concerns about security."

"*I can understand that. You seemed to be close to certain individuals just as their shit hit the fan. You wouldn't have been the mysterious hero that disappeared from the scene of Zafir Abdulaziz's arrest, would you?*" Alex doesn't answer, just continues to try and think of something sensible to say, his strategy has been lambasted by Charlie's direct and flagrant approach. "*Well maybe we should get together for a little chat. There are some things that I want to know, and there may be some things that I can tell you. Meet me Sunday evening, eight o'clock, at the Half Moon in Clapham; you might as well book yourself in at Lambourn Apartments on Wandsworth Road, it might be a long night.*"

"I'm not sure if I…" but Alex is talking to a dead line.

*

Alex walks back into the ops room, doing his best to radiate an aura of satisfaction with his progress. "Who's pissed on your chips?" Blakey asks as he looks up.

"No one, I'm fine. I just chatted to that potential intelligence lead. I'm meeting her Sunday."

"That's good. Should we delay the next meeting until the evening then?" Cliff asks.

"Well, I might not make it back until the morning."

"I knew it! Our prince of the pork sword's at it again." Blakey booms.

"I'm telling you, it's not like that." says Alex, trying not to giggle, or blush, but failing on both counts.

"Okay, so scratch Sunday, we'll do it Monday." says John. "What are you doing for the rest of today?"

"Nothing planned, I might try and do a bit of my own research in the meantime."

"Fancy coming with me to visit Blunt's mum? I've got an address. Maybe you could work some of your magic on her?"

6

Motherfucker

John takes a sharp left onto Danford Lane, not quite beating the red light, and narrowly missing the Kawasaki Ninja rider who had jumped the green from the right. "Fucking hell, do you always drive like this?" John doesn't acknowledge the question. He has the two-year-old white Audi A6 on almost permanent, unofficial loan from a friendly car dealer, so doesn't much respect it, or the road, or its other users.

As they head north towards the residence of Mrs Blunt, the two men discuss what lines of questioning they might explore and what the realistic chances of them discovering anything are.

"Just take everything that she says with a pinch of salt," says John, "and I mean everything."

"Do you know her then?"

"She was a Para groupie; she had an Army quarter on the patch in Aldershot. Word was she trapped Tony's dad into marrying her by getting up the duff, who knows; Tony might even have been his. They split up when Tony was young, but she hung around like a bad smell around the 'shot and would shag anything with wings on. She was one of the many reasons that Tony never got any respect from the lads when he eventually joined."

"You had wings on, John - something you want to tell me?" John just grins and shakes his head.

*

John uses the car park outside the shops in a street parallel and to the south of the address. He and Alex walk around the block and along Constantine Avenue until they find house number 211. They stand and survey the area, which has not been well looked after. There is rubbish everywhere, not so much in the street, but blown into the unkempt gardens; there are crisp packets, bottles and fast-food wrappers woven into the out of control plant life. The area seems to be a place that has given up; there are half finished building projects, with burst bags of cement spilling out onto the pavement, an almost empty, rusty old skip occupies the next house's driveway. The semi-detached houses look dated and uncared for. "What a dump." says John. The target house has the same shitty red brick walls as all of the others in the street, it does not have the shiny white window sills that most of the neighbouring house have, but flaky, old, gloss-painted rotten frames, covered in algae and mildew.

The two walk down the path at the side of the front garden, trying to avoid the brambles reaching out from their tangle with the neglected hawthorn bush. The front garden had been neat and tidy flower beds around a lawn at some point, but is now a patch of wild meadow, with a disintegrating roll of carpet for a centrepiece. They stand at the door, which has no bell, and the letterbox is missing its flap. John leans forward and knocks on the red panelling of the old, but sturdy looking door. They wait a few seconds - John knocks again.

"HANG ON, WAIT A TICK LOVEY. I'M COMING." shouts a haggard voice from within; its sound channelling at them from the aperture of the letterbox. John and Alex look at one another and smile, the randomness of this Friday afternoon task striking them simultaneously.

The door opens, and a caricature of a figure emerges from behind it, "Hello my lovelies." There is a puzzled look on the overly made-up face of the lady in her early sixties, doing her best to look as though she's in her twenties, but resulting in her looking as though she is pushing into her eighties. "Who are you?" she says grasping the collar of her leopard-print bathrobe, which doesn't quite cover her knees.

"Hello Mrs Blunt, I'm John, do you remember, I was a friend of Tony's in Aldershot?" The old lady squints at him, with no flicker of recognition.

"Sorry, darling', I've not got my specs on. Come in, the pair of you, and I'll find 'em." She turns and goes back into the house. John and Alex watch her bare, skinny legs with fluffy brown slippers disappear up the stairs. Again, they look at each other with amused expressions and step into the hallway.

*

The inside of the house is as untidy as the outside, if not worse. There are piles of stuff everywhere, every surface cluttered with papers, clothes, all kinds of household detritus. Not even just on the furniture, her belongings and rubbish are heaped on the floor too. What can be seen of the carpet is threadbare and filthy, probably covered in stains, but it is so thick with dust and grime, the colour of it cannot even be determined. Alex and John wince at each other as they walk into the living room. Alex looks at the equally disgusting sofa and armchairs and dreads the anticipated invitation to sit down. They hear mumbling chatter as Mrs Blunt struggles back down the stairs in her high heels. She has changed clothes into what look like what might be her best 'going out' gear. Her make-up is another layer thicker and her lipstick glowing fluorescent.

"Now lads, let me have a look at you." she says, grabbing her glasses from the mantelpiece above the, frankly, dangerous looking gas burner. "What did you say your name was, young man?"

"John. I was in 2 Para with your Tony, Mrs Blunt." Mrs Blunt reaches up and touches John's cheeks and looks deep into his eyes.

"Well, well, well I never. Johnny G. You never called me Mrs Blunt back in Aldershot did you Johnny? I was always your little 'sweet cakes', wasn't I Johnny?" Alex almost chokes on his tongue as John reels with embarrassment.

*

The awkwardness quickly faded, Alex and John were soon sat drinking tea from disgustingly dirty old mugs as Mrs Blunt told them about Tony's dismal life. Tony had fallen into the same trap as his father, Mrs Blunt did not describe it in such terms, but he had apparently been snared by a local Colchester girl, soon after the Battalion had moved to the Air Assault Brigade's new home, who quickly fell pregnant - before he knew it he was married with two young kids, struggling in work after an Afghan tour of ups and downs and with no real friends. He didn't put up much of a fight when his wife demanded that he leave the Army. Tony had held down a low-paid factory job for a while, but then got made redundant. He had wanted to bring his family back to Solihull, where his mum had returned by then; Alex guessed that this was because she was no longer having her way with her chosen prey of young soldiers. His already confrontational wife had not taken to the idea, and refused to budge, cutting him off, turning on him with venom, treating him like a golden goose that had stopped laying. She had also revealed that the kids were not Tony's – how true this was; Mrs Blunt couldn't be sure.

Without a job, access to his kids, still no friends, and suffering with depression - possibly Post Traumatic Stress Disorder, judging by the manifestations that Mrs Blunt was describing, Tony began to fall apart. He lived with his mum, in the shitty house in which they were now sat, a situation that could not possibly have helped his mental state. He tried desperately to make friends and find work, he caught a break and was employed as an 'apprentice' welder, learning on the job. There didn't seem to be any accreditation or paperwork involved, just long hours for low pay, but he learned a bit of a trade and was getting some experience. He spent his evenings mixing with the wrong type of friends, friends that sounded more like a disorganised gang. Mrs Blunt described how Tony had been influenced and led into trouble, culminating in him being sent to prison for manslaughter. He had lost his temper with a young lad who had been trying to boss him around. Tony's significant strength and training being too much once he had lost control; he broke the lad's neck when gripping him around the throat; Tony had only wanted to be left alone.

Once out of prison, three years later, he had become distant, and even odder than he had always been; he was into religion and growing 'that awful beard'. He moved straight out into his own place, never to be seen again by 'his poor old mum' nearly a year ago. Mrs Blunt was kind enough to let the lads look through Tony's things in what had been his bedroom. The only thing that they found, that might have been of some potential use, was Tony's old, broken laptop. John offered Mrs Blunt £100 for it, but she let him take it for the price of a hug.

"Maybe he wouldn't have turned out like this if he'd had better friends in the Regiment, eh Johnny?" she says with undertones of accusation in her voice, as they step out of the house. Mrs Blunt cuts a sad figure, stood in her doorway as they walk up the drive. As odd as Tony might be, he has left a painful gap in her life. Now well past her best, she has nothing and nobody. As amusing as John's history with her is and how random the afternoon has been, neither of the men leave the house smiling. John takes a final look back at her. She raises her palms either side of her mouth as they disappear around the corner; "Maybe Zafir was a better friend to him than any of your lot ever were?"

*

John accelerates hard out of the parking space into the smallest of gaps in the fast-moving traffic, getting a long horn-blast for his troubles. "ARRRGH FUCK OFF." he shouts out of the window. Alex feels his heartrate increase as John raises two fingers to the driver behind him and gives him the eyeball in the rear-view mirror. Alex is thankful that they take the next left and the car behind goes straight on, giving a cowardly honk as it passes through the junction. "So, what did we learn from that little visit?" John asks, breaking the tension.

"That you're a dirty, dirty man?" Alex laughs. John laughs back, he has no defence.

"Done a lot worse in Aldershot, mate." Alex's laugh turns into a grimace as he envisages the types of horrors that John is talking about.

"Seriously," John says, trying to bring the conversation back on track, "it sounds like Blunt was groomed in prison, starting about three years ago, then he comes out with a whole new focus and sense of belonging."

"And funding too. If he moved into a place on his own straight out of nick, he must have been getting money from somewhere." Alex surmises.

"Whoever it was, they were investing in him for some reason. I don't imagine him capable of masterminding anything; they must be planning to use him for something at the pointy end."

"He might have already served a supporting role in the Gardens' attack?" suggests Alex.

"Possible." John agrees.

"Still an asset at large and connected enough to make him a certainty for the compromise of our last mission." says Alex.

7

Human Traffic

Tony sits at the desk in the safe house in London. He is immersed in concentration, looking to optimise his target window of opportunity - *When are the peaks in numbers? On the way in or on the way out? What routes do they take? In which environment can I cause the most damage?* Thinking back to his military training, he considers where channelling might take place, where the concentration of force and confined conditions maximise the impact of a high energy release. He thinks about the sociocultural groups who might be in transit on the day - *Are there any religious occasions taking place that may be favourable or unfavourable? No own goals.* His focus on the screen freezes over and his mind travels back to his few minutes with Malala, as he thinks of inadvertently harming anyone like her. Her kindness, and that shown to him by his new friends, gives him pause for thought.

Tony recollects his arrival in prison, the stark reality of the cells and bright, benign walls; he had drawn parallels with some of the nicer accommodation that he had called home in Afghanistan. He had an advantage over most new prisoners; the sparse habitation and lack of friends were not new to him. Being spoken to like shit, under constant threat in an aggressive, abusive culture – it hurt less when it was at the hands of strangers, and not at those of people that should have his back.

After making no friends in his first month inside, a young Asian man had reached out to him and offered him solace. Tony was invited to join a religious group, strong in number, that thrived within the confines of the prison. All the group's members were positive, reassuring, and respectful to him. Tony regaled them with his horrific experiences in the Army and lifted them with his tale of meeting young Malala and her family, and how her family had welcomed him, and likely saved his life by offering him shelter for those few minutes.

Tony's sentence seemed to pass quickly, as life became more enjoyable than he could ever remember it being before; having real friends to talk to and to command the attention of. As the months passed, the conversation within the group had moved on from religion, and there seemed to be less time dedicated to praying, and more time discussing how their repressed lifestyle on the outside might be improved. The need for their voice to be heard and to have a place in the national conversation was debated. Tony felt that this new approach to life that he was enjoying deserved a place in British culture. Comparisons to how the Irish Republic Army had partially achieved their aims by securing attention through a campaign of terrorism and violence before buying their place at the table with the offer of peace; it all began to make a twisted sort of sense to Tony, who now saw his place as with this new family of friends.

The day came when Tony's new best friend was to be released, the one who had reached out to him. This was the first time, since the day that they had met, that Tony had felt sadness; losing the one who had brought him to this happiness hurt. "Will I see you again, Brother?"

"Of course, Tony my friend. Our network has arranged work for me near to where you live. I will be waiting for you when you get out, we will carry our mission forward together."

Tony smiled. "Take care, Zafir."

8

Tainted conscience

Alex walks slowly along the broad pavement of Old Town, Clapham. This is London doing its best to feel like a village, the miniature trees drenched in snow-like blossom and every spare corner decorated with greenery. He sees the garden of The Half Moon pub, its railed wall draped in trailing vines in bright pink flower. The facia of the pub protrudes forward of the rest of the original Edwardian brick building. Creamy pillars are interspersed with mahogany coloured window frames - he can't quite tell if they are real from a distance. The place looks comfortable and welcoming, but he fears that this liaison will not be so warm. Knowing that the lady that he is about to meet is a fearsome prospect, he focuses on summoning all of his mental strength and tries to switch himself on to the potential pitfalls of conversation, the boundaries and self-imposed constraints of what information he should not allow himself to give away.

As he pushes against the door, he realises that he doesn't actually know what Agent Thew looks like. In his mind, she is an industrious looking woman with an abrasive expression wearing a tired-looking business suit - an image of a stereotypical northern lass, as developed in the mind of a stereotypically ignorant southerner. He enters the bar, glances around the tables, most of them unoccupied. He passes by a young couple at a table for two, flirting over their shared bottle of wine, beyond them in the corner is a foxy-looking cougar of a woman dolled up to the nines, sporting the look that Mrs Blunt might have aspired to achieve in her prime, she doesn't even look up from her phone, busily scrolling through whatever social media feed that she is engrossed in. *Maybe I'm early, maybe she's late.* He walks through to the back bar, taking just a quick glance to realise that there is no one in there. He turns on his heels back through the door and stops with a shocked jolt as the cougar lady stands in his way. "Alex." she says sharply, as if calling him to attention; this is not a question - she knows who he is.

*

Alex reels on the spot, overcome with surprise that this delectable woman is his potential intelligence feed, unable to reconcile her looks with responsibility for matters of national security. In an instant, he feels himself to be a 'small m' misogynist. "Well? Cat got your tongue?" Alex has been expecting this to be a daunting encounter, but he has not anticipated feeling so cripplingly nervous.

"Hi, Charlie?" he says eventually.

"Yeah, be a love and get me a large Malbec." She pivots on one of her sharp stilettos and returns to her table; already back to her phone screen as she finishes the sentence.

Alex has another attempt at gathering himself as he stands at the bar, ordering himself a double whiskey, as much to try and outwardly show a bit of masculinity, as to steady his nerves.

The young couple walk out of the pub hand in hand as he approaches Agent Thew's table. Charlie throws her phone into her expensive-looking handbag and stares at him with a look somewhere between uncertainty and disdain, as though trying to decide where to begin a conversation that might well be a complete waste of her time. As she holds the pause, Alex takes the time to look at her in detail – her shoulder length hair is a mix of autumn browns with subtle blonde highlights, perfectly layered, framing her sternly attractive face and complementing her brown eyes. She is fashionably attired in a summery dress, light and leafy, revealing toned arms and well-tanned legs. "What are you looking at?" she snipes at him. Alex feels like a naughty, curious school boy that's just been caught looking up his teacher's skirt.

"Sorry, I'm just trying to figure you out. You're not what I was expecting."

"Did y' think I was going to be some sort a geek?" Charlie's strong Mackem accent is unfamiliar and adds a further level of complexity to the conundrum that is Agent Thew. The people of Sunderland have long been known as Mackems; as a historical centre of industry and productivity, the Geordies of Newcastle would say 'you mak'em and we'll tak'em'.

"Well I certainly didn't expect a beautiful lady of high fashion." Alex begins to relax and feels his natural charm flowing back into him. It seems to have an instant affect, and Charlie's stiffened posture melts gently; she picks up her glass of wine. As Alex begins to see her as a woman with all the natural needs and motivations; he feels the balance of power in this conversation moving slightly nearer to the middle.

"I'm working with the multi-agency team looking into the recent high-profile incidents." Charlie wastes no time at all in getting down to business. "All the focus within my organisation at the moment is on our captive, there's no link to either of the events to anyone that you're looking for, so I'm having trouble getting the spotlight to shine that way."

"Are we talking about our friend Tony?" Alex hopes that they are on the same page. Charlie tilts her head forward, her eyes locked onto his.

"Everyone else seems to think that he's a random weirdo, but he is a lead that I want chased." says Charlie, leading the conversation in the direction that Alex wants it to go, but it is now a game of words maintaining a level of deniability.

"The group that I'm working with are definitely interested in finding out more about Blunt, but we are having trouble locating him." Alex fishes for a hand up, knowing that Charlie has information and resources that would be of use.

"SIGINT from Zafir's phone shows that they were communicating."
SIGINT – Charlie references Signals Intelligence, any clues derived
from communications devices or networks; incorporating data and
the internet, this is now *the* growth sector within the world of
intelligence.

"Not any more though." Alex says.

"No, and the phone went dead well before Millbank, but the phone
records tell us a lot." Charlie says with a glint in her eye.

"I'm guessing that you've triangulated likely locations of residence?"

"Of course, that costs nothing."

"But?" Alex asks.

"But without him having done anything, and with no evidence of a
real 'Interest Group', as you have termed it, for him to be involved
with; there's no appetite to go after him - I can't get the boots on the
ground." Charlie takes a long flirtatious mouthful of wine. "I know
what he means to you and your friends though."

"So, will you give us the location?"

"I will," she says with an air of the theatrical, "under certain
conditions." Alex smiles, he doesn't ask, he swigs a hard gulp of
whiskey, doing his best to suppress the grimace that follows, not a
hundred percent successfully. Charlie smiles at his attempt to act like
the big man. "I'll need to have an element of control over what you
and your team get up to. I can't let ya loose with that information
without knowing what's gunnan on."

Alex smiles, Charlie's accent is growing on him, and is thickening with
every mouthful of wine. "So, we'd be reporting to you?"

"Not formally, you just keep me in the loop, anything important, and
if you tell me anything that has an impact my end; I might make some
requests of you - more of an agent-handler relationship than a direct

report." Charlie looks down into her almost empty wine glass as she talks and swills around what is left in the bulb of the glass.

"And if anything should go off on the ground? If anything were to happen to Blunt for example?" Alex is apprehensive; he has already said more than he had wanted to.

Charlie smiles, "You'd be one of my assets, I'd look after you. I can protect you." Alex feels a wave of satisfaction come over him. He has achieved his aim, he has successfully negotiated a working relationship with a Security Service officer, or he has slotted into Agent Thew's plan as she had always intended - however it is framed, he is happy.

"Can I get you another drink?" he asks.

"Did you book that apartment?" Charlie asks. A question out of context, Alex is a little confused.

"Yes."

"Then no thanks. Let's go and sort out this information exchange."

*

Alex holds the door for Charlie as she pulls a delicate shawl from her bag and covers her shoulders. They turn right out of the pub and head north on the Common's North Side Road with a ten-minute walk ahead of them, possibly longer Alex judges looking at Charlie's heels. He needn't have worried; she sets the pace in a way that reminds him of Lucy, but for the infrequent scraping shrieks that her heels make on the unfinished concrete of the pavement. He reopens the conversation to expunge the thought of Lucy from his head. "How did you get into this job then?"

Charlie smiles nostalgically. "Eeeeeee," she says through her teeth, "I was a young computer programmer for a gambling company, just out of university, you remember when the tabloids all had the bingo cards in 'em back in the day?" Alex has no idea what she is talking about and shrugs his shoulders. "Well I developed some of the software that helped to upscale the games for national distribution. I won an award for it and got invited to some fancy dinner in London. I was recruited, there and then, by some smarmy fella in a tuxedo – eee, he was like James Bond, I didn't take much convincing."

Alex laughs. "So, you're a technical officer then?"

"Was, I got more and more involved with cases out on the ground as my early career went on, getting called forward to support technical exploitation in the field. I enjoyed it, much more than being tucked away in some office somewhere. I started looking for more practical opportunities; it was easy back then, they always needed girls, the lack of diversity had an impact on our ability to complete intrusive field work - there are places men can't go and things they can't get away with saying, particularly to female targets. I'm back in the office more now though - getting old." She looks at Alex as they walk side by side.

"You're not old." he replies, obliging with the almost expected complement. "What are you, mid-thirties?" Alex is slipping into his 'internet dating' mode of flirtation. He hadn't expected this when he entered the pub.

"Try forties love. I'm old enough to be ya muvva."

"MILF?" Alex says as a reflex action, almost without realising it - he panics. Flirting is one thing, but this may be a step too far. He is blushing; he can see that Charlie is a little stunned.

"Pah." Charlie laughs. "I'd eat ya for breakfast." Alex feels like he's back to square one, luckily the deal is done, it's now just a case of the rest of the evening potentially being a little less comfortable. The thought crosses his mind to put what he said into context, to justify it, but his track record of trying that under pressure is not good; he knows he'll just end up digging himself into a deeper hole. "Have you got anything to drink in the apartment?" Charlie asks.

"Err, no. Sorry." Charlie breaks right from her march, turning directly into the doorway of a corner shop, she thrusts the door inwards, clinking the old-fashioned bell mounted on the frame, and disappears within. Alex stands on the pavement still in a state of bewilderment. He doesn't move for the minute or so that she is inside. The door clinks open with another chime of the bell. "Feeling thirsty?" he asks, as she stands facing him holding a paper bag with two bottle-shaped bulges in it.

"I work better when I've had a glass or two. You drink red I take it?

"I'm an ex-squaddie; I'll drink anything." he smiles back at her. *Maybe all is not lost; maybe she took it as flattery after all?*

*

"Are there any glasses in this place?" Charlie takes two bottles of Shiraz from the bag and stands them on the lounge coffee table as Alex retrieves his laptop from the bedroom of the compact apartment. "Watching your saucy videos in there were you?" Charlie says with a smirk. Alex laughs coyly.

"I'll get the glasses." he says as he places his computer down next to the wine. Charlie picks up the nearest bottle and reads the label; she looks at it without expression as Alex returns. "Looks pretty cheap and nasty?" he suggests.

"There wasn't much choice. Have you got a pen drive?" she asks.

"Sure." Alex says. He places the small, plain wine glasses down in front of Charlie and returns to the bedroom. Charlie twists the lid off the bottle with a snap and serves it without spillage, though a single droplet rolls down the outside of the bottle; she tilts her head and licks the neck all the way up to the thread. "Good technique." Alex says with a grin, hoping that the sexual banter is now flowing openly in both directions.

"Eee, shurrup." Charlie puts the bottle down and leans over the arm of the brown, two-seater leather sofa, unzips the centre section of her handbag, pulls out a palm-top computer and places it, open, on her lap. Give me that here." She snatches Alex's pen drive from him as he sits down beside her. "This is cosy, isn't it?" Charlie shuffles into a comfortable position with her hands raised, using her arms to help wriggle herself low in the seat. Alex looks on with amusement.

"I'll make no comment about the size of it." Charlie says as she inspects the pen drive. She plugs it into the side of her computer and slides it across for Alex to enter his password.

"I've not had any…" Alex pauses as he sees a window open and all the files on the pen drive getting sucked across into the memory of Charlie's computer. "What the hell was that?" He asks, with anger and desperation in his voice.

"Oh, sorry, it's set up to do that automatically, it's for covert ops. I was supposed to have asked you if it there was anything on it before I plugged it in. Nothing sensitive on there I hope?"

Alex shudders with the fear of realisation of what he has just allowed to happen – *how can I be this stupid?* A raging mix of anger and anguish burn through his body; he is paralysed by it. His filtered copy of the Watch List is on that drive, as is the back-up of the caller groups and message threads from the secure voice and messaging application that his team had used to command and control their mission. This information is evidence that links Alex to the mission and he has given it on a platter to a Security Service agent.

"Are you all right? You look like you've seen a ghost."

"Oh, no, I'm fine. I just need that glass of wine." Alex considers his options; say nothing and hope that she never looks at the files, convince Charlie that she needs to remove the files from her system or gain access to the laptop and remove them himself – *let's see where these two bottles of wine get us.*

Charlie opens a folder on her screen titled 'Abdulaziz-Zafir'. Clicking into that; there are several sub-folders, she selects 'mobile phone interrogation'. "We've generated a number of reports based on the data from Zafir's phone records." Alex can see from the file names that text, geo-data, and call lists are included and there is a written report.

"What are the headlines?" Alex asks, hoping to cut to the chase. He struggles to see how this will be a long night's work if this is all there is.

Charlie takes a long drink of wine; "Top that up, will you?" She hands him her glass and clicks open the only text document in the folder. "Call records show that Abdulaziz was only talking to five or so people, but consistently and frequently - this phone has only been in use for three months and only called this same group of numbers – classic 'burner phone' characteristics." Charlie plays her own devil's advocate; "It could be a new phone, he might only have a few friends, but when we look at the geo-data of this number and the distant end numbers; it paints a remarkably clear picture." Charlie takes her glass back and immediately starts sipping. Alex takes a drink and finds the wine easier on the palette now that the taste of whiskey has had a chance to dissipate, and is beginning to feel the warming effects of the combination of drinks; he allows his shoulders to relax and lets himself enjoy the briefing that is being delivered in the most intriguing, and strangely relaxing of voices.

"This handset made calls to two numbers that were answered mostly in London, and three in the Birmingham area, one of those was usually picking up in the Solihull area."

"Blunt's area." It was not a complex puzzle for Alex to piece together.

Charlie smiles – "So what do you know about Tony Blunt?" she asks with an officious tone, giving Alex a feeling that he has given something away. He doesn't feel up to the challenge of playing mental chess with an opponent as fearsome as Charlie. He quickly analyses what knowing about Tony Blunt might tell Charlie about what he has been up to and trusts himself that she is just being her bolshie self.

"Tony Blunt? He's a former 2 Para soldier who appears to have been radicalised. Colleagues of mine had a run-in with him a couple of weeks ago, but since then he seems to have disappeared." Charlie eyes him suspiciously for a second, seeming to know that there is more to it.

"Don't be playing me, young man." she says with a threatening, but simultaneously sly humorous tone. "Anyway," she goes on, "Zafir appears to be close to Blunt. Not only did he call the number assumed to be Blunt's, but he made calls from the vicinity of Blunt's house to some of the other numbers picked up in London."

"So, he spent time at Blunt's place, as well as spoke to him on the phone?"

"Exactly. Similar analysis of what we think is Blunt's number shows him making calls from near to Zafir's address in Hodgehill." Charlie pauses, looking at Alex until she feels that his mind has processed what she has told him. "There's more." she holds his gaze, "Blunt's number made calls from the vicinities of post codes PE3 and HP13 amongst others."

Alex says nothing, he is stunned into silence. Charlie matches his silence, not wanting to expand, not wanting to spell out the depth of her knowledge. Alex recovers to confirm what Charlie already knows; "Blunt was at my flat, he was at Lucy's flat?" Charlie nods. "What about Millbank?" Charlie shakes her head, "No; we don't think Millbank was planned until after this phone went dead, and if we had evidence that he had been there on some sort of recce, then that would have been enough on him for me to make him a priority suspect - as it is; he's the lowest of those on Zafir's contact list. What I've learned about what you, Lucy and your friends were getting up to, has had to stay off record, so I haven't acknowledged his involvement with you in any of my reporting – for your protection." Charlie gives Alex a searching look with her deep brown eyes. "You can say 'thank you' if you like?"

Alex winces out of his partial stupor. "Sorry, Charlie, thank you."

Charlie spends another twenty minutes talking through the possible leads, but mostly dead ends, generated from the interrogation of the mobile handset and the data taken from phone records of all the numbers called from it. Whilst the discussion is complex and takes most of his mental capacity to manage, Alex feels comfortable and is beginning to enjoy the cerebral workout, as he senses the pressure ease from Charlie, who now seems to be firmly on his side.

"It's just a shame that all of these numbers, including Blunt's, are now dead." Charlie says with an air of resignation and seemingly bringing the overview of the analysis that she has completed to an abrupt end. Blunt's phone died around the date you say your friends had a coming together with him. The others vanished from the network on the evening before the Millbank bombing, just before 159 terror suspects were mysteriously killed." Alex can feel Charlie's eyes on him, looking for clues in his body language. He feels supremely self-conscious once more - there is nowhere to hide. He tries to swallow; it feels like he has a rock in his throat. He edges around a little in his seat, aiming himself a little more towards her, doing his best to exude confidence.

"So, what have we got then?" he asks, in an effort to deflect, "The probable locations of the accommodation that Zafir, Blunt, a couple of characters in Birmingham, and a couple in London were using?"

"That's the long and the short of it. No other real tangibles." Charlie closes her palm-top down and places it back in her handbag. She picks her glass up and turns towards him, "Top us up again." Now almost face to face, Alex feels a different type of heat; he feels like a rabbit trapped in the headlights, but not in a bad way. He feels dominated; at the mercy of this seductive and undeniably attractive older woman - a woman who now holds enough evidence to link him to the killing of 159 people. Outside of such circumstances, his feelings, still live for Lucy, would prevent him from getting any closer than he already is, but he feels compelled to play on.

He pours the wine, first her glass and then his. Spurred on by his liberated carnal desire and with a subdued determination to develop another excuse for taking this liaison further; he drinks a little faster as the conversation develops away from terror suspects. Charlie seems excited by the tale of his brief and fairly uneventful time in the Army, and Alex is genuinely impressed by the limited detail that Charlie gives him on her steps up the rungs of her MI-5 career and some of the high-profile jobs that she has been involved with.

As Alex pours the last dregs of the second bottle, he senses a change in Charlie's body language, they lay back slouched together, both in states of reduced inhibition. "Oh yeah, you, as for 'MILF' – I haven't got kids." Alex isn't sure how to react – *is she happy with that being the case? Is it a sad thing?* He decides to take it in the context of the situation; the drink, the flirting, the apartment that she had suggested he book, with only one king-sized bed.

"What does that make you then? A WILF?"

"WILF?" she says with a confused squint and a cock of her head.

"Just a 'woman' I'd like to fuck." Uncharacteristically boldly, Alex rolls towards Charlie and slides his hand up the side of her neck and up into her hair which feels as silky as it looks. As he carries his momentum forward and moves in to kiss her, she grabs his wrist and lurches at him, making him slide down to sit on the carpet; she straddles his lap, now holding both of his wrists up against the front edge of sofa cushion. She looks him in the eye with a stern look.

"I told ya, I'll eat you for breakfast." almost as a challenge. Alex cannot sense what might come next. Charlie leans down harder on his arms and pushes herself up momentarily before descending on him, violently pressing her lips against his with animal passion.

9

Eyes on

The white Ford Fiesta hasn't provided the most comfortable of rides for someone Tony's size, but it has provided a low profile, and that is all that matters. He indicates to leave the A1(M) and follows the signs to the services, up the slip road, right at the roundabout, over the motorway to the east, and into the almost empty car park.

Tony drives towards the outside of the small cluster of cars that have been lazily abandoned around the entrance to the facilities. The car comes to a halt in a bay that is empty on the left and to his front. There is plenty of space on the right for the small car's surprisingly long door to open; the owner of the expensive-looking Land Rover in the adjacent spot has parked over their right side line, either through bad driving, or as Tony cynically assumes; deliberately, to prevent anyone parking within scratching distance of their prized motor. *I'd score the whole side of that bastard with my key if it wouldn't attract attention.* He grabs his small rucksack from the front passenger seat and gets out of the little car. He locks the door, then looks at the thick hexagonal head of the key to the old Ford, but manages to suppress his raging urge to deface the immaculate dark metallic green surface of the over-sized Rover's passenger door.

Using the huge, badly parked car for cover, Tony checks his surroundings; there is no one around that is taking any notice. He puts the car key into a small pouch at the top of his rucksack as the next car passes by, then heads towards the edge of the car park. As he steps out onto the open tarmac a jet-black Vauxhall Corsa, with body-kit and screeching engine, lurches towards him as though threatening to run him over. The driver honks long and loud on its horn as Tony jumps back with a jolt. A flash of adrenaline jets through him and he snarls with anger – *I'll follow the little cunt into the toilets and end him there and then*. Again, Tony finds himself gathering himself from an internal storm of rage. He takes a deep breath, finds his composure, and walks out of the car park.

Tony heads roughly east, crossing the road that heads south into Great Gonerby. He navigates the arable countryside easily, hand-railing hedges and tracks, avoiding designated footpaths and dwellings. After ten minutes he finds himself walking in a deep furrow at the edge of a potato field with a thick, rich green forestry block on his left side. He reaches the end of the small block of greenery and looks through the draping canopy of low branches of the last trees. He sees what he is looking for – at a range of about five-hundred metres, in the middle distance north-north-east, he makes out the farm complex - a homestead, barns and other buildings. He sees the silhouette of the house through a layer of trees, from the rear left. On the north side of farm, across its access lane, and only just visible to Tony, is a commercial property – *the foundry*.

Tony is as close as he wants to get in plain view. He retreats back along the wood line and takes the long route around the outside of the potato field, heading east along its southern edge, then north at the corner, bringing him back towards the farm, shielded from view by the small copse of trees to its rear – classic rose-petalling; moving in and out of range of the target to gain different and better lines of approach and views of what you want to see.

The route to the back of the property is in perfect soft cover, a wall of green hides Tony from view. He finds his way into the trees, breeching an old, low barbed-wire fence; the type that he has noted creating obstacles throughout the landscape. As he climbs over the fence, the rotten post threatens to crumble under his weight, Tony catches his glove on the wire as he jumps clear, "Fucking hell." he says under his breath, baring his teeth and snarling outwardly to nobody.

He makes his way over the difficult ground towards the northern edge of the copse, taking his time to step down on the brambles and nettles, but guiding his toes between any fallen branches that might snap and give him away – the lowest level of tactical movement as taught in the Reg. The small area of trees seems to have been long forgotten; most of what lays on the ground has decomposed into a soft mulch. Tony slows further as he nears the treeline that faces the house; he becomes aware of a full, rich smell of the countryside. He looks out from the trees to see the back of the farmhouse about fifty metres away. Between him and the house is a large garden, split into a well-kept vegetable patch to the left and a flower garden, in full bloom, to the right. The garden is lined on both sides with thick hedges.

The smell would seem to be coming from the compost heap to his immediate front. There are three pens separated by sheets of flimsy, brittle corrugated plastic, staked in place with long steel spikes. The waste matter in each of the pens are at varying degrees of decomposition, the one to his left is fresh, with tables scraps, sprinkled liberally over grass-cuttings, still moist and green, and a good bucket's worth of horse shit that hasn't found its way much past the front of the pen. The middle and right pens have been sealed off with a layer of grass-cuttings, the middle pen looks similar to the fresh cuttings of the first pile, but with a sepia filter over them – discoloured over time. The top of the third heap has clearly been untouched for years, the individual blades of grass cannot be made out; it looks like a drab papier-mâché hilltop that has been left out in the rain, the plant fibres appearing rough and dusty. Tony notes that this pile has been recently used; there is a gaping hole at the front of the heap. From what he can see from his view from the rear; the compost is extremely rich and has a moist treacle-like quality. The smell almost seems to become directional from this spot – *note to self: don't try and climb through that.*

The copse offers good cover and might make a good location for an observation post, but he needs a view inside the farmyard. He continues to his right, in line with the end of the garden, and to the end of the small block of trees. Tony takes a minute to observe what lies beyond; a wheat field, its crop of lush green beginning to show signs of yellowing, extends out to the south adjacent to the potato field, and north as far as the lane, where there is a low hedge. A thick hedgerow of hawthorn, brambles and nettles lines the border between this field and the eastern edge of the farmhouse garden and farmyard. Tony emerges from the copse and follows the line of the hedgerow beyond the garden and past the gable end of the farmhouse. Through this hedgerow, north of the house, there will be views available into the yard – *this will be it.*

Tony checks in all directions that there is no one in view, then gently pushes the nettles and long grass aside with the edge of his boot. He gets to his knees, pushes his hands out in front of him in a diving motion, then lets himself fall slowly forward into the hedge. He bites down, anticipating the thorns and branches digging into his arms and top of his head, but reaches the floor relatively unscathed. The hedgerow is mature, unkempt and burgeons to nearly four metres thick. He shuffles himself forward, with a caterpillar-like movement until he is most of the way through to the other side - there is sufficient room for manoeuvre, and he is able to stand without too much difficulty - *perfect view of the farmyard, but is it too near? I could sneeze or fart and be heard… or smelt; keep looking.* He reverse-shuffles back out to the wheat field, shakes himself down, and continues north towards the lane. Forty metres beyond the farmhouse there is a break in the hedgerow and a well-rutted few metres of dirt track joins the yard to the field.

Tony takes a few seconds to exploit the view and get a partial appreciation of the farmyard and its assets. He can see most of the yard, which extends beyond the farmhouse, possibly as far as the end of the garden, where there are what looks like large corn stores at the back, to the south, which form the limit of an annexed corner - this area has assorted tractor attachments strewn across it; ploughs, rollers, a hedge-cutter and a couple of bulk fuel tankers. Scoping round to the right; there is a continuous line of low sheds along the western side of the yard. The buildings in this row then jump in size where the yard opens up to its full width, becoming a tall, open-fronted structure – a machinery shed, housing a combine harvester in the first and largest bay, then three tractors of varying sizes in the adjoining bays, a further two that he can see house other agricultural machinery and paraphernalia. The row continues all the way to where the yard spills out onto the lane, though Blunt's view is skewed by the front of the enormous silver barn that stands opposite the farmhouse.

Tony steps past the gap and continues to follow the hedgerow north towards the lane. He can see the back of the large barn behind the broad, ancient hedge; it extends to the corner of the field where the hedgerow meets the lane and adjoins to the lower, thinner, greener hedge that tracks the lane to the east. Tony assesses that the older hedgerow continues around the corner, behind the barn, following the line of the lane to the west. Tony dismisses the idea of identifying any further potential hide locations, based on what he has seen across the yard, and what he knows from his internet map recce of the north and west. He is interested in what lies to the north of the lane, but this is for another day.

10

Sitrep

The men take their seats around the conference room table, each nursing a brew. John leads the meeting, kicking off with a back-brief of what he and Alex had learned from Blunt's mother, painting the picture of Blunt's poor mental state and loneliness, leading to pent-up anger, and culminating in him snapping at a young lout and getting sent to prison.

"We should look at press articles from the trial, maybe try and get a hold of the transcripts; there could be all sorts of leads, names of the other gang members for a start." says Blakey. "I'll take that on." he raises his eyebrows towards John, animating his enthusiasm for the task.

"Yeah, go for it." says John. The room is quiet in anticipation of who will give their back-brief next. Alex sits back and waits to hear the full read-out from everyone else before making his contribution. "So how did you get on?" John asks the others.

"We got on all right at the previous employer's gaff," says Cliff, "they confirmed that Blunt had worked there, they didn't want to say much - I don't think that their working practises are up to much. They said that he had become a competent metal worker, and that they were sorry to have to let him go when he was charged and held on remand. He never came back for his job after he was released."

"And they didn't have any onward contact details for him either?" Spence asks despondently. Blakey pinches his lips and shakes his head.

"I take it you didn't get anywhere with his place then Spence?" John asks. Spence shrugs his eyebrows, sitting back in his chair; he says nothing more about this slice of the investigation, but exudes his sense of shame at not making any progress on what might have been considered a simple task for a man of his considerable experience. "How did your meeting go with the intelligence source?" he deflects to Alex.

"Yeah, Alex, did you get your hands on anything juicy?" Blakey laughs, cupping his hands over his chest, squeezing his pec's like breasts; everyone laughs, even Spence.

"It was interesting, I'll give you that." Alex concedes. "I can shed some light on the location of Blunt's address for a start." Everyone nods an acknowledgement, signing that they are impressed. "I've got some details that can really help us out, but the crux of my meeting," Alex pauses for effect, "is that if we want to keep this Security Service source alive; we will need to reciprocate, send information the other way." Again, Alex pauses, this time to gauge the feeling of his colleagues. He doesn't sense any reticence, so pushes a little further; "They also might want to have some level of input into the direction that our venture takes." Body language around the table changes immediately and there is a lot of shuffling in seats.

"Classic MI-5." says Spence. Alex doesn't understand and looks to John and back to Spence.

"What do you mean?" he asks, sensing his own naivety.

"Letting us do their dirty work with no culpability or come back on them, but collecting enough evidence to stitch us up if it all goes tits up."

"I don't think it's like that." Alex retorts, grimacing at the apparent cynicism of his colleagues and knowing that his lapse in security, allowing Charlie to access his files, would not go down at all well in present company.

"Oh, it is." says John. "We need their help, but we'll need to be careful, Alex. How far did your 'relationship-building' go?" Everyone smirks. Alex is glowing in anticipation of the roasting he might be about to get; he needs to provide assurance that things with Charlie are as smooth as possible, but doesn't necessarily wish to go into the detail of how far things have gone with her. His mind flirts with the idea of letting some clues of his prowess slip, in an egotistical moment of self-indulgence, but it passes.

"Look, fellas, this agent knows enough about what Lucy and I got up to during the last mission to have me put away for a long time; I've got her trust, and she's got mine. I won't be sharing anything that she doesn't approve of, and I won't be giving away any of your identities." Alex feels that he is winning them over. "I get a real feeling that Charlie's motivations, and desired outcomes, are aligned to ours – her help, and even direction, might get us to where we need to be. Blunt's address might just be the start of it. If that comes up a blank; we'll be back to square one and out of leads without a decent intelligence feed."

"Okay, Alex." says John with a calm, considered voice, his eyes down, playing with his pen. He looks up and points the nib of his Biro at Alex to fix his attention. "It seems like you're on to a good thing here, but just be mindful; this 'Charlie', she's using you, and that's fine, but she'll give you the rope you need to hang yourself, probably us too – think about what you tell her and why, every detail."

"Roger, will do." says Alex.

Spence stirs uneasily and tilts a nod to Alex; "If you can get any sort of record of her giving you information or instructions; that might serve as some sort of protection, a bit of back-up."

Alex nods back, "Got it, no problem."

Feeling satisfied that he has the authority of the group to maintain the proposed arrangement with Charlie, Alex tries to use what he has learned from her to enhance the group's sentiment towards her. He explains to them how Zafir's phone had been interrogated by The Security Service's tech team and that it had revealed the link to what was thought to be Blunt's old phone.

"So, they pin-pointed the signals of those phones accurately enough to give you Blunt's address?" Blakey asks. Alex smiles as he thinks about how best to explain the expected level of precision offered by the triangulation.

"What we have is a spot on the map, which happens to be on a property in a Solihull neighbourhood. That spot was arrived at by compiling individual triangulations of a mobile phone signal every time that it had been pinged by multiple mobile phone masts using the data from over the course of a couple of months. Sometimes it might have been only picked up by three masts, sometimes it might have registered on five or six – we are lucky that the density of the population in the residential area means that the density of masts has to be higher to cope with the weight of phone user demand, so the individual pings are more accurate than might normally be expected. This amount of data should mean that the accuracy of the triangulation is reliable to within five metres, and it *should* be our target building."

"That sounded like a big 'should', Alex?" Cliff interrupts.

"Well, if the phones were used consistently in the same place, then any interference or refraction might consistently give an inaccurate reading, consistently off in one particular direction." Alex answers as honestly as he can.

"What are the chances of that?" John asks.

"I'd say negligible."

"What makes you so sure?" asks Cliff.

"A couple of things, but the biggest factor is that Blunt and Zafir's phones were on different networks, but yielded locations in the same building."

"So, the masts were in different positions, but calculated almost the same spot for their respective phones?" Spence ventures.

"Exactly."

"That's good enough for me." says John. "What's the plan then?"

Spence has relished the chance to get his teeth into a chunk of the mission; "We stake the address out for an afternoon, make sure we've got the right place, then enter after dark and go through it like a dose of salts." Positive glances are exchanged around the table.

11

The Solihull address

"I'm still not sure how I got this gig." Alex says slumped over the steering wheel of the ageing, faded metallic-turquoise Volkswagen Passat. It is late on a Tuesday afternoon and they are illegally, and therefore conspicuously parked; there is no on-street parking at all in either direction on either side of the road.

"Broadest possible cross-section of experience; you and me." Spence says without breaking his gaze, which is firmly locked on the target house.

"What do you mean?" Alex asks.

Spence turns to look at Alex with a smile. "No point sending any of the others, we've had basically similar training when it comes to this type of job, I've had more if anything. Having you here gives us some diversification, what wit' your technical know-how." He smiles at himself, pleased with his improvised answer. "Non-too-shabby this place our Tony got for himself don't you think?" The broad residential street is lined with some fairly desirable detached homes. Some of the buildings are the original bungalows, over sixty years old, a few added to with extensions and porches, other houses are new and unique shapes - complete rebuilds, some bulging to the boundaries of their allotted space, others are smaller and more discreet – the target property is one of the latter, in fact, it is possibly the smallest house on the entire road, certainly within view, but looks well built. It is of a dark brick with wood effect-brown plastic window sills. Most of the front garden has been sacrificed for a double driveway, and what is left of the borders are overgrown with weeds and grass, choking whatever bedding plants had been there before, less for the strong, bushy lavender near to the path on the left side of the neat small-block paving.

"What do you think? A spacious two-bedroom, or slightly more cluttered three-bed?" Alex doesn't answer, just smiles. "What's t' matter wit' ya?" Spence asks curiously, perplexed at Alex's spontaneous amusement.

"I can't believe you're not Irish with that accent." Alex turns to Spence, hoping to prompt a conversation. Spence laughs mutedly as he leans on his left elbow against the grubby beige door trim and rests the knuckle of his forefinger above his top lip, brushing the philtrum beneath his nose.

"I done some time in the provinces all right." He says meekly. "I toured there as a young Highlander and found it strangely enjoyable. I went on to do the Hereford course and went back there, I got heavily into the under-cover stuff, agent handling – that's the kind of investment you can't easily walk away from." Spence gives Alex a wry grin and looks back towards the target house.

"So, the Army kept you over there?" Alex asks.

"Yeah, but not like I was forced to stay there; it became my life. Ya heard of 14 Intelligence Company?"

"14 Int?" Of course he'd heard of it, it was one of the most legendary military units that had ever existed. "Only the myths and legends." Alex's eyes glint with anticipation, eager to hear more from someone who had actually served with a unit that had been thought of by some as a Government sponsored death squad.

"Well, my lad, most of those stories ain't myths. I was with the Det for what seemed like a lifetime." Spence's accent seems to thicken as he stirs the memories. "We got some serious work done over there, and we saw a lot of soldiers leave tha' place in boxes, I'll tell ya."

"It must have been intense?" Alex asks somewhat redundantly. Spence tuts a laugh, underlining Alex's understatement.

"You had to be three steps ahead of the enemy, all the time, night and day." He flicks a look over his shoulder and then focuses back on the house. "You certainly wouldn't park on a bare-arsed feckin' street like this in broad daylight." Come on; let's get da fook outta here."

*

Alex drives on south-east, past the house, both men keep their eyes fixed on it as they pass by. "It looks empty and abandoned enough." says Alex.

"I'd imagine Blunt left in a hurry after his coming together with John and co in Hodgehill. I'd doubt he'd even have come back here after that, so he wouldn't."

They follow the road just a hundred yards or so to a T-junction. "Left here, fella, then immediately right into the sports centre." The car park exit is almost opposite their junction, Alex sees the entrance as he pulls out onto the road. He indicates right and waits for a car coming the opposite way to emerge from under the narrow tunnel under the railway bridge. They park near to the entrance, Spence pays at the machine and they walk out of the leisure centre grounds, and onto the path of the main road. The bridge on their right carries the rail tracks over the road where it continues behind Blunt's row of houses. Between the track and the fences of the back gardens is a footpath. The entrance onto the footpath from the road is across from them. They cross and disappear into the greenery.

"Handy for trains." Alex says. Spence doesn't reply, he's checking the path in front to make sure that they are alone.

"That's convenient." Spence says as they near the back of the house. Alex sees the small cluster of three or four small trees outside of the fence at the back of the property.

Spence walks into the low foliage of the trees, disappearing from view. Alex pauses, unsure of what is expected of him and fearful of making any novice mistakes in the presence of a seasoned expert in such operations. "Getcha self in here ya eejit."

Alex pushes himself through the soft branches, protecting his face with a raised elbow. Inside, he is surprised that there is open space which appears to be well used. Any inwardly pointing branches have been snapped off long ago and the earth is exposed, all grass and greenery worn away, the soil is cracked and almost polished to a shine in places, likely caused by the slide of backsides over it by its usual frequenters. There is litter in the peripheries, primarily lager tins, sweet wrappers and empty tobacco pouches lodged in the tufts of grass. Spence is on his tiptoes peering over the fence; at about six feet tall, he can just about see over it. The view of the house is partially broken by the leafy overhanging branches, but the cover is welcome.

"The curtains are all open, no sign of life at the moment." says Spence. Alex stands next to him and looks for himself. The back of the house is in much the same condition as the front; stylish, but unloved. There is no sign of a conventional back door, but there is a small six-sided conservatory blistered on to the left side of the back of the property, which has a door on its right side. There is a large-block patio in the space immediately outside the conservatory door – the flag stones are green with algal growth. The rest of the garden's length, fifteen metres or so, is mostly lawn that hasn't seen a mower in at least a year, it is peppered with weeds and meadow flowers and a few odd saplings springing to about waist height.

"What's the plan then?" Alex asks. Spence steps away from the fence to face him.

"There was one car in the drive at number fifty-three," Spence points to the house to the left of the target building as they look at it, "but no sign of anyone in at either of the neighbouring houses." Alex hadn't thought to look at the neighbouring houses, either when at the front, from the car, or now from the rear. Spence's experience and depth of knowledge is clear in everything that he has said and done so far; Alex feels his confidence in mission success bolstered in his presence. Spence goes on; "I reckon we give it an hour to be sure that there's no one in the target house, or any nosey neighbours either side, then breech entry from the rear." Alex is a little surprised that things might move on so quickly, he had mentally prepared for a long period of watching and waiting, but he trusts Spence's assessment of the situation and the associated risk – *there's probably more risk of being discovered by junkies in here than there is of being caught going into the house in broad daylight.* "That'll have us in there before the neighbours start coming home from work. We'll be inside for a good few hours and leave under the cover of darkness."

*

The next hour passes without incident; there is a near miss with a dog-walker, but no movement in any of the houses. "Right." says Spence, signalling that it is time for action. He puts his back against the fence, bends his knees and offers his palms, one on top of the other, to Alex as a step up. Alex shuns the offer and uses his 'party piece' talent, vaulting the fence in a single leap, pressing hard down on his hands on the top edge of the fence to launch himself into the air – he clears the fence without touching it with his feet, he controls his flight through the air with his firm grasp of the top of the fence and lands confidently on both feet in the long, scruffy grass of the neglected garden.

Alex gets used to his slightly altered perspective on the space as he waits for Spence to join him. He sees Spence's fingers grip the top of the fence and his head and his right foot quickly join them, he is soon up on the top of the fence, the weight of his leading leg dragging his body over – he slides down gracefully, and dusts himself down as he turns to face Alex.

He leads Alex up the garden, staying to the right side, the fence offering good cover from view on this side, but they are exposed to anyone who might be watching from the left. Alex feels like the naughty schoolboy in a neighbour's garden retrieving his football. He makes his way towards the side door of the conservatory. Alex watches with intrigue as Spence plants his feet in a firm stance with his body in line with the door handle – *what clever method is he going to use to break in?*

Spence grabs the handle with both hands with a firm grip, getting both the palms of his hands behind it. He lifts his right leg and places his foot on the door frame, then lunges backwards and yanks with all his might, wrenching the UPVC door open. "Feckin cheap shite." He says over his shoulder with a grin. They step inside; Alex pulls the door to behind him.

*

The conservatory is a bright space, despite the grimy windows. The cheap wicker furniture is splintering at the corners and the blue patterned cushions are bleached from continuous exposure to the sun's rays, to the point where the material on the tops of the seat backs are almost white and beginning to fray. There is a small, circular, glass-topped top table, with a white enamelled frame, with nothing on it, pushed up against the side of one of the armchairs. Everything has a thick layer of dust and grit on it. "Keep your eyes open for a brush or a hoover, we'll need to get rid of those." Spence points a lazy forefinger from his already downward pointing right arm at the marks left in the dust by his first few steps.

They move on through the screen door into the small living room. It is neat and tidy, but similarly to the conservatory; the furniture has an 'entry level' appearance, cheap and cheerful as might be expected in a 'buy-to-let' property. "He doesn't take after his mum." says Alex, referencing the shit-state of her place. Spence doesn't acknowledge his comment, he is focused on the task in hand, scouring the place visually for any immediate indicators, clues, or items of intelligence value.

"Remember the 'victim operated threat'." Spence says, reminding Alex that the last residence that he had searched was booby-trapped. Alex immediately puts himself on a heightened state or alertness.

"We've got all the time in the world, so take your time, and don't go wandering off, best we stick together."

Alex and Spence systematically sweep through the property from the bottom up. Owing to Blunt's tidiness, and despite Spence's painstaking thoroughness and clever insights into where things might be stashed or secreted, they are soon on their way up the stairs to the bedrooms, having found nothing of interest on the ground floor. The smaller of the two bedrooms shows no sign of occupation; no bedding on the yellowing mattress of the standard double bed, and empty cupboards and drawers. They move through into the bathroom, it appears unused, not even a toilet roll on the holder. Spence is impressed by Alex's suggestion to crack the facia off the front of the bath to check the space beneath the tub, it dawns on him that Alex had searched Zafir's flat just a couple of weeks ago.

Still without any findings of note, they enter the master bedroom. Apart from the decomposing food in the kitchen, this is the first room in the house to show any sign of inhabitants. The bed is made up with a faded navy-blue quilt-cover and pillow set, it looks to have been slept in, but pulled straight. Spence lifts the edge of the duvet and slides a hand under, running his palm over the sheet. "What are you doing?" Alex asks.

"A mattress can hold body heat longer than you'd think. If anyone had been in this bed last night; I'd be able to detect a subtle temperature change between the middle and the extremities." Spence's negative body language tells Alex that it is not the case.

There is a white Formica bedside table to the right of the bed and a matching desk under the window. On the left side of the room there is a walk-in wardrobe and the entrance to an en suite shower room beyond that. Spence signposts Alex towards the wardrobe with body language that shields the bedroom furniture, he turns and takes a knee in front of the bedside table, opening the larger bottom drawer with care.

Alex fears that there will be nothing to find in the wardrobe, as the rail to his right is empty of clothes. There is a pair of old, but clean, Army issued black boots on the floor tray, in the far corner beneath the rail; Alex checks that there is nothing hidden inside them. To his left, there are two large cupboards either side of mirror and a bank of drawers under each of the cupboards. The gap beneath the mirror has a shelf, which is intended as a small dressing table, but there is no chair, and nothing adorning the surface.

Alex takes a deep breath and opens the left cupboard slowly and gently. He peeks inside as it clicks open; he is initially pleased to see something, but then disappointed as he realises that it is only clothing, scruffy old jumpers, and a waterproof coat. He moves across to the other cupboard to find jeans, walking trousers and jogging bottoms. He has no success from the drawers either, only thread-bare underwear and socks with holes and strings of elastic hanging from them. He returns to the main room.

"He's kept this place pretty sterile." Alex offers. Spence gives him what is becoming a customary, and now almost expected ignoring, remaining trained on the contents of one of the desk drawers, which he has pulled out and placed on the carpet. Alex looks over Spence's work so far; the other two drawers from the desk are parked underneath it and a few items lie next to them in the shade. The two drawers of the bedside table have been removed and are placed, one on top of the other, beside its remaining carcass; there doesn't appear to be much by way of contents in them. "Found anything interesting?" Alex tries again to provoke some interaction.

"Possibly." Spence says eventually, "Take a look at these." he hands Alex a small booklet, stuffed with scraps of paper of varying sizes that he has separated from the other drawer contents. Alex takes the booklet and eases himself down to Spence's level, rolling into a seated position against the wall on the right side of the desk. He ignores the booklet for just a few seconds, taking the time to appreciate Spence in action; his furrowed brow full of concentration, examining every item, trying to ascertain any potential macabre uses for each item in turn, or any possible way that each item might hold additional information that might otherwise pass them by. Spence's long greasy black twists of hair hang down over his face, masking his apparent age, possibly bringing it back to about where it should be, as the rigours of his life have aged his features, though not yet greyed his hair.

Alex opens the booklet and removes the first of the cuttings; he shudders inside as he sees the words of the headline *"Pavilion Gardens' event receives a boost"*. Alex leafs through the rest of the cuttings, they all reference Pavilion Gardens, the venue of the festival that was hit by a savage hostile vehicle and bomb attack just over a month ago. The attack had provided the impetus and motivation for Alex to follow through on his idea to steal the UK Terror Watch List, and to take it to Craig. It becomes clear to Alex that Blunt is not only the man who caused that mission to take losses, but that he is also now deeply implicated in the planning of the atrocity that killed sixty-nine people, a toll which may yet rise further. "Shitty death." Alex says once the shock has washed over him.

"Certainly seems like he might be a proper bad-lad." Spence says, again without looking up.

"Is there anything else?" Alex asks.

"Nothing. He's been well disciplined apart from those."

"I wonder what Charlie will make of these?" Alex says wafting the cuttings in the air.

"Well, we'll have to have a think about what we're going to tell our Security Service friends now, won't we." Spence has arrogance in his voice, making Alex feel undermined and robbed of his perceived authority of the intelligence situation. Alex thinks through what passing this information across to Charlie might mean for the team. His initial reflex response had been that flagging this would help Charlie attract more resources to tracking down Blunt. With further thought, he begins to see Spence's natural consideration; with Blunt as a central figure in the Gardens' incident, their unofficial team would not get a look in. Blunt might come to justice eventually, maybe even more quickly, but not at the hands of the likes of John or Spence, or any other of the hoods that he has fallen in with. Alex would rather avoid rough justice but considers that their approach may be more likely to discover any further connections that Blunt may have, that he may be less likely to give up to the authorities.

The pros and cons of the operational implications are complex and blurred, but nothing in comparison to the effect that with-holding information might have on his working relationship with Charlie. He would be forced to lie, which he is no good at anyway, but he assesses the risk of a master analyst, such as Charlie, finding him out as a certainty. His other option would be to lie to the team and not tell them that he has passed information to Charlie; the repercussions to the mission could leave a lot of explaining to do. Alex considers that he might claim that The Security Service could have found their own evidence against Tony, which has a ring of credibility about it. He feels this to be an easier lie to tell, but that would be to betray his new and hard-fought friendships. He puts it out of his mind for now.

*

"So, is that it? Are we just waiting here now until after dark before we leave?" Alex asks, looking out through the net curtain, observing one of the neighbours from the house next door to the left pulling into her drive. Spence laughs quietly as he slides the last of the five drawers back onto its runners in the bedside table.

"You think we've found all there is to find?" He asks by way of a reply.

"Well the place is hardly lived in, there's nothing much else too search is there?" Alex watches Spence as he calmly strides past him.

"We start from the bottom again, thorough this time." he says as he heads for the stairs.

Over the next four hours Spence gives Alex an insight into 'deep search'. Every piece of furniture is dismantled into its component parts, the carpets are stripped, sofa cushions, pillows, curtains, and clothes are cut, and hems unpicked. Skirting boards are jimmied from the walls, the few electrical items are unplugged and busted open. Everything on both floors of the property is completely destroyed, the place is a shell of walls with piles of detritus littering the otherwise bare floor. "The landlord's going to do his nut." Alex says, surveying the mess. "And we've got nothing else to show for it."

"We've not quite finished yet." Spence says looking out of the main bedroom door and up to the ceiling of the landing. He walks through into the main bathroom and turns on the hot water taps of the bath and sink before returning to the landing.

The badly painted square board pushes out easily from the loft hatch, it is not hinged down. Spence rotates it through 45 degrees, flips it up on its short edge and lowers it to the floor, standing it up against the wall. He reaches back up with both arms, grasping both sides of the hatch frame, pulls himself up off the ground and uses the toilet door handle to push against with his foot; in seconds he has disappeared from view, uncannily nimble and strong for someone his age. His face reappears at the hatch. "Come on, up ya get." he beckons Alex to follow him.

Alex makes the manoeuvre of getting into the loft look laboured compared to Spence's slick action, possibly due to inflated over-confidence brought about by Spence's example, but he manages eventually. He gets to his feet in the confines of the space, brought into dim light as Spence locates a draw-string light switch, illuminating the meagre forty-watt bulb. A narrow channel, between the two mirrored series of joist sections, has been boarded with thick ply wood. The remaining floor space has a thick layer of glass fibre wool over it, the rolls fitting neatly between the hard-wood joist beams. "You lift the insulation out, check in it and underneath it, one strip at a time. Stay on the beams." Spence says as he retrieves his multi-tool from the small pouch attached to his belt and extends the flat-bladed screwdriver tool. He lifts the lid of the water reservoir tank, the gushing noise increases in volume as he does so – he makes an adjustment to the stopcock, quickly silencing it.

Alex decides that rolling the fibre wool back up into rolls, as it had come from the factory in, would be the most effective way of searching, enabling him to feel if there is anything concealed within the blankets of wool, whilst clearing them from the channels that he will be able to search as he goes.

As he completes the third channel of insulation he looks over to Spence. The boarding has now all been lifted - it must have been laid before the insulation, as the cavities are empty. There are no signs of any findings from Spence, who moves on to the water tank which has now drained. With nothing found inside the tank, Spence moves on to help Alex with the strips of wool quilting, beginning at the other side of the house. Alex works past the central strip where Spence has lifted the boards from. He curses the unforgivingly sharp edges of the joists as they cut into his knees. As he nears the loft hatch, he feels something solid in the wool roll; he pauses to investigate, letting the roll unfurl back between his knees. There is a pocket in the right side of the fibre roll; he tugs at it gently to lift the top plies, revealing the corner of a small, beige cardboard backed notebook. "I've got something."

12

What to do?

"Hi Sandy, is there anyone in on the third?" Alex asks the delightful receptionist. "Yes, John's up there, I've not seen Cliff or Paul today, Spence went out earlier." Alex is not sure who Paul is, but figures that it might be Blakey's first name. He recollects old Army friends that he would consider as his closest of mates, whose Christian names he has never known; a strange little quirk of military life.

He makes his way up the stairs, tiring and dizzying as he spirals onwards and upwards; he can see himself quickly getting bored of them if he has to come here many more times – *I wonder how fast the lift is?* Arriving on the third floor, he gives a quick courtesy knock and enters the ops room.

*

John is sat at the nearest of the four desks. "How did it go at the house?"

"We found a couple of bits. Did Spence phone you?"

"Yeah, he gave me the low down – some serious shit. Did you find anything worthwhile in the notepad?"

"Possibly, I found some old passwords and login details; I'm hoping one of them will unlock that old laptop." Alex points over to one of the tabletops at the far side of the room where John had left Blunt's broken computer. "Where are the boys?"

"Blakey and Cliff are on the ground chasing leads, trying to track down some of those gang-bangers from the estates. They're trying to find anyone who knew Blunt well enough to know where he might have gone, but not well enough to want to protect him."

"They'd need to like him quite a lot, to not tell those two monsters." Alex jokes. "What about Spence?"

"He's nipped down to London, trying to nail us down a bit of sponsorship." John says coyly. Alex doesn't feel the need to know the details of what finances the guys are trying to hook up; he's happy to self-fund his involvement whilst it is just a cheap bed and breakfast for a few weeks. Maybe he'll take more interest should the costs start ramping up. "I'll get the brews on while you get cracking."

Alex places his laptop bag down on the fourth, and least cluttered of the four desks and fetches the broken laptop belonging to Blunt from the table just beyond it. Alex's initial analysis of it, is that the power connection has been lost. A common problem with this model is that the port that the power lead plugs into is fixed directly onto the motherboard of the computer. The board is a brittle laminate of fibreglass and copper threads - careless handling, placing lateral pressure or stress on the power lead jack, can cause the mounting of the port and the metal connections to snap off with a chunk of the end of the board – damaging the computer beyond economic repair.

Alex takes a small wallet from the front pouch of his laptop bag and from that, takes a small screwdriver. He flips Blunt's laptop over and undoes the twelve tiny screws that hold the body of the computer together. "Cheers." Alex acknowledges the arrival of his brew on the table. John sits perched on the side of the third desk, watching with interest.

The base comes away from the laptop with a few clicks of the plastic, Alex removes a further four screws before gently lifting out the hard drive unit and disconnects the rubber-hooded cable terminal. He places the drive beside the laptop, reaches into the main body of his bag and pulls out another old-looking laptop, remarkably similar to Blunt's.

"Where'd you get that?" John asks.

"Cash Converters; sixty quid." Alex answers.

"Nice." Again, John watches on in silence as Alex performs the same operation on the second computer. He takes the second hard drive and places it on the first laptop.

"You can bin all that." he says to John, who immediately picks it up and places it on the desk behind him. Alex fits and screws down Blunt's hard drive into the surrogate laptop, then clicks the base back into place and does up four of the twelve screws to keep it in place. He plugs the power cable into the side of the laptop as John plugs in the other end of the lead at the back of the desk. Both men hold their breath as Alex firmly presses the power button. An LED flashes next to the button and a purr of life is audible as the hard drive fires up, but after only a second; it dies. Alex tries again but holds the button down a fraction of a second longer this time, and the purr whizzes on and gains strength.

The computer needs to get to know its new drive and the boot-up process seems to take a fragile eternity. Eventually the old Windows operating system login screen appears. Alex lifts the front cover of the notebook; on the inside there is a column of words with numbers and symbols interspersed amongst them, they all seem to be variants of the same two names Chantelle and Phillip. Each of the passwords is scored out, except for the bottom one. Alex types it in; P-h-i-l-l-1-p-0-7. The login sequence initiates to both men's delight, and the desktop screen begins to load.

Alex gives the system a few seconds to properly run itself up, but all manner of update requests and system obsolescence messages are pinging up on the screen. After uploads, upgrades, installations and three system restarts, Alex is able to continue unhindered alone as John has become bored and returned to his own desk.

Alex opens the internet browser and hits 'Control H'. The last date that the application was used was 7th February 2013, Alex's heart falls, as hope for any useful intelligence seems to disappear. He continues with it in mind that there may be information held by the computer that may still hold significant clues to how Blunt had lived his life, and who he was in contact with, prior to being sent to prison.

Blunt's browsing history makes for interesting reading. Between the frequent visits to youporn.com and redtube.com, seemingly his two favourite sites, there are daily hits on brothersofbrum.co.uk.

*

Mid-afternoon and Alex has busied himself with lead after lead generated from links picked up between web pages, using the history on the computer and the pre-populated login details for many of the sites held in the hard drive's cache - the only gaps in information had been filled with a quick search of the notepad's inside cover. For all the piecing together that he has done, he has not found much to incriminate Blunt, but then he is still to find uses for some of the passwords in the book.

The ops room door bursts open; Cliff, Blakey, and Spence bundle in amidst nipping banter between Cliff and Blakey. Spence is his usual quiet self, lagging behind them. "Anyway, I never touched your sister." Cliff finishes the conversation. "Afternoon, gents." he greets John and Alex.

"Any luck?" John asks.

"Not much. It's like he's a ghost after coming out of prison. No one's seen him or spoken to him." says Cliff as they all take seats circled around the outside of the four desks.

"We found one of the lads that was listed in the court transcript as one of Blunt, and the dead lad's, social group." Blakey takes up the story. "He told us that Blunt joined their gang after he had bought some of them booze. They'd initially been impressed that he had served in the Paras, but soon figured him to be 'not all the ticket' and started taking the piss out of him. He reckons Blunt was getting more and more frustrated and there had been a few bites and flashes of anger, then one day he just lost it completely; he grabbed his mate by the throat and started throttling him. It had clearly shaken this other lad, he said he'd never been so scared, it was like Blunt was possessed; said he was a nutter."

"And neither him nor his mates have seen him since he got out?" Spence asks to reaffirm Cliff's point. Cliff just shrugs. "Alex and I, we went through Blunt's house like nobody's business, we found materials linking Blunt to the Birmingham attack and a notebook, but that was all; that's pretty good discipline for someone that's supposed to be a bit of a numpty."

"Whatever happened to him in prison, it seems like it's been a bit of a learning curve for our Tony." says John. "Nothing else from the house?" he asks.

"The only other thing might be to speak to the landlord to see if they know anything; I don't imagine Blunt was paying his own bills, we might be able to track down someone else in his network." says Spence. John nods enthusiastically. "I'd best be getting on wit' that before the fecker gets eyes on the place." Alex stifles a laugh as he thinks about the state that they left the house in. "What about the laptop, Alex? Has that notebook been any good t'ya?" Spence asks.

"Yes, I've got quite a bit off it; all historical though, this thing's not been fired up since before he went away in 2013." Alex taps the body of the laptop above where the hard drive is housed. "Aside from a lot of porn,"

"Standard." Blakey interjects.

Alex goes on, "Blunt was active on a Muslim community chatroom." Eyebrows are raised around the room. "All seemingly innocent stuff, nothing controversial, nothing 'anti-western', certainly nothing you'd note as extreme. Blunt was getting a lot of love and sympathy from a broad section of other members on the platform and was participating in multiple message threads." Alex pauses briefly. "In one of the threads he gets invited to the Hodgehill Mosque." This information means nothing to the other blokes, but for John, who quickly realises the relevance.

"Maybe that's where he met Zafir." says John. "Maybe we should pay the Imam a visit?"

"I'd best steer clear. I met him when I was staking out Zafir's place, he'll be wary of me."

"I'll take Spence." John tips a nod to the Irish-sounding Scot.

Alex goes on to describe Blunt's online profile as it was four years ago. No trace of Islamism, radicalisation, jihad, or even anger. It is the profile of a man looking for friendship, looking for someone to listen to him and understand what a shitty life he's had; looking for someone to make him feel better about himself. Alex had noted the confidence and positivity that had built through the messages that Blunt had posted in over a year of engagement on the site. From a life of being the butt of every joke, of receiving no respect from colleagues, peers, family; even his kids, Alex can see that this online community had given Tony something that he had never had.

Alex talks though Blunt's email account, the only items of note being monthly newsletters from the Hodgehill Mosque, the first of which had been received April 2012. No meaningful traffic had been sent or received from the account since early 2013.

Alex summarises his findings to his comrades; "No signs of radicalisation, nothing nasty at all really – he got involved with a seemingly harmless, friendly, local Muslim group; end of." The looks on the faces around the room show no hint of surprise, but then no sign of willing acceptance either. Alex senses that the men are finding it hard to obtain a mental image of Blunt being anything else but a fanatical jihadist. "Does like his porn though." Alex adds, to lighten the mood.

"With an impressionable mind, filled with depression and anger, and with an affinity for Islam, all cooked up in a prison-shaped cauldron for three years – I'd say that was a pretty good recipe for radicalisation." says Spence. "John, you and I'll pay a little visit to this Mosque. What other leads need chasing?"

Alex raises a hand, like a curious schoolboy. "I need to get some of this to Charlie." Anticipating Spence's remonstrations, he states his case; "I want to see if she can get any deep analysis done on the notebook and the laptop. I don't think it's a good idea to let her know about the stuff linking Blunt to Birmingham, not yet anyway." He is careful to add that caveat. "I can give her a 'warm and fuzzy' feeling that we're making good progress by telling her that we've spoken to his mum, his former employers, and the lad from the gang. Maybe with that, she'll trust us more and let a few other things slip." Conciliatory nods from Blakey, Cliff and latterly; Spence, signify to John that they agree.

"All right, Alex, you go and give Charlie her 'warm and fuzzy' feeling." The men snigger, "Let's see what else we can get out of her."

13

Hooked up

"It sounds like it's going well." Charlie's voice is spiked with a hint of sarcasm, but Alex knows that the team's progress is pleasing to her. Alex grips his phone tightly in his hand, pressing the corner of it into his temple, knowing that he needs to stay on top of the conversation. There are mind games at work and the situation is further complicated by his decision to get physically involved with her. He tries to imagine what is going on in her head, what her motivations are, what her goals are, more importantly, what priority order they lay in – how much might his 'swordsman-like' performance have bent those priorities out of shape? Alex still has an issue with trusting her, despite developing their bond through physical indulgence, he cannot determine whether banging hips with her assets is par for the course with Charlie, or whether it might actually have meant something to her.

The next step of the game is agreeing to the deep analysis of the notebook and laptop – *will I have to ask her to do it, or will she offer to get it done?* Alex has a split second to come up with a strategy. "I'm not sure that we're going to get much further forward unless we get a surprise from John's meeting with the Imam. I've got what I can out of the laptop, but it needs a proper look. The exploitation programmes that I have are only the commercially available ones; I might do more harm than good to the hard drive."

"I've got just the bloke you need for that; he happens to be nearby and is already aware of the case." says Charlie.

That was easier than I thought it was going to be. Alex wonders if Charlie is beginning to see Blunt as a lead truly worth pursuing, whether she might have new information from her end, or if her team's other leads are starting to dry up and that Blunt is simply rising in priority as other names are struck from their list.

"This operator - one of your gang?" Alex asks.

"No, he's with a Joint team working under the West Midlands Counter Terror Unit. It's a specially formed group looking specifically at the Gardens and Millbank incidents – I'm the Service Lead Liaison Officer for it. They're stashed in the middle floors of the West Midlands Police Headquarters – I'll make you an appointment; ten tomorrow morning okay?"

"Ye…" but she's already gone.

*

Alex jumps off the 94 bus a few hundred yards away from the Force Headquarters building. He takes the slightly longer route, cutting down and in through the north side of the main shopping precinct, glancing past the grounds of St Philip's Cathedral and approaches from Colmore Row and north onto Colmore Circus Queensway. A tingle of deep-seated fear comes over him as the ominous building comes into view. There is a good chance that the team that he is on his way to visit, may well be looking into the unknown group of aggressors who took action against over 150 members of the UK Terror Watch List just a few weeks ago – the mission which Alex had co-masterminded and oversaw the execution of. The fear that he had felt when walking into the pub to meet Charlie is more than matched as the unimaginative cube of eighties concrete comes into view. The benign architecture and drab building materials somehow translate in Alex's mind into a fearsome and imposing prospect. *Have I been set up? Has Charlie just been keeping me busy until she has enough evidence against me to send me down? Will I be cuffed as I walk into the building?* He feels as though he is walking into the lions' den, rather than heading for a meeting with a partner organisation. His only confidence comes from the memory of the night of no-holds-barred intimacy that he had shared with Charlie – *she wouldn't stitch me up, would she?*

Alex approaches the entrance of the building and notes that the facia of the ground floor belies the rest of the building; a recent face-lift intended to try and rescue the building's appeal; it looks out of place. He steps in carefully through the smoked, revolving glass doors, over-thinking the pace of their movement and kicking the bottom of the door blade in front of him, causing the mechanism to pause. The suited man following him bashes into the glass as it stops, Alex senses his frustration and embarrassment without needing to turn around, "Sorry." he says as they both emerge into the headquarters' lobby. The man is mixed race, a similar age to Alex - in his late twenties, with expensive, translucent-framed glasses, he strides past Alex and disappears into a waiting lift – *prick,* Alex thinks as he heads over to the reception desk to sign in. He is reminded of the MoD Main Server Building where he had met Lucy just over a month ago; the age and wear on the building's interior, the minor damage that had not been addressed. This building lacks the heritage and structural refinement, but it is another piece of real estate that has not been looked after by the occupying public sector body, which has higher priorities for its resources.

Alex follows the laborious sign-in procedure guided by a bright young Asian lady, who smiles at him kindly as she takes his details, photographs him using a camera tower that stands to her left, and issues him a visitor's pass, onto which his glum-looking face has been printed. "Please take a seat, someone will be down to collect you in a minute or two." she says, pointing to the bank of linked cream plastic chairs beyond the lift doors.

"Thanks, Inaya," he says with a smile. "I hope I pronounced that right?" She smiles back at him.

"Perfectly."

Alex turns and walks across the lobby to take a seat; he chooses one with good fields of view, facing towards the lovely Inaya, but from where he can also see the entranceway, the doors that lead in behind the reception area, and with a minimal twist of the neck; the secure entranceway to the ground floor offices behind him to the right. He sits in anticipation, unsure of what to expect. Neither Charlie, nor Inaya, has given away any clues as to who will be meeting him. He assumes it will be someone meeting a similar description to the prick from the revolving door; some 'up-themselves' high-flying geek of a young cop, looking to build a reputation and get things done. Either that or an older, established civil servant who thinks he is still current, but is unlikely to be truly 'on it'. Alex sits, waiting and watching. Every time one of the two sets of stainless-steel lift doors open, he scours the disembarking occupants to try and spot any likely candidates, challenging himself to identify them before they identify him. By 10:06 he has lost focus on monitoring the traffic from the lifts and is looking at the news feed on his phone, when the right set of doors open. He half glances at the three people exiting the lift, no suits, but something more striking, he double takes a second look back. Caught completely unaware, his heart seems to freeze in his chest. Walking directly towards him with silkily smooth steps, wearing a tight black, knee-length skirt and a softly draping grey blouse is Lucy.

Alex is in shock; he is completely overcome with a barrage of emotions. He is unable to process his feelings and what her presence here means – what it means; to him, to the mission, and to the status quo with regard to any potential investigation into the previous mission. The considerations and concerns fall behind his overriding thought of how much he wants her again. She stands out as spectacular in this dull and tired setting – she truly sparkles, framed by the gaping lift doorway, the downward pointing spotlights giving the effect of a halo around her. She has a look on her face that tells him that she is pleased, but not surprised to see him. Alex knows that this moment is important, she will judge him on how he reacts to her presence; his response may be defining in terms of how things might develop between them. He stands up, having to concentrate to control his body and stop if from shuddering. "You're the last person I expected to see here." he says as nonchalantly as he can in a deliberately quiet, calm, and unemotional voice. He gazes at her, without staring, with an understated and thoughtful, but not desperate smile - He feels as though he is getting away with it as Lucy struggles to find the words for a reply – he doesn't rush to fill the gap in conversation.

"It's good to see you Mr Gregory." she says broadening her smile.

"You too, Corporal Butler." Alex returns the professional façade.

"It's Sergeant, actually." Lucy says with a cocky smile. Alex raises a questioning eyebrow, not having expected her to get her promotion for months yet. She goes on; "After the shenanigans with the missing laptop, they just wanted me out of Main Server, and when Charlie Thew told me she had a new team that had a space for an Int Corps sergeant; I jumped at the chance." Lucy hushes as another group of people shuffle out of the lift and file past her on their way out of the building. "It's only my third day." She says quietly as the lobby empties. "Shall we?" she gestures towards the open lift doors.

Alex follows Lucy into the empty lift. She presses the button for the sixth floor and the doors close on them. Alex knows that this might be the only time that he has alone with Lucy and considers telling her how he has missed her, but he knows that now is not the time.

"I've missed you, Alex." she says looking him in the eye, in the reflection of the mirrored door of the lift. She slowly raises her hand behind him, watching him to read any reaction – Alex just gazes back blankly, tweaking a half smile as her hand comes to rest on his back. Alex breaks his fixed look away from the mirror and turns to look her directly in the eyes. They move towards each other slowly; Alex braces himself as their lips come together. The lift stops with a mild rattle, the pair return to their forward-facing positions; they eye one another in the door for the briefest moment before it opens with a jolt.

*

"Welcome to the sixth floor." Lucy says as they walk into a small lobby area, which is simply a small chunk of the expansive floor that has been sectioned off with partition walls. The walls are mostly glass, the windows giving a clear view of the vast open-plan office space which is bordered on each side of the floor with lines of offices, this layout and all of the characterless office furniture reminds Alex of the Contingency Group building. There is desk after desk, hundreds of them in block clusters of different sizes and configurations. Most have occupants, some are tidy, others a mess. The place is alive and buzzing with activity. Alex wonders how many of these people are involved with the investigation into the Pavilion Gardens' attack. Lucy talks as she walks; bursting through the double-doors and into the main floor area. "This is basically the working guts of the West Midlands Counter Terror Unit." she says, striding down a clear passage through the middle of the room. The building footprint is similar in size to a football field, continuing the analogy; they are currently walking from the dug-outs and along the halfway line. "The officers in these clusters are working on different work strands; Counter-terror and Financial Investigation teams, Surveillance, Forensics and Tech." Lucy points at the clearly defined groups of desks to give Alex an idea of who is where; he makes a mental note of where the Surveillance Team work from – *The watchers who watch those on the Watch List?*

Lucy continues the whistle-stop tour, "Security Advisors, Analysts and Prevention are all over there." She waves her right arm over the entire quarter of the room. "Each team has an allocation of the office space around the outside, but most of this wall," she points to the left, either side of the lifts, "is Training and Exercise Planning."

As they reach the centre spot of the floor, Lucy turns left and heads down another clear channel towards a large office that's not far off the size and position of the ten-yard box. "This is Operation Wayland, here." She grabs the door handle and holds it as she talks. "This team was only stood up last week, but it is quite well staffed. It's a multi-agency group brought together with the sole aim of tracking down the rest of the perpetrators of the Pavillion Garden and Millbank attacks. I'll introduce you."

*

Lucy pulls the door open. Though the room is lit by the same tube lighting as the rest of the floor, it seems a shade darker. The windows are coated with a translucent, non-reflective film, Alex is distracted from the initial introductions as he ponders the point of the window film — *what possible risk can there be on the sixth floor? Do they think the Russians will be flying drones to peer in? Maybe it's just to keep the sun out?*

"ALEX." Lucy snaps him out of his daydream. "This is Dev." — *the prick from the revolving door.* They exchange contemptuous looks as Alex shakes his hand lightly. Alex fails to concentrate on the other introductions; prevented from focusing by the insipid atmosphere of the dingy room and his internal grievance with himself for making a cock of himself with the apparently arrogant and obnoxious guy who seems to sit at the heart of Lucy's new team.

He switches back on to catch the last of the names and nods a hello to the older chap whose name he has already forgotten as Lucy talks him through the members not currently present. Alex is tuned back in and listens intently as she talks, whilst taking in the room. On the left of the office there are two clusters of four corner desks, both arranged to form a circle of outwardly facing workstations. On the right there is a large conference table with ten chairs tucked in around it. There are two doors in the wall beyond the table, Alex can see that they are access to small meeting rooms. Lucy stops talking, and Alex gets the gist that most of the departments from the CTU are represented in the team, these, plus Lucy from Military Intelligence, and Charlie from the Security Service; together make up quite a team of capabilities; *this is certainly a good bunch to have on side.*

"So, to what do we owe the pleasure, Alex?" Dev tilts his head and raises a cupped hand in the air to emphasise his question in a way that further irritates Alex.

"Charlie asked Alex to stop by. He's come across some items belonging to an individual who might be linked to Zafir Abdulaziz." says Lucy, seeming not to pick up on the tension between the two men. "Alan, are you free for a few minutes please?" she asks the man behind the desk nearest to the external wall. Alex recognises the focus of the man who continues to tap away on his keyboard, oblivious to Lucy's enquiry.

"Alan… Alan… Alan… ALAN!" Dev shouts in frustration. "You're wanted." He nods with his eyebrows towards Lucy as Alan's eyes flick out of his trance.

"Alan, could you come and have a look at something in meeting room one for me please?" Lucy gives him the biggest smile as he breaks himself away from his keyboard. Alex assesses that he is never away from it for long; he has a pale, unblemished complexion and seems to need to peel himself from the tailored office chair.

*

Lucy leads Alex around the conference table and into the room at the back-left corner of the office; Alan follows them in.

Two tables back-to-back and four chairs fill most of the space; Lucy walks around to the back of the room and takes the seat farthest from the door. Alex takes the opportunity to play it cool and sits on the near side, diagonally opposite her, he does this with a positive grin, so as not to look like he's trying to send a message. Alan sits next to him.

"Alan, as you know, we're not getting very far with our investigation." Lucy states as an opener.

"Can I just butt in their please, Lucy?" Alex asks. Lucy nods. "Could you just expand on what you team's terms of reference are, please?"

"Sorry, yes. Our mission is, in collaboration with partner organisations, to identify and bring to justice the conspirators of Majid Jaleel, the Gardens' attacker and Zafir Abdulaziz, the Millbank bomber and possibly the mastermind of the Pavilion Gardens attack." Lucy smiles at Alex, as if to thank him for his interest. The subtext of him knowing so much about what had gone on in both incidents, more so than Alan is likely ever to know, makes this something of a game to both of them.

She turns back to Alan and goes on; "Alex, here, has recovered items belonging to a possible associate of Abdulaziz's, one Anthony Blunt." Alan is yet to move; he sits slumped over with his fingers interlocked in his lap. Alex has genuine concern that he may not be all right and looks across to Lucy with a slight shrug of his shoulders. Lucy responds with a subtle grin. "He's got Blunt's notebook and a hard drive taken from an old broken laptop." Alex takes the verbal cue and removes the book and the surrogate laptop from his own laptop bag and places them on the desk in front of Alan – still, he doesn't move or acknowledge anything that is going on around him.

After a brief pause, Lucy tries to stimulate some response, "Will you be able to have a look at them for me, Alan?" Lucy dips her head to try and get into his eye line.

"Yes." he eventually says timidly. He gathers up the two items and clutches them to his chest.

"Thank you, Alan." says Alex. "I've done some basic searches of the drive and checked all the passwords in the notebook against potential logins held in its cache. I've detailed what I've found." Alex slides a single, folded sheet of paper sideways across to Alan, "That'll save you doing the same work." Alex pauses, but gets no response, he flicks a look at Lucy, who is still smiling. "If you could do a deep analysis to find anything that's been hidden or deleted – that would be great." He pauses again, not really expecting a reply. "Same with the notebook – if your guys can get anything from it, it would be really appreciated." Alan gives a sharp, shallow nod, or at least that's what Alex assumes it is, but he supposes that it could just as easily have been a nervous twitch – *I'll take that.*

"Can I go now?" Alan asks sheepishly.

"Yes, Alan, of course you can; unless you've got any questions?" Lucy says kindly. Alan, snatches up Alex's page of notes, snaffling into his grasp with the other items. He gets toe-tied with the table and chair legs as he rushes to stand, turn, and step off all at once, nearly tripping – Alex and Lucy look at one another bemused as he exits.

*

"Where'd you get him from?" Alex says with laughter in his voice as Alan closes the door.

"He's just a little nervous. Apparently, he's worse around me." Lucy says.

"Yeah, you have that effect on people." Alex says warmly, hoping that their natural, if slightly thorny, banter will return.

"You should see him when Charlie's here – he practically melts." Lucy says laughingly. Alex does not laugh in return; far from it. He is now imagining Lucy and Charlie in a room together, and not in a good way. The smile drops from Lucy's face too, but Alex cannot tell if it's because she knows about their night together, or if she's just preparing to talk business. He considers putting it out there; just telling her, whether she knows or not, it would no longer be an issue, it would then cease to bother him – *what if she doesn't care; I'll look like a bragging twat.*

"What's Charlie told you?" he says, thinking it might come out in the wash.

"She said that you and some of the guys had got together and were looking for Blunt. She thinks you're onto something – nothing's come of Zafir's other known associates so far. You could find yourself 'on point' for us." She looks at him for a reaction, but he's not sure what she expects from him. The look on his face is wry, but it's not a smile, it's not even a grin. They sit in silence for a few calm seconds.

"The last thing we need is the pressure of this lot on our backs." He says turning his brow towards the bustling teams through the windows. "It would be really useful if you could act as our filter." he ventures. "If we can keep the essential information flowing between us, we can keep things light and agile, and get the result that we all want." Alex intimates towards the unofficial climax that he knows will appeal to Lucy. "Charlie seems to be setting things up to go that way,"

Alex has a stern demeanour; there is no doubt that this is a serious request, which he expects Lucy to respect the candour of.

"You're not going to be happy until you've destroyed my career, are you?" Lucy says in good spirit. "I'll do what's best to achieve the aim. If that means protecting you and the guys; then I'll do it." She smiles at him the way that she had done across the desk at Main Server Building when they'd first worked together just a few weeks ago, the same smile that had captured him. Alex yearns to ask her if she regrets ending things with him; if she wants him the way that he wants her, but he won't do that to himself, he'd rather agonise than be told 'no'.

14

Walking the ground

Tony drives the same route, parks in roughly the same area of the services' car park and walks the same way towards the farmyard as he had done last Sunday. Now, just after midday on Friday, he reaches the south-east corner of the forestry block. He turns right to follow the hedge line anticlockwise around the potato field and into the dead ground behind the farmhouse. It is a warm day, and his pack is not heavy, but its mere contact with his back, and the pace at which he is walking, causes his plain black t-shirt to become clingy with sweat. He begins to daydream about situations that he may face in the coming days, about being compromised while on the second phase of his recce, by the occupants of the target building or dog walkers. His mind runs away with itself, coming up with outlandish solutions and ultra-violent ideas of how to put an end to unwanted attention, but he wakes himself up from it - *focus on the job in hand, you belter*. His attention is back on the route and his surroundings.

Periodically glancing over his shoulder and scanning the horizon to check that he is without company, he makes it up to the small clump of trees directly behind the farmhouse garden. He crosses through the hedgerow that he has hand-railed at the most convenient point, as recced last week, and continues north the few yards to the rear of his favoured observation post site. He paces back and forth, trying to identify the exact spot that he breached into the hedge; he finds the slight gap between the swathes of vegetation, and plants his pack on the ground in line with it to mark it. He gives the location a confirmatory sanity check to make sure that the spot stands up to the criteria of a good hide location. If anything, the foliage of the hedge has grown thicker; he feels confident that he has chosen well.

He drops to his knees and pauses for a minute with his eyes shut. He listens for any sign of movement or activity coming from the other side of the hedge. There is nothing close, but he can hear a heavy diesel engine revving in energetic bouts, as it is put to work on some task or other on the far side of the yard. This is a better scenario than an empty yard – whoever is operating the machinery will certainly not be able to hear someone snapping a few twigs over fifty metres away, even anyone in the vicinity of the house would struggle to hear him - he decides that it is safe to proceed.

Tony takes off the Army issue bergan that he has procured from an Army surplus store, and holds it in front of him, then allows himself to fall forward into the foliage, pushing into it and crawling into the space at the centre of the hedgerow. He picks an area of ground free from lumps, bumps, and insect nests, and takes a few seconds to clear it of sticks and twigs. He unclips the top flap of the bergan and pulls out a large, dusty, old pattern camouflage rectangle of nylon material – a 'basha'. Technically speaking, the basha is a finished shelter, which requires bungee ropes and tent pegs to complete, but Tony is only interested in using it as a ground sheet to protect himself from any moisture from underneath and to keep the bugs off him. The sheet is rolled, with a thin picnic blanket inside it. He unfurls it and spreads it out, covering the area that will be his home for the next few days. The weather forecast is good; no rain, and overnight temperatures not to drop below twelve degrees – he is going to enjoy this.

He unzips the large pocket on the outside of the top flap of the pack, feels inside, and pulls out a pair of secateurs and a large Leatherman multi-tool. He threads the Leatherman pouch onto his belt and continues to set up his temporary home. He takes the secateurs and begins to snip away any potentially irritating or even dangerous protrusions. He moves systematically and methodically around the space that he will be occupying for the next forty-eight hours, possibly longer.

Already feeling more comfortable and settled into his new environment, Tony sits next to his pack and sorts through its contents

- there isn't much to it, but he removes the sleeping bag, placing it over his legs, then arranges everything else inside the body and in the lid of the bergan so that he will be able to locate any particular item in the dead of night without any artificial light. Aside from the sleeping bag and the ground sheets, everything else will remain stowed in his pack for the fastest possible extraction in the unlikely event that he becomes compromised. He calculates that with the extremely low chance of rain or being disturbed, it is acceptable risk to leave the sleeping bag out permanently; this would be a huge no-no if still in the Paras. He figures it will take a matter of seconds to stuff the three items back into the pack and make his escape – *no Platoon Sergeant here,* he smiles to himself.

Tony slides his new, green 'roll mat' out from the body of the bergan. What had been a two-metre-long curling strip of foam, is now cut down and folded in half long-ways, and then concertinaed into three - the six rectangles open out to cover enough floor space to shield Tony's body from the heat-sapping properties of the ground on a cold night, leaving the extremities of his legs to fend for themselves. With the current warm weather, it is primarily for comfort whilst sleeping and during the prolonged periods that he will be in his watch position.

Tony moves forward to within a metre of the farmyard-facing edge of the hedgerow, he opens his mat up and places it down, orientated towards the centre of the yard. He lays on it, flat on his belt buckle and considers what he can see and what might be seen of him. The vegetation at the west-facing verge of the hedge is thick with grass and nettles – he cannot see anything; this is a good start point. He gradually adjusts his position, getting taller on his elbows, onto his knees, then swinging his legs around to try the seated position – *perfect.* He removes a notebook and pen from his right map pocket and sets to task.

*

"Henry, HENRY." Mrs Duffield calls to her husband. She doesn't expect him to hear her; he never hears her, even when he's sat next to her, let alone when he's driving the tractor. She walks from the farmhouse door out into the yard, carefully carrying a cup of tea towards where her husband is working in the mouth of the open silver barn to Tony's right. She waddles slightly, not necessarily from excessive weight, but from stiff joints. She waves to get Henry's attention – there is nothing wrong with his eyesight, he spots her from the cab immediately and gives her a wave back with his usual loving smile. Mr Duffield skilfully places the enormous cylindrical bale of hay onto the trailer alongside seven others – the last two stay in the barn until after his break. He reverses the old Massey Ferguson, withdrawing the two deadly, metre-long spikes from the bale, then parks it up, so as ready to continue after his cuppa.

"Thanks, love." he says, himself hobbling with the effects of arthritis, or maybe just a lifetime of hard graft, wear and tear, or a combination of both.

"Why don't you take a proper break, Henry?" Her voice rings with concern.

His old face answers with a hint of despair, "I'd love to, Dear, but it won't do itself." He waves angrily at the trailer, spilling his tea as he does so, further adding to his frustration.

"Come on, Henry, just come and have ten minutes, I'll get the biscuits." She places a loving hand on his shoulder. He smiles at her, and they walk together back into the farmhouse.

*

The afternoon has been long and uneventful. Tony has half a page of notes in his A5 book; descriptions of Mr and Mrs Duffield, timings and details of a couple of deliveries made to the farm over the afternoon, but no other callers to the address. Now 01:00hrs, the lights in the farmhouse have long since gone out. Using touch alone, Tony takes a head torch from the top flap of his bergan, moving slowly and carefully, he does this in silence, putting it into the map pocket of his left trouser leg.

He carefully crawls backwards through the hedge, feeling tugs on his micro-fibre fleece as he goes, he is now more worried about making noise than he is about sustaining scratches. He slowly stands, taking his time to adjust to the open ground conditions. The moon is three-quarters waxing and there is not a cloud in the sky, he has no problem seeing where he is and where he is going to go. He tracks the hedgerow south and breaches the hedge to come out behind the copse that borders the farmhouse's back garden. As he walks, Tony takes mental notes of distance, landmarks, any possible undulations or potential trip hazards; this information may never be required, but he might find himself on this route again with less light – 'ready for anything'; the first thing that he had learned in the Parachute Regiment. He follows the old fence along past the trees and continues around to the right, behind the farm buildings that house the tractors; the buildings that he has been looking at the other side of for most of the day. He reaches the next corner and identifies the end of the narrow country lane that services the farm and the business to its north. The lane ends abruptly into the wheat field that extends from his left, all the way round behind the foundry to his right, the far side is not visible; the crops just disappearing over the horizon.

As Tony steps off the rutted soil of the field and onto the cracked, disintegrating tarmac of the lane, he gets his first look at the premises on the north side of it. The building sits back from the lane, with a small decorative garden in front of it. A wide concrete drive leads up to the near side of it, past the brick facia of the office part of the building. The drive splits out to the left into a small car park, and straight on to the huge shutter doors of the warehouse building. The larger steel structure, painted in green, which has faded to a powdery, pastel-like duck-egg colour, sits conjoined to the back of the company office building, dwarfing it in size; Tony grunts to himself with disappointment – it looks a lot more modern and secure than he had hoped that it might be.

Tony walks out onto the lane, which widens and is increasingly dusty where the entrance to the farmyard and the foundry's driveway converge with it across from each other. The verges show evidence of years of heavy vehicles turning in the wet; causing deep ruts and splurges of mud, now set solidly in waves and troughs at every corner of the double junction.

Tony turns his attention back to the farmyard and slows as he rounds the corner into it, checking that there is no one unexpectedly present. Immediately to the left of the entrance is the back corner of the big barn, on his right is the long line of sheds which line the west side of the yard - the buildings that he has just walked behind. They are old and clad with corrugated iron that is flaking a dandruff of black paint, exposing the patchy galvanised surface beneath. He takes his time to inspect the contents of each bay; the first appears empty. As he walks into the bay he notices that the ground inside the barn unit is dry and dusty, and crumps under his feet like snow; it reminds him of the well-worn vehicle tracks of the camps in Afghanistan – he shudders with the flash memory of stepping in front of the weapon loading bay in one of a few Forward Operating Bases that he has had the displeasure of inhabiting. He is angry at himself for being distracted for even a second by a ghost thought from his time wasted in that place; his entire Service is a period in his life that he'd rather forget.

As he gets further towards the back of the bay the light level decreases. He takes the head torch from his pocket and pulls the strap down around the circumference of his head; he tilts the torch's masked red lens forward on its hinged mount so that it points down at his feet, then clicks it on. He adjusts the lens angle so that the constrained beam points to just below his natural eye line and continues his search. He finds nothing of interest and systematically moves on along the row.

Blunt identifies the newish, green John Deere as the largest of the tractor units, but considers that it has reduced utility when compared to the smaller, red Massey Ferguson, which Mr Duffield has stowed back in its bay with the bale spike still attached. The machines are all locked, but Tony conducts a visual recce of the mechanics of the Massey through the glass of the door – four pedals, the middle two seemingly connected, and a funny little one on the right that looks like a motorcycle gear shift pedal. There is not too much complexity to the control panel, though it appears weirdly narrow compared to the dash of a car, there are a couple of simple levers to the right of the driver's seat, which he assumes control the forks. He makes a note in his book of the vehicle's make and model and moves on to the yard annex.

The first shed-sized section of the smaller structure, after the combine harvester's bay, is a workshop, with workbench, vice and all manner of tools in boxes, trays and hung on the wall, their outlines drawn around them; a place for everything, and everything in its place – *this could come in handy.* The next 'room' has a low bench covered with specialist agricultural testing kits, weighing scales, a tiny flour mill and almost decorative scatterings of grain and course-looking flour. This, nor any of the other huts, hold anything of interest for Tony, mostly stored junk, as best he can tell. On the south side of the yard annex, adjacent to the back garden, is a large double barn, though together, still nowhere near as big as the silver barn. It is split exactly down the middle. Peering in through the cracks between the pairs of doors; Tony finds them both to be empty.

The yard annex itself is home to some items of interest. Tony walks around them and circles the rigid and unforgiving blades and spikes of the array of ploughs; the shapes and curves have an artistic quality to them, appearing eerie and mysterious in the moonlight, like agricultural sculptures; their strange beauty given an edge by their potential power and destructive capabilities – *I wouldn't fancy having that dragged over me.*

Tony notes the bulk fuelling trailers inconspicuously covering the gap between the grain stores and the huts. The one on the left is newish, painted black and is marked as diesel. The tanker on the right is in a much sorrier state. Though painted red, that was likely over forty years ago and it is now peppered with blotches of dark rusty scabs, which have bled out streams of orangey-brown residue. What remains of the paint has scaling layers of grime, algae and bird shit caked over it. It now blends in with the vegetative growth that is emerging from behind it on all sides, though the growth is subdued somewhat underneath the chassis itself by the poisons of spilled fuel. There is a large drip tray under the tap, where it joins to a perished hose, but years of splashes and splurges have meant significant contamination has taken place. Tony locates the gauge near to the pump and sees that the container is nearly three-quarters full; about fifteen tons of fuel.

Tony continues his tour of the yard, moving back into the main part of the complex. He pauses to look at the farmhouse and to consider his next move. Attempting to gain access to the house is the riskiest element of the recce. He is still far from confirming all the other things that he needs to make this project viable, so decides that the house can wait and heads over towards the silver barn.

The Duffields have clearly made a huge investment in the new shining steel structure. The walls and giant doors of the barn are still industriously pristine. What can be seen of its concrete footings still exhibit a glow of white-grey residue that is yet to be washed or worn away by the elements.

Mr Duffield has completed his task, removing the remaining bales of hay, leaving the doors open to allow the barn to air. Blunt strolls casually into the vast open space and admires the building's construction, which is more on the scale of a warehouse than a barn. He takes the time to identify the longest, sturdiest component parts of the super-structure; the girders running the length of the front and back walls are the longest sections without joins, making the base of the triangular roof trusses, but they are relatively light, and integrated well into the structure, as are the six upright beams along each of the two side walls. Tony walks to the back-centre of the considerable space, his steps echoing eerily, he reaches out to touch the central pillar of the rear wall. He runs his palm over the front surface of the girder; it is stone-cold to the touch, and much broader than it had looked from a distance. He looks up to see that it is relatively clear of fixings into the rest of the structure but for its termination into the rooftop and bolts securing the horizontal beam to its rear flange.

Tony walks back to the middle of the barn floor and holds his right arm out-stretched, opening the span of his thumb, fanning his fingers as far as he can; he aligns the tip of his thumb with the bottom of the main upright, he closes his left eye and edges backwards until the tip of his middle finger aligns with a point on the girder a metre short of where it bolts into the point of the roof. He halts in position, then rotates his hand through ninety degrees, lining the tip of his thumb up with the bottom right corner of the barn, and fixes his gaze on the point on the ground that the tip of his middle finger aligns to. He strides directly towards his measured spot and then paces out the distance from there to the corner – *nearly ten metres.*

*

Emerging from the farmyard, back to the lane, Tony gathers his focus on the next task - Austin & Sons. He scopes the frontward facing walls of the building – no obvious CCTV cameras to be seen. He walks up the inclined and grippy concrete driveway, the ornamental garden to his right, decorating the front of the grounds. It appears to have been lovingly cared for and incorporates mostly rose bushes, a lot of bedding plants, and two thick clumps of dark ferny shrubs featuring in the middle.

Tony turns right in front of the brick building. He peers through the large window to see a messy work environment; four desks each strewn with reams of paperwork, folders, and personal effects all over them. There is no view through to the workshop, but there is an interior door on the far wall which does not appear to have any locks or bolts on it, nor is there a keyhole apparent. Tony steps back and notes that the window is single pane in a wooden frame. He moves on past the window to a canopy construct, under which is the front entrance; he steps up onto the open sided porch and in to the recessed front door – it is painted red and is the kind of old wooden-framed door with a large window in the top half; reminiscent of that of a council house from the old estates of the West Midlands. The window pane is adorned with company branding that looks like it was knocked up on a home computer. Tony reviews the services that the company offers and considers what equipment they may have on site in order to deliver them. He assesses that he could put the door through with one solidly planted right boot, he leans hard against the top right corner of it and feels it flex in under his weight – *no top bolt.* He looks through the window into what looks like a small waiting room. To his left he sees the glow of an alarm panel – *shit.*

Tony continues in an anti-clockwise direction around the building, the pathway down the side of it is shielded by a thick, unkempt hedge. The brickwork ends at the front of the factory section of the building, where he finds a heavy metal fire door; it has no external handles and there is nowhere to gain leverage for access – he quickly moves on. The hedgerow ends parallel with the back corner of the workshop. The back of the building looks out onto the open plain of the wheat field. There are no windows or doors on the back wall; Tony continues. The westward facing wall is without cover, facing onto the car park, but is otherwise similar to the east-facing wall; though the fire exit is near to the back of the workshop, but equally impregnable. Around the final corner of the workshop building, he finds just the heavy roller-door, which he expects will only open by chain or motor operation from inside.

Tony walks back to the lane junction, stands at its centre and takes a moment to review his findings. He looks at the workshop and back over to the farmyard – *game on.*

15

In touch

Alan opens the notebook to the centre and uses forceps to bend open the two staples, turns the book over, then plucks them out from the spine. He places the cardboard cover in the jig directly beneath the large and expensive-looking camera and clips two of the edges down with pivoting spring-arms. He returns to the adjacent work station and presses a few buttons on the keyboard; the camera takes a rapid series of exposures. "Look." he says to Lucy pointing to his terminal's thirty-inch square screen – an image of the notebook's inside covers fills it. The image is supremely high quality and shows the texture of the card's finish.

"Wow," says Lucy in amazement, "that's unbelievable."

Alan laughs and watches her face for the reaction to his next trick. He clicks the mouse on a slider to the right of the image and slowly begins to move it down. As he moves, the image transitions through the colours of the spectrum, each band of colour showing up different marks and residues, which are almost exclusively on the left side of the spine – the front inside cover. He reaches the ultra-violet frequency, and several clear fingerprints glow bright white.

"Oh my God, Alan." Now he laughs a little louder in his funny little way, pleased that he has impressed her. Lucy sits and watches him work through the notebook pages, fortunately it is only thin, so doesn't take long, but not so fortunately; it appears to have pages missing, as they find the remaining half sheets towards the back of the book. It takes Alan less than fifteen minutes to complete the process.

"What's next?" Lucy says with enthusiasm, interested to see more of Alan's tricks.

"ESDA." he says casually.

"What's that?" Lucy says cluelessly.

"Electrostatic Detection Apparatus." Lucy doesn't bother to ask, choosing to simply follow him to the next bit of kit in the lab. Alan leads her over to a workbench around the corner from the camera unit, where sits an innocuous looking blue box about the size of a large shoe box. It has a bare aluminium exo-frame and lid, which is machined to be perfectly flat – no lip or curvatures to it at all. The machine has a blue trough-like attachment running underneath the left side long edge. Lucy wonders what magical mechanisms and workings might be inside the box, but she is soon to be disappointed. Alan clips the cover of the notebook down onto the lid surface, ensuring that it is as flat as can be, he then lifts the lid by the long edge on the right side, clicking it into place at a fifteen-degree slope.

"Are you any good with powder?" Alan asks, smirking. Lucy shrugs, not really knowing what he is getting at. "You Army people are so sweet and innocent when it comes to druggy jokes." he quips, and hands her an opaque blue plastic pot half full of black dust. "That's printer toner. Could you sprinkle a line of it along the top edge of the page please?" He points his right forefinger to where he means. "I usually get it everywhere when I do it."

Lucy does as she is asked, holding the tub between her thumb and middle finger, gently tapping it with her forefinger, causing a steady shower of the black dust, like snow in negative, which lands evenly along the edge of the sheet as desired. "Good technique." he says.

"Thanks." she replies, with a little too much pride for completing such a menial task; her happiness compounded by the developing rapport that she is building with him. "What now?" she asks. Again, Alan turns to face her, so that he can fully enjoy the expression that he expects to see on her face. Her eyes are transfixed on the card and powder as Alan flicks the small green switch on the front of the unit; it hums into life and the aluminium top plate vibrates invisibly – the only sign that it is doing anything is that the tiny black mountain range of powder flattens slightly and begins to slip downhill to the left. As the toner moves, it takes on liquid-like properties, like snow in an avalanche – the energy given to the particles by the vibration gives it life. Lucy soon notices that tiny traces of the powder are left behind, as particles are caught in the imperfections and indentations in the card.

"That's clever." she says, as the last of the moving toner drops off the edge of the machine top. With nothing much of interest being revealed by the process; she is clearly not half as impressed with it as she is by the camera.

"It gets better." Alan says replacing the cover with one of the sheets of paper that has come from behind a missing page and goes through the process again. Lucy watches intently, sensing that Alan is playing the part of a magician with something else up his sleeve. The right side of the leaf, what would be the seventh page of the notebook if it were intact, is obviously going to reveal a whole lot more. As the toner slides further down the page, Lucy is doing her best to try and count the layers of overlaid text.

"Oh my God." says Lucy once more. Alan is deeply gratified by her reaction. There is a pause as the two of them take in some of the more obvious words and numbers on the page.

"Once I have the digital images of these traces, I'll be able to separate out any of the text that we don't already have on the other pages. There might be more information in this book than your friend thought."

*

Alex sits back in comfort in one of the empty offices of the third floor of the Contingency Group building, his phone pressed to his ear. "He's been through it already?" he says with surprise.

"I'm telling you; he's on the spectrum, but he's a genius." Lucy replies. Alex is enjoying being back on terms with her, he hopes that he can keep his cool and not blow it.

"What did he find? Anything we can use?"

"He got a phone number from one of the pages of the notebook, it had either been rubbed out or was written on a page that had been removed, you wouldn't have spotted it." she says with a deliberate and playfully patronising tone.

*

Alex takes his seat with the others back in the conference room. There is a fresh round of teas around the table. "White and one, weren't you, Alex?"

"Yeah, cheers, Blakey."

"We've had a busy weekend by the sounds of it, fellas." John is buoyant and jovial. "Do you want to start Spence?" He looks across the table as Spence flicks his wavy black hair out of his eyes.

"I tracked down the owner of Blunt's house through public records. An Asian fella, he owns a shop in Hodgehill, of all places, so I paid him a visit. He wasn't that interested in talking to me to begin with, but I managed to convince him to give me five minutes." Spence grins to himself; the others in the room smile knowingly of what this might have entailed. "Still, though, he didn't say much; just that he'd never met the tenant, the bills were always paid on time and he never had any complaints."

"Did he say how the bills were paid?" John asks.

"Cash, he said. I didn't believe him though. Something wasn't right with him; he was flustered. He said the cash got paid into his account at the bank. It sounded like bullshit to me, but I didn't want to push him too hard just then, I didn't have anywhere else to go with the conversation. If we run dry; we can revisit him — a bit harder."

"So that remains an open lead then, Spence. We'll park it for now. Well done, mate." John says with a growing air of leadership. He senses the lull in morale by Spence's lack of significant progress and decides that he will report next. "Cliff and I paid a visit to the Hodgehill Mosque." he begins. "We met with Imam Abbas, lovely chap." John and Blakey smile at one another. Alex smiles and nods his agreement, as he recollects his warm welcome into the Mosque a few weeks back. His smile disappears as he remembers that the visit was also his first brush with Zafir. John goes on, "After the extensive pleasantries and green tea, he told us that Blunt had introduced Zafir to the Mosque soon after he had been released from prison. He said that Blunt and Jaleel, as well as Zafir, had been seen at the Mosque recently, but they were not regular attenders and never came back once he had warned off Zafir – that would've been a couple of days after Blunt disappeared and before the Watch List mission. He couldn't tell us much more than that, but interestingly he did say that some of the young lads from the Mosque have been in touch with Zafir by text message." John says, smiling at the acknowledgements of significance that tremor around the room.

"What, since he's been in prison?" Cliff asks, as the last of the pennies drop.

"Yarp." John replies mocking Cliff's slow response.

"If he's got comms with the outside world; I bet he's got comms to Blunt." says Alex. John is looking pleased with himself.

"Clearly we're not going to get near him, so I propose we throw this over the fence to the Counter Terror guys and see if they can run an operation to smoke him out and get us the data from that phone."

"I'll speak to Lucy." says Alex.

"LUCY." rings the reply from everyone around the table. Alex smiles, he is enjoying the reputation that he is building, despite things not being what they would apparently seem.

"She had to make a sharp exit from the Main Server Building, and Agent Thew wangled her a spot on this new team." John laughs and holds his head in his hands.

"There are two women on this CTU team, and you've knobbed both of them?" He laughs harder even without a response from Alex. "Do they know about each other?"

"I think Charlie knows I was with Lucy, but I'm not sure." Alex has had enough; now wanting to shrink away from the attention.

"You'll be getting yourself killed by friendly forces, ya wee eejit." says Spence with rare laughter.

John spares Alex any further blushes and moves the conversation on, confident that he has stolen the show with his revelation about Zafir's text messaging. "Any other updates from Counter Terror?"

Alex's facial expression quickly moves from embarrassed to smug. "Yes, actually. Exploitation of the notebook pages has yielded a whole host of information, but most notably; a phone number was discovered. The phone had been operating in the Bromsgrove area, and it was the last number in the call history of Blunt's old phone.

"No new information there then." John asks without asking; feeling that his findings still trump anything that Alex has turned up.

Alex smiles like a poker player with an unbeatable hand. "The word 'Murshid' was written above it." Everyone around the able looks at each other to see if there is a flicker of recognition on any of their faces, but there is none.

"We don't know a Murshid, do we?" says John.

Alex grins, "It's an Arabic word. It means 'mentor'."

16

Calculations

Sat at the old oak table in front of the laptop, Tony sends an encrypted reply to his mentor – '*I'll be there to collect it*', before returning for his third attempt to reconcile what he needs to understand.

He wishes that he had paid more attention at school, though he fears that whatever he had been taught, this level of technicality may still be beyond him. He rubs his eyelids, then the rest of his face, then massages his scalp – nothing seems to help him figure out what he is looking at. He grabs and pulls on his beard with both hands, wanting to inflict pain on himself as punishment for being so stupid. "Grrrrr, you're a fucking idiot." he snarls at himself; he lashes out, rapping the screen with the back of his hand. He snarls further as the ring and little fingers of his right-hand tingle with an irritating pain.

Tony is doing his best to get his head around the 'toughness and ductility' of steel; the amount of force it can absorb before it bends or fractures. Even finding a basic number is proving difficult, but then there are the added complexities of how that number changes with the application of velocity and inertia to the load. What effect does the angle of the steel and orientation of the surfaces of it have on the calculation? How much difference does the length of the subject piece make?

He stands from the chair, knocking it over as he does so. "For fuck's sake." He throws his hands up in the air and brings them down on the top of his head. "I don't even know what 'uniaxial tension' fucking means." He takes a deep breath and tries to calm himself. He bends down to pick up the chair, grabbing it by the front of the seat. As he pulls it forward and tries to tilt it back up on its feet, the rear legs slip on the carpet and the foot of the front left leg bangs painfully into his right shin. He erupts in a fit of madness, grabbing the chair with both hands and wrenching it into the air, he swings it wildly with a bellowing roar as he smashes it to pieces against the harsh corner of the hearth and the protruding corner of the mantelpiece. "FUCK YOU FUCKING FUCK." he turns to see the laptop screen glaring at him, unaffected by his display. "What are you fucking looking at?" He says to it with boiling anger. He takes two steps towards the table, grabs the laptop by the top of its screen with both hands, raises it over his head. He pauses for a split second – do I really want to do this? His anger wins over; he swings the body of the laptop down onto the edge of the table top so hard, that there is almost nothing left of the delicate machine. He tosses the limp shattered screen, with just one hinge left hanging from it, to the floor.

17

The Bromsgrove plan

"This is John." says Alex meekly, hoping beyond hope that he behaves himself. Back in one of the side meeting rooms of the Op Wayland end of the sixth floor, Alex makes polite introductions to Charlie, Lucy and Dev. John pretty much ignores Dev, but smiles as he looks from Lucy to Charlie, he injects a twist of evil through his eyes as he turns to Alex, knowing he can make this situation uncomfortably warm for him. Alex feels nervous and hopes to hurry on with the main points of business; Charlie comes to his rescue.

"We know your reasons for wanting to track Tony Blunt." she says speaking directly to John. "We're not that interested in him for the moment," Alex feels a pang of guilt as he thinks about the Pavilion Gardens materials found in Blunt's house. "but if you act on the 'mentor' based on information that's come out of this building;" she points the sharp, red painted nail of her forefinger into the desk, "then we have a significant interest."

"You don't have to worry about come-backs, Sweetheart, we're better than that." John smirks an arrogant smile at Charlie.

"Hmm." Charlie quietly fumes and picks up the papers in front of her. "I'll authorise a visit to the address in Bromsgrove, but I want it to be light touch and we'll lead."

"You'll authorise?" John barks angrily.

"YES." she snaps back. Alex laughs quietly inside as John sits back, taken by surprised by Charlie's ferocity. "I don't want any of your dickheads running around the place. Dev will go with Alex." Alex is shocked, caught unaware by the prospect of being out on the ground again.

Dev doesn't look any more pleased and throws his pencil down on his notepad. "I can't take him; he's a civilian." he complains.

"Relax, it'll probably be nothing anyway, probably just his spiritual mentor, but you might need technical back-up on the spot, and I can't see Alan coming out with you."

"Fine, he can wait in the car." Dev gripes.

"I better go too then." says Lucy. "You'll need someone to act as a distraction." Alex can't think of anyone better to occupy the mind of a male target. Charlie nods her agreement. John shakes his head in frustration, but does not argue any further, appeased that at least Alex is going - he sees Lucy as kind of one of his too.

"What are the terms of reference?" Lucy asks. John sees the need to get in early with his objectives before they get laid down for him.

"We need to establish that the resident is the person that was in touch on the phone to Blunt. Then we need to know what the nature of the relationship is. It'll need some well thought out tactical questioning. Any hint of shenanigans; then we need to detain him and get through the place with a fine-tooth comb. If this person is still in touch with Blunt; he'll put him on alert at the first opportunity, so we need to act fast and prevent any onward communications." Alex is impressed by John's decisive line. His larking about and informality make it easy for Alex to forget John's level of training and experience at the pointy end, but like Craig had once told him – he's the man you'd want on your side when the shit hits the fan.

"If," Charlie raises a single finger to John, "if he's significant, then of course he'll be treated accordingly – full isolation, the works, but after getting nothing incriminating from Blunt's place, or his laptop; I'm seeing this lead as fairly dead in the water as far as the Wayland operation goes." Alex squirms as his deliberate lie to the CTU team starts to become a factor. He looks at John, who grins back at him with a cocky smile as everyone else is focused on Charlie. Alex now considers that any potential threat that might be present in the property is now seen as benign by the team members who will walk up and knock on the door – Dev and Lucy, while he'll be sitting in the car.

"What about back-up?" Alex asks. Lucy and Dev have the dismissive look that Alex has feared might come.

"I'd still assess this as a low risk knock." says Dev. Alex writhes in his seat, not wanting to look weak or frightened, his mild streak of arrogance prevents him from further enforcing his belief that support should be on hand.

*

Charlie escorts John out of the room, making it a bit less cosy. Dev's posture changes immediately as he transitions his mind-set to that of the leader. "Right, so all we have to go on is an old phone number that's no longer in service, and an address where it was primarily used for a period of two months. The owner has been in contact with Tony Blunt – a bloke who's pissed off some of your mates, Alex. Is that it, or am I missing something?"

Alex knows he needs to temper his response. He fights his natural urge to hit back with a snipe, an insult, or try to impress him by demonstrating some of the knowledge that he has, but he also knows that knowledge is power and that if he gives it up easily; that power will be spent. Dev's tactics are a classic example of a detective trying to wheedle out information. Alex must be clever; he must give Dev enough information to hook him in, but not so much that he will want to steam-roll his team's claim on their objective. "Tony Blunt is certainly someone that you need to eliminate from your enquiries." Alex delivers the considered line with solemnity with just an undertone of macabre knowing, getting across the sentiment as intended, whilst telling Dev nothing at all.

What's your gut feeling about this, Alex?" Dev gives the impression that he is spiting himself to ask anything of Alex, but he had sensed the sub-text in the room when Charlie broached the topic of Blunt, and Alex's aloof and understated response signals to him that there is something going on.

"I'm not sure. Charlie might be right; it may just be someone from his religious community – perfectly innocent."

"But?" Dev asks over the top of his glasses.

"There's an outside chance that this mentor might be pushing some of the buttons on not just Blunt, but possibly others of interest too." says Alex. Dev's eyes light up; Alex has sold it.

"Is this part of Charlie's 'Interest Group' theory? He asks, pushing his spectacles back up the bridge of his nose with the middle finger of his left hand matter-of-factly. Alex and Lucy simultaneously look in to each other - Alex because he is surprised that Charlie has aired her ideas to the wider team, and Lucy to give him reassurance. "She was telling us that she'd worked with Lucy prior to Millbank, trying to identify members of some fanciful bunch who might be trying to coordinate an uprising – is that why no one at Five's taking her seriously anymore."

"What do you mean?" Lucy asks angrily, showing her loyalty to Charlie.

"Why do you think she's down here working with us plebs? Dragging in civilians? She can't get buy-in from her own chain of command, she can't get her own resources allocated; so, she blisters on to us." This is food for thought for Lucy and Alex, there is a long pause.

Lucy decides to press on with business; "In the current climate; we'll just need to drop 'Pavilion Gardens' into the application; we'll get a warrant without any issue."

"You're not wrong." Dev agrees. "Judge Hunter's daughter was injured in the attack." I'll make the application this afternoon and we'll plan to go in tomorrow morning.

"How's this going to go then?" Alex asks, unsure of the planning detail that goes into a call on an unknown suspect.

"We'll do some research here first; checking records, registers, digging into the history of the address and any previous incidents associated with it — develop a picture of who and what might be waiting there for us." says Dev. "You can do us the map recce and a route card if you like - you can do that on open source." he says to Alex with a condescending tone. "Lucy, you make a start on the real research; I'll go and sort the warrant." Dev gets up and heads back to his desk.

*

Are you okay?" Lucy asks.

"Yeah, I'm just thinking about the possible threat in this house." Alex is as worried about telling Lucy that he has been holding back, as much as he is about putting her at risk - again. "We think that Blunt might be a bit more… err," Lucy tilts her ear towards Alex and raises her eyebrows, hoping to prompt him on. "a bit more involved with things."

"What things?"

"We found some signs at his house that he might have had more than an informing role with whatever organisation it is we're chasing."

"Signs? You mean evidence?" She frowns as she awaits his answer.

"Nothing conclusive, but it looks as though he at least knew about Pavilion Gardens, probably well ahead of time looking at the dates on the materials he had collected."

"Bloody hell, Alex; no wonder you're wanting back-up for this knock. Why didn't you say something before?"

"I didn't want to give away too much to the wider team, certainly not to that prick."

"I suppose I'll have to 'find' something in my research to warrant an up-scaling then."

Alex grins a little, "Either that or I get some unofficial back-up jacked up?"

"Roger that." Lucy says with an unforgiving scowl.

He shifts in his seat. "What did you think about what Dev said about Charlie?"

"I wouldn't worry about that... but then again; maybe I would." she says with an unusual grin.

"What do you mean?" he asks.

"I had quite a frank discussion with Charlie when she recruited me for this team." Lucy takes a more serious tone, looking down to her hands on the desk as she goes on. "She really believes that we're on the right track. She also believes that there is too much red tape and process in the Security Service to get this done the way it needs to be done - the way we want it to be done." Alex thinks through what Lucy is saying. "Maybe she's right, if what you're telling me about Blunt is true."

"You mean she wants less accountability?" Lucy says nothing in reply, she just smiles. "What about the rest of this Wayland bunch? What do they think about that?"

"Dev's a cock, but he's ambitious, not one for corners, if you know what I mean, and blood-thirsty ... for a cop. He might grow on you." she shows him another kind of smile. Alex worries that Dev might have grown on her, knowing what a show of strength from a man can do to her.

"Alan – well Alan won't leave the building. Then there's Terry." Alex is yet to see or even hear of Terry until now. "Terry's old school. Not *old*, just *old school*. He's always out on the ground and has a contact network like you wouldn't believe. He's lovely." Alex doesn't feel the need to worry about Terry as a further threat to his chances with Lucy; he can tell by the way that she is talking about him that he is just 'nice'.

"What's the score with you being on the team? For field work I mean." Alex asks.

Lucy smiles and explains; "I was sworn in as a Special Constable on my first day." They both laugh. "That gives me all the powers that a Constable has and gets around all the red tape instantly."

"I always said you were 'special'." They laugh harder.

18

Breaking point

Tony finally gets around to picking up the pieces of the laptop, having put it off for a day, not wanting to touch the fragmented outcome of his absolute loss of control. The sight of the aftermath has been increasingly irritating over the morning to the point where it has surpassed the level of revulsion that clearing it up will bring. He picks up the biggest chunks of the debris, the battery, its housing, what is left of the motherboard and some of the under-side casing. As he gets down on his knees, he gets over the feeling of embarrassment at his tantrum, and revels in the release that it had brought him. He snaps one of the larger pieces of the plastic trim in his hand and growls at what is left of the subject of his fury, that had caused him such frustration. "Not so clever now, are you? Fucking piece of shit."

He throws the pile of computer pieces in the kitchen bin and slowly heads back into the living room-diner to face the next big challenge of the day. Tony picks up his mobile phone and thinks to himself for a long moment before he commits to making the first call. He closes his eyes and takes a deep breath. He feels the handset in the palm of his hand as he thinks about what he might say, what he might want to get from the conversation. He imagines it going well, gaining salvation from the road that he is on, the realisation of a greater love than the path that he has chosen. His mind battles over whether he wants to make the call or not.

Tony opens his eyes and firmly presses the numbers into the phone from memory and settles himself on the sofa in an upright position in total focus. His throat feels swollen as he waits for the call to go through, swallowing is difficult, his mouth is dry, and his palms are sweaty. It rings; Tony's sense of panic heightens further as his brain tries to summon the things that he wants to say and place them into an order of importance. He knows that he should have planned this before dialling, but he knows that he would never make the call if he were to put any serious thought into it. It rings a fourth time; his finger hovers over the button to hang up.

"Hello, who's this?" comes the answer from a grumpy young girl, full of attitude far beyond her twelve years.

"Chantelle, it's me, it's your dad." Tony says hopefully, trying to sound upbeat and positive as best he can whilst looking down into his lap. His face is ripping with exposed emotion, his vulnerability making him feel naked. The pause is filled with pre-teen angst, Tony can almost feel the sulky look coming down the line. He has not received the loving response that he has dreamt of; he hopes that she will find him in her heart and end this pause that has stopped his world.

"Fuck off, you fucking loser. You're not my fucking dad." Tony is crushed, the poisonous words seem to be coming straight from the mouth of the girl's mother – he hates himself for leaving the two of them in her care.

"Who's that?" Tony hears Phillip say from afar.

"It's Tony." she says loudly and directly into the microphone. Tony's own first name is a hammer blow to him. A tear collects in the lashes beneath his left eye as a feeling of utter rejection consumes him.

"Tell him to fuck off, Charn. FUCK OFF you useless prick!" The words from the mouth of his youngest sound obscene, his ex-wife has not only ruined his lovely little boy but reprogrammed him to disown and hate his dad too.

"Don't call again, you fucking loser." Chantelle hangs up, leaving Tony in disarray.

He begins to sob into his hands, the sockets of his eyes buried into his palms, his fingernails scratching deep into his scalp, the pads of his thumbs press hard into his temples. He squirms and whines, conscious of his starkly clear weakness in the otherwise silent flat. His anger at himself exceeds that of his self-pity and his cries of heartache turn to cries of rage. He grasps the phone in both hands and twists it until he hears a crack. He is acutely aware that this phone is his vital link; he thinks again and throws it as hard as he dares into the back of the sofa's matching armchair – it bounces back at the reflecting angle and lands somewhere under the table. He jumps up from his seat, turns and kicks the sofa. He bends to grab underneath the front edge of couch with both hands; with an immense burst of energy he launches it into the air, spinning backwards, hitting the ceiling with a crunch and falling onto an empty cabinet which buckles as the soft, but heavy mass of the sofa impacts against it. The sofa comes to rest looking broken and limp on the carpet, having suffered structural damage on its short, but violent journey. "ARRGGH, FUCKING, FUCK!" Tony is yet to expend his fury. He kicks out at his dining-room chair, it clatters against the underside of the table and lands back in its place. Tony turns to his right and smashes a fist into the wall. The plasterboard puts up no resistance and his hand goes straight through, meeting the brickwork with a sudden and finite stop. The pain shoots up his wrist to his brain, overcoming his adrenalin, shocking him to a stop. His rage is satisfied for now.

19

Soft knock

Alex sits, mulling over his concerns in the back of the unmarked Police car as it gently cruises south along the M5. He is momentarily distracted by the fine stitching in the leather in the back of Dev's headrest; he wonders how much this nicely spec'd 5 series has cost the country's counter-terror budget.

"The property is registered to a Mr Sayeedi, a 74-year-old businessman with several interests in manufacturing in the area."

"He must have done all right for himself with such a nice place." Dev adds.

Lucy continues her review of what they know; "No record to speak of; a bit of a history with HMRC, a few tax discrepancies, but nothing criminal. The property history is clean too."

"He's come up clean on all other searches, from all other partner organisation databases. I really think we're flogging a dead horse with this one." says Dev. Lucy glances over her shoulder, letting Alex know that she shares his concerns that this job is being taken a little too lightly, with too little conviction. Alex doesn't want to come across as the scared civvy on the ride along, but he must wake Dev up to the potential threat.

"I think you're right, Dev; this probably is dead end lead, it probably is just a pensioner sat in front of his telly, but I would like to see how you guys execute an operation professionally – how about, just for my interest, you give this your full investigative attention and show me how it's done?" Alex says in a not-quite condescending, but commanding tone.

Dev scoffs a short arrogant laugh and eyes Alex in the finely shaped and tinted rear-view mirror, "Sit back and watch a pro in action, Mr Gregory."

*

Lucy leads Dev down the long and lavish driveway. The grounds are set at the apex of a rather exclusive close, giving a generous amount of space around the large, detached house, that isn't quite a mansion. The garden is beautifully maintained with blossoms and flowers that would appear to have been planned in detail to give an exquisite range of colours and textures that suit the space and house perfectly. There is a brand new, sparkling silver Mercedes S-Class sat perfectly square in front of the left door of the double garage, a racy-looking A-Class adjacent to it on the near side. The garages constitute just a small fraction of the left side of the beautiful brownish rustic brick house. "This is nice." Dev comments as they approach the solid-looking front door which is set in a heavy frame. He knocks firmly on the tall window to the right of the door, ignoring the doorbell ringer. There is no immediate reaction; as the wait goes on, Lucy looks at Dev as though hoping for inspiration for what to do next. He moves forward to knock a second time but drops his fist as he sees movement through the window. He steps back into position a polite distance from the door. The handle twitches with a failed attempt to turn it, then lurches down with a satisfying crunch as the locking mechanism disengages.

*

The door opens to reveal an elderly man, draped in a creamy form of Asian attire, his white hair is well-trimmed and is in stark contrast to the dark, tanned wrinkled skin of his face. He is stooped over, clearly suffering from the effects of old age. He gradually looks up to see their faces, as he does; the bright expectant smile drops from his face. "Oh, who are you?" he says with surprise.

"Mr Sayeedi?" Lucy asks.

"Yes. Who are you?" he directs his question, again, at Dev. The old man's body language denotes his suspicion of them.

Dev takes the lead, "My name is Detective Devansh Jackson; this is Special Constable Lucy Butler." Mr Sayeedi flicks the faintest of fearful looks at Lucy – barely noticeable, but Lucy picks up on the micro-gesture - *maybe just a cultural thing?*

"What do you want?" he says abruptly.

"Mr Sayeedi, we are investigating the possibility that someone in the near vicinity has been in contact with a person who might help us with our investigations. Would you mind if we came in for a chat please?" Dev is firm and clear, but he senses that he is being met with equal determination from the old man.

"Well it's not convenient at the moment, I'm about to leave for an urgent meeting, actually."

"Really Mr Sayeedi? Who with?" says Dev.

"Well, that's my business."

"I'm afraid we're going to have to insist." Dev says pulling the warrant from his inside pocket.

"This is an outrage; Commissioner Braidy will hear about this." Sayeedi says with as much venom as a man as old and infirm as he can muster.

"Of course, you are perfectly within your rights to register a complaint with whoever you wish, Sir, but please…" Mr Sayeedi's frustration and anger quickly dissipate as he accepts that he has no choice but to allow the officers access to his home. He opens the door begrudgingly. Lucy rocks forward a touch, in anticipation of stepping forward into the property, but Dev holds fast. "Is there anyone else at home, Mr Sayeedi?"

There is a pause, Mr Sayeedi glances over his shoulder as he holds the door open; he looks up the stairs. "My wife is visiting her sister. My son was here, but he has gone out."

*

Dev steps into the broad hallway. There is a double door to the right to what looks like the main living area, an ornamental staircase that splits left and right on its way to the upper floor. To the left and back from the stairs there is another set of double doors, on the last wall to Dev's left, is a bank of three single doors. The floor is a course, but expensively heavy marble, the details of the internal architecture and décor are ornate and have a definite Arabian flavour to them. "You have a lovely home, Mr Sayeedi, how long have you lived here." Dev says, trying to relax the atmosphere.

"I had it built nearly thirty years ago." he replies. "Please come through to the kitchen." he says leading them through the double doors to the left of the stairs. Dev fights his natural response to go the opposite way to where the subject of investigation wants the search to go, but he feels that there may be more utility in making an effort to develop at least a little rapport with the old man before taking full control of the situation. "Would you like some tea?"

"No, thank you, Mr Sayeedi." Dev says politely.

"I'm fine thank you." says Lucy, despite him not making it clear that the invitation might be extended to her. Her voice draws his attention as he walks around to the far side of the large oak table that seems to be providing Mr Sayeedi with a day-to-day workstation.

"You don't mind if I just message my son to tell him that you're here?" he says, picking up a mobile handset from the table.

"Actually, Sir, we do." says Dev with authority. "Would you mind switching the phone off while we are here please?"

"Yes, of course." he replies with poorly masked anger apparent in his tone. He continues to thumb at the screen; Lucy spots what he is trying to do.

"MR SAYEEDI, put the phone down now." Lucy's surprising energy makes the old man jump; he half places, half drops the phone back onto the table. Dev is already in the process of pulling on a latex glove – he picks up the phone; there is a message window open to 'Naith', the only text entered is 'pol', Dev can guess where this was going. He instinctively presses the button near to the top of the right edge of the smartphone; it begins to switch off, he presses again to confirm and then places it back on the table for now.

"Mr Sayeedi, if you haven't done anything wrong, then there is nothing to fear from us, we simply want to eliminate you, and your address, from our enquiries." Dev hopes to reset the tone of the discussion.

"Sorry, Detective. How can I help you?"

"Mr Sayeedi, do you know someone by the name of Anthony Blunt? Known by most as Tony Blunt?" Dev asks. Lucy watches intently for any flicker of recognition.

Sayeedi isn't giving anything away; he holds his plain expression and shrugs, though his drooping shoulders barely move. "No," he shakes his head, "I've never heard that name. Should I have?"

"We've traced calls made from a phone used by Mr Blunt, made to a mobile number that has been used at this address. Might your son know him?"

"How am I supposed to know?" he answers with frustration. Lucy assesses that he either; doesn't know him, he is a good actor, or he is venting frustration at something else. "My son is the youngest of six, he is a very fine businessman, and he'll be the last to leave my home. If this 'Mr Blunt' is a businessman, a professional person; then maybe my son does know him. Maybe you should come back when he is here."

"Thank you, Mr Sayeedi, we understand. We'd just like to have a look around though if you don't mind." says Dev as he begins to look more closely at the papers on the table.

"Well actually, I do. I really must be getting on with my affairs, I have lots to do. Could we make an appointment?"

"NO, Mr Sayeedi. May I remind you that we have a warrant issued under the Counterterrorism and Security Act 2015, which gives us the freedom to search this property in fine detail should we feel it necessary. I must urge you to comply and conform to our requests; else you risk being arrested under Section 89 of the Police Act 1996. Do you understand Mr Sayeedi?

"Yes." says the old man. All sense of playfulness has now evaporated, Mr Sayeedi stares bitterly at Dev, who holds eye contact, showing that any loss of good will is of no consequence to him.

Dev puts on his other latex glove, Lucy puts on hers, and they begin leafing through the documents on the table. Mr Sayeedi takes a seat on the chair nearest to the back door, smouldering inside; his face bearing an angry grimace, he stares at his phone. As Lucy moves from the table to the sideboard, there is a sound of heavy footsteps from upstairs. Lucy fails to register it as significant to begin with, but Dev is instantly alert to the fact that there is someone unexpectedly in the house. He locks eyes with Sayeedi - whilst old, there is nothing wrong with his hearing. As they both try to calculate what their next move should be, the footsteps turn into a more rhythmic bounding; whoever it is, is on their way downstairs. The old man jumps to his feet, faster than the officers had thought possible; "NAITH, POLICE, RUN."

*

Dev bolts, nearly yanking the door off its hinges and springing out into the hall way. He looks up to see a figure hurtling towards the bottom of the stairs. The assailant sees Dev, and quickly realises that he has no chance of outrunning the fit young officer; he stops himself against the banisters, turns and begins to run back up the stairs, two at a time, as fast as he can. He is out of sight around the corner of the left branch of the stairs before Dev makes it onto the first step. The thick-pile cream carpet soaks up the energy from the soles of Dev's heavy brogues as he charges up the first flight, just catching sight of a door slamming shut. He is up the second short flight in two quick bounds, in a second he is at the door; he clenches the handle and braces himself for what lies within, but something flicks him in the face – splinters; he holds his hand to his brow – blood, not much, but enough to awaken him to the turn of circumstances. He doesn't even hear the blast of the first shot, but he steps back just in time to hear the second as it rips through the centre of the white glossed door. He turns and runs back down the stairs. He leaps down the bottom five steps, as the third shot snaps and ricochets off the stone floor. A fourth misses over his left shoulder as he dives at the kitchen doors, he slams into them, bursting through and barrels across the hard floor, sliding to a stop against a solid oak leg of the table, leaving a smeared trail of blood behind him.

Lucy is wrestling with old man Sayeedi, having wrapped him up into an arm lock, her free arm clasping down over his shoulder, she keeps clear of his free flailing arm that lacks the strength and flexibility to give her a problem. Dev sees movement through Lucy and Sayeedi's legs, through the patio doors.

*

John hauls the sliding door open, having scoped the inside of the kitchen on his approach; he's straight to business. "Where's the shooter?" he says with all the aggression expected of a man willing to take on an armed assailant with his bare hands.

"Last seen; top of the stairs." Dev says, still on the floor, clutching his right upper arm, having located the source of the bleeding. John and

Cliff edge forward in parallel approaches, towards the double doors, leaving plenty of space between them. The silence gripping the kitchen is disturbed by the slightest of creeks from the ceiling. John signals to Dev and Lucy to move out of the likely arcs of fire, directing them with his waving hand towards the functional areas of the room.

Lucy pushes up on the arm she has locked, forcing Mr Sayeedi senior to stand. John signals again with a cupped hand over his mouth, for her to ensure that her prisoner remains silent. She reaches around with her left hand and smothers his mouth, being careful to apply pressure mostly with her fore and little fingers, making a nasty bite to the palm less likely. She begins to shuffle after Dev towards the gap between the breakfast island and the cooking stations, when a shot rips through the right of the two doors: John flinches as it passes within inches of his shoulder. The second round follows quickly and is aimed lower. Lucy tries to move faster out of the line of fire, but Mr Sayeedi is dragging his feet, in fact, he is making no effort to move at all, she realises that he is completely limp. She drops him where he stands and flees for cover.

John and Cliff hold their positions up tight to the walls, just outside of the door hinges. They look each other in the eye, and each gives a nod of readiness. Cliff tilts his head, trying to listen for the slightest of clues to the gunman's approach. The doors burst open, John and Cliff buffer them with their raised forearms, both count in their heads; *two, three,* the simultaneously fire front kicks at their respective doors, hitting the panels just inside the door handles. Cliff's door hits Naith's pistol and leading arm, knocking it inwards and out of the aim; but despite the force with which Cliff hits the door, Naith does well to hold on to the weapon. John flings his door open again and leaps at Naith, taking him down hard into the marble floor. The thirty-something businessman stands no chance against John, even with a pistol. John straddles his man, grasping his hand, trapping the handgun in his fist, and thrusts it up into Naith's neck. John hammers his free hand down, his fist splashing into the soft features of his target's face, two, three brutal blows. His victim barely conscious, he pulls the right hand, holding the gun, down, he rolls Naith over onto his belly, and pulls the gun up past Naith's shoulder-blade, all in one seamless movement, limiting the time that the barrel is pointed at him. John squeezes hard around Naith's hand, forcing him to fire off a round. The shot sounds surprisingly loud to those still in the kitchen, as the initial shock and adrenalin is already beginning to wear off. It certainly sounds louder to Alex, who has now made his way into the house and stands only feet away from John, his feet splashed with blood and brain, which have erupted from the top of Naith's skull like a volcano. "Cheers, John." Alex says, just a little in shock at what he has walked into.

John stands up. "CLEAR." he shouts out of habit more than anything. He has to restrain himself from recovering the weapon and making it safe – that protocol is certainly not appropriate, not without forensic gloves on.

*

"What happened?" Dev asks peering from behind the kitchen door.

"Stupid cunt shot himself in the back of the head." John says boyishly, still buzzing. "I'm guessing you never cleared the place before you started gas-bagging?" He asks Dev and looks on to Lucy as he walks back into the kitchen.

"No, he…" Dev stops himself from making excuses, he can tell that John is not the sort of bloke he will win over in debate, certainly not in this kind of mood. "Where did you come from anyway?"

"I was taking the 'big-dog' for a walk." he winks at Cliff.

Dev looks at Lucy with a dissatisfied frown. "How the hell am I going to write this up?" he says to no one in particular.

"I don't know," says John, "but best not include me, Cliff or Alex in your report; that could look bad on you." John straightens his heavy, black leather jacket and checks himself over for any signs of incriminating splash-back from the contents of Naith Sayeedi's head. "In fact, you should probably call in a report now, to stop every bobby in Birmingham from descending on this place." Dev takes his phone from his pocket and goes to the back of the kitchen to make the call.

"Guys!" Alex says timidly from the hallway, still frozen to the spot, conscious that any movement is going to spread fragments and particles of Naith wherever he goes.

John laughs, "Sorry, Alex mate, wait one." He replies and goes off into the kitchen.

"Are you okay Lucy?" Alex says from around the corner, as he waits for John to return. Checking Mr Sayeedi's neck for pulse, but without any luck, she is reeling at how close the low velocity nine millimetre round had come to hitting her; if it hadn't been slowed down by the door, it might well have come out the other side of the old man and hit her too. "Lucy are you okay?" he asks again.

"Huh? Yes, fine. What are you doing?"

"Just waiting for John to get me out of this mess." Alex is stood in a narrow cone of debris, mostly gooey chunks of bloody brain, interspersed with fragments of skull, scalp and tufts of black hair. The main pool of blood is slowly oozing from the exit wound. Naith's heart had beat on for a few seconds after the round had travelled through his medulla, soon running out of retained electrical impulse, so the initial spurting jet towards Alex had quickly slowed. The blood is now seeping out under the force of gravity, causing the sticky pool to grow in all directions. Alex hopes that John will return before it reaches him.

"Here; lift your foot up." John says walking around, with the body on his right, reaching out with a roll of cling-film in one hand and the loose end of the wrap in the other. Alex lifts his right foot into the air. John passes the roll hand to hand rapidly around Alex's shoe, covering it from ankle to toes. Alex hops out of the cone of mess onto his film-clad sole and lifts his left foot as high as he can without losing his balance – John repeats the process. "You love a bit of blood and guts you, don't ya?" John smiles up at Alex. Alex thinks back, not quite two months ago, to his first taste of a killing; a shiver runs down his spine as he recalls the lifeless face of that particular victim.

"Right, we've got about twenty minutes before an incident response team gets here." says Dev, hot off the phone from the control room. Terry's on his way, he should be here a bit quicker. Control has called an ambulance too, but there's no ETA on that yet."

"Oh yeah, sorry Dev. Are you all right?" Lucy asks. He pulls a frowning face that shows that he is fine but nonplussed about everyone's apparent lack of concern for him. He removes his jacket to reveal a sleeve and cuff soaked in blood.

"Looks worse than it is; the bleeding has stopped already." John says. He uses the lack of time to move things on and shape what is going to happen next. "Cliff, Alex and I were never here. Things happened exactly as they did, but instead of me jumping on the fucker – it was you." he points a finger in Dev's face, "Got it?" Dev looks back at John, he is processing what John has said through his mental constructs of ethics and morals. John can see that he is not comfortable. "You'll get a medal for this. Unless you want to go with the truth; then I'll get the medal, and you'll get a discipline for having us three here. It's up to you." Dev is silent as things start to move around him.

"Let's use the time we've got to good effect then." says Alex. He takes two more pairs of latex gloves from his pocket. "Take those thick things off and put these on." he says passing a pair each to John and Cliff.

"Dev, if you wouldn't mind making yourself useful, and rub your leaking arm on this fella's back and around the gun a bit for us, would ya? There's a good chap." John is as sarcastic and condescending as he feels that he needs to be for tactical effect. Dev commits in his head to what he feels needs to be done and complies with John's request.

"Let's go guys. We are looking for computers, phones, drives, notebooks, diaries, documentation – anything that might contain a link to Blunt. We need to get through what we can before the incident team arrives; the shit might hit the fan when they get here. Dev, you check in here, save spreading your claret any further. Lucy, you take the downstairs living areas. Cliff, John, you come upstairs with me."

"I bet you say that to all the boys." John says in a camp voice as they dodge around Naith's mess and head up the stairs.

*

Alex enters the first room on the West wing of the upper floor, John takes the second; the room from which Naith had fired from, Cliff takes the third.

Alex finds himself in what he assumes was Naith's room. It is a generously sized bedroom, sparse of furniture, which makes the standard double bed look tiny. The bedspread is shades of navy blue, albeit of a high-quality material, which Alex cannot place, it looks almost damp, maybe some sort of silk mix. The room decoration lacks imagination, solid magnolia on all four walls, the carpet, though no doubt expensive, is identical to that throughout the rest of the carpeted parts of the house. Before he has a chance to begin his search, he hears John shout from the next room.

"JACKPOT."

Alex can't resist going to see what John has found, he comes together with Cliff at the perforated door, despite his size advantage, and the fact that he could crush Alex under his thumb, Cliff gives way, knowing that Alex is more than likely going to have the most useful skill-set in this situation. "What have you got?" Alex asks before his eyes have even registered on the trove of devices that lay before him on the bed. John simply waves his arm over them. Alex's eyes fix on the 'chip-shop' poor quality labels on one of the laptops – *classic MoD* – "That's Lucy's and that's mine." he points at the two laptops in the middle of the bed successively. The casings are loose; they've been tampered with. Alex has no doubt that they are the assets that were stolen from their hotel room just prior to the execution of their last mission. His eyes wander further, he spots two smartphone handsets; they are a match to the model of phone that they had used for the mission, "No doubt they're our phones too."

Alex pauses in thought as he considers what this means. Naith, possibly his father too, were part of the group that had gone after him and Lucy, each on two occasions. Naith himself isn't likely to have been involved with the dirty work, but it is near enough to the knuckle to give Alex an intense sense of vulnerability, knowing that someone was sat with his phones, his and Lucy's laptops. "Is there a pen drive? Just a tiny little metal thing." Alex holds up a forefinger and thumb barely a centimetre apart.

"No, this is it, everything off that desk and in the drawers." John says confidently.

Alex surveys the room, there are scant few other places to hide anything in the box room, which still isn't crowded with the three of them in there. He walks over to the desk and checks the drawer.

"You think I'm a fucking mong, Alex?" John snaps angrily. Alex doesn't want to insult John, but he needs to check for himself.

"No, John, but what I'm looking for doesn't look like much, you wouldn't even know that it's a drive." He flicks the few bits and bobs from one side of the drawer to the other in frustration. "It's not here. My raw copy of the Watch List isn't here."

"Well not to worry, Alex; we've taken down the worst of those fuckers already." says Cliff not seeing the issue.

"The reason they wanted the list wasn't to try and stop us, it was to gain direct access to the other 22,000 potential soldiers – it is their perfect recruiting list."

*

Alex, John, and Cliff come down the stairs and meet Lucy and Dev around the breakfast island. "Anything down here?" John asks.

"Nothing much to speak of aside from the old man's laptop and phone; a couple of phone bills." Lucy replies.

Dev's shrug shows that he concurs. "Anything upstairs?"

"You could say that." Alex holds aloft a clutch of translucent blue evidence bags each containing a single item from their hoard. "Including four phones and three laptops," he pauses for effect, "one of which is a Skynet model." Alex chooses his description so as not to tip off Dev to the origins of the items.

As the same thoughts rush through Lucy's head, as had rushed through Alex's upstairs, everyone tilts an ear to confirm what they think they can hear. A distant siren becomes clear; "We need to make a move." says John.

"What shall I do with this?" says Alex, raising aloft his clutch of evidence bags.

"I'll take them." Lucy says, holding out her hands.

"No." says John sharply, raising his palm to Lucy. "We'll take them. After this debacle, your 'Op Wayland' might end up on ice for at least a few days, and we need to get cracking on the gen from that little lot while it's still useful."

Gen, from intelli'gen'ce - every soldier wants the gen, and wants to know if it's 'pucka gen'. The gen from the evidence seized from this house may well be useless unless it can be brought to bear before any of the suspects that it might identify, find out that the Sayeedis have been compromised.

Dev's position is becoming increasingly more difficult, the pressure shows in his expression. Flecks of blue light bounce off the high sheen surfaces of the expensive kitchen and the siren gets ever louder. He has seconds to make his decision. No one wants to get shot for a lost cause, but letting evidence leave the scene of the investigation in the possession of civilians may be a career-ending faux pas. His overriding desire to get a result drives him, as heavy vehicle doors slam outside. Dev holds his stare, fixed on Alex. There is a hammering knock at the front door and shouting from the ambulance crew. "Okay, get it to Alan, no messing about.

20

Too close

Alex stands looking over his bed debating whether to open the bags and have a preview of their contents. Having decided that he doesn't want to go strolling into the Police HQ carrying a wealth of what is effectively stolen evidence, he has decided to wait a few hours to see what is going on with Operation Wayland. His phone rings in his trouser pocket; taking it out, he sees from the screen that it's Lucy; he fumbles to answer it quickly. "Hi, are you all right?"

"I'm fine, you?"

"I'm cool, what about Dev?"

"He's been patched up; it was just a flesh wound. Where are you?"

"I'm back in my hotel. I got the lads to drop me off here; I thought it was best that these bags moved as few times as possible, cut down the risk of getting caught with them; I'm nice and close to the Police HQ. Where are you?"

"I'm in a hotel too. The Army is sourcing me a flat, but I'm in the Claymore Royale for now."

"The Claymore Royale off More Street?" Alex asks.

"Yes, that's the one. You know it?"

"Know it? I'm in it." Alex's heart lifts at the thought of being so close to her, at the coincidence of her being in the same hotel, like it's meant to be. He knows that he has to fight his natural urge to be too over-bearing, to be too much of a pest. He knows what she likes, and it isn't to be smothered or pressured. There is an awkward pause, Alex's minor panic fades and he decides to ignore the fact that Lucy is in the same building and to crack on with business as usual. "What was the fallout from this afternoon?" he says coolly.

"Oh, urm," Lucy's surprise at his lack of reaction over their proximity gives Alex a smile. She goes on; "Terry was the next to arrive after the ambulance; he was great, but once the Response Team arrived, he had a row with the Operational Firearms Commander. Anyway, the inevitable happened and they've notified the Complaints Commission. Charlie's applying pressure from her end, but we're basically shut down for at least a day or two until we can get through the red tape."

Alex picks up one of the evidence bags containing one of the Sayeedis' mobile phones, looks at it, assessing what it might represent, and thinks about what the operational pause means for the pace of its exploitation. "Are you all suspended then?"

"Effectively, we can't go into our offices and we're not to perform any further investigation on the ground, just supposed to be doing admin from hot desks. Dev's taking a day off sick tomorrow."

"What about Alan?" Alex asks.

"He's a funny one." she says, not referring to his personality, *"He's not a dedicated team asset, so he's still working on other cases."*

"Can you convince him to bend the rules for us and get him to look at some of the things we lifted? I'd have a go at them myself, but I don't have access to the tools that he has, and I'd risk destroying some of the digital forensics." There is a pause as Lucy considers the complex and rigid rules that Alan's funny little mind tends to stick to as his day-to-day coping mechanism with life.

"It's risky to even ask. Even if he does it for us; he's got no filter, he might tell anyone what we've asked him to do." Lucy's level of concern is clear from the stress in her voice. *"I'll arrange to meet him in the labs first thing*

tomorrow and sound him out. Can you be on hand with the kit if I give you the call?"

"Of course." Alex is confident that Lucy will be able to work her magic. "How are you after today? It was pretty grim."

"It's still not really sunk in yet. The bullet that hit the old man was on its way to me; what if it had've gone through him, or under his arm, and into me? It doesn't bear thinking about." Alex can hear that Lucy is upset. All he wants is to be with her, to comfort her, to tell her that everything's all right.

"Well, I'm here if you need me; room 127." he says. There is another long pause, Alex senses that she is considering more than the shoulder to cry on.

"I'm here for you too; room 123." She hangs up, leaving Alex in a quandary. He thought he'd played the master stroke by giving her his room number, putting the ball firmly in her court, but she had countered him perfectly. Her proximity to him enhances his feeling that their coming together again is fate.

Alex lies down beside the evidence bags and contemplates the permutations of what might happen next, what Lucy might do, what he might do, what she would read from whatever he does. He'd like nothing more than to stride down the corridor, give her a big warm hug, then take her to bed to take her mind off everything that is going on. He knows that this fantasy daydream isn't the way to console Lucy. He knows that she likes a strong authoritative man, but timing is everything – he isn't even confident that she still wants him at all.

After staring at the ceiling for fifteen minutes pondering the situation, Alex gets up, picks up the evidence bags, two by two, and places them on the sideboard next to the efficient little kettle and brew set. As he turns back to the bed, there is a knock at the door. He freezes, he has not considered that Lucy might come to him since she gave him her room number, but maybe playing it cool has paid off? He isn't quite conscious of the quickening of his heart, but the dizzying effects of the surge of blood around his body make him giddy and nervous; this is compounded by the shadow thought that the visit to the Sayeedis' house may have re-awakened the mysterious Interest Group's interest in him – could they have found him already? Might they have been following him, again?

Alex moves quietly to the door, there is no peep hole. He is almost certain that it will be Lucy and decides not to ask who it is; he takes a firm boxer's stance, with his right hand clenched in a raised fist. He opens the door in a swift movement but is relieved to see Lucy stood looking uncharacteristically vulnerable in the corridor. He steps into a relaxed stance as he moves out of the way of the opening door.

*

The pair stand looking at one another briefly - Alex in disbelief that she has come to him; Lucy not wanting to give away any more. Alex breaks the silence. "Are you okay?" He resists his urge to invite her in straight away. He does not want to appear arrogant and assume that she is here for his company, or anything more, but at the same time he doesn't want to appear blasé at her presence.

"Not really." she says looking into her hands. Without a question or anything else to offer; Alex takes this is a green light.

"Do you want to come in?" he says in an unassuming, sympathetic tone. She smiles and gives a barely visible nod, and steps past him into the room. As he closes the door and turns to follow her, she grabs him in a firm hug. "I've missed you." she says with a real depth of feeling.

"I've missed you too." Alex doesn't want to reveal just how much; it would be too good to be true if her missing him was all that compelled her to come to him, and he's sure that's not the case. He anticipates that her emotions are in a bit of a mess at present, so decides to do his best to maintain his policy of showing minimal interest in rekindling their relationship. "It's been another tough day at the office, huh?" he says, partially breaking their embrace and looking down at her closed eyes. She looks up to him with an expression more comfortable than he had expected to see, softening what had been a stressed face, just moments ago. He runs his hands up her back and onto her shoulders. "Do you want a drink?" He drops his hands free from her, prompting her to do the same, and he walks over to the small fridge under where the evidence bags are.

"Have you the same shit white wine that I've got in my room?" Lucy asks unenthusiastically as she perches herself on the side of Alex's bed.

"Yes, but I can order up." He calls reception and requests a bottle of their best Sauvignon Blanc and two glasses. "It'll be with us in a minute." He sits pivoted on the end of the bed, angled so that they are side on to one another.

"So, do you really miss me," he says coyly "or do you just miss 'someone'?" he asks, showing a little more pessimism than he'd aimed to.

"That's not fair, Alex." she says defensively. "The only reason I put 'us' on ice was because of the fallout from the mission." Alex feels immediately guilty; he's fallen into the trap of making it all about him again.

"I'm sorry. All I felt was the rejection. I don't just miss having someone," their eyes come together as he pauses, "I miss *you*." Lucy leans towards him and reaches across, placing her hand on his. She continues the motion towards him - he gravitates towards her. Their lips meet; Alex revels in her touch, her taste, but their tryst is interrupted by a sudden, hard knock at the door.

The atmosphere softens with the distraction provided by the arrival of the wine. Alex fills the glasses and joins Lucy back on the bed. They recline next to one another propped up by plump cushions and pillows. "Cheers." he says, casually raising his glass towards hers.

"What are we drinking to?" she asks.

"How about recovering stolen assets?" he says nodding towards the evidence bags. They clink glasses with light smiles.

"Does it look like they got anything from it?"

"Hard to say, but they've had a good go at it. They've been into its guts. My biggest concern is that they've got into my pen drive and it's been moved on to bigger fish."

"You think that's why it wasn't with the rest of it?" she asks as she takes another slow sip of her wine. Alex nods solemnly. "Maybe we'll learn more from their material." she says optimistically. Alex doesn't acknowledge her; he is deep in thought. "What's the matter?" she asks.

"I'm just thinking." Alex says slowly. "What if we get a lead that takes us off in another direction?"

"That's fine; we go where the mission takes us." Lucy says, not seeing a problem.

"Fine for us, for Operation Wayland, but John and the blokes seem convinced that Tony Blunt is the key and is responsible for the death of Craig and the others. I'll have a problem talking them onto higher priority suspects."

Lucy's sigh indicates her level of understanding. "They're not going to make much progress on tracking him down without you, or should I say the intelligence that flows through you." she says knowingly.

"You mean if we turn up anything on Blunt, we just don't tell them?" he says almost at pains. Lucy smirks and drinks some more wine. "I couldn't do that to them. They'd kill me."

"Literally!" Lucy laughs. Alex sees the funny side and laughs with her. They lean in towards each other, and Alex decides not to hold back, he runs his hand up the side of her neck, on into her hair and pulls himself in for a long hard kiss.

21

Exploitation

Alex rolls over as his 07:30 alarm goes off. He is gratified to see Lucy still lying beside him. He runs his hand up the outside of her silky-smooth thigh, over the top of her beautifully curved hip and settles in the dip of her narrow, toned, but still womanly waistline. He sighs with deep satisfaction that he is back on terms with this goddess of a woman. Whilst feeling totally mentally content, his physical happiness with the situation is making itself known with a warm prod in her lower back. "Hello." she says, moving her hand towards his crotch to confirm his excited state. "I'll be on top for round two." she says, much to Alex's delight.

*

An hour later, Alex escorts Lucy into the hotel dining room. "How come I've not seen you at breakfast before now?" he says as they take their seats at Alex's usual table, a sensible distance from the self-service buffet counter.

"The Army online booking service got me 'room only', despite breakfast being free with any civilian booking." she says cynically. "I've been having cereals in my room; I never eat much for breakfast anyway."

"I know." Alex says with a fond smile. Their brief affair over the course of the Watch List mission had lasted only days, but it had left its mark on Alex. "So how are you going to play it with Alan?"

Lucy smiles and gives him a seductive look. "I'll use my natural leverage over him. Try and make his underlying natural urges overcome his beset need for rules and routine."

"Does that go some way to explaining your choice of wardrobe for today then?" Alex smiles broadly, looking down at her chest. Her perfectly formed C-cup breasts are receiving ample support from some sort of miracle bra; her soft, tanned, silky skin is pressing at her pink, open-necked shirt. She just smiles confidently.

"I'll text you once I've talked him round, then meet you at reception again." Lucy stands up, walks around to Alex's side of the table, and leans down to kiss him goodbye. She rests her hand on the top of his inner thigh, just tickling the end of his little fella. "See you in a short while."

*

Alex sits at his table basking in his satisfaction with how things are going, sipping a third cup of coffee. He takes his phone from his pocket to check that it is not silenced; he notes several icons on the notification bar and opens them, quickly dismissing unimportant emails. The third icon is from his encrypted messaging app. He swipes it to open the text – it's from Charlie – *"Hi smoothie, we're due a catch-up."* the message ends with an emoji of two clinking wine glasses. Alex's face flushes an incredulous red and he feels the sweat seeping out of his scalp – *why can't anything ever be simple*. As he goes to place the phone away, it vibrates in his hand; a text from Lucy, *"Bring the bags over now x."*

*

Alex walks into the West Midlands Police Headquarters lobby, carefully trying to minimise the profile of his bulging rucksack. He sees Lucy jumping up from her seat. "You took your time. Are you okay?" she asks. The thought of the 'Charlie issue' has clearly had the same effect on his outward demeanour, as it is having on his mind.

"Yeah, great, just a bit nervous with the payload, if you know what I mean." he does his best to feign a smile.

Lucy signs Alex in at the reception desk and takes him down to the basement floor in the shimmering lift. They exit into what looks like the dumping ground for the whole building; a broad corridor cluttered with boxes and stacks of paper, old promotional stands and paraphernalia, the walls are painted in an awful speckled 'slime green' gloss paint, or spray on liner of some sort. Lucy presses a buzzer, which is quickly answered by someone not visible through the glass into the labs. "Hi, Special Constable Butler, here to see Alan Walton, please." She holds her temporary identification up to the camera that's next to the microphone. The door clicks and Lucy leads Alex through into the large workshop. Lucy shows Alex the bits of kit that she has seen Alan operate, before Alan emerges from one of the changing rooms that lead through to the more sensitive areas, where lab coats and hair nets must be worn.

"Hi, Alan." Alex says, sounding as friendly as he can. He takes his rucksack off and opens it on the top of a robust steel-framed table with a solid black resin work surface. He lays the evidence bags out.

"I'm not touching that one." Alan says sharply in his funny little voice, pointing at Lucy's Skynet laptop. "It's OGD, I'll get the sack for that." Other Government Department: the political consequences that would usually go hand in hand with interfering with equipment known to belong to a partner agency would run far above his, Lucy's, or even Charlie's pay grade.

"You don't have to worry too much about that one, Alan. That's my laptop that was taken from me a few weeks ago by some quite nasty people. We just need to know if the security has been breached. You can do that for *me* can't you?" Alex steps back to leave Lucy to work her magic.

"I'm supposed to report it straight away and have it couriered to wherever they want it sending back to." Alan says, twitching a little at the left eye.

"Well, I can take it straight back to where it was issued from at Whitehall, it's still on my flick, so it's not really an issue, is it?" Lucy takes a deep breath, arches her back, and massages an imaginary itch in her ribs. Alan stares, and seems to lose concentration for a second. "Thanks, Alan, you're my hero." Alan seems to shrink slightly but offers no protest.

Alex points to his laptop, "That one's mine, it was taken at the same time, we need to know if it has been accessed, and if it has; was anything copied from it, similar for those two matching smartphones." Alan nods with a thinly vailed smile.

"The other stuff belongs to the Sayeedis – we need anything that you can get off those. We're primarily looking for any connections to the Pavilion Gardens and Millbank incidents, or to Tony Blunt." Lucy adds. "Remember, this is no longer under Operation Wayland, this is working directly to Charlie – for The Security Service." She pats Alan on the shoulder, and winks at Alex, as she moves out of Alan's field of view, allowing him to get focused on the task before him. "How long will you need?"

Alan looks at the items one by one, holds a finger up in the air to them briefly, then tilts his finger over and looks at his watch. "Come back at 1500 hours." He takes a fresh pair of latex gloves from the box at the end of the table and sets about his work, taking no further notice of Lucy or Alex. The pair shrug their shoulders at each other, then head for the door.

22

Pinpointed

"Don't spare the horses." Alex says as Lucy pulls her brand-new little two-seater Mercedes convertible out of the hotel car park. It is a little past 15:30 on a Friday afternoon; the traffic is going to be challenging to say the least. "I like the new car; it's very 'you'."

"I chopped in my A-class the same day I started here, my treat for promotion."

Alan's exploitation has revealed a web of connections that warrant further investigation, including a possible direct link to Blunt, but with the Sayeedis lying dead on slabs, this information is time sensitive and approaches its limit of usefulness with every minute that ticks by. The team is faced with a complex intelligence scenario with multiple leads competing for priority. Alex can feel the argument with Lucy coming.

"We need to focus on the possible upward chain of command highlighted by this new information." Lucy says sharply, as she exits the roundabout to follow the A38 out of the city centre.

Alex seeks to distract her away from the difficult line of conversation; "Where are you taking us? I thought Solihull was south of here?"

"The south side of the city will be rammed; it'll be quicker heading out on the M6 and around the M42. Plus, I get to stretch her legs." she says, squirting the accelerator and bursting past the traffic as the A38 turns from dual carriageway into a three-lane motorway.

The atmosphere in the close confines of the little car's beautifully crafted leather cockpit is clouded; Alex doubts that the conversation about the direction of the investigation is over – he's not wrong.

"I know the guys are hung up on Blunt, but frankly, we've got bigger fish to fry." Alex is inclined to agree, but that doesn't necessarily mean that he is willing to manipulate his new mates; he is determined to find the middle ground that will satisfy everyone, as he is usually able to.

"The blokes aren't going to be interested in going in cold on under-developed leads, not while Blunt's on the loose."

"He's always going to be the distraction." Lucy says with frustration as she finds herself agreeing with Alex's logic.

He goes on, "We don't have enough guys on the team immediately available to be going after all the new possibilities anyway. We're better off eliminating Blunt from our enquiries, as it were. We can crack on with chasing down the Interest Group with him out of the way, and with the full force of Op Wayland back in the game." Lucy gives him a weakly submissive smile.

*

"Gent's, this is Lucy." Alex introduces her to Blakey, Cliff, and Spence.

"Lucy played a big part in our last mission, providing the vast majority of the intelligence feed… one way or another." John smirks, knowing that Lucy is still a little sore about how the Watch List was taken by Alex on her watch, prior to her joining the team. John's smirk turns to an evil smile directed at Alex as Lucy leans past him to shake hands with the others. Alex fears mischief from the man who has quickly become a close comrade. They may be getting close, but Alex remembers that every soldier loves nothing more than a good 'cock-block'. They all move into the conference room, Cliff and Blakey fetch the brews.

John takes his seat at the centre of the left side of the long ovular table and gets things underway, "What have you found on our friends, the Sayeedis, then? No heartbeats I take it?" his evil little chuckle to himself suits the darkness of his humour.

"No pulses present," Lucy feigns a weak smile, "but a good bit of information regarding their network. Analysis of their devices indicates that they were covertly communicating with a closed group over encrypted channels."

"What does that look like?" Cliff asks.

"A similar messaging and voice application to the one that we used for the last mission. There is one particular conversation that displays classic coded language traits, and each of the addressees changes their phone number over the course of the conversation history – it does include one of the phone numbers that Zafir Abdulaziz was using at the time." Eyebrows are raised around the room. "This thread only goes back six weeks; we assume that this was when Sayeedi last changed his phone, as the messages are in flow at the beginning of the thread. Zafir's number was newly added, that's why it wasn't picked up from the sim that was found in his flat."

The men all seem impressed and interested, but Alex and Lucy can both tell that they are itching to see if there is anything that might lead them to Blunt. Lucy decides to indulge them, having conceded to Alex's argument. "In this message thread, Sayeedi mentions his 'Talab' on a number of occasions. Talab is Arabic for student." Lucy pauses.

"Or maybe one being 'mentored'." says Alex. Everyone in the room clearly sees the significance of this, as it was Blunt's mentor note that led them to the Sayeedis in the first place.

Lucy goes on, "We cross referenced the date-time groups of the mentions of this name in the thread, with other calls and messages made through any available channels of communication that we could find." Lucy's royal 'we' meaning 'Alan', "We found record of a voice call, just minutes before one of the 'Talab' instances, to the number Blunt was using until he disappeared. That call was made on the seventh of June."

"The day we gave orders at Hodgehill; that makes sense." John says, massaging his smooth scalp with the tips of his fingers. "We had that phone number anyway, it's dead. How does this get us any further forward?"

Lucy smiles with glee as she comes to her crescendo, "Subsequently, we found calls made from the Sayeedi's landline to a London-based landline number, which also tallied with mentions of Talab in the message thread."

"You think Blunt is answering the phone somewhere in London?" Spence asks.

"Yes." says Lucy resolutely. "We have a Police analyst working on getting us an address, the distant end line isn't covered by the warrant we have."

"Sweet." says John. "I trust that with Op Wayland on ice, and the time-sensitive nature of this intelligence – not to mention the fact that you're here briefing *us* - that we're in the frame for paying this address a visit?" John says with an excited grin on his face.

"Well, we'll need to clear that with Charlie." Lucy says cautiously.

"You don't need to worry about Charlie." John's hawk-like features are stark and scary in the bright conference room lights, "I know exactly what Charlie wants, I've already spoken to her about a chance like this." He gives Alex a knowing wink. Alex is surprised by John's comment, he has been caught unawares by the idea that Charlie would speak directly to anyone else in his team – he suddenly doesn't feel so special.

"There'll be no time for any surveillance or any kind of hanging about on this one, word of what's happened to the Sayeedis will be out now, so we need to move fast." John has it all figured out, "We've already got a van together, we just need to identify a forward basing area, then hard knock at zero two hundred hours tomorrow morning, pull him out and get him back to base for a little chat.

"Lucy, when will we have that address?" Everyone around the table is shocked to varying degrees by the speed to which John has come up with the scheme of manoeuvre.

Lucy is caught off guard, "Uh, I err, should have it in the next hour or two." Everyone looks at John; the blokes for further direction, Lucy in wonderment as to what he has in mind for Blunt, and Alex, well he just can't put his finger on what is not quite right about the way John is acting.

23

Supplies

Tony walks slowly down the first aisle of the hardware shop, the peak of his grey baseball cap pulled down close to his nose. He keeps his chin down to his chest, with most of his beard tucked into his big, baggy hoody. The hood is down; draped over the top of his large, non-descript, black ruck sack. He is suddenly conscious that he's making too much of an effort to conceal himself; he's failing to meet his aim of hiding in plain sight. He flicks his beard out and tries to relax, speeding up his movements, adding a little swagger, swinging his empty basket. The place is not busy, only a few tradesmen industriously going about their business and wanting to get back to their jobs; no one's taking any notice of him – he just needs to avoid the CCTV.

Some of what he needs to complete his mission will be available on location, but he cannot be sure what will be lying about in the foundry and he'd prefer newer kit than is available from Farmer Duffield's shed. The first item is a pair of wire snips – toughened steel and super sharp; he takes a pair from the rack and tests their movement, which is smooth and well-sprung, despite the fold of branded plastic packaging getting in the way a little. He throws the snips into his basket. The tools get heavier duty as he reaches the end of the aisle. He finds bolt cutters in a range of sizes; he opts for a medium sized pair, with extending handles – Tony is confident that his considerable strength doesn't need a great deal of multiplying.

He moves on past the end of the row; the back wall of the shop is where he finds clothing and personal protective equipment. He takes an extra-large set of navy-blue overalls from the shelf, shakes them out and holds them up against himself to check their length.

"They'll just about get around that big chest and those guns, fella." says the friendly old shopkeeper, appearing from the end of the second aisle. Tony grunts a polite, but brief laugh, nods, then turns back towards the shelf. The old man takes the hint and leaves him to it. Moving on, he comes to well-spaced racks of gloves. He selects a thick, grey leather set – the label trumpets their heat retardant qualities; they go into the basket. Beyond the gloves are boots. Tony's feet are hardy, after years of punishment in 'the Reg', especially in the early days, when the issued boots were cheap and hard. He isn't looking for comfort, just protection; as tough as he is, he'll not achieve his mission with a crushed foot. He selects a cheap and common brand with a good safety rating.

Tony walks back along to tops of the aisles, looking for items 'by the metre'. He sees the rack that he is looking for down the third lane on the left. On his way to it he sees something else that's on his list – ropes. He picks up a fifty-metre coil and checks the label – *'tested to 2400kg.'* He throws it into his basket, then takes a second coil and chucks that in too. He edges along to the dispensing unit containing every kind of wire and chain imaginable. He goes directly to the heavy end and unreels three metres of the highest gauge chain available into his basket. Tony decides to use his new croppers to cut the chain, rather than the dispenser's integral cutting mechanism, giving him a chance to test them. There is a satisfying click as the link is sliced cleanly, followed by pattering thuds and clinks as the end of the chain drops down onto the thick brown card of the boot box.

Tony takes two chunky, hardened steel padlocks from the rack along from the checkout kiosk and drops them in with his other items. He stands and waits for someone to come and serve him. The old man totters from the back of the store, "Sorry, I'll be right there." Tony doesn't reply, just tips the faintest of nods, not wishing to reveal any more of his face than he must. The shopkeeper walks behind Tony, around the back of the counter and takes his place stood by the till.

Tony places his basket on the low counter and takes his rucksack off, holding it ready to stow the items as the old man scans them. "So, what were you?" says 'Mick' if his name badge is accurate.

"Sorry?" Tony replies, confused by the question offered without context.

"What were you?" he asks again boldly, "Engineers? Marines?" Tony looks up to eyeball the man but says nothing. "Once you've served; you can see it in others – I could see it the moment you walked in." he smiles – still Tony says nothing. "It takes more than a beard and a cap to hide it." Mick laughs, slightly unnerved at the muted response. "I was Royal Engineers, did my full twenty-two before I retired and opened this place." Mick's voice slows and quietens as he looks at his customer's expression and realises that the chirpy chat that he'd hoped for isn't going to happen.

"Not me pal, I've never served." Tony says, handing over a fan of twenty-pound notes. He takes his change and receipt, and leaves.

24

Base camp

"What's going on John?" Alex asks, as the transit van cruises south east down the M40. This is the first opportunity that Alex has had to get him on his own since the meeting back at the team headquarters.

"What are you talking about?" John says coyly with a steadfast grin.

"You seemed pretty sure of yourself when we told you about Blunt's location." Alex eyes him sideways from the passenger seat of the van; he doesn't relent. John's grin breaks into a full-on smile, he's almost laughing.

"Yeah, well, I've been doing a bit of liaison on the side with our Charlie, ain't I."

Alex laughs aloud; he finds the thought of John 'smoothying it' with any female hilarious, but him and Charlie coming together, well, that is something that his imagination would rather not play with. The humour of the situation is enhanced by Alex's elation that John is potentially giving him top cover with regard to his own interlude with Charlie, and that it might divert any attention from it. Putting aside whatever physical interaction John might have had with the Security Service agent, Alex is interested to hear more about what they've spoken about. "What have the two of you been liaising on?"

"We've been talking a lot about the back channels of the operation. We agree that this Wayland pish isn't going to get us the result we need."

Alex nods, "I told you; she hadn't got us involved without reason.

"You had fun, right?" Alex looks in for John's reaction. He laughs, nods, even blushes.

*

Alex jumps out of the van into the dark and onto the dusty ground of the yard. Skip trucks are parked nose-to-tail in the 'L' shaped area of land that disappears around past the corner of the shell of a building. He looks in to the shadowy expanse of the open-ended warehouse-come-shelter; the right side of it houses neatly organised stacks of skips of all sizes. There is a small, prefabricated office in the rear left corner. "Where the fuck are we?" he asks.

"Royal Docks." John replies. "We're about twenty minutes south of the target address.

"Chips' Skips?" Alex reads from the side of one of the truck doors.

"Yeah. Chips was 1 Para, he got attached to us for the back end of our 2008 Afghan tour, took over as my Section Commander when ours was killed." John looks to the ground; Alex can see that he is reliving a memory - it is the first time that he can remember seeing John express any kind of emotion other than anger, with the exception of their brief chat in the café about Craig's demise. "When we asked him for use of the place to have a little word with the bloke that we think stitched up Craig Medhurst; he couldn't do enough for us. When he heard it was Tony Blunt; he even offered up disposal services."

"Bonus." Alex says insincerely, cringing at the thought of what that might mean for Blunt. The troubled look still plagues John's face. Alex wonders what is going through his mind. He is about to ask when he sees headlights approaching the gates of the yard. His initial reaction is to panic, but he soon realises that the tired-looking black Skoda Octavia is being driven by Cliff, Spence in the front passenger seat, Blakey in the back.

*

The battered Skoda pulls up next to the van. "Fucking traffic." Cliff says as he gets out. He strides over and pulls open the side door of the transit.

"Bollocks," John replies, "I saw you pull off into the services." Cliff sniggers as he grabs two steel-framed folding chairs from the back. He takes the chairs and places them against the corrugated iron wall over to the left side of the covered space. The five men gather around the bonnet of the Skoda.

"I'll be leading on the 'lift op'." says Blakey. "Cliff, you'll be the door man," Cliff nods his acknowledgement. "Spence, you'll be with me as first assault pair – I'll be on point." Spence gives a similar nod. "John, you'll follow on with Cliff in reserve as second assaulting pair if needed." Alex clears his throat, hoping to remind Blakey that he exists. "Alex, you're lookout; you stay on the street. Make sure you've got arcs up and down the A112, and onto Church Road." Blakey points out the ground that needs covering on an image on his phone screen. Alex cannot conceal his disappointment at being left out on the street, yet again, when the action will be going off.

"The ground in general is urban city, H-hour is 0200 hours, so it will be quiet, but not completely dead, there is no significant night life in the immediate area, so we shouldn't be bothered by members of the public. Street lighting will mean that it will be light, no visual aids required, ambient light should be sufficient once inside.

"The ground in detail is twenty minutes' drive north of this location, set on the north junction of a triangular one-way system. The flat complex is on the north-east side of that junction. I believe that the flat is the second door on the left on the ground floor. We have no intelligence on what the neighbours will be like, but it could be a rough mix, so stay alert and expect idiots.

"The mission is to capture Tony Blunt and bring him back to this location for interrogation, in order to determine his involvement with the killing of Craig Medhurst and our other lads." Blakey repeats, this mission statement over again, as is traditional for British Forces' commanders when delivering orders, this means that everyone is clear on what the over-arching objective is.

"Scheme of manoeuvre." Blakey moves on to describe an overview of how the mission will be achieved. "We move from here in both vehicles. The route in will follow the A12 north, coming in from the west using Oliver Road, then onto the one-way system on Church Road. This will leave the vehicles pointing the right way for a quick extraction south, straight down the A112." Blakey does his best to show the route on his phone, but the men get the gist and have done their homework, they all nod with an air of impatience to show that they are content. "We get into the building – John; you're responsible for getting us through the front door. Then Spence and I will line up behind Cliff outside the flat door," Blakey nods at the smiling hulk. Cliff gives a glimpse of his war face. "Cliff will bust us in, then I'll locate Blunt, assuming he's present, between me and Spence; we'll put him to sleep, plasti-cuff him, then get him out into the van." Alex itches to ask a question but knows that he must wait for the right time in the process. "The route back will be directly down the A112 to West Ham, where we take Manor Road, then follow your nose all the way back in here." Having completed the outline of the plan, Blakey goes back through the key actions of the mission in enough detail to ensure that everyone knows the part they will play. He adds in contingencies and 'actions on' to be taken should likely risks be realised. Alex remembers Craig's orders from Hodgehill, and how important it was for everyone on the team to know what to do if things did not go to plan. It was less of a concern to him then, but he features in some of the scenarios, and he knows that he must be tuned into the expected actions and be ready for anything.

"So, we get up the road taking the scenic route to the west, John gets us in to the building, quietly if possible, it goes noisy as Cliff gets us in the flat, then Spence and me goose-neck the cunt. Zip ties and hood on him, then in the van and back here on the direct route. From then on, we'll leave Cliff to do his stuff. Everyone happy?"

Alex recognises this as his time to speak. "Once you guys are in the building, can I follow you in? I'll need to check for any useful intelligence." Blakey says nothing, just looks at John.

John pauses, knowing that Alex is keen to get amongst it, but he also sees the sense of the idea. "All right, Alex. Once we've got Blunt under control, I'll come out and relieve you, and you can give the place a scan. Make sure you've got gloves – there's some in the van.

Blakey then goes through the remaining relevant headings of the orders format, covering detail on the logistical elements of the mission, command and control; this takes but a few moments, as most of it is already in place, it is simply a verbal check to ensure that they have what they need to hand, and every member of the team understands who will be making the call for specific decisions.

25

Packed

Tony checks over the equipment and supplies that he has gathered over the past week since his recce of the farm. Everything is laid out in a smart and uniformed order on his bed. He closes his eyes to think through his plan of action to ensure that he has remembered everything. He doesn't get far through his scenario, when his eyes open calmly and he thinks about the only item that he has resisted the temptation to purchase himself - the one thing that he has arranged to be procured on his behalf to avoid possibly becoming flagged as suspicious.

He begins to load the items into his old pattern Army bergan. He starts with the things that he will need least frequently. The lengths of chain are not ideal in terms of weight loading of his pack, but this is of little consequence to Tony, having just a short distance to cover; they sit loose at the bottom. Next, he takes the two lengths of rope and drops them into a thick plastic rubble sack, then places that into the bergan. The weather is expected to be good, but rain cannot be ruled out – the rubble sack will keep everything that isn't individually water-proofed dry. He reaches into the sack to press the natural coils of the ropes snuggly into the corners of the pack, on top of the chains; creating a pit for the other items to sit in. He lines the rope nest with his heavy gloves. He drops in a small bundle of clean clothes; they are almost vacuum packed in a resealable polythene bag that he has squashed the air out of by sitting on it, they nestle nicely between the gloves. Before the body of the pack becomes too full; he slides his folded roll mat down between the back and the rubble sack – this is a convenient place to stash it, and it will protect his back from any lumps and bumps that might protrude from his load.

Making sure that he keeps the sides of the rubble sack from crumpling down under his things, he continues to pack – boiler suit - also in polythene, spare water – three two-litre bottles, sleeping bag, already inside the bivvy bag and with as much air squeezed out as possible. He stuffs it all in, pushing down hard on it with his knee, he gathers the top of the rubble sack together and rolls down the excess plastic on itself. He uses the two drawstrings of the bergan to secure everything down, just about within the planned capacity of the bergan body.

He places all of his bits and pieces, his niff-naff and trivia, into the top flap of the bergan; sunglasses, notepad, pen, contact gloves, knife, filtered head torch with spare batteries, some cash, a new phone sim card, mostly useful items, but some trinkets that might help to pass the time of day – *only time I've ever missed having webbing*. He does his best to pack it in a way that will minimise any rattling.

He places all his food, up to a week's worth, into the first of the two side pouches that he has zipped back onto the flanks of the bergan. He layers the items in terms of daily supply, so that he never has to dig too far for what he needs, with snacks and boredom food between main meals, the ten-litre pouch is completely filled; he struggles to close the zip.

The second side pouch is home to his two-litre water bladder, he shoves his water-proof jacket in next to it, then his 'softie jacket'; a Forces' favourite - the plain green nylon jacket of a thousand layers that has given many a soldier warmth on long winters' nights over the decades. He picks up the two padlocks and the snips, and pops them into the small water bottle pouch on the front of the main body of the bergan; he is not happy that they are loose to rattle around, so he takes the beanie hat from the top pouch, rolls the padlocks in it and then stuffs them back in next to the snips.

All that remains on the bed is the bolt cutters and a roll of black electrical tape. He grabs the cutters by the business end and wedges the ends of the handles between the body of the bergan and the left pouch, having to force it down the tight gap until just a couple of inches of its nose is exposed above the top of the pouch; which he then tucks under the edge of the top flap concealing it from view.

Tony stands to see if the pack passes visual inspection; he tugs at the top flap to straighten it so that it looks neat and well-balanced, but he notices some excess strap hanging from the flap buckle – he addresses it with the black tape. He may no longer be, or wish to be, a Paratrooper, but some things you just can't unlearn. He threads the first two fingers of his right hand through the pack's collar hook and lifts it up with his elbow high – *thirty kilos*.

Placing the pack down again, Tony sits on the bed and puts on the new industrial boots. He has been pleased with the fit, but now he will see what they are like under load. Tony threads his left arm through the shoulder strap of the pack and swings it around onto his back, shuffling to get his right arm through the other strap. He bounces it into position high on his back and tightens the easily adjustable straps as far as they will go. He bounces on his heels to settle the load and to get himself balanced with it. He can feel the chain pressing into his lower back, but it is not too uncomfortable. The weight on his legs takes him by surprise, but he knows that it is easily manageable for the couple of kilometres that he has to cover.

Finding himself stood in an empty flat, almost 'mission ready', Tony feels a significant milestone being reached, he has only one more item on his agenda in London, then he will be away. He secures the doors before heading out, around the corner to stow his tightly packed bergan in the car ready for the early morning start, then heads off to make his collection.

26

Move to strike

The men load up, back into the same vehicles that they had arrived in; this time John waits to follow on in the van as the lads' car pulls off. The drive north is quiet, as one would expect, into the early hours in this part of the city. Alex looks at John; his demonic features softened by thoughtful sadness, clearly still troubled by the memories dragged up by speaking of his time in Afghanistan. Alex considers it maybe best left alone at this sensitive time before the lift operation launches, but then it might do more harm for John to have a clouded head. His interest forces his decision. "Was 2008 your first deployment then?" he eases into the conversation.

John grimaces, but he's too much of a man to brush it off. "No. I did the seventh turnaround of Op TELIC in Iraq as a tom. I'd just got bumped up to lance-jack for Afghan."

The noughties were a turbulent period for the Second Battalion, some of John's colleagues had earned five medals with less than three years in the unit during that time. From his third annual report, John had promoted from Private to Lance-Corporal; about right for a 'top-third' infanteer, the only place you'd expect to find someone who went on to Hereford two years later with a further promotion already under his belt.

"What role were you in for HERRICK?" Alex asks, addressing the tour by its operation name.

"I was a section two ice-cream in a Rifle Company." Alex just about understands 'two ice-cream' – '2IC' - 'second in command'. "Blunt was in my section." John says unprompted and with disgust, hateful that he knows him - that there is even a connection between them. Alex says nothing, just waits for John to go on. "He's always been a weirdo, never quite the full ticket." John almost laughs, "He was fucking useless, completely untrainable – he'd always be dropping us or himself in the shit for something." John's smile disappears. "We didn't make it easy on him to be fair." John looks straight on up the road to the back of Skoda as he talks on, "We were out on a patrol one day in Sangin, Blunt went forward to check out a suspected IED, next thing we know, the Commander was dead and the rest of us were taking incoming like you wouldn't believe. They had us proper pinned down, we lost another three dead and Blunt was missing in action."

"Jesus. Where'd he go?"

"We thought he was dead, but then just as we were about to run out of ammo and be put to slaughter; he came up behind the enemy and hosed them all down – killed them all outright."

"So, he saved you then?"

John's face is spiked with anger. "That's one way of looking at it. The cunt was hiding somewhere - he just disappeared and left us to it for a good ten minutes. If he'd have done what he'd done straight away; maybe three more of my mates would still be alive now."

"Where did he say he'd been?"

"Some bollocks about protecting civilians, but that was shite; the only people that needed protecting were his mates." John catches an ironical glitch in his words knowing that the way they had treated him; Blunt wouldn't have seen any of them as his 'mates'. "We let it go though. Like you say, he saved our lives, but we never let him forget that those of us who survived that ambush knew he'd fucked us. We never let him get too much glory – anytime anyone started going on about it, we'd slip a bit more information out about what really went down."

Alex thinks over the complexity of what John has just told him - *his head must be doing somersaults; moving in on an operation to lift a bloke that got three of your mates killed, saved your life, and then in all probability, ended up getting your best mate and mentor killed too.*

*

Tony steps up onto the low wall and skips over the railings that protrude from the top of it and lands two footed amongst the foliage of the trees of Walthamstow Cemetery. He walks north following a row of ancient graves, hand-railing the road that leads to the Chapel. As he reaches the corner, where the road breaks left and right around the solitary building, he sees his contact. The two men exchange nods, neither of them knowing, nor want to know, each other's name. Tony takes the package, gives another nod, then turns and walks away.

*

The car turns right onto the one way system of the A112 and immediately pulls up onto the curb right outside of the small two storey block of flats that merges deep-set into the more conspicuous buildings either side of it; the flats look like they've been more recently build, probably just to fill a gap. The van bumps up behind the Skoda, undramatically rolling to a stop. Of the two or three pedestrians in view; none take any notice and carry on their merry way to wherever they are going without even looking up.

Alex jumps out of the van and opens the sliding side door, standing clear for Cliff who retrieves a large, red, heavy metal door ram. Alex looks down to see the tip of a cosh barely visible resting on the inside of Blakey's cupped hand – *I wonder how far up his sleeve that goes.* Spence doesn't appear to be armed, but then Alex wouldn't expect Spence to be so overt. John leans into the body of the transit and takes a full-sized iron crowbar and hooks it onto his thick nylon waist belt. He takes a savage pair of knuckle dusters from the map pocket of his walking trousers and presses them firmly onto the webs of his fingers with the palm of his other hand, baring his teeth with a horrible leer as he does so. Alex fears for Blunt's chances of making it out of the building alive. "Cuffs, hood?" Blakey says to Cliff. Cliff nods, and that is all the communication needed.

John grips the crowbar firmly in his right hand, it grinds against the brass of his new accessory, he leads the team off across the open paving at the front of the building. Alex moves along to the left of the flat, far enough to be able to see clearly down Church Road and north up the A112 towards the cricket ground. His primary concern is diverting any pedestrian interest, but it doesn't look like he's going to have to worry. He settles, trying to act casually against a conveniently placed street lamp, as he checks the approach routes again, he is startled by a sharp splintering of timber. His eyes shoot back to the team as the front door of the flats swings open. Cliff moves through the doorway grasping the ram with purpose. John remains as the link man, maintaining eye contact with Alex for now, tipping him a reassuring nod.

There is a pertinent pause; Alex envisages Blakey and Spence lining up in formation ready to spring forward once Cliff clears the door. Another second passes and the distant sound of heavy metal smashing against Blunt's flat door is followed instantly by the shattered rattle it makes as it gives way and bounces off the wall behind it. John disappears from the doorway in an instant, leaving Alex on his own. He self-consciously checks his arcs again, before allowing his attention to fix back on the doorway. He hears a shout of 'room clear' from deep within the building. The boom of the explosion almost passes Alex by, had the front door not have nearly ripped itself off its hinges, he might not have noticed. He stands in shock, not sure if he has seen what he has seen, not sure if it was a part of the plan that he has failed to pick up on. He hesitates, unsure of whether to remain at his designated post or to investigate. Smoke begins to trail from the building's entrance. Alex stumbles forward, then, gathering a sense of what has happened, runs to his team-mates.

Alex stops in the doorway; he sees someone running into the flat, but another on the ground. "JOHN." he shouts as he makes out his unmistakeable figure through the haze; laying spread-eagled but moving, reeling in pain. Alex darts to his side, sliding to his knees over him. "John, can you hear me?"

"Help Cliff, he gasps." vaguely pointing into the flat.

*

Tony had been surprised to see the vehicles outside his flat as he had emerged from his shortcut home down Vicarage Road. He had been relieved to see their lookout distracted by their own team going in. He had been startled by his security device initiating in his flat. He now stands considering his options from the cover of a bus shelter on the Church Road junction. He lifts the package that he is carrying up in front of him and unwraps the cloth at the heavy end, exposing the ferociously sharp cutting edge of his enormous new felling axe. Tony pauses, relishing the idea of hacking to pieces whoever it is that has come for him. There is too much risk of becoming embroiled, too much risk of compromise, too much risk of jeopardising his mission. He tucks the cloth back over his new toy and walks to his car.

27

Fallout

The uniformed officer shows Alex into the poorly lit interview room. "Take a seat please Mr Gregory." Alex's charm has all-but dried up; his frown attempts to morph into a smile of acknowledgement, but barely makes it. The officer closes the door on her way out. Having been arrested at the scene as a matter of course, he has been starved of information, the lifeblood on which he survives, not least when his mates are in varying states of injury. It had been clear that Blakey had died instantly, catching the full force of the blast and blaze. Alex had helped to recover Spence out of the building, but he was in a bad way when they loaded him into the ambulance. John had walked clear of the building, but Alex suspects that he had sustained more than just the obvious burns to the face; he had been put into a separate ambulance just as Alex and Cliff were being arrested.

The door twitches; Alex flinches. He looks to his left to see who might appear. He can hear the female officer who booked him; "We have Mr Gregory in here for you Ma'am." The door swings open.

"Thank you, Constable, that'll be all for now." says Charlie as she bursts into view. Maybe he's just tired, maybe it's because he's so pleased to see a friendly face, but Alex is taken aback by her aura.

"Am I glad to see you." he says, closing his eyes in relief. She glints a cocky smile at him. "How do you look that good at... what time is it?"

"A few minutes after six." she replies. "Hairspray and lippy, the rest falls into place."

"Have you got any news on the blokes? Are they okay?" he asks tentatively. Charlie's face does not fill him with confidence.

"Spencer," she begins.

"Spence?" Alex says, half questioning, half correcting.

"Yes, Thomas Spencer. I'm afraid he didn't make it. He was dead on arrival at the Hospital."

Alex takes a second for the realisation that he'll never see the quirky Scotsman, with the thick Irish accent, or Blakey, the loveable bear, ever again. He tries to remember the words Craig Medhurst had once said to him, "*We're the gamblers that choose to be at the table. If blokes like us die – it'll only be sad if it's not in the fight." something along those lines.* Alex feels himself to have unwittingly stepped into the shoes of the gambler; his immediate sorrow of losing two friends is usurped by the realisation of the danger that he is putting himself in.

"Are you all right?" Charlie asks, as much to wake him up, as an expression of her concern.

"What about John?" He asks with more optimism.

"What about him?" Charlie says with surprise and a hint of defensiveness. "Oh, right, yeah, he'll be fine, the big dafty." Alex manages a smile; the bad lad must have made quite an impression on her to get her so distracted in the current situation. "He's got a nasty burn over his eyebrow and his throat and lungs are inflamed where he sucked in the blast – he's in Whipps Cross University Hospital, I popped in on the way here from the scene and saw him, he was asleep, but I got the Police guard stood down off him."

Alex doesn't feel too bruised at being down her pecking order; he is glad to hear that his friend is alive and as well as can be expected. "So where do we go from here?" Alex says despondently, "Op Wayland suspended, our team decimated – this mission is on its chin-strap."

"Eeee, don't you be letting your head go down young man." Charlie smiles, "We're not as far off track as you might think." Alex's gaze rises from the table where it had skulked to; dragged up by his intrigued eyebrows.

"How so?"

"My Section Chief hadn't seen the value in the Blunt lead, that's why I agreed to work with West Mids CTU on the Interest Group – so I could add a bit more of my own spin on things. I've been a bit naughty playing mum off against dad, and getting you boys involved, but now we're in a great place for me to second the bits of Wayland that I want, keep John and his lads on board as my unofficial solution, and have whatever other company resources I need on demand to help us track down Blunt."

Alex is having trouble computing all of this. He's still trying to come to terms with being banged up for the night. He's lost two friends and he's had about an hour's sleep. "What about me and Cliff? Are we not under arrest then?" Charlie smiles some more and shakes her head daintily. "So, what are we still doing here, then?"

"I just thought we'd have a chat while they try and wake Cliff up. Come on, let's go and give him a kick.

*

After treating the men to an early morning greasy spoon breakfast, Charlie leads Alex and Cliff into Ward 23 of Whipps Cross Hospital. A residual benefit of John's initial Police guard is that he has been accommodated in a large, single-sleeping side room – ideal for the level of privacy that they needed. Charlie enters first, "Hiya."

Cliff is next in and goes straight in for a man hug, but John raises a palm, "Whoa there, big fella." Cliff settles for a hand-clench. They exchange looks that shares more sentiment than either Charlie or Alex notice or could possibly fathom.

"Hi, John, you all right?" Alex asks, quite redundantly. John shrugs, grins, and shakes his head all at the same time. The three visitors pull up chairs and make themselves as comfortable as they can. Whilst the chairs are no doubt designed for the comfort and relaxation of lone patients, they make conversing with the bedded down patient awkward.

"I'll be a hundred percent in a couple of days." he pauses to cough, "I'm just waiting to see the consultant, then hopefully they'll let me out." John's wheezing voice doesn't instil confidence that he is anywhere near fit enough to be discharged.

"You take your time fella." Cliff says with brotherly concern.

"We're not likely to get any gen back out of the evidence from the flat until Monday, though there doesn't look to be much in the way of pickings – the latest from the Scene of Crime Team doesn't inspire much hope, they only came up with a smashed laptop in the communal bins, that looks like it matches fragments of plastic that they've found in the subject flat." Charlie says, doing her best to manage expectations, while taking the self-induced pressure off John to get back to it. "They found a phone handset and a snapped sim card in the same bin, so I guess any hope of tracing likely phone signatures from the property isn't going to lead us anywhere."

"What have we got to go on then?" Alex asks. Now Charlie does have a look of concern on her face.

"What about Zafir?" John splutters. "He's tight with him, he's one of the only other people that Blunt's been in touch with over the past two months." Charlie sees a spark of potential.

"What do you think, Alex?" she asks, "You know more about Zafir than anyone."

Alex thinks the situation through. Since the direct lead to Blunt from the Sayeedi's, he'd forgotten about the Imam's talk of Zafir's communications. "If he has access to communications, then yes."

"Access to communications?" Charlie quips, "He's in a British prison; he'll be more connected than an Indian call centre." Everyone laughs, it causes John to break into a painful fit of coughing. Cliff passes him a drink of water.

"Well, yeah. Depending on what Blunt is up to, Zafir is the obvious person for him to be talking to – the booby-trap at the flat is classic 'Zafir'." Alex thinks back to finding a similar device in Zafir's flat when he deployed for a brief spell on the ground on the previous mission.

"I'll arrange for the prison to search Zafir's cell and see if we can turn up any phones or devices." says Charlie. She has a look that says she has more to say, the three men wait with bated breath, but she is coy. "I don't want to trample on the memory of Blakey and Spence, but how are we off for replacements?" she eventually asks.

"There's no shortage of volunteers, and that's before last night." says Cliff confidently.

"It's Craig's funeral on Friday; we'll be seeing about 500 blokes that would fit the bill." John adds.

28

Track record

Having travelled back north through the early hours of the morning, Tony had managed to snatch a couple of hours sleep in his hide location, just a few metres from the farmhouse. He had laid in his sleeping bag meditating as long as he could bear after being woken by the early morning summer sun and had arisen well ahead of time for the day's task.

He takes his notepad and pen from the top flap of his bergan and places them in the left map pocket of his black, civilian walking trousers, the snips from the water bottle pouch go in the right. He undoes the string from the parcel and unfurls the cloth to reveal his pride and joy, his new felling axe. He holds it flat over his lap and rubs his hands up and down the thick wooden shaft of the handle; it is a beautifully made thing – everything about it smacks of quality. He admires the flared curves of the outside edges of the blade, caressing them with his fingers, then plays with the cutting edge with the pads of his thumb – *I can't wait to swing this at something.*

He rolls over onto his knees and crawls to the partition in the hedge, stands the axe up on the base of its handle and pushes through behind it. He partially emerges out into the wheat field and takes a methodical scan around it to check that he is alone. He heads off south, back past the farmhouse, following the perimeter of the field to the corner, retracing the route that had brought him here last night. On this occasion, at this juncture, he turns left, heading east towards the corner diagonally across from the farm. He turns the corner to head north up the other side of the field. He follows the trees, which extend for not quite a hundred metres before thinning into clumps of bush and bramble. Tony vaults the wire fence, using his axe to steady himself. This fence has been recently replaced, the wire is still yet to rust, and the timber posts are a fresh, virginal yellow. He walks between the bushes; the ground falls away to the right and the greenery thins further to tufty grass within thirty metres. He can now see clearly down into the railway cutting to the track – four simple lines of steel that required so much engineering to put in place.

From this nice clear area, he tracks back up the embankment to the fence. He eyes up a spot at the base of one of the fence posts. He positions his footing to give him the best shot at the post without incurring a tangle in the wire. He takes a firm two-handed grip of the axe handle and is about to draw it back but is taken by surprise.

"HELLO THERE." he hears a shout. He looks back to the track and follows its line south to the mouth of a tunnel. He sees a flash of white hair under a flat cap just visible above the top of the wall of the tunnel entrance. The old man waves enthusiastically at him. Tony freezes momentarily as he considers how to react. He slowly raises his left hand, waves, and contorts his lips to the shape of a smile, but it is most certainly doesn't carry the sentiment of a smile.

He walks back into the cover of the thickets; the solitude offers him greater freedom to think about what his next move will be. He plays out a variety of scenarios in his head before making his decision. Tony climbs the short distance through the bushes, the going gets easier as the trees spring up, leaving a thinner undergrowth beneath them as he approaches the retaining wall of the tunnel. As he summits the bank, he sees the old man sat in a camping chair. "Nice spot." he ventures as he observes the view of the track from directly above; the tracks stretching away into the distance under the lane that leads to the farmhouse.

"Isn't it a beauty?" the old man says proudly, "I've been coming here for five years and you're the first person I've ever seen here."

"Really? That's interesting." says Tony, "You never bring any company up here?"

"No, I've not really got any friends. My wife and I kept ourselves to ourselves. Since she passed away, I've been pretty much on my own."

"That's sad. No kids or family?"

The old man shakes his head with a bitter-sweet bite of his lip. He leans over and picks up a Thermos flask. "Would you like a cuppa? Sorry, what did you say your name was?"

"No thanks, I'm all right." He hesitates a second. "I'm Tony."

"Oh, well nice to meet you, Tony. I'm Andrew – not 'Andy'." He laughs. "What brings you out here? Looking for some logs?" he says, admiring Tony's axe.

"Yeah, it's as much for the exercise as it is for the wood."

"Have you asked Farmer Duffield about that?" Andrew says with a mock scowl. "He's the landowner, though I'm sure he wouldn't mind."

"Do you know him?" Tony asks, sensing an opportunity to pick up some local intelligence.

"Know *of* him. I've met him once or twice – Henry and Rose are about as sociable as I am!" Tony senses that there is nothing more of use forthcoming.

"What about you?" Tony nods to the tired-looking notebook, resting on the top of the tunnel wall. "You spotted anything worth seeing this morning?"

"No, nothing out of the ordinary, just the usual weekend passenger traffic heading down to London, or up to Scotland. Not many 'rare cops' to be had on this section of track."

"Do you still write everything down anyway?" Tony asks, peering over to try and read Andrew's neatly completed table of entries.

"There wouldn't be much else to do if I didn't. I've got nearly five years of records, but these lines are so busy that it's a fixed routine I'm afraid; it never really changes. I get the occasional bit of excitement when they swap out one engine for another when they require servicing. Still I enjoy the fresh air and the view."

"What do they call people like you?" Tony asks, stepping back a little.

Andrew laughs, "Oh, we get called all sorts; foamers, anoraks, trainiacs, gricers." The ground beneath their feet begins to tremble, then vibrate. "here comes one now." Andrew says, leaning forward on his hands against the wall. "In the states I'd be a ferroequinologist, that means 'student of iron horses'." he says, looking up sideways at Tony. He is shocked to see him stood with his axe raised high above his head.

"No, you're just a boring cunt." Tony brings the axe down with all his might, chopping down ruthlessly into Andrew's neck as the train fires out of the tunnel just feet below them. The weight of the blow kills him instantly, despite it being far from a clean slice. The power of the blow smashes Andrew's face down onto the wall, caving in the front right quarter of his skull, if the broken neck hadn't killed him, the head injury would have. The thick collar of Andrew's wax jacket has prevented the blade from making too much progress through his flesh, but the vertebrae in his neck are smashed to pieces and the spinal cortex within is severed conclusively.

Tony pulls the axe from its tangle with the collar of the jacket, this drags Andrew's buckling body awkwardly sideways from between the chair and the wall; it slumps and rolls onto the ground. Tony picks up his notepad, which has dropped to the floor, to prevent it from getting sullied with any of the blood, which is now oozing from Andrew's wounds, leaching through the layers of well-trampled grass.

*

Tony walks back from the body into the trees, looking for somewhere suitable to dispose of the old man. The morning sunlight cuts through the canopy, taking Tony's focus away from the task in hand; he finds himself enjoying the brush with nature. The perfect silence, interrupted only by the occasional warbling of a morning songbird, allows his senses to focus on the visual. The myriad of colours is amplified by the mix of bright filtering light and darker areas of shade. Tony knows that he only has five hundred square metres of forestry block to find somewhere suitable, so he takes his time to look thoroughly, he is also cognisant that the further that he searches; the further he will have to drag the body. He is thankful to see a large fallen tree laying right to left. The base of the trunk of the tree is a metre off the ground, kept raised by the huge clump of roots which have blistered out of the woodland floor. The root base of the tree stands over three metres in the air and leaves a well-shaded crater; Tony walks around to inspect it and climbs down into it to explore its deeper recesses with his boot – *perfect.*

As Tony emerges from the trees back to the scene of devastation, he finds himself shocked and saddened at the sight of Andrew, face-down and lifeless before him. He thinks about how bright and friendly he had been just a few moments ago; how kind he had been to pass the time of day with him, even offering him a brew – a bump of guilt sticks in his throat as he figures out how best to take hold of him. The sight of another train appearing from under the lane a few hundred metres up the track snaps him back into focus.

*

With Andrew safely stashed out of the way, Tony sits on the old man's slightly buckled chair watching out over the track. His notepad remains in his pocket and he looks with intrigue over the recent pages of Andrew's book. He checks back through the past month of Saturday mornings, looking for the patterns and regularities. Andrew had only been present a few days each week according to his records, but Saturday mornings had been one of his regular windows. He had been correct about the routine of the trains and Tony is content that what he finds will suit his plan.

29

Belmarsh

Less than a kilometre, as the crow flies, from Chips's depot, Charlie and Lucy sit in Governor Davidson's office at Her Majesty's Prison Belmarsh. He returns to the spacious office, watched all the way by both women. Despite being in his late fifties, both find themselves admiring his charismatic manner and his impeccable turn-out; his grey suit complements his tight, neat haircut and perfectly groomed handlebar moustache. He takes his seat. "Tea will be with us in a minute." he says rocking back in his plush black leather chair. He has the confidence of a man who knows the power that he wields – if there was ever a man that had complete control of his 'trainset', then he is that man. "Now, how can I help you ladies?" His charm borders on the misogynistic, but his age lets him get away with it, even with these two fiery women.

"Governor Davidson," Charlie begins.

"Please, call me Rod." he interrupts.

"Rod, we believe that one of your prisoners on the High Security Unit, Zafir Abdulaziz, is in possession of an illicit communications device. We believe that he is using that device to communicate with, and possibly abet, an active terror suspect."

The Governor listens intently, unshocked by what he hears. Though it would be slightly unusual for one of his remand prisoners to become engaged so industriously, so quickly, it is certainly not unheard of, or surprising to a man of his considerable experience in the Prison Service.

"And you'd like me to have his cell and... how shall we say – other hiding places, searched?" The Governor smiles, making it clear that he is only too happy to oblige.

Charlie smiles back, but then pushes on, "Not quite Rod. You see, Abdulaziz, despite his youthfulness, is quite a senior player. We don't think for a moment that he would risk keeping hold of a phone in his own cell, or up his own arse for that matter." Rod's head rocks back on his neck, as experienced as he is with the oddities of prisoners, he's not used to hearing such language from a 'lady' - he's not quite prepared for Charlie. "He's cleverer than that. What we want to do is try and catch him in the act of using it."

Governor Davidson runs the tips of his right thumb and middle finger down the sides of his moustache as he considers how best to achieve the outcome that Charlie requests. "We have something of a well-developed snitch network at Belmarsh;" he says, sitting back again in his chair, at ease with his proposed solution, "if you could come up with a fictitious piece of information that you think Abdulaziz would not be able to resist passing to your suspect, or whoever else, then we might feed that in through a suitable inmate." Charlie and Lucy nod at one another, then at Rod. "The only potential problem with this plan, is that we don't have gangs of officers stood about, on call to observe and jump on him if he should take the bait, and there's no telling how long he might wait to make the call, or where in the unit he might make it."

"I have funding, Governor, I can underwrite whatever overtime costs you incur." Charlie says flatly, hoping to head off any possible showstoppers.

"It's not the money, Agent Thew, I just want to manage your expectations that even in optimal circumstances, there's a strong possibility that we might miss catching him in the act."

Charlie locks eyes with the steely old gent, tempting herself to flirt with him. "I have faith in you, Rod, and your men."

He smiles back, he too not shy of a little flirtation, "And women, let's not be sexist." he grins.

Charlie and Lucy both laugh with him, but more at the irony of Rod calling out the sexism. "How soon can we get this done?" Lucy asks.

"Give me three of four days to arrange the additional staff, shall we say, Friday, possibly Thursday at a push?"

Lucy and Charlie have the same look of frustration on their faces but are both keen to maintain the flow of goodwill that they are getting from the Governor. "Rod," Lucy says delicately, "We would have done it yesterday if we could have got an appointment with you on Saturday afternoon." she pauses to let that sink in. "I know our urgency doesn't constitute your emergency, but there is a potentially serious threat out there, that we risk losing track of with every hour that passes. Is there any way that you can make this happen tomorrow?" The seriousness drops out of Lucy's eyes the second that she finishes speaking and they melt into her best puppy-dog baby browns. Charlie joins in with her legendary pout; the poor man cannot bring himself to let them down.

"Tomorrow." he says with authority, trying to show some level of control, "We'll put the word out at nine a.m., an hour before his usual exercise time. I'd say that would be the most likely opportunity for him to get away with something."

Lucy writes something in her notepad, tears off the page and slides it across the desk to the Governor.

30

One call

"I've got Cliff here with me at our hotel. Is everybody on?" Alex asks over the encrypted group call.

"I'm here, still on the biff." croaks John from his hospital bed.

"Dev and Alan, here at West Mids." says Dev.

"I'm here at Belmarsh with Charlie." says Lucy. It's 08:30 on Tuesday morning, everything is in place to launch the operation to seize Zafir Abdulaziz's phone. A lot has emerged overnight as the investigation into the explosion at Blunt's safehouse has unfolded. Charlie chairs the virtual meeting from the staff meeting room of HMP Belmarsh's High Security Unit to bring key members of the team up to speed.

"Now then, you lot." Charlie stamps her unique northern mark on the meeting. "The device that exploded at the Blunt safehouse in the early hours of Saturday morning, killing our colleagues, Spence and Blakey, was a small charge of plastic explosive.

"The improvised explosive device was victim operated; as Blakey opened the door into the bedroom of the flat; the main charge was initiated by a rudimental pull mechanism that operated from a pulley attached to the door frame – the blast from the plastique was devastating to anyone directly within its cone. Blakey and Spence never stood a chance."

The line falls silent for a moment as they remember the fallen two. Cliff sifts joyous memories of good times with Blakey, one of his closest mates from the old days of Support Company, 3 Para, then meeting up again on the other side of Selection, bumping into each other when off the ground in Hereford.

Alex cannot help but envisage the two of them crashing in through that doorway, like lambs to the slaughter; he flinches at the thought of the blast hitting them, how their broken bodies looked in the aftermath.

Charlie goes on, "The residues found indicate that the particular types and blend of nitroamine and plasticiser don't match any military or commercially available formula, suggesting that it is homemade. There's no exact match, but Lab's reckon that it was made to the same recipe as the explosive used at Millbank and Pavilion Gardens.

"Here's the big news you've been waiting for." she says as though the bombing link wasn't enough, "Tony Blunt's fingerprints were found throughout the property. The explosives and his presence in the flat give us the conclusive evidential link between him and the Interest Group that we've been looking for."

"We know we're not chasing ghosts now; we know he's our man." John says hoarsely.

"Exactly." Charlie replies. "We get this phone link from Zafir, and we're another step closer to bringing them down." Just from the moment of silence that follows, Charlie senses that certain participants on the call are neglecting to focus on the bigger picture. She can live with their short-term objective of taking down Blunt, in fact; that operational level of focus is useful to her, so she allows them to relish the thought of getting hold of him. What is now bugging her is that even though Blunt most probably left the flat for the last time without knowing it; he had still left so little information behind.

"Did he leave any clues as to where he might have gone?" Alex asks.

"No – in a word." Charlie says bluntly. "Some of the memory from the smashed laptop has been recovered, but there had been nothing much saved on the drive; there was one recent document listing tourist attractions in London. His browsing history had been deleted; DSTL are still working on recovering that. Based on the tourism sites, and the location of his flat; we're thinking he might have a role in target selection and that he's scoping sites of high visitor population density in the London area."

"Fuck," says John, *"they're already moving on to new targets?"*

"And he's ditched his phone, and we have no idea where he's gone?" adds Cliff.

"Correct... at the moment," Lucy says, "but if he's going to maintain contact with anyone; it'll be Zafir. Hopefully, we'll gain access to that link within the next couple of hours."

*

Lucy and Charlie are escorted to the High Security Unit's Central Control Room. It looks like the command console of a battleship; walls and fittings are painted a beige-cream and there are screens covering most of the walls – the state-of-the-art LCD flat screens look almost out of place against the old-fashioned, but well-engineered switching. They are offered seats at one of the side terminals, which has less controls around it, but crucially has a solitary dedicated twenty-four-inch screen.

"That's your window into our world." says Governor Davidson as he enters carrying a tray of brews. He takes a seat behind them. "The message from your note has just been passed through my staff to a grim little cretin who's known for keeping the jungle drum beating. I've no doubt that it'll make it to Abdulaziz's ears within the next hour." The three of them sit, eyes firmly on the screen.

"What are we looking at here?" Lucy asks.

"This is the camera nearest to Abdulaziz's cell. That's his door there." He points at a barely visible slip of a shadow in the wall. The picture is well defined, but the camera is at an oblique angle to the door.

The Governor fills the time by giving Lucy and Charlie some background information on the routine that the High Security Unit's prisoners go through and how it differs from the rest of the prison. "HSU is effectively a prison within a prison, it only takes the highest risk inmates, and that's either high risk of escape or doing damage to others, or highest risk of being taken down by other prisoners or by themselves. All cells are individual occupancy, and we have an isolation area where prisoners can be kept completely alone; never seeing another inmate, if the need arises – which it does."

As Lucy takes a sip from what's left of her almost cold cup of tea, she sees someone hesitate on the corridor just outside Zafir's cell; he pokes his head inside, then disappears within.

"If he's in there for more than a minute; I'll get the officers in." Rod says calmly looking at his watch. Before Rod properly notes the time, he steps back out of the cell onto the landing facing into the cell, his back to the lens. He has one hand drooped in his pocket and his head sagging lazily towards the floor, he disappears under the camera and out of the field of view. The Governor leans across to the officer manning the main control station, "Track him." The officer clicks a button on his mouse and the picture on his centre screen changes – the prisoner who has just left Zafir's room walks across the shot.

"That wasn't the informant that we gave the message to, but he's dressed like one of Abdulaziz's. It could just have been a quick social call, but it would be my assessment that the message has been passed." Rod says confidently.

"What next then?" Charlie asks.

"Abdulaziz will have told his visitor to summon the phone carrier, either to his cell, or more likely to a secluded corner of a communal area. We just need to sit tight and watch for his next move.

The tension builds over the next fifteen minutes as the Watch Officer continues to track the prisoner from cell to cell, seemingly knowing that he is being watched and diligently laying a smoke-screen of cover over his activities, evermore convincing his observers that he is the carrier of the message and something to do with the provision of the phone. After the fifth cell that he has visited; there are too many potential 'phone holders' to keep track of, so overwatch remains focussed on Zafir's cell.

"Here we go." says Lucy, as a figure darts from the cell and disappears from shot to the right. His face is not visible, but his shoulder sling marks him out. Having been tackled to the ground by several elite and Special Forces veterans outside the venue of the Millbank bomb that he had just detonated, Zafir's arm had been smashed and then almost wrenched off – there had been so much damage done to the blood vessels by the splintering bone; he had been lucky to keep it.

"All stations, target prisoner is heading towards the recreation area." The Watch Officer tracks the figure to the end of the landing, then catches him coming down the bottom of the stairwell and through the doors into the recreation area. It is a large indoor yard with a thin coloured glass roof that lets in maximum daylight. The floor is AstroTurf and there are large banks of gardening troughs and workbenches for the prisoners to enjoy a little horticulture. There is a third officer on duty in the recreation area today, as the cameras track the unsuccessfully illusive figure across to the distant gardening area, a fourth officer enters the covered area behind him. The four officers hold their positions, doing their best not to look conspicuously at the far corner – they patiently await their Governor's signal.

"Can you zoom in on him?" Lucy asks, her instincts telling her that something isn't right – why would such an important player be left waiting for his phone? He looks up to check his surroundings just as the camera settles into focus at maximum magnification. "That's not Zafir."

"What?!" Governor Davidson blurts, almost leaping from his chair.

"Get the screen back to that last room." Charlie snaps at the Watch Officer.

Rod grabs the spare radio handset from console, "All officers on HSU east wing, deck one secure cell 343 now."

A wave of excitement ripples through the High Security Unit as the officers surge from their stations, many of them already pre-positioned on the first floor in anticipation of being needed at Zafir's cell, they run to the opposite end of the floor.

Lucy, Charlie, and Rod crowd the screen in the control room, watching intently as the officers pile in, one after another. The fifth to arrive pauses at the door, realising that the room is already well over its reasonably expected capacity. He continues to guard the door as the two prisoners within are secured.

*

"You do it." Charlie says with her face screwed up in a grimace.

"I'm not touching it." Lucy sneers back with an equally disgusted look. The pair have the liberty of the staff meeting room again. They are faced with the mobile phone that has been recovered from cell 343. Zafir and his accomplice had been interrupted too quickly for them to properly stash the handset and the first officer into the cell had seen the mattress springing back into place – it was an easy find. The further search discovered a used, and rather smelly, condom, giving an all too clear indication where the phone may have been secreted, hence the two women's lack of appetite to lead the analysis.

"Go on with ya, Army chick, you should be used to this sort of thing." Charlie cracks a smile at Lucy. She offers her the pair of latex gloves that have been thoughtfully left by one of Rod's officers. Lucy shakes her head and takes the gloves.

The handset looks almost new, less for the smears and residue of lubricating fluid. "It's not exactly the most slimline phone, considering where it's been stored." Lucy says with a grin.

"There's got to be some perks to the job; is it set to vibrate?" Charlie laughs.

Lucy switches the phone on and begins to systematically review the available information. Charlie sits ready to enter the detail into her laptop to instantaneously crosscheck anything found on the device.

"No messages, no stored numbers, and the only call history is a single call made the minute before the officers stormed the cell." Lucy says disappointedly.

"What was the number?" Charlie says hopefully.

"If my memory serves me correctly; I'd say it's Blunt's old number."

"Fuck." says Charlie "Read it off." Lucy reels off the number; it takes less than a second for the Security Service's database to confirm that it is the number associated with Blunt up until Friday night.

The two women take a moment to think through how else value might be extracted from the asset. "It's not even been four days yet; Blunt still might try to reach Zafir from a new number." Lucy says hopefully."

"What are we going to do? Sit around this phone and hope that he gives us a call?" Charlie says rhetorically.

"What are our other options?"

"We'll clone the phone and monitor the line, like you say – there's a good chance he'll make contact. We'll do a proper exploitation of the handset and check the line account to see what's been deleted off the call lists." Charlie reels off the remaining potential that the phone still has, but there is something in her voice that tells Lucy that she is thinking along another plane entirely.

"What about having a little chat with our Zafir?" Charlie says seductively.

"How do we stand on that legally?" Lucy asks.

"It's a fu'kin' minefield." Charlie says, not wanting to sugar-coat it. "I suppose if we can get him to sign up to talking to us off the record, with only potential leniency to get out of it – he might go for it without a legal brief present."

Lucy shrugs, "Let's ask our mate Rod to put it to him."

*

Lucy and Charlie sit waiting in the HSU Governor's office; it doesn't bear much resemblance to Rod's. The desk, fixtures and fittings are all of the same mark, but it's significantly smaller and hasn't seen the personalisation that the top man's has - the chair is nowhere near as nice. Charlie sits back in it, kicking herself side to side off the inside panels of the drawer units.

"He doesn't know about Blunt's change of number and, I'd assume, change of situation – he might not yet know about the Sayeedis either." Charlie says, thinking aloud, as she begins to strategize for the imminent interview with Zafir.

"It's been a long five days." Lucy says reflectively, "Their channels of communication do seem very narrow; it's quite plausible that there might not be anyone else to bridge the gap between Zafir and the Sayeedis. When are we going to be getting a full readout from Blunt's sim?"

"The only other number they found on it was dialled once for a brief call, a contract-free line. It was answered and has remained active in the Colchester area."

"Promising?" Lucy asks with a heightened level of stimulation in her voice.

"Not really – the working hypothesis is that it was a call to one of his kids; highly unlikely that we'll get anything of value from them. There's a uniformed unit on their way round to investigate."

The wait goes on for the prison staff to prepare Zafir for them. Charlie remembers what she had meant to ask Lucy; "What did you put in the note you gave Rod?" Charlie asks with intrigue.

Lucy smiles, "I made up a current home address for Alex Gregory."

Charlie stifles a laugh, "That'd do it." she says.

The door of the office opens and Rod half steps in. "Ladies, we have Prisoner Abdulaziz in one of our counselling rooms ready for you."

Charlie and Lucy follow Rod from the office through a brightly lit, creamy corridor. Lucy feels the dread welling up inside her. Zafir had been involved, at some level, in her abduction – part of the Interest Group's effort to obtain the UK Terror Watch List from Alex. These efforts had also included as smash and grab on their hotel room, where she had suffered a heavy blow to the head. Alex had been forced to concede to her that Zafir had also intimated a threat against her when he had been restraining him prior to his arrest at Millbank.

They walk the short distance past a series of plain, numbered, pine doors, all on the left. The wall on the right is the prettier side of the stark and perfectly flat outer wall of the unit building. The inside's inoffensive cream paint is decorated with printed boards, with images showing prisoners doing constructive tasks, such as gardening, welding, and carpentry. Lucy tries to let them distract her; she thinks how they look slightly less lame than the average Army poster campaigns.

Rod opens the fourth door along the corridor and stands with his arm out in front of him, ushering them in. Lucy hesitates, taking a half step behind Charlie. Rod looks at her, "Are you okay?" he asks.

She pinches a dry smile. "Fine."

31

Bring Zaqqum

Zafir fixes Charlie with a hard stare; his frustration at being caught with, and subsequently losing his phone, evident on his face. He has a mix of menace and intrigue in his eyes, his anger being suppressed by his thoughts of what information he might be able to glean from this situation. Charlie can tell in that instant that he is going to give nothing away willingly, and he is only here to learn from them and antagonise them — *we'll see about that.*

His expression changes drastically as Lucy steps into view; changing to wide-eyed shock, which is rapidly replaced by a spiteful sneering grin. "Corporal Butler." he says gleefully.

Lucy fakes her best, friendliest smile; she doesn't feel convincing, but she drives on through her fear. "Mr Abdulaziz, how's the arm?" she smiles again, a genuine one this time that she allows to parade across her face. He glares back at her, his anger getting the better of him; he cannot fully repress his snarl, the right corner of his top lip curls, the bridge of his nose trembles and his nostrils flare.

"Mr Abdulaziz, thank you for agreeing to talk with us off the record today." Charlie interjects, hoping to take some of the negative energy out of the conversation for now. "We take it from your attempt to get in touch with Mr Blunt this morning, that you are as yet unaware of his change in circumstances?"

Zafir says nothing; his head and eyes flick from Lucy to Charlie and he freezes. His only movement is now the tiny darts that his pupils make as they scour the Security Service agent's face for clues. His brain goes into overdrive thinking about what might have happened to his friend, whilst trying to figure out what to say, what to ask, but most of all - what not to give away.

"Do you know a Naith Sayeedi, Mr Abdulaziz?" Charlie throws another layer of complexity into the information battle being fought in Zafir's head. "Are you aware of *his* change in situation?" Charlie smiles, her eyes locked on his, as hard as his are locked on hers. The subtle tells of confusion and the lack of anger in his features, tell Charlie what she needs to know about the start-state for this game of chess. She holds most of the cards, but are there cards that she does not yet know about? A win in this game is to find that out conclusively – she may not leave this room knowing everything that Zafir knows about Blunt, but she is determined that she will know whether there are any secrets remaining – that will inform her decision on whether to sanction further, more formal questioning. Being off the record is not to her advantage; she has little to threaten him with in this interview, however she is confident that her years of interrogation experience give her the edge. She has plenty of information to act as bartering chips, but she knows that she must use them wisely.

"We've visited Mr Sayeedi with a warrant, we know that he has been directing Blunt's involvement with the new project. We've seen his messages; we know what they're up to." she lies. "There's an opportunity for you to fill in a few small gaps in information for us, maybe save us a day or two of investigation – it could work out well for you when it comes to your sentencing." Charlie enjoys weaving mistruths into the narrative, knowing that they are a reliable way of peaking the egos of interviewees who love nothing more than pointing out the mistakes of others.

"I haven't been convicted yet." he says cockily. Charlie laughs gently back at him, her head tilted down with a wildly manic look. Lucy notes that Zafir appears disconcerted. Charlie is enough to make anyone doubt themselves – Lucy is glad to see the effect being taken on Zafir. Charlie's calm approach and her complete lack of urgency have a hypnotic influence; drawing out Zafir's interest in what she is going to say.

"So, Naith Sayeedi - is he a friend of yours?" Charlie asks. Zafir again fails to respond. Charlie looks intently for the micro-gestures that will give him away, but not a hair twitches.

"How did you come to know Mr Blunt?" Charlie asks. Zafir says nothing, his arms folded, cradling his broken arm, which is still missing its sling. Charlie gives him time for the answer that she already knows is not coming, then serves it to him; "We know you did time together at Winson Green nick." Still no response from Zafir. "We know that it was in your company that he formally converted to Islam." An absent-minded grin creeps onto Zafir's face.

"What we were really wondering is why you've latched on to him. His military record shows that he's pretty much the worst soldier that has ever made it through the system. He appears to have got through basic training only because he was too stupid to quit. His base level of fitness and numbness seem to be all that carried him on to a field unit. His reports say that he is barely trainable - he was sent back in training for remedial coaching and retesting no less than four times over the twenty-eight-week course, spending forty-seven weeks at the Catterick depot." Charlie flicks through the pages of documentation in the folder before her. "He nearly got himself killed by not following the drills on his first parachute descent – the only reason the Army kept him on was out of pity; he had nowhere else to go. And your little gang thought that he might be useful? What are you doing with him? Are you using him to be some sort of stooge, or a mule?" Charlie is almost laughing at Zafir, mocking his judgement of character and ability. Lucy note's Zafir's facial expressions becoming gradually tetchier. Charlie is cognisant of them too but pretends not to notice; she just grinds on at him. "Based on interviews with his Army colleagues, past employers and family, our Tony's profile has been assessed as benign. We don't believe that he is capable of doing any harm, not since his experiences in Afghanistan - that seems to have taken it out of him. Whatever you think you're lining him up for simply isn't going to happen, not if this 'numb-nuts' has anything much to do with it."

"How can you be so wrong?" Zafir explodes. "He may no longer be a threat to innocent Muslims, but he's going to kill plenty of you infidels." Lucy and Charlie are both struck by his outburst, both hit with the realisation that the threat that they have been chasing down now looks to be credible, and not the wild goose-chase that they thought it might be. If what Zafir has said is true; the impetus on the mission to find Blunt will need a significant shot in the arm, certainly from the security services' side. Thankfully Zafir keeps his eyes locked on Charlie. Lucy wouldn't make much of a poker player; her gawp of despair would have been a shot scored if he were to notice. As it is; Charlie holds her calm outward composure.

"Is that a fact?" Charlie says dismissively. "He sounds like the kind of fuckwit that blows himself up in the garage while putting on his vest. Are you sure about your selection processes? Or do you just take any old mug who'll fall for your rhetoric?"

Zafir's face seems to charge with sub-surface rage; he trembles with anger. His need to express power, now constrained to words as a prisoner within these walls, makes him want to combust. "You won't be laughing next week. Tony Blunt is a skilled craftsman, and he will be putting those skills to good use – you will know Zaqqum this weekend.

Charlie doesn't know what Zaqqum means, but the intent in Zafir's words transcend any language barrier. Whatever Blunt's plan involves; Charlie sees the Interest Group's vision of bringing hell to earth.

"You can come back next week and tell me how useless my brother is. Should we make an appointment? I'd like that." Zafir says, taking an advance in comfort from his faith in Tony delivering on his task.

There has been a subconscious and simultaneous step change in Charlie and Lucy's attitude towards Zafir. They know that he is a dangerous man, but his incarceration, his injury, and the way in which

Charlie's tactics have ridiculed and mentally softened him, had reduced their impression of him into an unthreatening and weak individual, but the longer the interview goes on, and the more he reveals; the more dangerous he, and his group, seem to be.

"Tell me, how do you come to be here begging me for information on the whereabouts of my incompetent friend?" Zafir says smugly.

"Like I said;" Charlie retorts, "you are one of many lines of investigation, you should take the opportunity to work with us before the chance dries up – it's only a matter of days, if not hours before we find him."

"He is not the fool that you think he is, he knows how to stay hidden." Zafir says gravely, "The next time you hear from Tony Blunt; it will be in the news."

Charlie ignores his comment, authoritatively drawing a line under his posturing with a disinterested glance at her folder before moving on. "We recovered Blunt's internet browsing history from the past couple of weeks; it looks like his target selection ideas include some headline attractions in the London area. He wouldn't be so stupid to think that he could get anywhere near one of them with anything more meaningful than a firework, would he?"

Zafir shakes his head and smiles, "You people just keep looking for a big bomb, or even a hostile vehicle, somewhere nice and obvious." he says sarcastically, "Keep thinking that we are stupid, incompetent and predictable."

"You've already intimated you know when a terror attack will take place, and you do know what the target is, then?" Charlie says, showing no hint of being impressed or threatened by Zafir, and over emphasising the action of taking a note on her pad. Zafir looks edgy; it hits him that with his posturing and bragging; he may have said more than he had intended. "That's enough for me to draw up fresh charges of conspiring to commit an act of terror; I'll have you as an accessory if anything does go down." she lays it on thick, knowing that this off-the-record chat would hold no water with the CPS. Zafir shifts in his seat, his body language signalling clearly that the interview has reached its conclusion.

Lucy feels brave and leans forward - "Where did you disappear to that night?" she asks; the mystery of where Zafir and eight of the other 177 targets marked for death, had gone still plaguing her. Zafir smiles, his eyes flick to the ceiling for less than the blink of an eye - Lucy doesn't spot it, but Charlie does; she also knows the context of Lucy's question - how had Zafir eluded his would-be assassin on the night of the Watch List killings.

"He was in the attic." Charlie says calmly.

Zafir laughs, with a self-congratulatory twist in his jowls, pleased that his ability to outwit his hunter had been so ridiculously simple.

"Who chose the nine of you who got warned?" Lucy asks, hoping to find out more about the Interest Group.

Zafir tilts his head to look at Lucy, weighing up what he has to lose and gain by answering her question. "My network is extremely selective, despite what you might think about Mr Blunt. There is no question that we would allow any of our affiliates to be taken by your clowns."

"But you didn't have a copy of the list by then; did you move everyone in your network."

"Everyone who had earned their place. You did us a housekeeping favour with some of those on our peripheries – they earned their martyrdom."

"So how many are in your group?" Charlie asks speculatively. She watches, focusing acutely on his pupils as she goes on, hoping for a reaction, "Twenty? Thirty? Forty?" She is sure that she sees a slight twitch on 'forty'. "So, forty then?" She gives a presumptive, confirmatory grin and writes into her notepad – again Zafir has a mild look of panic, that he's given away something else that he had no intention of giving away.

"How do you plan to get back in touch with Blunt?" Charlie asks. Zafir shrugs, forgetting for a split second too long about his broken arm; he winces as the pain fires through him. "Without you or Sayeedi to help him; who's he going turn to?"

Zafir limits his reaction to his eyebrows this time, raising them to show his careless ambivalence. "Mr Blunt needs no one. His plan is in place. I'll wait for his message in the newspapers next week."

32

Taking stock

"Welcome to the big smoke." Alex says to Dev mockingly as he approaches him at the coffee machine.

"Hi, Alex. Sounds like here's where it's at." he says, turning to greet him with an open hand. Alex shakes it with as much warmth as he can muster. His first impressions of the guy having been somewhat expunged. "We're honoured to get invited into this place." Dev says, raising a hand to the innards of Thames House, albeit the lowest classification area of the ground floor. The Security Service's headquarters building, just two hundred metres south of Zafir's Millbank bombing.

"Come on you two, I've paid for your drinks, follow on." Charlie chirps as she leads Lucy and Cliff off. A large area of the ground floor of the south wing is taken up by the trendy, comfortable coffee lounge and a good quality restaurant. A large amount of official business gets done in liaison meetings that cannot take place in the deeper offices and annals of the building – a large informal area, well-spaced, with semi-private corners and booths, is essential to facilitate optimal business. The next level of privacy up can be found in the meeting rooms that lead off through the restaurant. The hallway leading from the restaurant further into the south of the building is poorly lit, with no natural light. The floor is beautifully worn white and blue marble, dating back to the buildings 1930's origins when it was owned by ICI and used for a variety of purposes, by a variety of lodger businesses. Becoming a listed building in 1981, it was procured by the Government in 1994 for the sole purpose of accommodating MI-5.

*

Charlie uses her swipe pass to open a solid white glossed door into a spacious, contemporarily, and expensively furnished meeting room. Her laptop is already jacked into the room's projection system; she takes her seat nearest to the screen at the far end of the large mahogany stained table. The screen is simply a white rectangle painted onto the grey wall.

Cliff drops his massive, muscular bulk into the chair opposite Charlie. The smoothly shaped chair bowl is made of the same plywood as the table and is an almost exact colour match for Cliff's skin. The chair appears to be at its limit of strength, bending to his shape and just about holding his weight as he comes to rest; Alex appears dwarfed as he sits next to him. Lucy sits next to Alex. Dev closes the door and sits along from Charlie, leaving the middle chair empty. "Have I got bad breath or some'in'?" Charlie says feigning offence. The laugh breaks the ice that has frozen over the rest of the group just by being present in this iconic and mysterious old building.

"Welcome to Thames House. In light of recent developments, the Security Service has taken full control of Operation Wayland and added significant resources to it. The horsepower we now have should help us to follow all existing and emerging leads to their rapid conclusions."

Alex feels a little condescended to, and that their unofficial part of the team has become somewhat surplus to requirements. He wonders how much time Charlie is going to allocate to what is, as he sees it, a side-briefing.

"As you know; Lucy and I oversaw a sting operation to intercept Zafir Abdulaziz in the act of attempting to communicate with Tony Blunt." Charlie and Lucy give the group a swift canter through the operation and the subsequent interview.

Alex is preoccupied with thoughts of Zafir, flashing back to the moments before the Millbank blast, when he had chased him down on the way out of the building. He thinks through the realities of what happened in the room that he had just run out of, the carnage inflicted on Craig and his friends.

"In summary," Charlie says loudly, looking squarely at Alex, all too aware that his mind hasn't been on what she's been saying, "There is strong potential for a terror attack by Blunt this coming weekend. Crimestoppers have put out alerts to the public through all their channels with his mugshot and there will be a request for anyone who's seen him to come forward on the local news in London this evening. He may be operating completely in isolation; making this an extremely dangerous situation, being that we have no evidence of any current means of communication that he may be using and no idea where he may be residing. We know that members of the so called 'Interest Group' potentially have access to plastic explosives in large amounts, though there was no forensic evidence of any stash, outside of the small amount used in the booby-trap at Blunt's safehouse. Zafir also hinted that whatever Blunt is planning may not be a typical blast or hostile vehicle attack. We need to think about what that could possibly mean for targets based on large concentrations of tourists in London.

"Zafir also let slip that the Interest Group has around forty members, that means that there are forty potential leads to Blunt out there somewhere, but also forty potentially dangerous people in their own right. Unfortunately, since the Sayeedis met their end, all contacts in their suspected leadership address group on Naith's phone have gone dead, and all properties associated with the numbers have been rapidly vacated. Predictably, there are no forwarding addresses and no signs of any of the names reappearing elsewhere. We're not even sure if these properties were registered to real names."

Everything sounds hopeless to Alex. The Interest Group is clearly on top of its 'information game'. His mind is in overdrive trying to work out what signs and indicators to look for left by the mistakes that they might have made. He assumes, hopes really, that they do not have a deep technical understanding of the ways to keep themselves completely digitally anonymous.

Sometimes things are so obvious that they get overlooked. Taking this mission on in isolation and focusing too heavily on Tony Blunt has blinkered Alex, Lucy, Charlie, and Cliff. One of these things occurs to Alex and brings him to life. "What about the nine disappeared targets from the Watch List mission?" There is an air of quiet over the team. Dev looks confused, not being party to the details of what went on just twenty-six days ago. He had seen the headlines in the news, he had received the lengthy overview at a daily briefing a few days after it had come to light, he'd even been on the lookout for any evidence of vigilante activity as part of his work routine over the past few weeks. He now considers that this unofficial group that Charlie is courting, might have had something to do with it. He eyes Cliff and Alex with suspicion. Charlie's brain is faster than any of the others; she knows Alex has made a mistake.

"What are you talking about Alex?" she says, trying to let him know that he's pretty much dropped himself in it.

Alex sees the flicker of a snarl and a flick of her eyes towards Dev, he takes the hint. "Err," he fumbles for a bluff, "that press release about the suspects from the UK Terror Watch List getting killed. It said that they killed 159 out of 178 – maybe the other nineteen got tipped off. If they were part of an organisation that managed to get prior knowledge; they might have disappeared before the strike."

Dev knows that Alex is lying, his investigative intuition won't let it go that easily. "Why did you say nine then?" he asks.

"I've been doing some work on that." Lucy says matter-of-factly, flicking over a page in her notebook, "I've been filtering down the Watch List, trying to figure out how they picked their 178. I managed to find the right combination of traits to get all 159 inside the top 178, then removed the names of all those who died. I did a bit of digging around the nineteen survivors, and it seemed that nine of them had been living in their listed addresses up until the night of 15 June, but then left and have never returned. I've got a working theory that they were tipped off by the Interest Group, because they are members. I was going to brief it after Charlie had finished, but it would seem that Alex has stolen my thunder." She turns to him and feigns an angry scowl. Alex slides his hand across and gives her thigh a thankful squeeze.

"That's great work, Lucy." Charlie says, hoping to draw a line under Dev's suspicion. "So, we have nine real names that might be put to our mysterious group. That's a crackin' start." Charlie makes a note on her laptop. Whilst Alex's idea is clumsily communicated, it is exactly the kind of oversight that she had hoped this meeting would expose.

"What's the plan then, Charlie?" Cliff asks.

"We've got several work strands on-going, more now with what Lucy's just said. Our best shot is Zafir's phone. Although he doesn't have Blunt's new number, Blunt has his and we're hoping that he'll try to re-establish contact with him before he makes his move. We have monitoring in place with help from the phone network. We're doing the same with the Sayeedis' phones. I've got our tech bods on the case doing some deep analysis with the handsets. If there are any links to anyone who might be one of Zafir's forty – we'll be on them."

"You should have just sent them to Alan up at West Mids; he's the best there is." says Dev, full of confidence in his geeky colleague.

"I'm sure he's brilliant," Charlie says, not completely dismissively, "but the handsets are with our specialist team down at DSTL, Porton Down."

Alex, Lucy, and Cliff each raise an eyebrow, knowing something of what goes on at the Defence Science and Technology Laboratories. Porton Down's reputation still suffers from the urban legends of human testing of biological and chemical warfare agents from decades ago. No one serving in recent times, outside of certain circles, knows how true these rumours might be, but they bear no resemblance to the organisation that DSTL has evolved into. The only thing that hasn't changed is that it is still cutting edge in everything that it does. These days that includes every kind of materiel exploitation.

"We had DSTL field labs deployed with us at Camp Bastion; they're miracle workers. Give them a laptop burnt to a crisp, and they'll recover the whole hard drive. They'll find DNA or prints where you'd never expect to find them." Lucy says, thinking back to the amount of kit and equipment they had crammed into their pristine expandable box-bodies – the tour of their facilities had been one of the most memorable things she'd done in Afghanistan.

Charlie smiles. "Well imagine that with all their home comforts and jacked up with Security Service levels of network and record access - that's our special little corner of DSTL."

"There's also the possibility that Blunt might have been stupid enough to test or even use a new mobile before he set off for wherever he's gone. We're checking the mobile networks for any new numbers that might have pinged the masts in the vicinity of Blunt's safehouse within the forty-eight hours before the flat went boom.

"We're looking at CCTV local to the flat to try and spot Blunt moving to and from it. The forensics team has found fibres of coarse nylon, similar to that used in the carpets of cars, so there's a strong possibility that he may be mobile; hopefully we'll find some footage of him getting into or out of a vehicle. It could be a car that he has the use of, or it might lead us to an associate if he's been getting lifts."

"What about more traditional methods of investigation? Is there anything *we* can actually do on the ground?" Dev asks, hoping to do some 'proper policing', as he sees it.

Charlie welcomes the enthusiasm; they are the specialist boots on the ground that she has cultivated them to be. "Blunt's likely to have been in and around the safehouse flat for a little over a month now. Someone will have seen him, or seen him get into a car, or even spoken to him. We've got uniforms on the streets, knocking on doors, but they're only asking the basics and looking for the obvious. I want you guys to get into the space he's inhabited, think about what he was thinking about and seek out what he was up to. There's nothing much to go on from what was found in the flat; all the food in the cupboards was either fresh produce, or big brands, so we haven't even been able to identify where he was shopping. No one in the nearby shops admits to seeing him." Everyone seems a little elated at the sniff of something real to do. Charlie can feel the frustration dissipating.

"The obvious question is 'where is he now'. If his target is going to be within Central London he won't have gone too far. We're checking out the identity of the landlord of the flat. We're fairly sure it'll come up as a spoof individual or company, but there may be other properties under the same name that we can look at or maybe financial leads from the property that might take us somewhere. We've asked the Met to mobilise its informant network – a ginger giant with a big fluffy beard can't just arrive into a community and not be noticed by someone.

"In broader terms, we've recommended to the Home Secretary that the terror threat level be put up. The Police have been advised to anticipate the move to 'critical' and increase their presence at all the big tourist hubs in the Capital."

"This is all great," says Cliff, "but what are the actions on contact for us?"

"To put that into civilian language; what do we do with him if we get hold of him?" says Alex.

Charlie gives Alex a friendly sneer, "Thanks, Alex, I could probably have worked that out for myself." she says, buying time for herself to work out how she is going to word her reply. The frank terms of reference that she has discussed with John behind closed doors cannot be repeated in present company. "We need to ensure that he cannot complete his mission and get him into custody as quickly as possible. We should be able to secure a conviction on 'causing an explosion', if nothing else, but hopefully we'll have more on him by then, and find him with a whole lot more." This rendition satisfies Dev with its legality, and just about holds Cliff's expectations together; in his mind he has his own rules of engagement for the man that has both directly and indirectly caused the death of several of his friends and had nearly taken him out of the game too.

33

Break

"Where do we start?" Cliff asks, standing on the pavement outside the block of flats where two good friends had been taken from him. The only sign of the explosion that rocked it three days ago is the boarded-up windows of the front door.

"I did a map recce on the way here;" says Dev, "the main areas of interest, where he might have been out and about, appear to be north and south of here. Shopping centres and community areas mostly to the north, a few to the south, but the train station is that way too." he says nodding to his left, down the short one-way section of the A112.

"Shall we split up then?" Cliff asks.

"I'll go with Lucy to the north." Alex says without hesitation.

"You and Lucy seem to have all the inside information on this case, maybe you should share the love?" Dev says, with a hint of distrust in his voice. "I'll come north with you." he says to Alex, "Lucy, Cliff, are you okay with scoping out around here and to the south?"

"Fine." they both say in unison.

"Uniform have knocked on all residential doors within 500 metres and spoken to all retailers and businesses in the same area. We should start by looking at supermarkets and convenience stores. The staff at the train station might be a good shout too; nothing came of Monday's interviews, but we might get lucky if other staff are on duty." says Dev. Looking over Lucy's shoulder at a closed down DIY shop, an idea enters his head. "Electrical, DIY and hardware shops are probably worth a look too; if he's planning an attack, he'll need some sort of materials."

*

"What the fuck's going on, Alex?" Dev asks aggressively as soon as they're out of earshot of the other pair. Alex says nothing, playing dumb, waiting for Dev to narrow his question, looking past him through the bars of the park fence, pretending to observe the people within. "Don't take me for a mug. You and your bunch are in the thick of this Interest Group thing. What is it all about? Were you working with Craig Medhurst? Been party to murdering 159 people, have we?"

Alex squirms a little in his skin as he walks but comforts himself with the knowledge that he has the Sayeedi incident over Dev; his panic melts away. "John and Cliff are old mates of Craig's, so were Spence and Blakey. They want to get justice for Craig and the others who died at Millbank. It's more than that though, we all know how dangerous these people are – they need taking off the streets. Whatever we can do to make that happen, then we'll do it." Alex says, hoping to throw a veil of innocence over himself. "All you need to know is that Charlie has us vetted and approved to work with the Security Service."

Dev walks on in silence as the individual shops meld into more of a recognisable retail area; still mostly charity shops and dirty looking fast-food restaurants. "I want people like Blunt off the streets too, but murdering unconvicted civilians is not going to happen on my watch."

"It won't come to that. I think Charlie's initial idea of having us around to track him down has run its course; it seems to be well back into the hands of the 'Alans' of this world. This expedition seems to be an exercise in futility designed to make us feel a bit better. Honestly, what are we going to find of value – he's long gone."

"Don't be so sure about that. I'm no 'old sweat', but I've been a cop long enough to know that getting back to the basics can turn up all sorts of data, information and intelligence – facts, clues and leads as they used to say." Alex appreciates Dev's efforts to cheer him up; his morale having been in need of a bit of a lift.

They walk on to find the first bank of proper high street shops, still well within the 500-metre radius of the safehouse. Dev finds that each of the four takeaways, the Spar shop, the Sainsbury's, and the petrol station have all received a visit from uniformed officers earlier in the week, and Blunt's face hadn't been recognised at any of them. As the A112 becomes Leyton High Road, the reports of Police calls cease, but they have no better luck with anyone recognising Blunt's mugshot. Some of the shop managers offer their CCTV footage, but neither Alex nor Dev fancy watching that back; they take contact details and promise to have someone get in touch in the next day or so with instructions on how to submit the files.

*

The morning ebbs away. Whilst they are meeting some interesting characters in some interesting shops, no one has seen Blunt. Alex and Dev stop for a late lunch in the last coffee shop on Hoe Street, which is the local name of the A112 as it emerges from the north side of Leyton's central retail area. Dev asks the proprietor, a skinny, haggard looking lady in her fifties, if she has seen the man in the photo as she makes their drinks.

"Sorry, love, I'm sure I'd have remembered that beard." she says, barely glimpsing at it. Dev suppresses his frustration and repeats what he has said about him possibly having made changes to his appearance, but she is doing that classic old Londoner thing of only hearing what she expects to hear and getting carried away with what she is saying and doing. Dev gives up on her, thanks her for the drinks and joins Alex at a table at the back corner of the cafe.

"How's that 'back to basics policing' working out for you?" Alex asks with a smirk. They both laugh together. Their laughter stalls as the breaking news scrolls across the bottom of the wall-mounted television screen; '*PM raises UK terror threat level to CRITICAL*'.

"Shit gets real." says Dev.

"Zafir must have been convincing." Alex says. The magnitude of effect that the subject of their investigation has had on an entire nation gives Alex a sudden sense of intense pressure being placed on the team – on him. Again, he finds himself wracking his brains to come up with a new, novel, innovative way of locating Blunt, but he just can't make the breakthrough.

"I wonder how the others are getting on." says Alex.

"Same, I'd guess. I'm sure they'd have messaged us if they'd turned anything up." Dev says taking a bite from his sandwich.

"I'm sure we're missing something really simple. There must be something we haven't thought of." Alex's frustration is making him angry at himself. "In the Army we have an estimate process we go through that prompts us and reminds us not to forget things when we're making a plan. It's the same with the orders process; everything fits into a template that we follow religiously to make sure we've not left anything out. Do you guys have investigative techniques and tools like that?"

"Of course we do, though we're well off template with this fucked up situation. Taking 'locating Blunt' in isolation from the Interest Group, as the investigation in question, we'd be in the initial investigation stage. What we're doing now is the important stuff that might get us a quick result – the 'fast-tracking actions'. If Blunt is really going to strike this weekend; these are the only actions we'll get round to taking."

"Is that it? Is there nothing more detailed to help you check you've not missed something?"

"There are procedures for all of the elements of the investigation, it's not as simple as your headings in your Platoon Commander's Nyrex." Dev says with a smile. Alex is taken by surprise that Dev's knows of the 'font of all knowledge' that is the junior commander's A4 waterproof folder, used for the formulation and delivery of orders in the field. "I did two years of Officer Training Corps at uni.

"Initial search, scene management, material, communication, investigative interviewing, they're some of the basic headings we're using in this case, each has its own bespoke set of acronyms, mnemonics and wire diagrams to assist officers to negotiate a systematic and ordered investigation. Charlie will be following similar, if not identical conventions."

Alex is not surprised that organisations like the Police and the Security Service have such protocols, but he takes comfort from hearing about it. "You'll have to give me a look at your Nyrex sometime."

"Any time." Dev replies.

Alex looks to his phone and explores the map of the area. There are two DIY shops around the corner towards Knotts Green, maybe we'll get a bit of luck.

*

"Well that was a fucking waste of time." Alex says angrily as he and Dev step out of the second of the two shops that they had pinned their hopes on. Dev wants to reassure him that something will turn up, but even he is feeling his words wearing thin, as they near the limits of their assigned search area.

"Keep your chin up. We'll follow this road back across the A112 and see if there's anything interesting, then cut back down Vicarage Road to meet the others."

"Shortcut?"

"Six and two threes, but it'll be a change of scenery."

The walk down Lea Bridge Road is far from scenic and only yields one small electrical shop, the owner of which has not seen Blunt. They walk on as the buildings become exclusively residential.

"It looks like we're waiting on Blunt to try and call Zafir, then." Alex says with resignation as they walk under the arches beneath the overground railway track.

"There's plenty of leads to work through yet." Dev says, looking at Alex, but Alex is focused on something over the road. A red cuboid of a building sticks out from the Victorian town houses and modern blocks of flats that surround it.

"Tool Town?" Alex says, reading the bold sign over the top of the large pane windows. The store is bigger than any of the other four DIY shops that they have visited. "How come this didn't show up on the search?" Dev just shrugs and strides across the road.

*

The heavy, steel-framed door sounds an electronic chirp as Dev pushes it open. They walk towards the single till where the only customer in the shop is being served.

"Thanks Mick." the man in paint-stained dungarees says as he turns and walks past Dev and Alex, giving them an inquisitive stare.

"Let me guess, you need some overalls?" Mick says, smiling contently appreciating his own brand of humour.

"Good afternoon, Sir. I'm Detective Constable Dev Jackson, this is my associate Mr Gregory. Are you the Manager?"

"Manager, owner, lackey, whatever else you want to call me." Mick beams: Tool Town is his pride and joy.

"I wonder if you might be able to help us. We're looking for this man." Dev holds up the mugshot. Mick eyes it carefully, with a thoughtful expression, wanting to ensure that his genuine aspiration to help them will come across, but instantly he is gratified; real recognition strikes him and his face returns to its natural, cheerful state.

"Yes, I've seen him. He was in here at the end of last week – miserable git, he was."

Dev and Alex exchange looks, both amazed at their luck.

"I remember him clearly because I would have sworn that he was a soldier, but when I asked him; he said he'd never served. Even with that horrible beard, it was clear to me, you know; takes one to know one." He looks Dev and Alex up and down, "Maybe you don't."

Dev laughs aloud turning to Alex. Alex frowns, raising his eyebrows at Mick. "Ten years Royal Signals, formerly *Sergeant* Gregory." he says, not boastfully, but causing Mick to further question his intuition.

"Royal Signals?" Mick says quizzically, "Well that's hardly soldiering, is it?" He breaks into a belly laugh, Dev joins him. Alex can't help but laugh too. "Sorry, no offence – I've known some pretty warry scaly-backs in my time to be fair."

Mick begins to give Alex a blow-by-blow account of his military career, which both he and Dev might usually have the good manners to endure, however time is of the essence. "Mick, we'd love to hear about it another time, but our investigation has some urgency to it; we really need to track this guy down."

"Sorry, yes." Mick blushes a little, cognisant of his tendency to gabble on, "Wife says I could talk for England, especially when it comes to the Forces."

Mick recounts his interaction with Blunt from start to finish. Dev takes copious notes of Blunt's appearance in the shop five days ago. Mick is able to answer every question that they pose to him in impressive detail. Mick is also able to seek out Blunt's transaction on the computerised till and prints them a copy of the itemised receipt.

"I've got the CCTV up there;" he points up over his left shoulder to the camera mounted in the corner above the shopfront window, "I'll sort a copy out for you."

"Brilliant, thanks, Mick. We'll send someone along for it tomorrow if that's okay?" says Alex, mimicking Dev's party line that he's heard several times today.

"Nonsense, I'll have it on a pen drive for you in a tick. Eng'ers can do data too, Siggy." Mick walks hurriedly to the back of the store and disappears through a door.

"Cash payment." Alex says, hoping to prompt some thoughts from Dev.

"Inevitable – in line with the methods he's been using. There are some interesting items on his shopping list though; I'm sure we can read something from them with a closer look."

Mick returns and hands Alex a pen drive. "I've copied and edited the footage down; from the moment that he walked in, to the moment he left – all three cameras."

"Thank you, Mick. We'll be in touch if we need anything else." Dev says as he and Alex shake his hand. They head towards the door, but Alex spins on his heels to face back to Mick.

"By the way, he was in the Army – 2 Para." Alex can see that Mick is delighted to hear it, restoring some of the lost faith in his sixth sense.

34

Elementary

The team reconvenes back at the Thames House meeting room and the task of unravelling Blunt's plan begins. As well as Dev and Alex's findings from the hardware store, Lucy and Cliff have a less solid sighting of Blunt, potentially purchasing a military bergan and a few other items of field kit, that the shop assistant was unfortunately unable to recall. With a lack of itemised records, or any well-defined CCTV; that is about as good as it is going to get from the search of the local area.

The whiteboard sees a lot of action; fishbone diagrams and other analysis tools and techniques get an airing. They apply the 'five whys' to possible uses for the items known to be in Blunt's possession and bounce partial ideas off one another, trying to reason how the items might be used together to perform an act of catastrophic destruction and mass murder.

"The most likely actions we've identified so far," Charlie summarises, skipping through their findings matter-of-factly from her laptop screen, "securing of access-egress doors, breach entry into a fenced off or padlocked area, some sort of heavy duty metal-work, or a disguise for entering industrial area, and 'multiple kidnapping'." She says this last possibility with emphasised inflection; the thought of Blunt holed up with a group of captives at his mercy doesn't sit well with her. "We also have notes to look at venues with high structures or ceilings, and strategic level utility sites."

The silence in the room tells Charlie that she's not going to get anything productive out of them for the rest of the day. There are a lot of possibilities and many more ideas to come, but they are not going to be effective in figuring them out stuck in this room, despite the building's rich history, these four walls lack inspiration.

"Okay, let's knock it off for today. Get out this evening and enjoy the city, keep thinking about what Blunt might be up to, group message any ideas, something might spark." Charlie says, patting the lid of her laptop down.

"John got out of hospital this afternoon," says Cliff, "shall we all meet up with him for a bite and a beer?"

"Will he be up to it?" asks Dev.

"It's John; what do you think?" laughs Cliff.

*

"I didn't think we'd be getting any down time this week." Lucy says, stepping out of the shower. Alex looks up from his laptop to take in her perfect curves as she stands drying herself in the soft, cloud-like towel, further enhancing her angelic appearance.

The move into London had not come with any offer of expenses from Charlie, so Alex had chanced his arm and asked Lucy if she'd mind him sharing her accommodation. This would have been a no-brainer, bearing in mind the natural way their relationship has reigniting, but for the fact that he still has his interlude with Charlie on his conscience.

"Are you getting in the shower?" she asks.

"Yes, I'm just running a few searches for likely target venues. I can't get my head around us not being able to pin him down – with all the resources we have on our side; we should have him by now." Alex rubs his eyes and slides his fingertips up into his hair to massage his aching head.

"He'll turn up. The whole country is looking for him now. It's going to take the analysts time to follow up on all the Sayeedi contacts, and it's odds on that Blunt will try to call Zafir at some point before he strikes; we just have to be ready to react."

Lucy's words provide him with some comfort but having been in close proximity to the Millbank bomb, and having lost some good friends to it; he is placing himself under immense pressure, taking ownership of the responsibility to prevent it from happening again.

"You need to chill out, you little stress-head." she says, allowing her towel to slip as she sits beside him and rubs his shoulder affectionately. The sight of her breasts and the warmth of her touch are enough to distract him. He tosses the laptop aside to give her his full attention. Their lips come together as Alex slides his hand down her side.

"Do you fancy another shower?" he asks, caressing the delightful curve of her hip, slipping round for a cheeky feel of her bum - all his worries forgotten for the moment.

*

"There's Dev and Cliff." Lucy points to the guys, standing chatting behind the left pillar of the iconic and colourful Chinatown Gate. They greet each other in turn, and each describe what they've done with their few hours of spare time. Alex and Lucy fail to mention that they've been together, but all four have otherwise been unable to get the investigation far from their minds.

"PUT HIM DOWN!" Cliff bellows as he catches sight of Charlie and John arm in arm; they both quickly let go of one another as everyone else in the street looks around at them. John's face is healing well, but there is a collective wince as they approach the gate.

"That looks sore, John." Lucy says, inspecting it closely as she gives him a hug.

*

The team of six head on through the gates looking for somewhere to eat. John and Charlie seem close as they lead the way. Charlie peers in through windows and looks over the menus mounted at the doorways of the restaurants, making everyone laugh with her critiques of each establishment; giving spurious reasons not to go in. Eventually she makes her recommendation of a place she's been to a few times before; an unusually spacious, dark, and ornately decorated restaurant with authentic, ancient artefacts from the motherland.

"Looks suitably expensive." says Cliff, signalling his support for the choice.

They file in; Charlie exploits the genuine, joyous recognition displayed on the ageing, but astute maître d's face, making her demands for a table that best suits their needs; they are taken upstairs to a deserted first floor, where they have the choice of five circular tables. Charlie points everyone to the right from the top of the stairs, to the most secluded spot; a table on the balcony overlooking the hubbub below.

Alex and Lucy take the seats to the left and rear, John and Charlie go to the right and rear. "Looks like you're my date, Dev?" Cliff says with a grin, patting him lovingly on the back. Dev's face drops a little as the penny drops that Lucy is no longer available, it is quickly confirmed as he catches the pair looking at each other the way lovers do.

Drinks quickly arrive and the sizeable food order, dominated by Cliff's selection, is taken.

"I hear our Tony has been shopping?" John says to get conversation going on topic. "Any new ideas on what he might be up to?" intimating that Charlie has brought him up to speed with the afternoon's brain-storming session.

"I did think that he might be doing a replen' for your love cave, John." Cliff laughs. "Seriously though, I did have a thought about sewerage sabotage. We mentioned interfering with utilities but causing a major blockage of the sewers could have huge areas swimming in filth; there'd be shit and disease everywhere." Perfectly timed, the waiter plonks a dish of chicken satay on the table right under Lucy's nose.

"Thanks for that Cliff, a lovely image to go with my starter."

"What about a clothesline?" says John enthusiastically.

"Heavy duty one, you mean?" Cliff sounds like he's taking his friend seriously, "Like your mum has for her underwear?" Again, Cliff laughs to himself.

"Shut it, you mong." John says, batting back the big man's banter. "I mean a cross-road garrotte that'd take the top off a London bus, along with the heads of all the passengers."

Again, the waiter's timing is perfect, this time to catch the shocking content of conversation. The chat calms down until all the starters are on the table, three dishes of which are around Cliff's place setting. "I'm hungry." he says defensively as the others eye his choices with a degree of food envy.

Alex is enjoying the evening out with the team. He misses Craig and the rest of the core group from the last mission, but he has to admit to himself that he is more at home with this bunch. He is not the outlier here; he is at about the centre of gravity and a focal point of the group dynamics. He has developed his own unique ties with each member, building respect and earned each of their admiration – *I hope more of this lot survive this mission.* He rubs Lucy's thigh under the tablecloth.

Alex decides to take the conversation back to work in the starkest terms while they are assured of at least a few minutes of privacy from the efficient restaurant staff. "How do you rate our chances of tracking him down in time, Charlie?" His question kills the atmosphere dead. Everyone looks in to the Security Service agent with great interest in how she will field it.

"Eeee," she sighs out in purest Mackem, threatening to fall back onto her 'know-nothing-Northerner' regional stereotype. "You think I'm going to pull a rough percentage figure out me arse, Alex?" She stares at him with her twinkling smile. He feels a wave of embarrassment come over him and he immediately regrets trying to put her on the spot. Fortunately for him; she's just having some fun with him. "I'm sure that Lucy is aware, maybe even John and Cliff with their training, that when involved with serious investigations, as Dev and I are on a day-to-day basis; we need to be on top of understanding probabilities." Charlie's voice refines, whilst still maintaining an honesty to her Sunderland roots, her demeanour alters too. "If we assign a probability to each of the leads that might successfully deliver Blunt to us; we can multiply them together in a way that will give us a probability that we will achieve a positive outcome."

"What's your assessment?" Alex asks, excited that he might receive a tangible answer based on reality.

"I'd say that, within timelines of Saturday morning, maybe fifty-fifty that he phones Zafir, thirty percent that there's a valid public sighting, ten percent that our techies can find a direct link to him, and maybe twenty-five percent that he gets picked up on his approach to an attack by blue forces, what with the heightened alert state.

"Boom, that's it by my maths – hundred and fifteen percent." Cliff exclaims.

"That's proper Paratrooper maths." Alex smirks, bracing himself for a clatter from Cliff, who just laughs back at him, knowing all too well that maths isn't his forte. "The quick way is to multiply the negative outcomes together then invert it." he says confidently.

"Good knowledge, Alex." Dev says, more to show that he also knew the formula, than to pay Alex a compliment. "Remind me never to play poker with you."

"A little better than seventy-five percent." Alex says after the swiftest of roughly rounded calculations rattle through his brain.

"Seventy-six point three seven five, actually." Charlie proclaims.

"Pretty good." John offers his opinion.

"Good, but not brilliant." says Alex, risking bringing the morale of the team down.

"You've not included any input from our efforts." Dev says, clearly annoyed. "We're not just going to sit on our thumbs waiting for Blunt to fall into our lap, pinning our hopes on him making a mistake, or some geek turning something up on a phone or computer. We've got the skills and knowledge to find him, or at least have half a chance – I'm not giving up."

"Our half chance makes it nearer eighty-eight percent." says Alex with more of a buzz in his voice.

"I'll drink to that." says John, raising his beer, "To catching the fucker."

35

A stroke of luck

Time had not been moving quickly for Blunt. The seconds, minutes and hours of the past four days seem to have ticked by at a snail's pace. Not wanting to risk being spotted, he had remained in the copse where he had stashed Andrew for the rest of the Saturday, moving back to his hide location that night. He had eaten and slept, and passed the time of day in complete silence, all the time; just metres away from the Duffields. Even with the old man busying himself around the farmyard, and two deliveries arriving; the additional intelligence gathering opportunity was too low in tempo to occupy even Tony's relatively simple mind. Having maximised his sleep, but still finding himself with an abundance of time to burn; it is becoming a struggle to keep his head together – his lack of patience had been cited, along with a number of other character flaws and skill deficits, in the report that had accompanied him back to his Company when he had been binned off a Regimental 'Drill and Duties' course aimed at developing junior leaders - he'd only been put on it, as a maturing soldier, to build his confidence, but it had had the opposite effect.

Any and every fragment of an opportunity to be tracked or traced by the authorities goes through Tony's mind over and over again. Each iteration of his internal review of his actions, and the trail that he has left burning behind him, seems to be more obvious and easier to pick up on. He has frequent bouts of cold sweats and flusters himself into minor panics each time that he allows it to cross his mind. A partial thought about any slip of information that Naith or any of the other elders might have let escape, or his car being recognised at the services' car park, grows in his head until he finds himself tremoring, doubting his own ability to continue to conclude his mission. Over the four days he has found himself able to break these self-inflicted attacks by living out the consequences in his head: resolving the issue with extreme violence. He now finds himself comforted by his axe – any flicker of doubt, fear or concern that enters his head is quickly dissipated as he grasps the handle of his instrument of power. He brandishes the handle, feeling the grain of the wood. He searches the top of the shaft and the beautifully shaped head for any encrusted drops of blood that he might have missed every other time he has inspected it, worshipped it, in return for the power and confidence that it has given him.

He has chosen this evening, Wednesday, twelfth of July, as the optimal night to test the security of the Austin & Sons' Foundry – not too far out from his D-Day to allow security services' hares to be set running, but far enough ahead for him to come up with a plan should things not go as he hopes they might.

He moves from his well-established hide, out of the hedge, and tracks north cautiously past the gap in the hedge, having a brief look into the empty farmyard, before heading on to the corner of the field where it meets the back corner of the barn and the lane. Pushing himself into the hawthorn behind the head of his axe, he disappears into greenery. The hedge is much narrower, but much denser than his hide location; he is forced to drop down to his belt buckle and half leopard crawl, half drag himself along the ground to the far side, using the axe to hook on to trunks and branches to haul himself along. He is soon sat comfortably with a perfect view of the foundry. He is in good cover provided by the uninhibited long grasses, nettles and cow parsley that spews up from the banks of the shallow ditch that runs between the hedge and the road. The generous foliage meets seamlessly with the swaying branches of the hawthorn; Tony is confident that he is invisible to any passers-by.

Over the course of the afternoon Tony has seen a slightly concerning number of deliveries and pick-ups made to Austins, but he is confident from his previous recce, that they will be closed on Saturday. From 16:00hrs he observes office staff and metalworkers leaving in ones and twos from opposite ends of the building complex. Blunt listens to the chit-chat and friendly banter between those that walk to the car park together; he is just within the limit of being able to hear what those with louder voices are saying. He picks up nothing of value from any of the chatter.

The clock ticks on past 17:30hrs, the workers' overalls have become harder worn and the office-ware has become more expensive; only the most dedicated, and highest paid staying late. Tony notes two cars remain in the car park; a slightly mature, burgundy Jaguar and an equally mature, but shiny black Land Rover Defender, Tony finds himself fighting the urge to desire the latter, the legacy of his taste from his former life feels like poison to his new ideology, his mind attempts to overpower his feelings for the vehicle, synonymous with military service, with revulsion – he convinces himself that it's a shit-bucket.

"Good night, Ted. Have a good weekend." The stout chap, in a nicely tailored suit, says to the bigger man in blackened overalls as he passes him on his way out of the office building.

"I'm off tomorrow and Friday, so I'll see you on Monday, Mick." Ted replies as he opens the door to the immaculate Defender.

Perfect, Tony says to himself delighted that Ted has pretty much reaffirmed what he hoped he'd known; that Austins is closed for business over the weekend. He watches on as Mick turns back into the doorway and presses a four-digit pin into the keypad mounted on the corridor wall on the left. Despite squinting and craning his head as far forward as he dares, as the Defender reverses around to face him, he is unable to make out the digits of the alarm code. *First figure might have been 'one', second could have been 'nine' – maybe a year of birth.* He puts it out of his mind for now.

*

Tony enjoys the brilliant golds and pinks thrown out by the sun as it sinks into the horizon behind him. The vast open field with yellowing wheat seems to shimmer in the breeze. As the last of the light fades, he slides down the short distance to the bottom of the ditch and shakes his numb legs out; the sedentary watch duty having taken its toll on their blood supply. He gets to his feet with the aid of his trusty axe, being careful not to disturb the greenery as he steps up and out onto the lane. Tony walks diagonally across the tarmac and jumps up onto the bank of the Austins' ornamental garden, making straight for the largest of the fern shrubs. He inspects it at close quarters, pulls it about and kicks his foot into it a few times – *that should do nicely.* He steps into the middle of the shrub, turns to face the foundry's front door, then squats down, disappearing completely into it – *perfect.*

He stands from his position of cover and steps through the flowers towards the front door of the unit. He wastes no time in getting to grips with the doorframe; already aware of the lack of secondary bolts and fairly sure that the alarm sensor will be at the top left of the door, he presses hard in that corner, flexing it back - he wedges the back of the axe head into the gap. It takes less than a second for the alarm sensor to register that his is more than a momentary blip, and the shrill, ear-piercing siren rings out. Tony calmly yanks out the axe, turns about and steps off the path back across into the centre of the garden, resuming his position in the shrub.

Tony makes himself as comfortable as he can, fully expecting to be there for up to an hour for a responder to arrive, if they are going to at all. He slouches back, unconcerned that he has no visual on the doorway at the moment, deciding that he will have plenty of time to position himself when he sees vehicle lights approaching. He is just about to shuffle his position to straighten his legs, when he sees a flash of light flick across the branches to his left – he freezes instantly. His eyeballs swivel in their sockets, glaring round to the left as far as they can without dragging his head around with them. Torchlight now illuminating the front of the building; he sees old man Duffield walking up towards the front door. Tony sees instant options for his plan emerging; he thinks them through as Farmer Duffield steps up to the door, he inspects it briefly, then walks back along the path and disappears around the left corner of the building. He soon reappears out of the shrouded darkness offered by the hedge at the eastern side of the front of the building having completed a circuit of the property, and seemingly satisfied that all is well; he takes a bunch of keys from his pocket, Tony notes the purple, rubber pom-pom keyring that hangs from them as Mr Duffield turns the key in the lock and steps inside. Tony leans forward to get the best possible view of the keypad, which fortunately is back-lit. He clearly sees the doddery farmer press the numbers slowly and deliberately, one, nine, five, eight. He closes the door and locks it but does not walk away immediately. He looks down at the shrubs, from one to the other, sensing that something is not right. Tony feels the cold sweat boiling all over his body; he moves his left hand slowly to form a strong, two-handed grip on the axe.

Farmer Duffield's gaze breaks from the garden and fixes down to his hands. He has an old Nokia phone, which beeps away slowly as he types in a message and sends it, before finally heading back to his bed.

36

Porton Down

Wednesday had been a day of chasing ghosts for the team; even Dev's enthusiasm had waned. The Crimestoppers' campaign had sprung reports on what seemed to be every ginger beard in the country. Only the best of the leads had made it through to the team, but even acknowledging just those into the inbox had been an unwanted distraction. The local street cameras had picked up Blunt on his way to and from Tool Town but had not yielded an footage of him entering or alighting a vehicle of any description. Thursday morning had looked like more of the same, but Alex and Lucy were relieved to be asked by Charlie to represent the team on a flying visit to Porton Down to receive a full back-brief on detailed findings from the Leyton safehouse.

"I'm glad I kept hold of my DV." Alex says, thinking that it can only have helped in getting him on the list for a visit to the secretive military laboratories. Holding 'Developed Vetting' status and a Security Service 'rubber stamp' had certainly saved Charlie some form-filling. "I couldn't have stood another day like yesterday."

Lucy keeps her eyes locked on the lanes of fast-moving traffic of the M3. "There was a lot going on; you only had time for six brew breaks?" she says, ensuring that her mockery isn't too subtle.

*

Alex and Lucy are both made to feel at home in the final few miles of the journey, seeing familiar places signposted at every junction: Andover, Tidworth, Middle Wallop, Bulford; there seem to be as many red military road signs as there are civilian. The infamous installation is discretely secluded amongst the young forestry blocks and tall hedgerows of the gently rolling hills north-east of Salisbury.

Lucy pulls into the car park, which is inside the outer wire, but not in the full security of the inner complex. They walk across to the guardroom, which is similar to the guardrooms of other high profile military establishments that both have passed through during their careers, though the four armed guards that Alex spotted as they had crossed the car park and the thickness of the security glass between them and the ageing Military Provost Guard Service Sergeant, has not gone unnoticed.

"Professor Banbury will come to collect you in just a minute. Please take a seat." the Sergeant says with a smile as he passes Lucy two 'escorted' passes.

Within a couple of minutes, the automatic doors to the right of the reception desk swing open, making way for a cheerfully bounding man in his forties, though he is dressed in his sixties. He has wavy tufts of almost-white blonde hair feathering behind his ears but is thinning on top. He looks straight past Alex and Lucy, then spins about in muttering confusion, looking to the sergeant at the reception desk for a clue.

"Jon?" Lucy asks, before the guard looks up.

"Lucy?" comes his startled reply. He looks her up and down, then smiles at Alex. "You're younger than your voice sounded on the phone." He thrusts out his hand.

Lucy cannot decide whether having an old voice is an insult, or a young appearance is a compliment. Jon's beaming smile, softly posh voice, colourful, teacher-like attire, and cues to social awkwardness, tell Lucy that there's not likely to be a deliberately offensive bone in his body.

"You're not as tall as you sounded." she retorts as she shakes his hand, causing him to smile and blush as he realises how these parallel comments might have caused mild offence.

"You must be Alex?"

"Hi Jon, nice to meet you." Alex shakes the scientist's hand, noting the respectable, respectful grip he applies. Jon's hand shows no sign of having seen any real hard work, like Alex's own.

"Follow me; it's just a short walk."

It is another bright beautiful day, this coupled with the beautifully tended gardens outside, of what looks like it may have been the Officers' Mess back in the day, make it difficult to believe that they are in the grounds of the revered camp. With the other mysterious and varied buildings within their gaze, and the quirky character that they were following around; Alex can't help thinking that oompa loompas might be spotted at any moment.

As they advance further into the grounds the buildings seem to get bigger, newer, and more industrial. The vision that Alex had nurtured in his head of this place being a few old pre-war sheds is fully dispelled. "Are the rumours about this place true?" he asks, mischievousness and a hint of malevolence in his words.

Jon looks at Alex, his smile still bright, but with a knowing look. "You Army boys, you love a good rumour." he laughs. "The things I've heard about this place; it's a wonder we get any visitors."

"So, it's all bollocks then?"

"I wouldn't say that." Jon's pace slows a little as he thinks carefully about what he wants, and is permitted to reveal, about Porton Down's history. "This place has been around under one name or another since 1916; through two world wars, fighting to get our servicemen and women a winning edge - I've no doubt the health and safety rules, that didn't even exist back then, might well have been breached."

"There are lots of new buildings." says Lucy.

"This place has grown arms and legs over the last few years. Lots of private and contracting lodger companies have been moved in, and with DSTL consolidating its resources, we now have all the munitions and explosives research here from Fort Halstead. That's been really handy, actually, for cases like yours that involve a blast or weapons – we have them on site to collaborate with.

Professor Banbury leads them into one of the disappointingly smaller buildings and in through an anonymous, unmarked door.

*

The professor invites Alex and Lucy to take seats at a double desk that faces on to a wall, onto which a huge interactive LCD screen is mounted. He takes a seat off to their left, at what looks to be the driving seat of this ultra-modern briefing suite. The smaller LCD screen of the computer terminal beams light into the darkened room as the mostly black login screen is replaced by Jon's desktop, covered with glowing white folder windows; he touches the screen, dragging an icon from one of the folders, and shoves it off the desktop towards the oversized monitor. A presentation opens as Professor Banbury launches into his introduction.

"You're here today as the field technical and intelligence leads in the investigation to locate Tony Blunt." he begins. Alex's self-esteem rises sharply at being recognised as such, but then sinks again as he wonders if that's just what Charlie has said to get him in the door. "We received items and samples recovered from Blunt's Leyton safehouse three days ago and have made some good progress. We've not found you a golden bullet I'm afraid, but there have been some notable findings, both physical and digital, which may prove useful."

Jon briefs on the exploitation processes and procedures that the information and items have been subject to, taking the opportunity to show off some of the facility's advanced technology. The Top Secret labelling assigned to most of the intelligence products that come out of institutions such as Porton Down, is almost always due to the method, process or source used to get to it, rather than the level of secrecy surrounding the content itself – protecting the secrecy of the route of intelligence is vital if it is to continue to be of value – once a method is known about; it can be mitigated against by potential subjects, devaluing its worth.

Jon moves onto the meat of the presentation; "The computer was almost new; purchased for cash from John Lewis in Stratford on Friday ninth of June. Charlie's people are already on the case with the store; trying to see if the purchaser can be identified."

Alex and Lucy look at one another, both hit by the same sentiment – *I thought we were Charlie's people.*

Jon goes on, "Our Security Service colleagues tell us that there was no fixed internet connection registered to the address, but we found a driver in the computer's system files that would have supported a Bluetooth connection to a hotspot. We've identified the network provider associated with the model of device that would have been used and have been working with them to isolate the traffic that went through it, but it appears to have been protected by the use of a virtual private network.

"Fortunately, we've managed to recover most of the laptop's memory; the hard drive was remarkably clean apart from the document that you're already aware of. We were able to recover the temporary cache and cookie files identifying most of his deleted browsing history." Jon points to the documents on the desk before Alex and Lucy – an extensive list of URL addresses fills the first three pages behind the cover sheet.

"How much of it do you think you've got?" Lucy asks.

"We've pieced together the date-time groups from the metadata of every individual interaction, along with the times of every other activity undertaken on the laptop, and we've discovered several large gaps of inactivity. We can't be sure if those gaps are missing data, or if he simply wasn't active on the computer over those times."

"Those gaps might be useful to the investigation in other ways." Alex says. "Can you give us the timings for the periods of inactivity?"

"If you look to page five of your handouts." Jon says, playing down his self-satisfaction at pre-empting the request. Lucy and Alex flick over to the page to a perfect representation of what they want to see; a horizontal timeline running down the page with blue spikes marking every period of digital activity registered on the laptop. "The parallel red areas of shading are his mobile phone periods of transmission, the column of notes on the right detail location movements away from the immediate area of the flat as evidenced by mobile phone antenna triangulation data."

"Nothing on the laptop after third of July? That's ten days ago." Alex says. He looks back along the timeline, noting frequent instances of activity through the vast majority of waking hours. There are two notable gaps in internet activity, which coincide with long outages in mobile phone transmission. "It looks like he was out and off grid Friday, thirtieth of June to Sunday, second of July for sure. The only other daytime period of any length is Sunday, twenty-fifth of June." says Alex, "This is good stuff, but I wish we had more recent data."

"You've asked the network about traffic content, but what about the data usage timeline?" Alex says looking at the graph.

"I don't understand." The professor says, "We're not sure that we have complete data on the laptop traffic, but it's fairly cut and dry that it was destroyed where the line drops off on the third of July."

Alex allows a few moments for Jon to use his imagination; soon enough, there is a ping of realisation on his face. "Another device?" he says.

"The phone doesn't move from the flat much up until the explosion; would you be sat in a hole like that with nothing to keep you entertained?" Alex asks.

"I'm rather partial to a book myself, but point taken." The professor looks annoyed at himself for the oversight. "I'll get on to the network this afternoon."

Strictly speaking; investigating whatever theoretical items that may have been used in the flat is outside of Banbury's brief. His mission was to exploit what had been presented to him, and without the hotspot device present; he has already gone above and beyond his remit, but it is an obvious implied task that he might easily have anticipated.

"Don't bust a gut, if there was a second device; it was clearly protected by the same VPN, and the chances are that its usage will just coincide with the presence of his phone. If there's any way of them identifying it though, particularly if it's a sim enabled tablet or smartphone; we could do with any details – if he believes it's clean, he might be using it as his onward means of communication."

Professor Banbury continues the briefing, leading into the recovered content of Blunt's browsing history. He summarises that Blunt was narrowing onto the top two or three tourist attractions in the capital; "Taking into consideration the research that he appears to have been doing on the properties of metals, and the items that he bought on his shopping excursion; I'd say that his most likely target is the London Eye."

"Can you imagine an icon like that coming down? That'd be up there with Nine-Eleven." Lucy says aghast.

Alex thinks through the possible scenario and how the known resources that Blunt has available might be applied to best effect on such a target. "If he could get access to the structure, rope himself up onto it and place a couple of decent sized charges; it could be carnage."

"It doesn't bear thinking about; going into the Thames stuck in one of those pods." says Lucy holding her arms tight against herself, wincing at the thought of it. "What's its capacity?" she says looking between Alex and the professor. Alex shrugs.

"There are thirty-two capsules, each can take up to twenty-five people – eight hundred people fully loaded. The wheel rotates twice in the hour, meaning that there is just under a minute gap between capsules unloading."

"No rapid emergency evacuation then?" says Alex, somewhat redundantly. The professor shakes his head gravely.

"That's a relatively easy one for us to nail down though." Lucy says, choosing to see the positive angle. "We can get the attraction security enhanced, surge uniformed foot patrols onto the bank and have an armed response team forward deployed to the immediate area."

Alex is keen to hear what else Jon and his team have found, not wanting to become too blinkered into chasing down just one course of action, regardless of how strong it might appear. "Was there anything else of note in his browsing history?"

"As I was saying, he had been looking extensively into the properties of steel; his searches included some quite complex terminology, and he found his way into some advanced materials. I've been trying to determine what it was that he was trying to calculate – what he might have been thinking that might point us towards how he might be trying to construct a plan, but I can't seem to find the relevance of anything that he was looking at – there was nothing that would tell him how structures would react to an explosion, the kit he has isn't capable of delivering anywhere near enough force to do any significant damage. I suppose he may have been looking at what effect tying the wheel would have, should the motor continue to drive it, but there will be fail-safes in place to counter that."

"Maybe he's just a dickhead?" Alex says. "If he's operating in isolation, and he's as much of a numpty as our John says he is, then maybe he's bumbling about in a dream world, without a clue how to do any proper damage." says Alex.

"We can't just write him off like that." Lucy says, scowling at Alex, disappointed with his attitude. "Blunt almost infiltrated Craig's Hodgehill gang, he killed two of our guys in Leyton, nearly taking out John and Cliff too, and you don't think he's a serious threat?"

Professor Banbury has the look of agreement with Lucy. "His efforts to conceal his digital footprint, the use of a VPN – I wouldn't say that is consistent with a 'numpty', certainly not one who is working in isolation."

Alex raises his hands, "No, all I'm saying is maybe his plan won't be as joined up as we might be expecting." He straightens himself up in his chair, physically trying to shed his negative position. He takes on a more upbeat tone, "Was there anything else from his browsing history that stood out?"

The professor leafs through the three pages of addresses, printed in font barely big enough to read, "Nothing sinister really. He did have a good look through the website of one particular metal foundry business, it stuck out, as it was the only real bit of detail, outside of the tourist spots, that he went into.

"Where's the foundry? Down in the Docklands?" Alex asks.

Jon frowns, "It's not in London, old boy, it's somewhere up near Grantham."

"Random." Lucy says, unsure if this might be information of value.

"I wasn't sure if he might have just gotten side-tracked and ended up there from his research, but he definitely searched the company by name on Google." Jon's uncomfortable body language tells that he is unsure of how much importance to place on it.

The lack of other leads automatically elevates this information's worth. "We'll see about sending some local uniforms around; see if they can find anyone who has seen him or pick up on anything that might attract a potential terrorist." For a tenuous 'Special Constable' Lucy is beginning to convince even herself in her Police role.

"Moving on to the telephone handset recovered from the communal bins." The professor clicks forward a slide, showing the rudimental device; a basic Nokia model - the typical 'burner phone'. "The handset has been forensically linked to Blunt, and I believe that you are aware that he has been in communication with both Zafir Abdulaziz and Naith Sayeedi?" Alex and Lucy both nod. Jon speaks a little more softly; "I don't want you to get your hopes up, but we're trialling a new technique that we've selected this case to be a bit of a guinea pig for." This sounds like the ground-breaking kind of thing that Alex had been expecting to hear within the walls of the famed establishment. He listens intently as the professor goes on. "I can't go into any detail, but it involves the characteristics of your 'Interest Group' network, a super-computer, a spot of data-mining and some slight contusions into privacy law, but if we can make it work; there's a possibility that we might be able to identify and locate the next crop of phones associated with your group users."

"Wow, that would be something." Lucy says, her mouth watering at the prospect. Alex's mind is not so much on the bigger picture; while he sees great value in such intelligence, he doesn't imagine it contributing towards intercepting Blunt, certainly not by Saturday. "How soon might you have a result?"

"There lies the problem." Jon says through a screwed-up frown. "We could be a month or more away yet; politics and tech issues both causing us hurdles I'm afraid."

*

Jon had gone on to describe the conventional forensic findings from the flat. How his team had worked in close partnership with the Met's Scene of Crime team. Blunt's DNA and fingerprints were all over the place. Prints and hair belonging to other individuals were found, but none had returned a match against records.

Jon's report showed in detail all manner of trace elements found within the fibres of the carpets, in the dust on the surfaces and within the nooks and crannies of the furniture. The assumption that the flat has been used as something of a transitory form of accommodation rendered many of the findings useless, but there were a few things that were deduced to have only been deposited there recently. Fresh seeds and pollen particles were found in the carpet and on the bed clothes, though mostly only from common weeds and meadow plants, not placing Blunt, or possibly one of his visitors, anywhere other than some generic area of greenery or another.

*

The drive back up through the countryside had been quiet so far, both Lucy and Alex reflecting deeply on what Professor Banbury had just taken them through at a canter. Alex leafs through the report, back and forth, Lucy silently concentrates on the curving country roads as she reconciles the data in her head, trying to extract some tangible intelligence from the facts.

"What do you think then?" Alex asks as they slip back into the monotony of the M3. "Likely target – the London Eye?"

Lucy seems to squirm in her seat, "I don't know. There's no smoking gun pointing to it, it's all circumstantial. I was kind of hoping for a blueprint with a big red bomb drawn on it." She laughs a little. "Maybe this is as good as the intelligence is going to get? All we can do is prepare for it. I'm certainly not convinced enough to stop investigating other possibilities; we need to keep our minds open and our senses sharp."

37

Inside the farmhouse

It has been another long, slow day for Tony. He had sat for most of the morning on the bank of the ditch, facing the foundry, to see if the previous night's alarm had triggered a visit from a technician or maybe even a security patrol. He had drawn stumps on his observations by lunchtime, returning to his lair to feast on a cold 'boil in a bag' of chilli con carne. He'd slept most of the afternoon, waking just before dusk feeling a slight unease.

He slowly feels around in the top flap of his bergan, moving silently to identify the items that he is looking for. He pulls out a powered-down smartphone and a tiny plastic envelope containing a sim card, still unbroken from the small board that it is etched from. He holds them together in his right hand, looking and thinking, weighing up the risks against the potential benefits of making the call. He sits in a meditative state, exploring his feelings, his motivations, challenging himself to be strong, whatever that means. He analyses his thoughts, the multiple layers of emotion, anger, confusion, desperation, hopelessness. Is he scared to make the call for fear of the response? Is he motivated to make it to give himself a way out? He places the phone and card back into the bergan lid – again.

*

The lights of the farmhouse have been out for an hour. Tony stands silently, perfectly still at the kitchen window, leaning on the end of the handle of his axe – it has become a metaphysical crutch to him; it has not left his side since it came into his possession.

He peers in through the glass, checking for any tell-tale glow seeping into the kitchen – all is black. He lifts the head of the axe off the floor and slides his hand up to its neck, tucking the end of the handle under his arm as he approaches the front door. His movements slow further as he reaches out to grab the door handle with his gloved hand, his mind willing it to be unlocked as he gently pulls it towards him to hold it into its frame, and then begins to turn it. The remote location makes the likelihood of the door being locked difficult to guess; roaming opportunists are unlikely, but then the farm would be a good choice for targeted rural burglary.

He feels the spring compress and hears it squeak and whine until the handle bottoms out at its limit of movement. The simple lock mechanism is independent to the handle and the movement gives him no clue as to whether it will open. Tony takes a deep breath as he moves his body weight forward, releasing the negative pressure on the door - it glides open. Tony moves it under control to its full extent; the air is still, and the door stays hanging firmly open wide. He walks into the dusty, stifled silence of the hallway, which is markedly different to the fresher, livelier silence of the yard. It is a light evening; the moon is three-quarter waning and is strong enough to provide enough illumination to move by in the hall.

He takes time to observe every item as he steps in; it doesn't take long for him to come to the main items of business – hanging from one of the hooks mounted on the bottom of an antiquated mirror is the large bunch of keys that he is looking for. He notes the dangly keyring, though it looks more grey than purple in the low light. Also hanging from the hooks, with similar rubber keyrings, are the keys for the farm vehicles.

He deviates from the hallway, turning about from the mirror, deciding to explore the kitchen before heading deeper into the house. He scoops aside the multicoloured ribbons of a fly curtain, letting them gently fall back into place as he enters the room. The kitchen is large, spanning the depth of the house. It has a Victorian appearance with few signs of attempts to update it, other than a fridge-freezer that

Tony judges might be older than he is. The room holds few surprises, just the expected knives and other assorted cooking implements, irons, and boards; unimportant but handy to have knowledge of. He passes back into the hall, pausing briefly at the bottom of the stairs – he listens, and hears noisy breathing, not quite snoring - just old people sleeping peacefully. The walls of the hallway have a few old, framed photos hanging on them, mostly black and white, no new ones, no signs of children or family; Tony's mild sense of sadness for the couple is quickly replaced by a gratitude for the assumed reduced risk of visitors.

Tony checks the cupboard under the stairs, finding nothing more than cleaning equipment and a small pile of ironing stacked neatly in a plastic basket. He shuts the door on it and continues round to the right, past the bottom of the stairs, he opens an old oak-panelled door into the living room. The room extends beautifully out into the back garden to his left with a homely, lived-in conservatory. The moonlight streams in through the back of the house negating the need for Tony to use his headtorch. The vintage sofa and armchairs, in garish patterned textile, don't look too comfortable, and the felt-covered card table doesn't look too stable. Tony feels the comfort of the Duffield's way of life. They seem to have a basic but peaceful existence that he could only ever of dreamed of. He'd never come close to finding the type of utopia that the Duffields have, he covets it more than he has realised up until this moment. His mind's eye sees them together, arm in arm hobbling together across the yard, he finds himself contemplating a way through his mission without bringing them to harm. Again, drifting into a daydream in the middle of business, Tony shakes his head to stir himself back into action.

He walks through the sparse, but somehow still cluttered living room, to its far side, where he opens the door to the study which looks out into the yard. Mr Duffield's office-come-cubbyhole is furnished with simple, but sturdy pine furniture. Uninterested by the mounting piles of paperwork and agricultural industry publications covering the desk, book cases and tables, Tony is about to dismiss the room, when he notices an incredibly robust-looking wardrobe to his right, secured with a heavy padlock – *armoury, bonus.* Instantly he is looking for the padlock key. He searches all the stupid places in the room first, knowing as a former soldier, only too well how lax people can be with their security, as evidenced by the front door. He checks the drawers of the desk, then looking down beneath the fan of papers to its left, he realises that this is not a table, it's a large safe – *ammunition magazine?*

With no sign of the keys, he makes a mental note of the manufacturers of the padlock and the safe and returns to the hallway. He checks through the keys on each of the numerous bunches until his eyes ignite with joy of seeing the word 'ABUS' on one of them, just next to it on the ring is what looks like a key that will fit the safe. He returns to the study to see what treasures await him. He takes his time with the tricky padlock, savouring the moment of the door swinging open. Before him is a vintage double-barrelled shotgun and a high-powered air rifle. A little disappointed, Tony had been hoping for something more voracious, but it is what it is, and still an unexpected bonus. He opens the safe to find a healthy stock of cartridges: birdshot, buckshot, and slug ammunition.

Happy with what he has found, all mission essential points ticked off, he leaves the farmhouse exactly as he had found it.

38

Laid to rest

"I feel like we should be doing more." Lucy says, her eyes flicking down to check the satnav.

"What more can we do?" Alex replies. "Nothing much new from the professor, nothing off the phones, and even super-sleuth Dev hasn't managed to turn anything up."

Lucy shrugs out her frustration. Jon Banbury's late evening update disappointed; there was no evidence of a second device being used on Blunt's internet hotspot. The troop of investigators brought in had spent hundreds of fruitless hours pawing over CCTV footage and following up on the reported sightings – not a solid lead or even clue to be had.

On their way east along the infamous A14 towards Bury St Edmunds, both are still wrestling with their decision to break from the investigation to attend Craig Medhurst's funeral, the Friday before the weekend that intelligence indicates that their targeted person of interest might be about to commit a terror attack. The first few hours of the morning had swung it for Alex, achieving nothing, skulking around between the Security Service briefing room and cafeteria, opening his laptop to begin a search before closing it again in exasperation, realising that his ideas were flawed or weren't even relevant. He and Lucy had talked each other into the need to go and pay their respects to the big man.

They turn off the A14 with less than a mile remaining to the destination, but as they leave the roundabout at the first exit, they see the jam of traffic clogging the route just a few metres down the road where they want to be turning left to the crematorium.

"I thought it'd be busy." Alex says, the pair begin to look for a suitable spot to ditch the car. Lucy follows suit of the car in front and pulls up onto the verge. On foot, they follow the row of abandoned vehicles round the junction to the left and join the march of mostly rugged-looking men, many wearing blazers, medals, and Regimental ties and head-dresses. Alex notes numerous Royal Anglian cap badges and signatory navy-blue ties with diagonal red and yellow stripes. The Poachers, whilst one of the Anglian battalions, are based in Rutland. Bury St Edmunds is the home of Third Battalion, the part-time Reserve battalion, but most Poachers hail from the local area, as do the 'Vikings' of the second Regular battalion who are based in Woolwich.

The growing crowd is peppered with khaki berets of Anglian veterans, and the odd sandy beret of Craig's former Special Forces comrades; he notes that the latter are worn by mostly older men, he has no doubt that many more of the younger SAS veterans and those still serving, are present, but with their inherent desire for anonymity yet to fade, they attend with little or no regimental branding. The pedestrian traffic becomes a slow-moving queue down the middle of the road, as marshals clear cars from it to make way for the inbound funeral procession. Alex and Lucy turn right in through the gates of the crematorium, weaving between the deserted cars that litter both sides of the road. The crowd swarms the building; there is well-mannered jockeying for position as Craig's closer colleagues attempt to get nearer to the building. Far from the sombre atmosphere of the family funerals that Alex is familiar with, the place is alive with the buzz of a filling football stadium as members of the veteran-heavy gathering catch up, and recount stories of 'when they knew Craig'.

"VETERANS FALL IN." The bustling throng is silenced, and everyone looks in to the tall, charismatic gent in immaculate Anglian veteran's rig. He waves a pace stick high in the air making it clear where he wants them to form up. The berets begin to regulate themselves into ranks; extended rows spanning the length of the route from the entrance gates to the crematorium building on both sides of the road, five, six deep at the centre, respectfully leaving room only for the group of mourning civilian family and friends near to the entrance of the building. All other well-wishers are firmly filtered out and guided back with questioning looks; the kind of looks that ask 'have you served'. The men, and occasional woman, shoulder to shoulder, unable to achieve proper 'drill spacing', continue to chat amongst themselves.

Whilst stood looking at the thick back of the enormous old infanteer planted in front of him, Alex thinks about the loss of Craig. He hasn't thought about him properly since the hunt for Blunt had taken off in earnest. Aside from working in support of Craig's team briefly in Afghanistan years ago, Alex had only known him for the two weeks of the Watch List mission, but he had grown close to him over that time. Craig had mentored him through the toughest of times; he'd been a proper 'military dad', showing him the way, leading by example, and providing inspiration. As he glimpses the hearse, as it comes into the grounds, all the veterans and uniformed serving soldiers of the bearer party are called to attention, Alex feels a tear well in his eye as the cortege passes by.

*

The service is broadcast through speakers to those outside who stand in absolute silence up to the committal. Alex leads Lucy around to the back of the crematorium to where he anticipates the mourners who made it inside will emerge from. The double doors slowly swing open and Craig's family are led out by the celebrant and accompanied by the current Commanding Officer and Regimental Sergeant Major of the Poachers in full Service Dress. Craig's ex-wife and his two daughters, both in their thirties, are sobbing in each other's arms. Alex and Lucy tip respectful nods in their direction, but they are not taking any notice. Alex looks beyond them to see John with a tight bunch of men all with arms around each-other, Cliff is barely recognisable in his suit.

John strides straight over to meet them. "You made it." He grips Alex in a strong man-hug.

"We had to." Lucy says, taking his attention, "We couldn't not come and say goodbye to Craig, and we were banging our heads off the wall in London."

John releases Alex and turns to Lucy for a hug, resisting the urge to ask about the investigation whilst the closing music of Craig's service is still playing.

39

Prelim moves

Tony should be happy, in fact, he should be delighted. Everything is going right, every element of chance in his plan has gone his way so far. Maybe it has been his lack of confidence that has allowed him to get this far without properly interrogating his belief in what he's doing. Maybe his lack of faith in himself to succeed is what has allowed him to stumble and bumble to this point. The window of opportunity for fate to intervene, to stop him from completing his mission, is rapidly shrinking. He now must face the reality that his plan will be executed - he will be responsible for significant death, destruction, and mayhem. The thought of the glory, the release of anger and frustration goes some way to allay his apprehension, but without the words of support of his mentor, or his friends; he is unsure if he has the conviction to go through with it. He takes the mobile phone and the sim card in his hand, once again torturing himself through the debate of whether to call or not.

*

The next step is clearing the way. A simple action he might have completed before being so rudely interrupted by Andrew. Tony returns to the railway cutting as the sun begins to sink behind him, drenching the fields and hedgerows in a magical golden-orange light.

Tony stands leaning on his axe, the wire snips dragging his right trouser leg down tight to the belt loops. He surveys the west bank of the cutting, looking for the optimal spot. He looks for the slope with the best access, clear from trees, with the shallowest decline, fewest lumps and bumps. After making a visual assessment from the edge of the field, he vaults the wire fence and walks the ground of his provisionally favoured spot. The ground is soft under foot, despite the dry conditions. A weave of rabbit tunnels makes the ground rough and unpredictable. "FUCK." he shouts to himself as he nearly goes over on his ankle. He is not pleased with the site, but the rest of the bank looks to be in the same state. "Fuck it." he says, resigned to this being the best option available.

He walks back, directly up to the fence, looks left and right – he selects the two fence posts nearest to his chosen route, takes his axe in a firm grip, and begins slamming the blade into the base of the first of them. Within a minute the section of fence is hanging limp, held up only by the taught wires. Tony takes his snips and cuts the three thick gauge structural wires, and the top strand of barbed, where they meet the next undamaged fence post nearest to the tunnel. He hooks the slack length of fence with the head of his axe and drags it back on itself, collecting it in a discrete pile of wire and posts the field side of the fence, away from the tracks.

Tony checks his watch as the sound of a rattling train registers in his ears. He sits in a patch of thick grass as it passes, then gets to his feet and walks down to the rails and heads towards the tunnel along the edge of the rough aggregate. He takes his head torch from his left map pocket, stretches it around his head and clicks it on. Confident that there are no trains due, having consulted Andrew's diligently kept records, Tony still feels deeply uncomfortable about being on the track, let alone inside the eerily dark tunnel. He proceeds two hundred metres, watching the ceiling and the tops of the walls the whole way; he notes the repetitive pattern in the concrete – *I can work with that.*

Walking back to the cutting, he climbs the bank to his hole in the fence and looks across the field to the gap in the hedge that leads into the farmyard – *all set.*

40

Wake

Since the family departed and left the soldiers to it; the wake has degenerated into a feisty affair. The early evening rolls on, the Poachers and Vikings have been completely honourable up until now, but the fun and games are really starting to get going. The men take the ale-fuelled opportunity to stoke their inter-battalion rivalry in the name of Craig's memory. For the most part, it has been in good humour, revelling in bar games and banter, only occasionally turning to fisticuffs, but even that has been quite well controlled by the senior blokes present. Alex and Lucy keep themselves to themselves at a quiet table past the end of the bar of the Angelica hotel.

"Excuse me, are you Alex?" says the man, unbranded as a veteran, but clearly of military ilk, as he approaches from a neighbouring table. Alex looks about, caught off guard.

"Err, yes." Alex feels a wave of insecurity rush over him. The thought had crossed his mind that some people might feel that it is his fault that Craig is dead; he had taken the list to Craig – some might say that Alex had instigated the pathway to his death. Alex stands from his seat, bracing himself for what's coming.

The stranger thrusts out his hand. "I'm a big fan of your work." Alex shakes his hand. "John tells me that you're in the process of tracking down the fucker that cost Craig and the boys their lives?" Alex says nothing, just returns a confident, knowing look. "Well if you need anyone to take care of business; there are plenty of us standing by." He taps Alex on the arm, lingering for a split second with a genuine look of subservience. "There's a drink behind the bar for you and your good lady." he says as he finally turns to walk back to his mates.

Word of who Alex is seems to spread through the Special and Elite elements of the remaining mourners as the evening goes on. More free drinks at the bar and handshakes are forthcoming, and appreciative nods are tilted in his direction.

"You're proving quite popular this evening." Lucy says, her smile showing that she is impressed by her man.

"Looks like we're set to chase down Blunt, and anyone else with Craig's legacy army." he says with irony, and a hint of reticent bitterness in his voice. He has been the reluctant champion of the fight against the UK mainland terror threat, and with John, leads the charge against the Interest Group, but since losing Craig, he has felt that the momentum is draining. He fears that the threat may well be successful in striking back with vengeance, whether through Blunt or others. It is becoming clear that John still has a powerful network in place to be called upon and that a war may well be brewing.

41

Cutting in

"That bastard alarm again." Mr Duffield says, looking up from his book.

"Now then, Henry, mind your language." Mrs Duffield says, playfully parrying at him with her knitting. "You'll have to have a word with Mick on Monday, that's twice in a week."

"Don't you worry my love, I will." He eases himself out of his armchair and gets his keys and jacket from the hall.

Old man Duffield dodders across the yard at a comfortable pace, muttering under his breath as he goes. He looks across to the foundry for any obvious signs of disturbance, but all is as expected. Almost disappointed, he goes through the routine of taking a closer look at the front entrance, then walks the perimeter of the building in a clockwise direction. Giving the side doors a nudge on the way round, he catches himself shivering with a chill down the spine as he emerges from the darkness, back out to the front of the office. He looks left and right, he looks at the garden, the shadows of the shrubs attract his eye, but he knows that he's just letting himself get spooked. He continues along and up onto the open-sided porch and takes the keys from his jacket pocket, moving as quickly as he can; the shrill alarm causing physical pain to his old ears. He turns the key in the lock, pulls the handle down and pushes the door inwards. He punches in the four-digit pin, halting the siren instantly.

Tony aims higher than he did when striking at Andrew; a good lesson learned, though the top of the doorframe makes the swing a little cramped and clumsy. Still, the magnificent, heavy blade of the axe swoops down mercilessly slicing into Henry's neck, just inside his hairline. Penetrating through his vertebrae and into his windpipe, he is all but decapitated, his head remains attached to his body by half the width of his oesophagus, the thin weak muscles, and the old-wrinkled skin of the front of his neck. The body of Henry Duffield falls into the tiny reception area of the foundry offices. The red door is matched by red carpet inside, which masks the amount of blood that is being ejected from the old man's neck. Tony looks over the scene as the rate of blood-flow slows to a trickle; he is pleased at the lack of obvious mess. He takes a knee over the farmer's legs and leans down to check the jacket pockets; he finds the tatty old mobile phone in the right pocket and places it in his right map trouser pocket. He places the axe just inside the door, leaning it up against the wall right by the alarm control panel. He grabs Henry by the ankles and drags him, without any due regard or respect, into the building, flipping him 'arse-over-head', his arms flail lifelessly. He dumps the body in the corner of the small waiting room, where it cannot be seen by anyone who might look in through the front door window. Tony takes the mobile phone from his pocket and presses the down arrow – as he'd hoped, there is no pin number. He navigates to the sent messages. Activity on the handset has not been prolific, the message sent to Mick two days ago is the last – *'Mick, alarm gone off, all clear, I've reset it. See you tomorrow, Henry.'* Tony taps in a message, now realising how pumped he is from the act of killing the old man; his fingers are trembling on the buttons, his mind is not as composed as it had felt just a moment ago. *'Mick, alarm gone off again, all clear and reset, see you Monday, Henry.'*

Tony pushes the front door to, then walks through the office. He finds himself wondering what it would be like to work in a place like this; a nice family business in the countryside, not like the places he's worked, run for maximum profit, with questionable working conditions and minimal regard for welfare and safety. The cluttered work stations look comfortable and homely, the family photos on the walls in the far corner make him ache in the pit of his stomach for his own children who he misses dearly. His emotions mix between sadness and anger as his mind fires through memories of them, from their births, all the way through to how they had abused him when he last spoke to them.

Tony finds his way out into the workshop, where his mind switches back to business. He circles the main working area in a clockwise direction, observing what equipment is available to him, and searching out the key piece of equipment that he needs. There are trollies full of tools, benches laden with specialist cutters and shapers, most of which he is familiar with. He spots a chained pen in the back-left corner, highlighted by numerous safety signs; the area is decorated in the hazard warning colour scheme of yellow and black chevrons. There are three pairs of huge gas cylinders, each on a wheeled frame, like over-sized golf trollies. Tony sets quickly to work checking the levels of each of the oxygen and acetylene tanks, unscrewing the taps on the torches before purging the values and then opening the flow of the tank. Selecting the trolley on the right, he checks the nozzle of the torch for serviceability, then wheels it out of the pen. He lifts a pair of goggles from the nearby rack and hangs them over the top of one of the tanks. He takes a final look around the workshop before dragging the gas cutting set through the office and over into the farmyard.

Tony leaves the trolley at the front corner of the enormous silver barn and walks towards the farmhouse, his bloodied axe over his shoulder. With emotion creeping into his head about what he is about to do, he tells himself that Mrs Duffield would rather die quickly now, than learn of what has become of her Henry, and live a lonely life without him. He thrusts the door open and strides into the house.

*

Tony staggers back out into the yard, shaken to his core. The previous two kills had been comparatively easy - faceless blows from behind. Mary Duffield had looked up at him with a begging face full of terror, tinged with sadness, a telling look that showed recognition of what must have happened to her husband. The handle of the axe had smashed through the weak arms, that she had raised in search of mercy, like they weren't there. The blade had sunk into the side of her head, the leading edge cutting all the way in to the inside of her eye socket. The axe head's continuing momentum had simply dragged her along with it, swatting her down to the kitchen floor.

Tony walks across towards the barn not feeling so closely attached to his beloved axe for the moment. He walks with it in a loose grip at the neck of the handle swinging it almost behind him. He shoves it into the gas trolley, like a golfer at breaking point, chucking his driver back into the bag after hooking his umpteenth tee-shot. He returns briefly to his lair within the hedgerow to grab his bergan, before dragging the trolley into the gaping doorway of the barn. He walks to the inside left front corner and turns on the band of lights at the far end of the building, then marches down the length of the lightly rippled concrete, dragging the trolley behind him, to the centre of the gable end wall.

Wasting no time, Tony dons his gloves and goes through the process of setting up the tanks, re-purging the gages, checking the levels, turning on the fuel, turning on the oxygen. He turns his attention to the torch, taking a firm grip of it in his left hand, he unhooks the striker that hangs from the frame of the trolley. Tony feels a thrill run through him as he opens the fuel and ignites it. He turns up the fuel until the sooty trail disappears from the flame, which grows in length and generates a roar. He then opens the oxygen tap, causing the flame to shrink and turn a powerful light blue; the roar quietens, but is far more intense.

Tony dons his eye protection and kneels next to the main upright of the super-structure. He begins to cut, at a sharp downward angle, about thirty degrees, through the left half of the rear flange of the substantial 'H beam'. The thickness and strength of the steel makes this a slow job, but he soon moves on to the right side of the back plate, continuing the line of the cut. He makes a concerted effort to cut a clear gap to ensure that there is no risk of the pieces joining back together. He makes a horizontal cut across the central thickness of steel where it meets the cut across the rear flange. The last of the 'easy' cuts, to be made from ground level, is to the front flange, directly parallel with the one made to the rear. Tony slows as he nears the end of the cut, low to the right side, the structure begins to creek and groan as its integrity becomes challenged. He shuffles back, operating the torch at arm's length, unsure how much confidence to have in the rest of the barn's structure. The beam drops an inch to sit just below and to the right of where it was formerly attached. Tony assesses that his cuts are as desired, creating a sharp double point to the right side of the girder.

Tony takes a deep breath, looking up to the other end of the beam, as a former paratrooper, the idea of working at height doesn't faze him, but he doesn't much fancy the effort that the next part of the task involves. He takes one of the lengths of rope from his bergan and uncoils it on the floor, walking it out, making use of the copious space available. He takes the two ends and runs them through his hands together, locating the centre of the fifty-metre length, then picks up the two loose ends in his other hand. He threads the centre loop of rope up through the handle of the welding trolley, then passes the two loose ends through the loop and pulls them all the way tight, creating a lark's head knot. He looks up to the top of the girder again, hoping that he has estimated the distance accurately enough, and that the rope is long enough to make it up and down whilst doubled.

He uncoils the second rope and ties one end around his waist using a figure of eight knot, something he learned when rock-climbing with the Army, then attaches the two ends of the other rope to the loop with a lazy overhand knot. Making sure that the trolley is as close to the central pillar as it can be, he begins to climb, trying his best not to put too much pressure on the cut beam. There is not much else to get a hold of, but as he gains height, his leverage over the beam decreases and he feels more confident about pressing his boot hard against it to gain purchase between it and the galvanised steel wall and its deep vertical grooves.

Reaching the uppermost horizontal beam, around ten metres from the ground, Tony sits on the top flange and hooks his leg around the giant central girder. Untying the double end of the rope secured to the trolley, he feeds both ends together up behind the beam that he is sitting on and pulls them through, allowing them to drop towards the floor below. He breathes a sigh of relief as they reach the ground with a couple of metres to spare. He then feeds the rope tied around him down the same gap until all the slack is gone. Tony reaches under the girder, grabbing his safety rope and whips it around behind him, taking it under his other arm. He lowers himself down off the beam and allows the rope to slip slowly through his grip until he reaches the ground.

Tony unties himself, leaving the two ends of his safety rope dangling from the girder and walks out of the barn, feeling slightly apprehensive again about the next part of the task. He takes the key for the old red Massey Ferguson from his pocket as he walks across the yard to where the tractor sits neatly in its port. He jumps into the driver's seat and looks over the controls, now feeling the annoyance of having smashed up his computer before completing his research. Two gear sticks, like those in an Army Land Rover, he guesses the prominent one on the left is the basic transmission and the other is the high-low ratio stick. The pedals are similar to those of a car, but for being split on either side of the steering column, again he guesses that they will be in the same order as with a car.

Tony turns the key in the ignition and the starter motor turns over, but the engine fails to fire. He tries several more times before considering that he might need to do something else, as the old man never seemed to have trouble getting it going. He feels his anger begin to surge; he looks around the cab for something to lash out at. Staring right at him from the dash is a small red lever; he instinctively pushes it in. Unwittingly disengaging the engine kill mechanism, he turns the key once more and the old Massey fires into life. The tractor shakes and rattles around Tony, he is unnerved at feeling comparatively still with just the soles of his feet feeling the buzz; the softly sprung seat keeping the vibrations from the rest of his body.

He depresses what he hopes is the clutch, it feels like a heavy clutch should, he flicks the big gear lever to the left and up. He begins to raise his foot from the pedal but realises that the hand brake is on. He looks left and right and identifies a lever near the floor on his right, he pulls on it, presses the button on its end and lowers it to the floor. As he releases the clutch, the tractor lurches backwards, Blunt's feet slip from the pedals as his orientation is lost in confusion. He gets a foot to the clutch and knocks the stick out of gear as the lift arms crash through the vehicle bay wall, Tony gets his right foot to the brake just as the huge wheels are about to burst through the thin corrugated iron.

He gathers himself, wiping the building sweat from his brow, looking around the cab for a diagram of the gearbox layout, but finds nothing, all advisory stickers long since worn away. He tries left and down; this time the vehicle lurches forward, jumping like a learner driver on their first lesson. He finds a steady rate of throttle, from the dinky little pedal to the right, and drives out of the shed. Tony decides to have a little play in the yard before trying to negotiate manoeuvres in the confines of the barn, notwithstanding its vast scale.

Tony feels comfortable with operating the machine after fifteen minutes, even having a play with the fork attachments on the front of the old Massey. He drives down the middle of the barn, stopping two metres short of the welding trolley, and lowers the forks down to a metre from the ground.

Tony loops the ends of the trolley rope around the back-stop bar of the bale spike forks in a figure of eight knot back onto themselves, then climbs back into the tractor and reverses it slowly. The ropes tighten and the trolley slowly lifts into the air. He backs up until the trolley handle wedges in underneath the horizontal beam.

Tony ties himself back onto the end of the second rope and, putting on the thick leather welding gloves, uses the loose end to haul himself up, his considerable upper body strength making light work of the ascent. He gets himself comfortable on the beam and sorts himself out for the next package of work. Removing a glove, he ties off the loose end of the safety rope to the horizontal beam with minimal slack, then reaches down to the trolley to retrieve the striker, googles, and torch.

Tony sets about cutting through the four bolts securing his beam to the one that he is sitting on, which proves more awkward than he had anticipated, particularly the two on the distant side from him, which require an uncomfortable amount of reaching around to. Tony's horizontal beam shakes as the second of its bolts are cut, but the strength of the steel wall is plenty to keep it where it is. He loosens his safety rope and stands on the beam for the final cuts to trim the upright from the structure.

Tony relishes the last inch of the last flange; he watches the metal burn away and the final thread melt and stretch as it drops free. The angled cut slides off its opposing face as the girder drops, sending it out to the side. The points of the girder strike the ground with the chime of a bell. The beam falls like a toppled redwood, almost in slow motion. Its long edge hits the concrete with a deafening clang that is so loud that it physically hurts Tony's ears, the shock of the noise causing him to flinch violently, dropping the torch as his hands race to shield his ears. All concentration is lost; he loses his footing on the beam and falls the short distance that the safety ropes permits.

Hanging upside down, but thankful that he kept the safety rope short, Tony looks to his next priority, the welding torch. He can hear it hissing, but as he looks down, over his shoulder, from his precarious, suspended position, he cannot immediately see it. He follows the gas tubes, which are just out of his reach, from the tops of the tanks, they spiral down together to the bottom of the trolley and disappear inside its frame – *shit*.

*

Doing his best to keep calm, Tony thrusts his chest upwards, grabs the safety rope and hauls himself towards the beam. He fights to gain purchase on the girder, but even with the rope there, this is now much harder without the huge vertical beam to get a grip behind. He eventually scrabbles onto the narrow ledge and shuffles a metre to his right and grabs at the hoses as far down as he can reach and yanks them. The torch comes into view, still within the trolley, still burning, pointing directly towards the oxygen tank. Tony is confident the danger is past having moved the position of the torch from where it had been burning for a good twenty seconds; *if it were going to go, it would have gone by now*. He gives the tubes a further tug and the torch pops out of the trolley, burning freely into the empty space of the barn. Tony reels the torch in slowly, hand over hand and turns off the taps on both the torch and at the tanks.

Panic over, he undoes the simple knot of his safety rope, and sets it around him ready to abseil, taking a second to focus, knowing that rushing in a situation like this, when his concentration has been knocked, might lead to a fatal mistake. He drops off the beam and lowers himself to the ground.

Tony lowers the trolley and spends the next hour cutting two much shorter sections of narrower girder from the standard vertical supports of the west wall of the barn, he cuts large holes in the end of each of these two sections, and widens one of the bolt holes near the flat end of the long section.

He rolls the long beam so that the point is uppermost. He threads the end of the heavy-duty chain through the bolt hole and then around the bar on the fork's assembly of the old Massey Ferguson, which he has lowered to the ground. He padlocks the chain onto itself, securing it loosely but strongly. He lifts the forks to shoulder height, then dismounts and wedges the larger of the two other steel pieces, which is just over a metre long with flat-cut ends, under it. He undoes the chain, then reverses, drops the forks below the end of the girder, then draws forward again until the girder is over the top bar of the fork assembly – Tony chains it back on to the bar in that position as tightly as he can.

Tony threads the loose end of the chain through the holes in the smaller pieces, the third piece is just about half a metre, also with flat-cut ends, and padlocks the chain in a closed loop. He raises the forks into the air and reverses out of the barn, dragging the long beam noisily across the concrete, with the two smaller sections quietly clanging against each other, like some kind of over-sized windchime. He parks the Massey with its rear wheels half filling the gap in the hedgerow, pointing backwards across the wheat field.

42

Getting messier

"I think it's time we left." Lucy says as a bar stool bounces off the wall just behind Alex's head.

"You think we'll get out of here alive?" Alex replies. The bar is reminiscent of a fight scene from a cowboy movie.

John and Cliff walk into the room, John grabs the hollering young soldier, who threw the stool, by the collar and slugs him playfully in the stomach, "CLEAR OFF, DICKHEAD." He throws the lad towards the door and carries on, joining Cliff with Lucy and Alex. "How are you enjoying the Anglians' hospitality?"

"They're a lovely bunch of lads." Lucy says smiling. Anyone who has served would know what to expect from soldiers when a recipe like this comes together; neither are surprised at how the night has unfolded. "We were just about to leave."

"Glad we caught you then." says Cliff, "What are you drinking?"

Alex smiles, knowing that they're staying for at least one more. "I'll have a Greene King, please." he has become rather taken by the Indian Pale Ale that is brewed just around the corner from the hotel.

"Another gin and tonic, Lucy?"

"Go on then, Cliff. Thanks."

Cliff returns with the drinks to a quiet table. The four reflect in silence, amongst the carnage going on around them; something of a metaphor for the 'on-going' Blunt investigation.

"He had a lot of time for you, Alex." John says, in the vein of a jealous big brother. "Since the day he met you at the boxing gym, he never stopped going on about you."

"Thanks, John." Alex says, meaning it deeply. It means a lot to know that Craig thought highly of him, but it means so much more to hear it from the likes of John. "He loved you blokes too," Alex nods towards John and Cliff, "I could tell you and Mark were his top boys, in more ways than one." Alex's bottom lip quivers as he thinks of Mark, the brightest and friendliest of the old crew who had welcomed him in and made him feel protected from the other ruffians.

"I'll be at that tart's funeral next week." The others laugh, John's bond with Mark was such that he still rips him after his death, "The family only want close friends and Hereford blokes to go."

"The other family, then?" Lucy offers.

"Yeah, family's all that matters at times like this."

43

Epiphany

The night had gone on into the early hours, Alex and Lucy feeling much more comfortable in the presence of the two men with monstrous physical presence, and their group had been joined by several other friends of theirs, all of similar build or reputation. John had gone to lengths to introduce them to several of his comrades, and generously described his talents and qualities. Alex had come upstairs with a warm glow, not just from the whiskey chasers.

He is woken by a soft, sensual kiss on the lips. "How's your head, tough guy?" she asks.

"What?" he asks, a little groggy and confused, and feeling like shit.

"You let your super-modest mask slip after about the third measure." she laughs at him sympathetically.

"I wasn't a complete twat, was I?" He lays, eyes closed, arms up over his head.

"No, they liked you, and knew you were drunk." She rolls over and hugs him condescendingly, but with a smile that says that she is proud of what he is becoming. "You're like one of the family now."

Never had the word 'family' meant so much to Alex in a military context. His troop-mates in basic training, and lengthy trade training had been close; they'd been through a lot together. He had good mates at the field units he'd served with, but having spent a lot of time in the gym as a physical training instructor; it had been a competitive environment and he hadn't got that close to them, only a few tight mates that he'd deployed with in small teams on operations. The concentrated, highly active period that he has spent with his new mates has developed strong bonds that will last a lifetime; he now understands better how these guys are so together, and feels honoured to be let into that, even just a bit.

The word 'family' rolls through his head over and over again, he thinks of his younger sister, what she's up to, his parents, in their own separate lives, both remarried and happy. The family that he's been taken into is completely different, more animal in nature, more physically protective, but more dangerous and vibrant. He feels disloyal about comparing his flesh and blood against his Forces family, but they are so different that neither is better or worse than the other. He thinks about Tony Blunt's family dynamics; the awful grouping that is his strange mother, horrendous ex-wife, and his two disaffected kids, enough to unbalance anyone, but apparently Blunt still hadn't given up on his kids - *maybe family is important to him too.* Having been rejected and abused by his Forces family, Alex is not surprised that Blunt has turned to an alternative family – his Islamist brotherhood – he wonders if what Tony feels for them is anything like what he feels towards John, Lucy, Cliff and the others who he has met. Through all his trials and tribulations, who would Tony turn to? Alex thinks back to himself – *when the shit hits the fan, who do I want to call most?*

Alex jumps up from the bed, "Blunt's mum and kids - are their phones on the monitored list?"

"His mum's is, but I don't think the kids are."

Alex grabs his phone from the side of the bed, "If he's going to call anyone, it'll be his mum or his kids." He dials. "Hi, Charlie, it's Alex, where are you?"

"Mornin' Alex, I'm at Gold Command in New Scotland Yard's planning suite. Where are you?" she pauses, *"How was Craig's funeral?"* she adds,

remembering Alex and most of the rest of the team taking leave of the investigation for something important.

"It was epic. Listen, I've had a thought; are Blunt's kids' phone numbers on the monitoring list?" There is only silence in reply. "Charlie?"

"I'm thinking, hang on, I'm on my laptop." there are some rapid keystrokes, *"How the fuck have I missed that?"* she says angrily, with hints of desperation and exasperation.

"You've got their numbers on record, can you have their histories checked over the last three weeks? Any new numbers in their incoming calls."

"Yes, Alex, okay," she snaps, *"I know how to do my job, thank you. I'll call you back."*

*

There are some rough faces on some of those that make it down to breakfast. Lucy laughs at Alex as his pained face hangs over the scant cooked breakfast from the buffet selection that offered so much more. "You look how I feel."

"Tell me again why we're out of bed so early?"

"We need to get back to London, Charlie needs us." Lucy says trying to enthuse him.

"Really? I don't think there's much we can do. She seems to have it all sewn up with the Police."

Well technically; I am the Police." she says, smiling sarcastically.

"Morning, pissheads." John says across the restaurant, causing everyone in the room to look around.

"Hi, John. You look fresh." Lucy says, genuinely surprised that he is even out of his pit, let alone bouncing around so spritely at 07:30hrs.

"I've been for a run down the river for a few miles to sort myself out, it's beautiful down there." He looks around the restaurant. "Anyone for a brew top-up?" John gets the drinks, a mountainous full English breakfast and sits down to join them.

Alex is no stranger to running off a hangover but has been so dehydrated by the whiskies that his head pounds every time he moves; his brain feels like a walnut rattling around inside his skull. The sight of John troughing down a huge fork-full of sausage and egg doesn't help. His phone buzzing in his pocket diverts his attention from the sickly feeling.

"Hi, Charlie." Alex says, looking at John for his reaction. He smiles and flicks his eyebrows up as he shovels in the next mouthful.

"*Alex, Blunt's daughter's number had an incoming call from a previously unknown number yesterday afternoon, the call went unanswered.*" Charlie's voice sounds a little nervy, Alex cannot tell if this is due to the pressure that she is under in London, or if this lead might be something real. "*The calling number is brand new to the network, it had never been used before.*"

This sounds promising, he has one question on his mind – *was the call made from London*, but he is taken by surprise:

"*Mast triangulation is not that accurate, due to the rural area, but indicates that the call was made from somewhere near Grantham.*"

"Shit. Blunt had searched a business in Grantham, Professor Banbury mentioned it in his back-brief." says Alex. Lucy's head shoots around at him.

"*What sort of business?*"

"A metal foundry."

"And you didn't think to mention this to the rest of us?"

"No, we thought he'd just stumbled onto the site as part of his engineering research." Alex and Charlie share a moment of confusion at what possible relevance a foundry, out in the sticks, over a hundred miles north of London might have to Tony Blunt. "Do you think it's worth checking out?"

"Yes, I fookin do. Dig out the address and get it to me, like; now." Charlie barks. *"I'll send a local unit to check it out, but I want you and John up there pronto – is he there?"* Alex hands his phone to John.

"All right, Sweet-cheeks?" John's smile quickly morphs into a focused stare into nothing as he listens intently. "Got it. Hopefully see you this afternoon." He rings off and hands the phone back to Alex. "Let's go." He shoves his half-eaten plate of breakfast into the middle of the table, takes a slurp of coffee and stands up.

"Where?" Lucy asks.

"Alex and I are going to Grantham."

"What about me?"

"You kick Cliff out of bed and take him down to London, Charlie'll direct you from there."

44

Value adding tasks

Tony had slept soundly, treating himself to a night of comfort in the Duffield's spare room. He had set the bedside alarm clock to a lazy 07:40hrs, not wanting to be up and about too early, pottering around, creating opportunities to fuck things up. The plan is simple, but his mind wonders as he lays in the downy soft bed, thinking about maximising the impact that his masterpiece will have on the world. This morning's activities will be largely about preparing a couple of neat additions to the plan that will make it truly horrific, that will make it a real message to those who think that he isn't capable of anything.

Fresh and clean out of the shower, clean underwear, but back in his stinking outdoor wear, Tony takes the keys to the big John Deere from the hook by the front door, picks up his axe and walks across the peaceful yard. The morning song of the birds the only sound to be heard, he finds it so much more enjoyable when it isn't waking him up.

The John Deere is a big green monster, and far newer than the Massey, it's like a giant Tonka toy. He turns the key in door handle, that's fitted neatly into the modern looking glass door, and climbs into the tractor. The cab looks like a cross between that of the space shuttle and an early learning play area – everything is rounded plastic in soft colours. The basic controls are in the same layout as the Massey's, but there is more information; labels and symbols embossed into things. He starts the engine; a puff of black smoke blows out of the over-sized exhaust that towers out of the bonnet. Using the nearest of three gear levers, he puts it into first, and drives out of the bay.

Tony heads right, then spins it round, arcing left, parallel with the front of the farmhouse, and reverses towards the towing eye of the dilapidated petrol tanker. The clear view from the back of the cab makes lining up the hook slightly less painful than it might have been, taking only two attempts to get it perfect. The weight of the trailer means that there is no possibility of wiggle room, but Tony has the hook perfectly in line with the eye, which is currently just above the height of the tractor's towing hook top plate.

Dismounting from the cab, he looks at the structure of the trailer; it is in an even poorer state than he remembers from his recce; the light of day showing deep rust scars on every beam. Fortunately, the jockey wheel mechanism had received a generous application of thick industrial grease, which has taken on a life of its own with all the grime, insects, pollen, and dust that had accumulated in it, but still serves its purpose. Tony turns the handle, which moves with ease, lowering the eye to just above the hook's tip. He hops back into the cab, reverses the small matter of centimetres, and then raises the hook. The trailer groans as its weight is again shifted. Tony secures the hook to the eye with a locking pin.

With the huge fuel cell attached to the tractor, he grabs his axe from the cab and moves to the off-side pair of wheels of the trailer. Rudimental chocks, cut from thick logs, are in place on the outside of both of the wheels on this side. Tony hooks the blade of his axe behind the front wheel chock and yanks it hard. The wedge crumbles into pieces as it is pulled free. Tony scrapes out the larger remaining fragments of rotten wood from the path of the tyre.

He doesn't imagine that old man Duffield will have bothered putting chocks on the nearside, judging from the trailer's proximity to the wall, and he doesn't much fancy checking amongst the thick vegetation that has grown there. He trusts that if a chock were to be present, it would crumble in a similar vein.

He jumps back into the cab and gently edges the big John Deere forward. The immensely powerful tug of the tractor is unforgiving on the old trailer, its forward movement, however slow in acceleration, puts strain on the decaying structure. The massively heavy fuel cell lurches as its partially seized axles begin to turn. Tony hears a loud 'pop' and looks back with concern, realising that about fifteen tons of pressure is now on one rotting tyre on the left side. It isn't possible to go much slower, so he continues regardless.

As the wheels move onto the rougher ground of the main square of the yard, the second left tyre pops, causing the fuel tank to lean heavily. The rims of wheel hubs scuff and scrape across the broken patches of concrete. Tony holds his breath, hoping that the trailer will hold together long enough to make it onto the softer ground of the wheat field.

Tony drives over the smooth bridge of dried mud adjoining the yard to the field, but his hopes for an easy ride over the wheat are dashed as the giant wheels of the tractor hit the first pair of tramlines; the deep pair of ruts formed by multiple passes, probably of the very same tractor that he is driving. Tony's route does not cut straight across the ruts, his bearing is east-south-east, meaning that all four wheels of the tractor hit each rut individually, making the vehicle buoy violently side-to-side, causing the green monster to yank at the delicate chassis of the old tanker trailer.

The front right wheel of the trailer thuds into the first big rut, snapping the rotten welds that hold the triangular bracket through which the axle threads. The axles and wheel assemblies are torn from the undercarriage of the trailer, leaving a twisted pile of metal and rubber squashed into the dirt and wheat. The tanker is now sliding over the crops on its underside, the beams of the sub-frame have become stabilising skids on either side. The ride is no more comfortable for Tony, but the fuel chamber is moving smoothly, gliding over the ruts effortlessly with gentle bobs and weaves.

Nearing the end of his four-hundred metre journey across the field, Tony straightens up, pointing the tractor unit to face directly onto the cutting slope, aiming at the right side of the gap that he has created in the fence. He jumps down from the cab and gives the tank a quick all-round visual inspection. There is no sign of the tank leaking anywhere and the tap is still accessible at the rear of what is left of the trailer. He picks up the end of the trailing delivery hose and stows it over the tap.

*

Tony enjoys the slow walk back to the farmhouse, swinging his axe playfully at the swathes of wheat heads. The long scar left by the tanker through the perfect pattern of the wheat field seems somehow satisfying, representative perhaps of his aim to cause disruption and anarchy. He taps the rear wheel of the old Massey Ferguson as he passes it on the way back into the yard, now filled with contentment that everything is falling perfectly into place, now feeling completely committed to what he must do if he is to earn the respect he deserves.

He strides back into the farmhouse as though it were his own. He places his axe against the wall and walks into the kitchen. "Don't get up, Mary." he waves the palm of his hand at the body laying prostrate on the floor behind the table and sets about the cupboards, quickly finding a stash of shopping bags. He selects a nice heavy Marks and Spencer's 'bag for life' and takes it with him into the study and begins to unbox the slug ammunition into it.

45

Cursory look

By the time the task filters down to PC Andy Harrison it sounds pretty lame, but having spent nearly twenty years patrolling Grantham and its backwaters; he isn't expecting his Saturday morning to be much more interesting than any other. His partner, newly assigned from training, is still full of energy and enthusiasm, and sees the adventure in everything.

"Sounds like a special mission to me – orders from London to track down a potential terrorist." Asram says, pulling the collar of his issued black polo shirt straight from underneath his fluorescent yellow stab vest.

"A wild goose chase, five miles out into the middle of nowhere to check on a business property that isn't even open?" Andy replies, regretting his cynicism before he has even finished his sentence. He has enjoyed his years of service; he remembers being young and excitable like Asram – *encourage him, don't do him down.* He smiles at the bright new copper, "Though you never know, we might get lucky, catch us a real villain – you might be a hero in your first month."

Turning left after the garden centre off the Belton High Road, the two officers mentally ready themselves; Asram for action - Andy for the anti-climax that doubtlessly awaits.

*

The Vauxhall Astra patrol car rolls along past the Austin & Sons' office front, the officers' eyes are all over the building, surrounding land, and hedgerows. Asram revs the engine a little more than is really required as he turns the wheel, taking them up onto the slope of the entryway to the car park.

"Looks quiet." says Asram. Andy bites his lip to withhold the 'I told you so' and channels his positivity to try and make this a learning experience for the lad.

"Stay alert. If this chap is about; he could be a handful." They get out of the car and get fresh eyes on the place.

"Shall I have a walk around?" Asram asks.

"Yeah but be careful. Shout if you see anyone."

"What, and you'll come running." Asram smirks.

"I can still move when I need to." Andy grabs the modest roll of belly that's sneaking out between his belt and his vest, "This is for momentum – there's no stopping me once I get going."

"I hope I'm in as good a shape as you when I'm your age." Asram says as he turns to walk towards the back of the building.

Andy watches him disappear around the corner, then heads for the path at the building's front. He looks through the window into the office. Seeing nothing of interest, he moves into the shade offered by the doorway's canopy and steps up onto the plinth to take a look in through the window of the front door. His eye is caught by the glow of the alarm panel; all seems to be in order there. He looks around the waiting room, the carpet looks filthy and stained, mostly covered by one large blemish that looks like someone has spilled an entire can of oil, the wet-looking patch, darker than the rest of the carpet.

"Everything okay, Andy?" He is startled by Asram, who appears, as if from nowhere, beside him.

"Yeah, all good. Anything round back?"

"Nothing; all secure and no sign of life."

"Let's go and see if old man Duffield's seen anything."

46

Who's there?

There is a heavy knock at the door. Tony freezes. He knows that old Mary can't be seen from the window, but he also knows that the door is unlocked. He opens the breach of the shotgun, loads two shells and makes his way into the hall.

"HELLO, MR DUFFIELD, ARE YOU THERE? IT'S THE POLICE."

Fuck. Tony is worried, not about being caught for murder, but for the risk to the completion of his mission. He edges closer towards the door, but not so close that he might be seen from the kitchen window. He looks at his axe but knows that it is his secondary weapon for now. He raises the long barrels of the shotgun to chest height.

"HENRY, MARY, ARE YOU THERE?" PC Harrison shouts. Tony's eyes flick to the door handle as it snatches down and the door hints at opening.

"It's not locked." he hears a younger voice say. Light streams into the hall as the door slowly opens. Tony locks eyes with Asram as he comes into view, his finger exerts the final few pounds of pressure required to release the shot, firing the composite slug into Asram's chest, sending him flying onto his back. Tony launches himself forward to the doorway, flicking the barrel selector across, and turns the gun on Andy. With time and range on his side, Blunt raises his aim to Andy's head. Andy is petrified, frozen to the spot – *say something, do something.* "Please." is all he can muster. Blunt pulls the trigger, taking the top half of Andy's head clean off.

High on adrenalin, Tony is barely aware of what is going on around him. He hears the gasps and gargles of the young officer. His first thought is to retrieve his axe, but he sees the copper reaching for his radio. Tony races forward and stands over him; he is similar in looks to his friend Zafir. "Are you Muslim?"

His eyes glaring with fear, Asram nods desperately as he coughs blood over himself. "Ana asif." Tony apologises. He raises his right foot high in the air, trying not to look as Asram uses the last of his strength to raise his arms in defence. Tony brings the thick welted heel of his boot down viciously on the constable's face. He repeatedly stamps down until he is sure that Asram is dead.

47

Don't spare the horses

John finally manages to pass a Skoda estate that has taken an age to overtake a pair of duelling lorries. The third lane is now clear; he accelerates, the needle springs towards the hundred miles-per-hour graticule. "Wish it was four lanes all the way." he says, having enjoyed the wide stretch up as far as Peterborough. John's phone rings through the car's hands-free system, the name 'Sweet-cheeks' comes up on the central screen.

"Is that Cliff?" Alex asks, setting himself off laughing. John looks mildly embarrassed. "Fucking nob 'ead." He presses a button on the steering wheel. "Hi, Charlie. I'm in the car with Alex, you're on speaker phone. We're on the A1 about twenty minutes away from the location."

"How fast are you going? You only left forty minutes ago? Anyway, listen, I've been onto Lincolnshire Police for an update, and they reckon they've lost contact with the unit they sent out to the foundry. They haven't reported in since arriving there, and they can't raise them. I've told them to send another car, but they don't have anyone nearby."

"Roger, understood." says John, "We'll ring you back when we get there." he ends the call.

Alex brings up the area on his phone, "It's pretty remote, it might just be a comms dead-spot." he offers.

"They checked in on arrival." says John.

"Fair one. Their Airwave system is pretty good too, it should work anywhere."

Alex zooms in on the image of the immediate vicinity of the foundry and begins to think on a tactical level. "It's fairly exposed. How do you want to play it?"

John takes the phone from Alex and holds it over the steering wheel. Alex is immediately on edge, as John's eyes flick between the road and the screen. "Ideally, I'd come in from the South and CTR from around the back of the farm, but I don't think we've got time for that. If it's just Blunt operating in isolation; then I'm happy to go in with a little more haste than I usually would." He looks in again at the screen and stretches out the image further. "The route in from the east along the track gets good natural cover from that hedgerow, I say we stop short to the limit of noise, run across the field and go in around the back."

The limit of noise is not a set distance, it is how far away you think you might be heard from. Good infantry fieldcraft is to place your sentries at the limit of noise, so that you can spot the enemy before they are able to hear you, moving them in or out, dependant on how much noise you plan to be making at any given time.

Alex takes his phone back, to have a look at the ground in detail. "Sounds like a plan."

48

Final positioning

The kitchen table barely conceals the mounting pile of bodies, but Tony is not concerned; in around forty minutes his masterpiece will be complete, a few extra bodies will be the least of anyone's worries, if anything it will act as a distraction while he makes his escape. He walks with purpose from the farmhouse to the Massey Ferguson, the reloaded shotgun in his right hand, his axe in his left, the bag of ammunition swinging from around its handle. He loads his weaponry onto the floor of the cab of the rearward facing tractor, climbs in and starts her up.

He sets off for the final time across the field, dodging around the wheel assembly of the fuel tanker, but then settling into the path already sledged through the wheat. The smaller, lighter tractor feels far less stable than the giant John Deere, reversing is further disconcerting, but the heavy ten metres of steel dragging behind it has something of a steadying effect, like a huge tail.

He soon arrives at the east side of the field, pulling up alongside the tanker. He steps down into the swaying wheat, grabs the shotgun and bag of shells, and walks in front of the John Deere, out of the crops and onto the slope of the cutting by the cut end of the fence. He looks over the ground down the hill to his right; he needs a decent bit of vegetation near to the tunnel mouth, but not too near. He picks his spot, ten metres up from the tracks, thirty metres north of the tunnel entrance, he places the bag down and lays the shotgun over the top of it. "Weapon loaded, safety off." he says aloud, announcing its state as if handing it to someone else.

The earth begins to shudder, and the associated whirring sound pounds, gradually louder as the 08:39 out of Grantham bursts from the tunnel, almost up to its top cruising speed. Tony watches as the engine and three carriages of the local train pass him by. He checks his watch; 08:42, *bang on time.* He sets his countdown timer to thirty-two minutes. "Let's get busy."

49

I don't like this

"We're within a mile. Any update on the cops?" John asks.

"No, still no sign of them, another unit's on its way, but won't be there for another twenty minutes at least. Keep me updated." Charlie rings off.

John decelerates rapidly as he reaches the corner of Gonerby Grange Lane, at the end of which is sited Austin & Sons' Foundry. "It's just shy of two K' down here." Alex says as the car creeps around the corner. The lane is shrouded on both sides with tall, thick hedges, giving the men hope that their approach will be provided with good cover, but this soon reduces and disappears, intermittently reappearing as they progress to the west along the narrow winding road. The countryside is rolling enough that visibility to their front is never more than a couple of hundred metres: ideal for their purposes.

Alex keeps check on their distance from the foundry, monitoring their location on the satellite image on the car's satnav. They drive between the red brick walls of a flat bridge, passing over the railway track. "About three hundred metres further." Alex says. John slows to almost walking speed. "It's on the right down here." Alex adds.

The bushes are opaque on the left, but light and patchy on the right which thins completely towards the foundry. Alex looks through them out onto open wheat fields, the verge on that side is low with no ditch. John pulls over onto the offside a hundred metres short of the target building. "It's that building behind the hedge." says Alex.

John assesses the ground; "The plan's good." He steps onto the bare earth left unsown at the edge of the field and walks quickly towards the foundry. Still without a line of sight to anything beyond the hedge, other than the rooftop, John leads Alex out into the wheat, cutting the corner to the north end of the hedge. The back of the building is a solid wall of panelling and is unremarkable, just the sight of it gives Alex a sad sense of reality, having built up his hopes that this might be a real lead, he realises that in all probability Blunt is long gone and the two officers have just become otherwise engaged. John seems more focused, his eyes hawking back and forth. "You head round that way; I'll check the car park."

Alex walks the path down the east side of the building, he presses on the fire door, but it is firmly locked. The passage is silent, not even a birdsong. The cover offered by the thick hawthorn gives him a modicum of comfort in seclusion, whilst simultaneously giving him a touch of the willies. Alex had only seen Blunt on one occasion, at the Hodgehill orders group; the day that he had later gone off grid. He had cast an ominous figure, big on the scale of Cliff, not so muscular, but had that look of natural toughness, he had a haunting look etched on his face that gave a clue that he was holding an inner power that was waiting to be unleashed. Alex has no idea what Blunt is planning, but he knows that he must be stopped, and he thanks his stars that he has John with him.

Alex slows as he reaches the front of the building. He cautiously sneaks a peek around the corner. Glancing over the ornamental garden, he sees the entrance to the farm, and into the first couple of its vehicle sheds, but that is all. Slowly stepping out onto the front path, confident that all is clear, he scopes the facia of the foundry office building; it seems as benign as the rest of the place. He relaxes a little more as the lack of activity becomes apparent.

Alex steps up onto the entrance's plinth, growing braver, he moves closer to the door. Looking through the window into the waiting room, he sees nothing of note, he looks left into the office, not seeing a great deal of detail through the adjoining doorway, he then moves along for a better view through the office window.

"Found anything?" says John, startling Alex as he emerges from the recessed doorway.

"Argh, ya fucker." Alex jumps. John laughs at him. "Nothing round there. Can't see anything in here. What about you?"

"Nothing much, all secure, but there's an abandoned cop car in the car park."

"Where the fuck are the coppers then?" The two men exchange concerned looks.

"Could be anywhere. I'd say inside the foundry itself or having a look round the farm." surmises John.

"The alarm looked set to me." Alex says, flicking an eye over his shoulder towards the front door.

"Let's have a look." John brushes past Alex and steps up to the door. "Yeah, that's set." He takes a closer look at the waiting room. John has more experience than most with blood, and concealing it, and recognises it in the carpet right away. "Someone's been murdered right here." he says with zero doubt in his voice. "Look." He points to the floor beneath his feet.

Alex can barely make out the narrow tyre track in what he assumes must be blood on the concrete step. He suddenly feels distinctly vulnerable. "What are we going to do? Break in?"

"No point. There's not likely to be anyone left alive in there, not with the alarm sensors on. Let's check a bit further afield."

"What do you think's happened?" Alex asks.

"Fuck knows. This was nothing to do with the coppers, it's not that fresh, but it stinks of Blunt. Maybe they're off chasing him somewhere, but it doesn't explain why they haven't reported in and are out of contact. Let's have a squizz at that farm. Are you tooled up?"

Alex shrugs, a little embarrassed, and waves his mobile phone back at John.

"Let's see how far that gets you." John says.

*

After another consultation of the satellite image, John decides to at least make an attempt to conceal their infiltration into the farm complex by heading anti-clockwise around it to the back of the farmhouse.

"Looks pretty quiet." John says looking through the greenery at the bottom of the back garden. Come on, let's get moving." John pushes through the branches and steps over into the middle pen of the compost heap and jumps down onto the grass, he takes a knee while he waits for Alex to join him, his eyes fixed on the farmhouse.

"Shit." Alex whispers as he sinks and slides into the sticky compost of the third pen. He joins John low down on the grass.

That'll keep you tactical, for fuck's sake, Alex; he'll smell us coming." John laughs as he moves off, keeping low as he gorilla-runs to the south-west corner of the house. He looks in through the window into the living room, he squints to see through the doorway into the study - "Fuck." he says under his breath. Alex looks at him, expecting him to elaborate. "There's fucking shotgun shell boxes all over the floor."

"The phone option isn't looking so bad now is it?" Alex smirks.

John looks at Alex with a mild amount of disgust and exudes the attitude of a man accepting a challenge. "You call Charlie and hurry the cavalry along if you like, but I ain't slowing down.

Alex redials Charlie's number, John slides a stout iron cosh out from a pocket inside his jacket sleeve and heads in through the unlocked conservatory door.

*

After giving Charlie the quickest of updates, Alex puts his phone back in his pocket on the hoof as he rushes to catch up with John. He ignores the stairs for now, only paying enough attention to reassure himself that no one is looking down on him. The corridor takes him straight to the front door, he tentatively looks to his right, into the kitchen. John is knelt over a pile of bodies behind the table, pulling the radio from the breast plate of a practically headless Policeman's yellow vest. He squeezes its pressel, "Hello, all stations, all stations, officers down, officers down, officers down at Duffield's Farm, north of Belton, out."

John drops the radio, pushes past Alex, and creeps along the hallway to the bottom of the stairs, he glides up them smoothly and silently. Alex can hear him moving between rooms but hears no other disturbance. John is soon back with him as he begins to feel less and less well, stood looking over the bodies. "Alex, get a grip fella, I need you to be on the ball." John grabs him firmly by the shoulder, turning him away from the carnage.

"How long have they been dead?" Alex asks, more to get his mind working, rather than to add value to their search.

John looks at the bodies and applies what he has learned from the terrible things that he's seen over the years. "Clearly the cops bought it in the last hour; they only got the task as we left Bury. The old lady looks like she's been drying out a while, maybe last night?" John can tell Alex is struggling, but he doesn't have the words or the time to counsel him. "Come on, mate, we've got to find this lunatic and quick." He looks Alex in the eyes with a hard stare.

"I'm on it." Alex says, trying to look confident. "Where next?"

"The yard." John says nodding out through the kitchen window.

50

Ramping it up

Jumping into the old Massey Ferguson, trying to keep control of his excitement, Tony puts the smaller of the two tractors into reverse. He edges past the big John Deere and across the threshold of the cutting. The angle of the slope seems far steeper from Tony's new perspective. Leaning backwards, he trusts the weight of the tiny front wheels, the forks and, of course, his perfectly cut beams, to stop him from tipping over down the hill.

He soon settles into the gradient and is most of the way down, when gravity takes hold of the ten-metre beam, shifting its pull against the forks into a push as its grip on the grass slips. Tony is not fazed by the slight change in balance, the chunky tall rear wheels are almost at the trackside and the tractor feels stable.

Tony feathers the accelerator and massages the clutch to coax the old Massey up onto the compacted layer of hardcore, then a little harder to get it over the first rail. Tony's soul is filled with an inherent sense of being in the wrong place. From his earliest memories he has had it drummed into him to 'stay off the tracks', the same as anyone, even in the midst of his terrible mission, he finds conflict with his natural good nature when doing something so fundamentally wrong as encroaching onto a railway.

He has to be aggressive with the throttle to bump the old tractor across the rails until its rear wheels both sit between the carriageways. Tony pulls hard down on the left side of the steering wheel, causing the front end to pivot round to his right, pushing the rear right wheel easily over the inside rail of the south-bound tracks. The right front wheel bounces up and over the same rail, and the tractor is positioned perfectly to continue its journey towards the tunnel. Tony is happy with the way that the driving has gone, as a completely novice tractor driver, but he is less pleased about his failure to calculate that his beautifully cut beam would not follow him across the rails. It hangs awkwardly off to the side, inside the inner northbound rail. He thinks about the weight of the beam, and what he has at his disposal to help him to quickly move it across two rails.

*

Having judged two-hundred metres distance into the tunnel, by counting twenty joints between the individual sections of rail, Tony stops the Massey. He jumps down and walks back, into the headlight beams of the tractor, looking at the unexpected task in front of him.

He moves to the pointed end of the girder and stands over it. Luckily, the angle that he has cut into the end of the girder provides a surface that will aid the lateral slide of the beam over the rails. The central wall of the beam also provides a good handhold.

With brute force, he drags it sideways over the inside rail of the northbound track without too much difficulty. The right point of the beam crashes down onto the knuckle of one of the fastenings that hold the rail down, it slips off that and crunches into the concrete of the sleeper that the fastener holds the rail to. Tony takes hold of the girder again and tries to lift it, but it doesn't budge. He focuses his effort, a second time he powers all his strength through his legs, back, arms and shoulders – he just about gets it to move a few centimetres. He stands up, breaths hard, and looks at his watch – *nine minutes, still plenty of time*. Tony walks over to the forks assembly and turns the key in the second padlock; both the small girders fall to the floor. He picks up the bigger of the two sections and takes it back to the point. Tony pushes three-quarters of the section under the problem piece, flange edges pointing down into the hardcore, and then levers it up. The ten-metre beam, nearing half a metric ton, moves with comparative ease towards the next rail. The rest of the way is not so easy, it takes Tony several failed attempts to get the beam up onto the rail, eventually getting it over with the help of the sole of a boot at the risk of a couple of toes. He shuffles the beam further over, so that it touches the inside of the outer rail of the southbound track.

Satisfied with the beam's position, he makes his way back to the tractor, he climbs the steps up to the cab, but stays hanging out of the door frame, looking up to the ceiling. He leans into the cab and searches the controls for a likely looking switch, he flicks a couple, hoping not to initiate any unwanted mechanics, but his luck is in and the spotlights mounted on the front of the cab provide a shock of light, illuminating the tunnel like daylight. He clearly sees the recesses in the concrete form of the tunnel sections – the next one is just a couple of metres behind the fork assembly – *perfect.*

Tony jumps down into the driver's seat and works out what he needs to do. He selects reverse and sets the tractor moving backwards slowly, at the same time he raises the forks, waiting patiently, his eyes almost closed, as he focuses on sensing the moment of impact. There is a light jolt, and a few sparks emanate from above the forks as the two corner edges of the girder flanges strike the ceiling – Tony kills the lifting mechanism and drags the beam across the ceiling until it hits the vertical edge of the ceiling section. This jolts on the tractor's chassis, Tony feels it tilt forward – he has the clutch down in an instant. He kills the engine and puts on the handbrake.

Tony picks up his precious axe on his way out of the cab of the Massey for the final time and locks its door. He picks up the shortest section of beam and moves towards the pointy end of the long beam. He picks his spot, under the main girder where he thinks his fifty-centimetre section will fit and stands it in the gap. It nestles nicely in the hardcore, leaning at almost the right angle to support a load coming down through the beam. Tony picks up his axe and uses the flat back of its head to tap the short beam firmly into place at the perfect angle. The metre-long section slots in just as nicely. Tony is ecstatic - the guts of his plan is in place; he just has the icing left to put on the cake.

51

Taste of prey

Alex falters in the kitchen doorway, unsure of how to proceed in an unarmed search for a murderer who is. John has no such qualms, if he does; he's not showing them – he hustles past Alex into the hall, grabs the handle of the front door and pulls it down under control. John opens the door slowly, his field of vision growing from right to left as the edge of the door exposes more of the yard as it opens.

All is quiet, most of the structures in view are open and there is no sign of life, not a noise, not a movement. John lets the door open all the way and beckons Alex out from the kitchen. "We'll search the place, but it seems dead," he laughs to himself, nodding back towards the kitchen, "literally."

Alex shakes his head, "I'll keep saying it, John, you're one sick puppy." The black humour is one of the things Alex misses most from the Army, but he had never taken it to the level that John still does.

"We'll start round that way." John points to the left; the only area they haven't had a clear view of so far. John moves fast along the front of the farmhouse, stopping on the corner to look around the yard's annexed area. He pauses for a few seconds, allowing his ears to adjust to the silence of being stood still, another few seconds to give anyone in the area a chance to move, to make noise – still nothing. They systematically check every building, finding no one. They begin to move faster as they simply walk past the open-fronted, and mostly empty, vehicle bays.

"Where's the farmer?" Alex asks as he goes over the situation in his head.

"He'll be dead somewhere, no doubt." John replies, not yet feeling that it's time to start analysing.

Alex instinctively looks out to the fields at the talk of the farmer. "What's that?" he says recognising that something is not right in the field.

John looks across through the gap in the hedgerow, between the big silver barn and the farmhouse. He sees the deep scarring in the wheat, and the fresh, white scar in the concrete leading to it. "That's it. I don't know what it is, but that's it." John says.

*

John runs over to where the scar emerges from inside the open silver barn. "He's dragged something out of there," he says looking into the barn, "and taken it over that field."

"Along with something else, that's missing its wheels." Alex says looking at the wreckage and the two vastly different trails scrapped through the crops. They run to the gap in the hedge, the nearer vantage point bringing the full field into view. They can see a green tractor with a giant, drooping bubble hanging from the back of it. They both stand in silence, watching as a tiny figure appears from the verge beyond it, the person approaches the tractor with something long in his hand. He walks to the rear of the trailer.

"That's fucking him!" John says. Alex hadn't thought it might be anyone else. The pair look at each other. "What the fuck's he up to?"

"That's the rail line." Alex says, his mind skipping back to the detail of the overhead imagery.

52

Race

Tony is happy with the condition of the tanker, from what he can see; there is no obvious damage to the important, and only remaining beams of the sub-frame. Standing at the back of the unit, he grasps the large, round aluminium tap and turns it anti-clockwise. He grabs the nozzle, unhooking the hose from behind the tap and squeezes the trigger; the hissing and splattering of running liquid gratifies Tony, who hadn't thought to test the tap or delivery system before going through all this additional aggravation. He flicks the locking mechanism over the trigger and drops the nozzle to the ground.

The petrol looks somehow dry as it seeps into the earth between the crushed stems of wheat; Tony steps back before it reaches his feet. He takes a slow look back along the stark scar that he has left across the field. He sees something unexpected - there are two people at the farmyard entrance. A thousand thoughts run through his head, who they might be: security forces, people from the foundry, or their security firm, farmhands, dog-walkers. He is unsure of how worried he should be; not worried at all if they stay where they are, but then, they start to run – "Shit."

*

Tony throws his axe into the cab and jumps into the driver's seat. He turns the ignition of the big green beast of a tractor, it rumbles into life. He throws the lever into gear and goes to set off at best pace, only just remembering in time the fragile state of what he is towing. He allows the revs to fall and gently lifts his foot off the clutch. The tractor rolls over the brow onto the bank of the cutting; Tony feathers the brake and looks behind him to see that the tanker is following dead straight. As it crests over the fulcrum of the top of the hill it slumps over to the right, Tony feels the tonnes of weight pushing the tractor forward. The beam of the sub-frame grips into the grassy bank, preventing the tanker from slipping sideways.

Tony releases the brake as the front of the tractor gets closer to the bottom of the slope, knowing that he will need a little momentum to get over the rails. The increase in speed and thickening of vegetation reduces the penetration of the beam into the soft soil of the cutting; it begins to slip, the fuel cell slides and rolls, twisting on the hook. Tony reacts by stepping on the accelerator, he steers right to try and put the tractor back under the tanker. The front of the tractor jumps as the sharp decline of the cutting meets the sharp incline of the edge of the hardcore. The tractor bounces and writhes as it struggles for grip on the rails whilst being tugged violently from behind by the tanker. Tony gives the accelerator more and wrestles the steering wheel round. The tractor's rear wheels bound over the first rail as the tanker thumps into the channel between the bank and the hardcore.

Tony is back in control but running out of time. He throttles up hard and turns the wheel half right, dragging the tanker up onto the rails. He has a strategy planned for how and where to place it, but now he is only concerned with getting it to the site.

He drives into the tunnel as fast as he thinks the tanker can stand. The rear strut of the tanker's sub-frame settles nicely on the inner rail of the northbound track; it scrapes along it almost smoothly, sending a steady shower of sparks the short distance down to the ground – they fizzle out just as the trailing pipe, still pissing petrol, slides on past.

Tony arrives at the long beam and turns the wheel to the left to head underneath it. The John Deere doesn't quite fit beneath the beam and Tony isn't going to risk his structure's integrity. He stops with the cab's roof as close to the girder as he can get it.

The rush is now back on. Tony grabs his axe, leaps from the cab, and sets off sprinting to the mouth of the tunnel. He knows that the distance across the field is over four hundred metres, he knows the distance to his shotgun is about two hundred and fifty – how slow was he down the tunnel in the tractor? How fast can those two men be across the wheat?

He pumps his arms, swinging his axe for maximum momentum - the light at the end of the tunnel burns brighter. As he runs, he feels the violence boiling up inside him, ready to defend his carefully laid plan. He shifts the handle of the axe up through the palm of his right hand and grasps it at the neck with his left, raising it to a 'high port' position, ready to strike at whoever threatens to get in his way.

53

Scrap

John reaches the brow of the cutting, his heart sinks to see the trails of debris converge on the track and disappear into the tunnel. "Oh, fucking hell." he says as Alex catches up with him.

"He's going to de-rail a train?" Alex says.

"It'll be worse than that, he's taken a fucking fuel tanker down there." Both men pause to contemplate the horror that this scenario conjures and come to terms with what they must do to stop him. "Come on." John says with a tap on Alex's shoulder as he turns and runs diagonally down the slope, just inches from Blunt's firing position. Alex follows him, but also fails to spot the shotgun barrels sticking up out of the long grass, and hares past them.

Stop the trains – the simple solution comes to Alex as he throws his arms out to steady himself as he jumps onto the hardcore from the grass bank. He takes his phone from his pocket, but falters as he sees a flash of light from beyond John – Tony Blunt, with a fucking big axe. John dives sideways to the right to dodge the blade. He lands awkwardly on his side on the outer rail. Alex braces himself for a confrontation that he has no idea how to deal with, but Blunt snarls at him, breaks to his left and heads up the bank. Through pure adrenalin, Alex gives chase and thunders back up the grass after him. Blunt dives on the shotgun, but Alex is on him before can get a proper grip on it.

Alex hooks his arm around Blunt's neck, grabs his own wrist with his other hand, forming a loose neck lock, and pushes hard off both feet to launch them both into the air. Alex uses his momentum to spin them round as they fall towards the unforgiving outer rail of the northbound track – as the ground rushes towards them, Alex lurches off against Blunt's body maximising the moment of impact. Blunt is stunned, but still conscious, and already thrashing his elbows back at Alex, whilst clinging to the shotgun.

A heavy black boot comes from nowhere, smashing Blunt's head back. "CHECK THE TUNNEL." John only has eyes for Blunt now; this has been the chance that he has been waiting for since being made a mug of at Hodgehill.

Alex rolls away from Blunt and gets to his feet – *my phone?* He looks to the floor – it's not there. His eyes search back up the bank, but he can't see it. "WHAT'RE YOU WAITING FOR?" John blasts angrily. Alex turns and runs towards the tunnel.

*

John swings another boot towards Blunt's face, but he is ready for it. He hugs onto John's lower leg and rolls over onto his knees, lifting John off balance. Tony surges energy through his legs and thrusts John over onto his back. He climbs along his body, keeping close to John's legs, so that he is unable to swing a kick at him. John fights to sit up and gets as much weight behind his fists as he can as he rains punches down on the back of Blunt's head. Tony weathers the storm and picks his moment; he strikes like a cobra, drawing back and firing a powerful punch at John's head. The blow lands perfectly on John's temple, causing him to switch from attack to defend. Tony strengthens his position, straddling John's mid-riff, he swings more punches to John's head.

John covers his skull with his arms and rolls away from the flying fists as they come at him. He breathes hard and focuses on holding his guard tight. The frequency of Blunt's punches slows as he begins to tire. The knuckles of Blunt's right fist slip off John's forearm, and John takes his cue; he shoots out both arms around Blunt's neck and hauls down on him with all his might. At the same time, he thrusts his right knee upwards, pushing past Blunt's clenching inner thigh. John scrambles his legs out from under Blunt's and rolls him over onto his back. He flings his weight forward and rotates his upper body, firing his elbow forward, smashing Blunt in the face – his nose explodes and is immediately streaming blood. John hits him from the other side with his other elbow with more success – he snarls into a frenzy, but his eagerness to finish the job offers Blunt a chance.

Tony feels John's legs loosen their grip around him, he burrows a fist down and hooks it up between John's legs, he shoves him upwards whilst trying to wriggle his way down. He kicks his newly freed legs over John's back and rolls backwards over his own shoulders. Now on top of John, who is face down in the hardcore, he lifts his leg back and drives a knee into the centre of his back. The blow lacks power as his strength is drained. He pushes himself up, stepping off John's shoulder blade and staggers over to pick up the shotgun.

John sees where Blunt is headed, he desperately scrambles to his feet and makes after him.

Tony dives for the gun and rolls over with it in his hands. His right hand is too low on the neck of the butt, he fumbles to find the trigger under the pressure of John bearing down on him. He squeezes off the action as John leaps at him. John gets a palm to the barrel just in time, his right ear takes the full volume of the blast, but the slug fires past him.

John charges on, now with both hands gripping the weapon, he pushes Blunt back, deliberately steering him right, onto the inner rail. Tony trips and falls. His natural paratrooper reaction is to roll with the trip, twisting his knees off to the left and arching his back out to meet the hard ground. He pulls the shotgun hard up past his chin to yank John over him and helps him on his way over his head with a push off the soles of his feet. John clings on to the stock with his left hand and stops mid-flight, he drops out of the air; the hard ground taking the wind from him as he lands.

Tony snatches the gun away from John and flicks the barrel selector across. He rolls into the prone position and takes aim at the top of John's head. John instinctively pushes down on all four of his limbs as has hard as he can to move himself out of harm's way as Blunt pulls the trigger. The slug tears into John's right thigh at a low angle, ripping a great chunk of flesh from his outer quadricep.

Tony gets to his feet and stands over John. "Not such a big man now, are you?" he says, with a decade of hatred in his voice. John rolls onto his back clasping both hands over the wound, his eyes clenched tight in agony. Tony looks at his watch, "We have a minute." he says sadistically. He walks calmly up the bank to his firing point and drops the gun on top of the bag of shells. He bends down and picks up his axe. Holding it high on the neck, he runs his thumb along the blade, feeling its sharpness.

John musters his strength and focuses his energies on what he can still do. He maintains his position on the ground, on his back, but shuffles around to orientate himself towards Blunt, feet first, resting his shoulders on the inner rail and ankles on the outer rail of the northbound track. Blunt comes at him down the hill, naturally gathering pace as he lets gravity take him, he leaps with his axe held high over his head.

As Tony swings for John's neck, he sees the injured man's body buck and legs flick into the air. John targets the gap between Blunt's hands to plant a two-footed stamp onto the handle of the axe. Tony is unable to keep his hold on the handle and the head hits him in the face, putting a deep gash in his left eyebrow. He lands awkwardly on John's legs, rolling off to the left. John rolls to follow him and hooks down with a powerful blow to the jaw, rocking Blunt to his core.

Tony's body shakes, he feels a tremble like he's felt from no other punch he's taken in his life. It dawns on him that the tremble continues, is getting stronger, and is coming through the ground. He looks to his right and sees movement far off in the distance, through the tiny gap under the road bridge three hundred metres to the north. Still traveling at over one hundred miles per hour, the Edinburgh to

London East Coast train has begun to slow on its approach to Grantham. The train takes Tony's attention, distracting him from John, who is on his feet and limping up the bank.

54

Clear the lines

Alex has lost all sense of reality and perspective inside the tunnel. Running into an unfathomable nightmare has evolved into a state of confusion amongst the lights and shadows of what lies before him. The headlights of the Massey Ferguson partially illuminate the tunnel, but their full glare is obscured by the enormous John Deere and its bulky payload, leaving a glowing corona burning around its mass.

The full detail of what Blunt has planned becomes clear as the light reflects off the side of the girder. The sinister construction, mostly in shadow, looms large from behind the tanker. The two top edges of the tall flanges creating a double-railed ramp that deviates steeply up and inwards from the track's natural path. The tanker straddles the south and northbound carriageways with the ramp over its left side.

Alex quickly determines that removing the ramp must be his immediate priority and runs around the tanker and past the massive green tractor. He notes that it is parked almost touching the huge beam. He turns to the door of the Massey Ferguson and yanks on the handle – the push-button door catch refuses to budge. No matter how many times, or how many angles Alex presses on it; it is locked, the keys, no doubt, with Blunt.

He feels the sense of panic that he'd had when entering the tunnel returning to him. He steps back and forth as his conflicting ideas of what to do next manifest through his legs. Eventually he runs to the door of the bigger, green tractor and gasps aloud as he finds it open, "Yes." He cannot believe his luck to see the key in the ignition. He jumps into the seat and starts the engine.

The controls are unfamiliar, a multitude of levers and buttons. Alex's technological brain takes over, he puts his foot on the centre pedal – *feels like a brake,* he presses the large button next to the stick marked with an 'A' and releases the brake, he feels the freedom of the wheels as the tractor edges forward, the chunky front wheels pressing into the inner rail of the southbound track. He looks up to see the beam of the ramp close to touching the top of the cab. Alex braces himself, then squirts the accelerator; the tractor bounds forward, up onto the rail, crunching the plastic shell of the cab against the heavy steel of the beam. The roll-cage lifts the ramp slightly and dislodges its two supports, but the tractor bounces off and rolls back, causing the tank to rock violently, it creaks and scrapes against the rails and the hardcore, emitting a flash of sparks.

A fireball flashes in Alex's mirrors and he is instantly aware of the continuing burning at the back of the trailer, the flicker of flames just visible. He floors the accelerator and holds it there, crouching as low as he can in the seat as the cab smashes into the beam. He pumps the throttle as the tractor breaks free of the girder and the wheels cross the rails, but then brakes suddenly as he realises that the ramp is going to be left intact once he has driven clear. He turns the steering wheel right hand down and drives head on into the old red tractor. The Massey slips backwards a metre or so, but the forks lock in tight against the ceiling of the tunnel, chips of masonry fall down in a cloud of dust – Alex panics once more – might he be making the situation worse? He selects reverse and drives back far enough from the smaller tractor that he can manoeuvre out, as he puts the John Deere back into drive, he senses vibrations that are unlike those of the tractor's engine - they are coming through the ground.

55

Blunt end

John collapses on his backside next to the bag of shells, he breaks the shotgun breach open and flicks out the spent cartridges. Blunt is on his feet and picks up his axe. John fights the urge to load both chambers and slots home a single slug shell into the right barrel, he slams the gun shut and trains it on Blunt who is almost upon him – he fires at the centre of mass of his target, hitting Blunt low in the stomach.

Tony is sent flying backwards into the air, his arms and legs like a starfish, but he maintains a grip on his axe. He lands broken and bleeding on the northbound track as the train hurtles closer, speeding down the southbound rails, it's reverberating roar now audible.

Enthused by the sight and sound of the speeding train heading to its fate, Tony channels his energy, ignores the pain and rolls himself over onto his knees, still holding on tightly to his beloved axe; he uses it to get to his feet.

A sudden roaring whoosh blasts from the tunnel, and a fireball shoots from the darkness, rolling into the air and over his head. He looks back to John, who has also made it to his feet; he readies himself to defend the next attack but fails to notice the residual trail of burning petrol at his feet. John sees it and bides his time.

The flames lick at Tony's trousers, he senses something, then the ribbon of flame dancing on the bank over John's shoulder catches his eye. He looks to his feet; John's patience pays off - he careers down the cutting as fast as his injury allows. John screams his best war cry and throws himself feet-first at Blunt, kicking, with everything he has left, hard in the chest. Tony is cannoned backwards onto the southbound carriageway, straight into the path of the train, still moving at over ninety-five miles per hour - in an instant he is smashed into a pink cloud of vapour, punctuated with bony lumps and chunks of flesh.

Coated in a thin film of Tony Blunt, John lands in the rut between the bank and the track holding his ears as the train's brakes screech with a deafening ferocity as the engine slides on locked wheels into the tunnel.

56

Impact

Alex steers the John Deere onto the right side of the tunnel; the tanker leans in to the middle as it slides along the inner rail of the north-bound carriageway, but it is clear of the southbound tracks. Looking back past the Massey, Alex sees the tunnel lit up with streams of sparks coming from the underside of the train, which is growing in detail and filling evermore of his view, its smooth movement is interrupted, it bucks up from its trajectory and bounces off the ceiling with a thunderous crunch, Alex's ears are overcome by the roar as the train crashes back to the rails, it seems to devour the ramp and tramples the old Massey, which is mangled underneath it.

Some of the pace is absorbed from the engine, but it seems to gain speed as its carriages push into it from behind. Alex puts the tractor into third gear and accelerates. The nose of the engine grinds past, gasping and wailing like a harpooned whale. It scuffs against the tyres of the John Deere, making Alex's input through the steering wheel irrelevant; the tractor is squeezed into the wall of the tunnel and dragged along it, the tyres bursting simultaneously in puffs of high pressure gas – he braces himself, with arms locked tightly, both pushing and pulling against the steering wheel, he feels his biceps and triceps spasming. The giant tractor now feels like an insignificant toy, being bullied by the massive, all-powerful train.

The groans and screeches gradually lower in their tone as the train's energy is spent and its speed tapers. The tractor stops, the train releasing its grip on it, as it slews back to the middle of the tunnel as it comes to a halt. Alex feels elated as he realises that he has survived the ordeal, but then remembers that he is around three hundred metres into a tunnel, in a tractor attached to a twenty-ton trailer of petrol which is currently on fire - he decides to put his victory dance on ice for now.

The wheel hubs have maintained most of their structure and have kept the cab away from the tunnel wall enough that Alex can escape. He steps from the cab, past the mangled black plastic mud guard, onto the shredded remains of the front tyre. He jumps down onto the hardcore, which is bathed in the light of the tractor's headlights.

It is eerily quiet, there are a few creeks and cracks from the train, like a giant, cooling clothes iron. Alex's ears accustom to the lower level of noise and he hears voices, groans, cries. Then a single loud voice shouting. He hears a door opening and the voices getting louder and clearer. "Ladies and gentlemen, please disembark from the train and carefully make your way along the left side of the tunnel – watch your step."

Alex considers the crash from the perspective of those on the train. Aside from the initial jolt and the rapid deceleration; it couldn't have been that bad. It might have been a different story if the petrol tanker had of gone up, but as it stands, they have gotten away with it – *Blunt is an epic failure.* Alex again realises that he is getting ahead of himself and he must help to get everyone clear in case the petrol goes up. He runs to the head of the train.

*

Alex can just make out a group of people stood around the first set of doors of the second carriage, milling around. "HEY, COME ON, YOU'VE GOT TO GET OUT OF HERE." He runs past the engine that looks ominously mischievous, sat across the rails at an unnatural angle.

There are twenty or so people congregated around the doors, Alex can see others stepping down from the next set of doors along and making their way towards them, but he knows that he needs to get people moving, or this bottleneck will only get worse. "PLEASE

EVERYBODY, YOU NEED TO GET OUT OF THIS TUNNEL
IMMEDIATELY, THERE IS A FIRE RISK, YOU ARE IN
SERIOUS DANGER."

No one seems to be listening, everyone is more concerned with
looking for their family members and friends. There are two women
stood in the doorway looking down, trying to spot members of their
groups; there is no sense of urgency, no realisation of the danger that
they are in. Alex spots the guard at the front of the crowd near the
doors, he pushes his way through to her.

"Excuse me, but you need to get these people moving." he says
firmly.

"Well, thank you, but that's exactly what I'm doing." she says angrily.

"No, you don't understand. This derailment is a planned attack. There
is a possibility of an explosion - any second. You need to instruct
these people to get out of this tunnel. NOW!"

"Did you say this was an attack? There might be an explosion?" says a
man in a linen shirt, clutching a laptop bag. A ripple of fear quietens
the crowd who now seem to be paying attention. Alex fears that he
may cause a panic, leading to people getting hurt, but then if they all
stand around while that petrol tanker cooks off - *they're all going to end
up dead anyway.*

"LISTEN, THERE IS AN IMMINENT RISK TO LIFE, YOU ALL
NEED TO MAKE YOUR WAY OUT OF HERE AS QUICKLY
AND AS SAFELY AS POSSIBLE." The mood in the tunnel
changes; some properly get the message and begin to run; others
scurry in circles looking with greater urgency for their missing loved
ones. Those that hadn't taken notice before are observing the action;
the penny drops for many and soon everyone is at least moving
towards the mouth of the tunnel, even if not at any great speed.

The guard turns her attention back to the doors of the train, responding to a call for help from a distressed woman, with blood pouring from her forehead and a child under each arm.

Alex watches with curiosity at the contrasting displays of chivalry and selfishness, some people taking the opportunity to be the hero, while others push past in their desperation to escape this terrible set of circumstances. Alex's attention is drawn away from the door - under the carriage the light from the flames seems to be burning brighter. It might be his eyes becoming accustomed to the lower light of this side of the train, it might be that his fear is enhancing the blaze in his head, but he knows that he needs to be out of here. He cannot bring himself to run whilst people are still struggling to get off the train, so he strikes a bargain with himself. He steps forward and takes the larger of the two children from the injured mother and waits as she steps down and takes her baby back from the guard. "Come with me, we need to get out of here and quick." he says with as much force as he can convey without scaring her too much.

"What's happened?" she asks.

"The train's been deliberately derailed and there's a tanker full of petrol on the other side of it – it could blow at any moment. Alex hopes that he hasn't said too much, and that she doesn't simply break down on the track, but this woman is made of stronger stuff; she has two kids to get through this. She throws her nappy bag, kicks off her shoes, and runs like a winger breaching the defensive line. Alex swings the toddler high up on his shoulder and does his best to keep up. He shouts encouragement to the people that they pass as they head towards the bright daylight of the outside world, but some of them have stopped. Alex sees an arm of one of them pointing out of the tunnel. He looks beyond them; to his horror, he sees the northbound train approaching.

57

Northbound

The first few people have made it to the fresh air at the south entrance of the tunnel, causing the confused driver to give a long blow on her horn, and ignore her ringing mobile phone. Having quickly achieved her cruising speed of sixty-five miles per hour, just three kilometres from Grantham, the warning would be too late anyway.

Alex and the young mum sprint past the speeding train. The children's screams are drowned out as the emergency brakes of the three-carriage train are applied. The final twenty metres seem to take an age to cover. "GET UP THE BANK, GET UP THE BANK." Alex screams at the passengers stood looking back into the tunnel, seeing what they can see of the imminent impact. The screech of the brakes is suddenly amplified and is overlaid with disturbing overtones of a crunching rumble as the second train strikes against the side of the engine of the first. As Alex bursts out from the shade, he dives to his left, onto the steep grassy verge of the bank, holding the tiny boy tight underneath him. The boy's mother and baby sister are a few steps behind him, she follows his lead and jumps to the safety of the cutting bank.

Some members of the small gathering of passengers stood around the mouth of the tunnel look down at them mockingly, but in that instant, they are all sent flying along the track by an immense blast wave, a split second later, a wall of shrapnel, hardcore, gravel and chunks of masonry are ejected from the mouth of the tunnel, this happens in eerie quietness, only the sounds of the fragments bouncing off one another and the ground, the deafening boom from the blast follows another fraction of a second after it. Alex throws his hands up reacting to the searing heat. The sonic wave is as powerful as the pressure wave, which goes through Alex, leaving him in total shock, he feels completely disconnected from his physical self, his hearing reduced to a ghostly monotone hum.

58

Aftermath

Alex lifts his hands from his face to see the track covered with lumps of masonry, wreckage, and bodies; most of the clothes blown from them, in varying states of mutilation and dismemberment, all covered in a sandy dust. Black smoke billows from the top of the tunnel's mouth, though not exclusively, the heavy, dirty particles fill the air, Alex lets out a weak cough.

Aside from the young family that he has saved, there are only eight other people that he can see alive; they are all flayed, laying on the bank in states of confusion and bewilderment, trying to find their bearings and reconcile what has happened.

Alex checks that the children haven't suffered any serious injuries – though there's not much he can do for perforated eardrums. The mother thanks him, or that's what he reads from her face and hand gestures, as he is unable to hear anything that she is saying. He tries to calm her, reassure her that everything is going to be all right, he uses body language and a kind face, as she doesn't seem to be hearing him either.

He stands up on the bank, feeling a sense of duty to the survivors, and a feeling that he must go back into the tunnel to offer help, but he is also thinking about the other end of the tunnel – *What's happened to John? Did he get the better of Blunt? If he did; would he have followed me into the tunnel?*

Standing deep in thought, Alex feels the heat on his face as the adrenalin begins to wear off; blisters bubble up on his nose, growing into his field of view. The soft skin of his eyelids and cheeks begin to sting as it dries and cracks in the hot air. He steps down onto the track; the footing is impossibly loose on the thickly spread fragments of concrete, he takes a few steps towards the tunnel, but he is quickly defeated by the acrid smoke and intense heat that emanates from it. He drops to his knees and breaks down at the intense sense of helplessness, and the fact that Tony Blunt has won.

*

Emergency service vehicles and personnel soon begin to flood into the field at the north end of the tunnel, setting up operations just metres away from where Blunt had set up his firing post. Alex and the other few survivors from the south end of the tunnel are escorted by ambulance crew members to the north entrance. The route cuts across two fairways of a golf course, leading them around the perimeter of a forestry block and through a gap in a hedgerow, into the field that Alex recognises as the one that he ran across about an hour ago. Carrying three-year-old Jamie, for his mum, Alex fights the urge to run to the cluster of vehicles and people.

They slowly approach the fleet of brightly liveried vehicles. Alex places Jamie back in the custody of his mother as she is quickly allocated an ambulance - the number of injured, is sadly dwarfed by the number of dead. Alex heads for the only Police vehicle with its blue strobes flashing, something he remembers from a UK Operations exercise; the only vehicle at the scene of an incident that should have its strobes on is the command vehicle. He figures that most ambulance crew are oblivious to this, and that the command truck is going to be a Police asset. He stands at the open side door of the incident support unit truck and waits for a gap in the busy bodies to appear.

"Can I help you, Sir?" He is greeted by a uniformed sergeant.

"I've just come from the south entrance. I'm looking for a survivor from up here; John Gallagher."

Joseph Mitcham

The policeman stares intently back at him, Alex senses that he is being sized up. "Yes, he's here. The officer steps out of the van and calmly takes Alex by the wrist and clicks a handcuff onto it.

59

Bedside manner

John's injuries are triaged at the scene as too serious for the local hospital to deal with. He is taken to Queen's Medical Centre in Nottingham, the nearest Major Trauma Unit, along with only another fifteen of the injured.

Alex relaxes into being processed through Grantham and District Hospital under Police guard, before being moved on to the Police station. No argument that Dev can put forward over the phone can convince the Custody Sergeant, or his local superiors, to release him. Alex uses the time to evaluate what had happened. He tries to take the positives but cannot stop thinking about how close he came to being axed by Blunt, crushed by the derailed train, vaporised in the explosion, pulverised by the shower of concrete or gassed to death in the tunnel's post-explosion toxins.

Alex distracts himself from the spine-tingling thoughts, by castigating himself for being so self-centred, and switches his thoughts to the passengers of the trains. He has heard no news, as yet, of how many died or were injured, but he does the sums in his head to try and estimate; fifteen carriages between the two trains, about sixty people on each one – *nine-hundred passengers, and what, forty survivors? Tops.*

*

Charlie pulls some strings in the car on her way north; Alex is free to be collected when she, Lucy and Cliff arrive at the station just after lunchtime. He walks into the reception area and into Lucy's arms. Overcome and unable to speak, he clings on to her.

"Oh my god, Alex, are you okay?" she asks, stepping back, raising a hand to touch the dressing over the left side of his face.

"Come on, let's go and find that other wally." says Charlie, taking the pressure off Alex to say any more. He remains silent and follows them out to a large black people carrier, a Security Service pool vehicle that Charlie had managed to requisition.

*

"Here he is." John says warmly, without his usual brashness, as Alex steps into his hospital side-room holding Lucy's hand. Though he is made up to see him alive, having shown extreme levels of valour, there are no high fives or cheering, just a firm handshake across the edge of the bed.

"Chin up fella, we did all we could do."

"You did more than anyone could have done in the circumstances." Charlie adds looking straight at Alex, from John's side. "From what I hear, no one would have made it out of the south of the tunnel without you there, Alex. If John hadn't have stopped Blunt; no one from the north end would have made it off the tracks." She leans over and kisses John on his badly scarred forehead.

"We saved about forty, of what? A thousand? That's pretty shit going, but we were lucky to get there at all, so the real prize is that we got Blunt." John says, knowing that this day's efforts will never be a success in the eyes of the public, the authorities, the families of the dead, but as far as he, the friends and family of Craig Medhurst, and the others killed at the doing of Tony Blunt and his 'Interest Group'; this is a sweet day – and just the beginning of his vengeance.

60

Total success

The media has its usual field-day with the body count, going over the numbers and personal stories during the periods with no real information of value to broadcast. They focus on the daily releases of names and back-stories of the victims as individuals' presence on one or other of the trains is confirmed. The situation being so complex, two totals are kept; the confirmed total, which counts the victims who have been confirmed killed by name, this number had crept up slowly at first in the tens, increasing at an inconsistent rate into the six hundreds after the five weeks since that terrible day. The second number being the estimated total number killed, which includes those missing and presumed present and therefore dead. The accuracy of this second number has become a subject of fascination, as cases of fare-dodgers who might or might not have been on board have emerged, and it has come to light that there is at least one case of a scammer claiming that a missing family member had been on board the local train.

The forensic investigation into how events unfolded in the tunnel that day is not straight forward and causes much frustration as the stakeholder groups demand to know what happened. The devastation was so complete that there has not been much to piece back together. There have been theories that some sort of 'super weapon' had been placed in the tunnel, as so much damage would have required an unfeasibly large bomb. Alex's eyewitness account has helped to straighten out some of the confusion.

The interim official findings are that the Edinburgh to London train had been deliberately de-railed by a lone terrorist, who had erected an improvised steel ramp and planted an incendiary charge with the intent of setting fire to the crashed train. Despite the two vertical stays, that he had placed under the ramp, being knocked loose, the ramp had successfully dislodged the train from its rails.

Approximately two minutes after the first train had come to a stop, the 9:14 train from Grantham had struck the derailed London-bound train, nudging its engine and first carriage off the northbound tracks, becoming derailed itself in the process. The smaller train's speed had been sapped from it, with only the momentum of three carriages, of lighter construction than that of the twelve of the high speed model cars that it had come up against, however it was still moving at nearly twenty-five miles per hour when it struck the stricken John Deere tractor, pushing it back into its payload of fuel, lifting the front and jamming the already dangerously over pressurised tanker between the crumbling ceiling and rock solid floor.

The ingredients of a perfect storm were present in the tunnel; the heavy loading of the air with imperfectly burned petrol and carbon monoxide, added fuel to the atmospheric mix, as well as the second train providing the additional pressure required to rupture the tank, the northbound train also brought with it a rush of oxygen-rich air to complete the chemical equation. The fuel cell burst like a balloon, and the reaction was phenomenally violent. The speed of the flame had travelled incredibly fast, matching the speed of the pressure wave of the escaping vapours, making this a detonation, rather than a simple explosion.

The military scientists of Fort Halstead some years ago had worked tirelessly to replicate conditions such as those present in the tunnel and weaponize them, leading to the development of the highly efficient 'air-fuel bomb'– Tony Blunt had managed it with a steel girder, a tanker of petrol and a couple of tractors. Resulting in a confined vapour cloud explosion on an epic scale, in a controlled space, and therefore exponentially more powerful than any military munition, Blunt's blast had exceeded any outcome that he could possibly have been anticipating.

The power of the detonation was such that it lifted the forest floor, bringing down a strip of trees over the top of the tunnel. A sixty-metre section of the tunnel collapsed over the epicentre of the blast, and the concrete lining of the tunnel had been shattered and stripped for almost the entirety of the six-hundred metres of the tunnel's length.

The damage to the trains and their passengers was devastating, the heavy steel chassis of the carriage nearest to the tanker was deformed beyond recognition and the bodies of most of the other carriages were completely destroyed. The manner in which the air-fuel mix had filled the tunnel as it ignited, meant that every part of both trains had been subject to the equivalent force of a conventional bomb blast.

If, however unlikely, anyone had survived in the trains, they would have died in seconds from breathing the burning, poisonous air that was left. The passengers making their escape on foot in the tunnel were either blown to pieces by the pressure wave, incinerated by the blast wave, smashed by the hail of masonry as it was fired from the ceiling and walls, or shredded by the shards of shrapnel ripped from the trains' carcasses.

The circus goes on and reality draws closer to prediction, with 671 named victims against a predicted total of 893. Many of the thirty-nine survivors have given their eye-witness accounts in exclusive interviews on camera and in the press. The interventions of John and Alex have been played down from the start, neither of them wanting any credit or public recognition. Media interest in the early stories that circulated about members of the public stepping in had quickly died off without faces to put to them, and their apparent failure to prevent the disaster.

The Interest Group are yet to claim responsibility for 'Belton Tunnel' as the incident has become known, or even announce their existence. Charlie has been shrewd with her messaging up her chain of command, and has come out of the investigation looking like the only one who had a clue about what might be going on, and the only agent to have an inkling about how to track down the Interest Group; she is the natural choice to be selected as the Security Service team lead for the onward investigation to hunt down the group with all the resources that she needs, including the direct secondment of Sergeant Butler, lifting her from her Police attachment.

*

The pace of life has gone into slow motion for Alex, from the lengthy periods of interview over the two weeks after the incident, to the long weeks of calm, staying with Lucy, helping her settle into a new flat in Central London, provisioned by the good people of Defence Accommodation Services. In terms of their relationship, the pressure is off; both are simply happy to enjoy each other's company for now.

Alex has been back in touch with Dickie, the guy who had put him on the contract where he had met Lucy and found the Watch List. Dickie has been delighted to find Alex some tasty little jobs to keep his mind occupied, having some projects he hasn't been able to complete, as his other engineers just don't have Alex's skills.

The work is taking his mind off the fact that there is still an organisation at large that is likely to be planning further attacks on the UK's public. He is learning to relax again and has been looking forward to tonight.

*

Alex looks out of the tube carriage's window at an obtuse angle, with intense interest in the inside of the tunnel, challenging himself not to shudder. "Where are we meeting them?" he asks, hanging from the over-head hand rail.

"Charlie's favourite Chinese." Lucy answers, wondering how Alex is feeling about his first rail journey since Belton Tunnel.

"The one we went to with the team?" he asks looking up from the window as the train emerges into the brightness of Leicester Square station.

"Yes."

"Not too much work chat tonight, hey?" he says.

Lucy laughs, knowing how futile that request is at the best of times, but with the four of them in the same room for the first time since their second visit to John in hospital, they both know he's wasting his breath.

*

Alex has seen John regularly over the past few weeks, him having taken some time off too, but the flush red scar over this right eye still gives him a mild shock as he sees him across the restaurant. He walks over from the bar in his trademark head-to-toe black outfit to greet them. Charlie follows him, looking like she's been for a makeover – life in a blossoming relationship seemingly agreeing with her. They each hug in turn with feeling. "How are you going, Alex?" she asks.

Alex might have been offended at the insinuation that he might be experiencing weakness if he hadn't been through one of the most terrifying experiences of his life. He is also cognisant that Charlie isn't one to care if she offends him, or anyone else for that matter. "I'm fine, thanks Charlie."

The pleasantries continue up the stairs and to their seats at the same table they'd sat at before on the otherwise deserted upper floor. Orders are taken and drinks arrive before conversation, led mostly by John, slips smoothly through; catching up with friends, the funerals of friends, before descending into 'avenging friends' where the conversation turns distinctly professional.

"We've got Professor Banbury from DSTL working with our team, he's doing some stella work towards helping us identify our target group." says Charlie. With Pavilion Gardens, Millbank and Belton Tunnel; the Interest Group has rocketed from unknown straight to the number one spot on the Security Services' wanted list in a matter of months. "We don't think it will be too long before we'll be in a position to go after them.

Alex smiles, knowing that Charlie is trying to tempt him. John is blatantly up for it, Lucy has it in her job description, it is only Alex whose interest requires piquing. "I've had enough, Charlie."

"What?" says John.

Charlie stares back at Alex, a perplexed look on her face, thinking through the levers and arguments available to her that might bring him round.

"Oh, come on, you're the heart of the team, Alex." Lucy says, seductively stroking his shoulder.

"It doesn't have to be so full on." Charlie says, "I can retain you on full expenses in return for helping us out when we need your skills. You'd be free to carry on your contract work in between time."

"What sort of 'full expenses'?" Alex asks - *it can't hurt to ask, can it?*

"Basically everything; all your bills, anything you buy - food to phones."

Alex thinks through the lifestyle he'd be afforded, in Central London with no money worries. It's tempting, but can he put himself through it again? "No, fuck that, I'll leave you three to it." he says, feeling an instant lift of liberation.

Charlie doesn't feel the need to press the issue, not here, not now. She knows she'll get him, or at least Lucy will get him for her.

End

Review?

Honest reviews of my book help bring it to the attention of other readers. If you've enjoyed 'Where is Tony Blunt?' I would be really grateful if you would spend just a couple of minutes leaving a review (it can be as short as you like) on the book's Amazon page or on your favourite readers' website. Thank you so much—you're a legend!

Follow my Amazon Author's page for news of more in the Atrocities Book Series – search 'Joseph Mitcham' on Amazon.

About the Author

Joseph Mitcham served with the British military in elite and technical units for over 16 years. His service, and life experiences since as a proud veteran, have given him a rich bank of knowledge and memories that brings his writing to life.

Having never written fiction before, the inspiration for embarking on the Atrocities Book Series project came from contemplating what might happen if a group of veterans got hold of the UK Terror Watch List. Using personal experiences from the roles that he has served in, and characteristics from some of the people that he has served with, Joseph writes with grounded authenticity, which makes his plausible plots utterly believable.

Printed in Great Britain
by Amazon

54439379R00192